A PIRATE'S LOVE

Johanna Lindsey

A PIRATE'S LOVE

Five Star
Unity, Maine

Five Star Romance.

Published in conjunction with Avon Books, a division of the Hearst Corporation.

April 1997
Standard Print Hardcover Edition.

Five Star Standard Print Romance Series.

The text of this edition is unabridged.

Set in 11 pt. Plantin.

Printed in the United States on permanent paper.

Library of Congress Cataloging in Publication Data

Lindsey, Johanna.
    A pirate's love / Johanna Lindsey.
        p. cm.
    ISBN 0-7862-0953-4 (hc)
    1. Caribbean Area — History — Fiction. I. Title.
PS3562.I5123P57   1997
813'.54—dc21
                                                96-54265

A
PIRATE'S
LOVE

Chapter 1

Bettina Verlaine was more than apprehensive when she entered the sun-filled drawing room that morning, and stood before her mother and father. It wasn't often that André Verlaine summoned her so early, and never before had he warned her to be present a day ahead. She knew that he must have something very important to tell her, something that would affect her life. She'd had the whole night to worry about it, but deep inside of her she knew what it would be. She was nineteen and marriageable.

She had expected to be married off three years ago, when she had come home from the convent school. Most girls from wealthy families were betrothed when they were only children, and married at the young age of fourteen or fifteen, as Bettina's mother had been. Many suitors had come to call on Bettina's father, though she had not been allowed to see them. But her father would consider none of the young men who sought her, for none was rich enough to suit him.

Bettina was sure that her future had now been decided. Soon she would be told the name of the man she would marry.

André Verlaine was seated at his desk and hadn't bothered to look up when Bettina entered the room. Could her father be deliberately putting off the task of telling her his decision? Perhaps he was feeling a trifle guilty about it now. But then, how could he? He was the same man who had sent her to the convent, saying she had become too troublesome to handle. She had spent most of her nineteen years away from home, and now she would be sent away again, forever.

Jossel Verlaine looked at her daughter anxiously. She had tried desperately to dissuade André from choosing Bettina's husband and thought she had succeeded until last night, when André had offhandedly informed her of his decision. Bettina wasn't like most girls; she was too spirited and too beautiful to be just given away. She might have chosen a good husband for herself, if only André had been reasonable. But no, André had to find a wealthy and titled husband for his daughter, and didn't care if Bettina found him repulsive or not.

Jossel sat before the open doors that led onto the terrace, as she did every morning, but today she hadn't been able to take one stitch in the tapestry before her. She couldn't stop thinking of the fate that awaited her daughter.

"Well, Bettina, this will not take long," André Verlaine finally said brusquely.

But he didn't alarm Bettina. Her father was never one to show tenderness or love for her, or for her mother, either. He treated them both as he treated the servants. André Verlaine was a cold man, obsessed only with increasing his wealth. And this consumed nearly all his time and thoughts, leaving little for his family.

"Why don't you sit down, *ma chérie*," Jossel said tenderly, before her husband had a chance to continue.

Bettina knew that her mother loved her. But she refused to sit, not wanting to appear relaxed and make it easier for her father. Bettina was feeling rebellious, and knew she had no right to be, for this was the way of things in the year 1667. It had been the same for centuries, and would probably never change. She just wished that her mother had not talked so much about falling in love and choosing her own husband.

Mariage de convenance was what daughters were for, at least daughters of wealthy parents. Besides, no eligible men lived in their small hometown of Argentan, only peasants and petty tradesmen. If Bettina had chanced to fall in love, her father would never have consented, and she had been kept isolated from young men of her own class.

"I have arranged for your marriage to Comte Pierre de Lambert," André continued. "It will take place soon after the beginning of the new year."

Bettina flashed her dark-green eyes at him angrily, one last show of defiance to let him know what she thought about his

8

crude announcement; then she bowed her head meekly as a good, obedient daughter was expected to do.

"Yes, Papa," Bettina said quietly, amazed at her own self-control.

"You will leave in a month. This will not give you much time to make your trousseau, so I will hire dressmakers to help you. Comte de Lambert resides on Saint Martin, an island in the Caribbean, so you will travel by ship. Unfortunately, it will be a long and tedious voyage. Madeleine, your old nurse, will go with you as chaperone and companion."

"Why must I go so far away?" Bettina exploded. "Surely there must be someone here in France I could marry."

"By the Blessed Virgin!" André shouted, his otherwise milky complexion turning quite red. He stood up and glared at his wife. "I sent her to that convent to learn obedience! But all these years were wasted, I can see. She still questions my authority."

"If you would only take her wishes into consideration, André. Is that too much to ask?" Jossel ventured.

"Her wishes are of no concern, *madame*," said André. "And I will not stand for any more of your opposition. The betrothal has been arranged and cannot be undone. Bettina will marry Comte Pierre de Lambert. I pray God he can curb her defiance where I have failed!"

Bettina bristled. Did her father always have to talk as if she were not even present, as if she were of no consequence at all? She loved her father, but sometimes — in fact, most times — he made her so mad she could scream.

"May I be excused now, Papa?" she asked.

"Yes, yes," he replied irritably. "You have been told all that you need to know."

Bettina hurried from the drawing room, wanting to laugh, for what had she actually been told? She knew the man's name, where he lived, and that she would marry him after the new year arrived, that was all. Well, at least her father hadn't married her off fresh out of the convent. No, it had taken him three years to find her a husband, a man who could make it possible for him to increase his own wealth.

Bettina was full of conflicting emotions as she quickly ran

9

up the stairs. She was angry with her father for sending her to a man who lived so far away. She would be in a new land, a land of strangers, and this terrified her. She wasn't really angry with him for arranging the marriage, for she had expected no less, and she was relieved in a way that it was finally done. She felt deep sorrow that she would be leaving her mother. But to counteract these feelings was a kind of joy — joy that she would not be completely alone on this journey. Madeleine would be with her, dear Maddy, whom she loved as much as she loved her mother.

Before going to her own room, Bettina stopped at the door next to hers and rapped softly. At the sound of Madeleine's voice, Bettina walked into the room, only a little smaller than her own. She crossed to the window where Madeleine was sitting, and took the chair beside her.

When Bettina didn't speak, but just stared pensively down at the empty street in front of the house, Madeleine smiled and set aside her needlework.

"Your papa told you, eh?" she asked softly.

Bettina turned slowly to the woman who had cared for her when she was a child, who had cared for her mother too, from the day she was born. Madeleine was fifty-five, slightly plump now, but still agile. Her brown hair was half-streaked with gray, a silvery gray that matched her gentle eyes.

"So you knew," Bettina said passively. "Why didn't you warn me, Maddy?"

"You also knew, my pet. You have expected this for three years."

"Yes, but I didn't know I would be sent across the ocean. I don't want to leave France," Bettina said, her anger coming to the surface again. "I will run away!"

"You will do no such thing, young lady!" Madeleine scolded, shaking a pudgy finger at her. "You will accept this and make the best of it, just as you finally accepted being sent away to school. You should be glad that you will have a fine husband. He will give you many children, and, God willing, I will be there to see them grow."

Bettina smiled and leaned back in the chair. Madeleine was right. She would accept this marriage, for there was nothing else

10

she could do. She was past the age of throwing tantrums to get what she wanted. The sisters had taught her to make the best of things.

Bettina had been a cheerful child until she began to wonder why her father didn't love her. This weighed heavily on her young mind, and she tried desperately to gain her father's love and approval. When she didn't succeed and he still ignored her, she began to be troublesome, just to gain his attention. It wasn't enough that she was showered with love by her mother and Madeleine. She had to have her father's love, too. At her young age, she couldn't understand why her father disliked her; she didn't know that he had wanted a son. And a daughter was all he would ever have, for Jossel couldn't have any more children.

So Bettina developed a temper. She began to throw tantrums, to be defiant and disrespectful. She hated her father when he sent her away to school, and continued with her troublesome ways at the convent. But after a few years she learned to accept her fate.

She realized that it was her own fault that she had been sent away. The sisters taught her to control her temper. They taught her obedience and patience. When she came home, she no longer resented her father.

Nothing had changed. Her father was still a stranger to her, but Bettina accepted this, too. She stopped feeling sorry for herself and gave up trying to win his approval. She had her mother's love, and she had Maddy. She learned to be grateful for what she did have.

But sometimes Bettina couldn't help wondering how different she could have been if her father had been a loving man. She might not have developed the maddening temper that she had to fight to control. But what did it matter? Only her father could drive her into a rage, and she would be leaving that cold, insensitive man very soon.

11

Chapter 2

Early in the evening, Jossel Verlaine came to Bettina's bedroom to talk to her daughter privately. She was still upset.

"I tried, *ma chérie*. I tried endlessly to dissuade your papa from sending you to that — that man." Jossel spoke nervously, wringing her hands, which she always did when she was disturbed.

"It's all right, Mama. I was upset at first, but only because I must go so far away. I expected to have my marriage arranged, so the betrothal came as no surprise."

"Well, it came as a surprise to me! André has been arranging it for months, but only last night did he think to inform me of it. Once he made his choice, he acted on it. He did not take into consideration that he is sending you to a man you have never met, and also forcing you to cope with a new land and climate at the same time." Jossel usually said what was on her mind, at least to Bettina, but she started to pace the room and seemed quite at a loss for words.

"Is there something you wish to tell me, Mama?" Bettina ventured.

"Yes, yes, there is," Jossel answered in heavily accented English. Papa and Mama both liked to speak English, since many of Papa's associates were Englishmen. And since Bettina had also learned that crude language at the convent, Papa insisted that English be used at all times.

Jossel was still hesitating, so Bettina tried to break the silence. "I will miss you terribly when I leave next month, Mama. Will I ever see you again?" she asked hopefully.

"Of course, you will, Bettina. If your new" — she paused, hating to say the word — "new husband does not bring you here for a visit, then I will persuade André to go to Saint Martin."

12

Jossel looked at her daughter with deep concern in her dark-green eyes. "Oh, my little Bettina, I am so sorry that your papa has insisted on this betrothal to Comte de Lambert. I wanted you to pick your own husband. If only André had allowed me to take you to Paris, you might have found a man you could love, a worthy man André might have approved of. There are so many to choose from in Paris."

"Comte de Lambert is a worthy man, is he not?" Bettina asked.

"Yes, but you have never met him, Bettina. You don't know if you will love him or not. You don't know if you will be happy or not. And that is all I want, for you to be happy."

"But Papa has chosen Comte de Lambert, and he wants me for his wife. He has seen me, hasn't he?"

"Yes, a year ago. You were in the garden when the *comte* called on André. But Bettina, you are a lovely child, lovely beyond belief. You could have had your choice of husbands, and found a man that you would want to spend your life with. But your papa is too fond of tradition. It would not do but that *he* choose your husband. It doesn't matter to him if you are happy or not."

"But that is the way it is, Mama. I did not expect it to be otherwise," Bettina replied, though wondering why it couldn't.

"You are such a good and trusting daughter, and it grieves me to think that you might spend your life with a man you do not love. It is because of this that I came in here to tell you something, even though it is against my better judgment."

"What is it, Mama?"

"You know that André was chosen for me by my Papa when I was only fourteen years old. I was, as you are, ready to love my chosen husband and to be a good wife. But after one year of marriage I knew it could never be. After another year, the situation became worse, for André wanted a son and I had not yet conceived. I was desolate, and I had only Madeleine to confide in and love. But she could not protect me from André's furious outbursts.

"So I began to take long walks and make trips into town, just to seek peace. On one of my walks I met a sailor, an Irishman with fiery red hair and dancing green eyes. His ship was docked on the coast for repairs, and he had taken leave to visit his parents, who had left Ireland and were then living in the country near Mortagne. I chanced to meet him when he passed through Argentan. He stayed here instead of going on to Mortagne, and I met him again and again until we became — lovers."

"Oh, Mama, it sounds so romantic!"

Jossel smiled, relieved that her daughter was not shocked by her confession. "Yes, it was romantic. Ryan stayed in Argentan for three months, and I met him regularly. Those were the happiest months of my life, and I shall always treasure the memory of them. I loved him with all my heart, and he lives on in you, Bettina, because you came from the love I shared with Ryan. He was your real father."

"Then Papa — he is my stepfather?"

"Yes, *ma chérie*, only your stepfather. I wanted you to know about the happiness I was able to steal those many years ago, the only love that I ever had. I wanted you to know in case you don't love Comte de Lambert. I pray that you will, but if you don't, then I pray that you will find someone you can love, if only for a little while. I want you to be happy, Bettina, and if you should find yourself in a loveless marriage, I don't want you to feel guilty if you should find love elsewhere. I am not saying that you should go out and look for it. But if love should come to you as it did to me, take it while you can and be happy. I only want you to be happy."

Jossel started crying, and Bettina went to her and embraced her tenderly.

"Thank you, Mama. Thank you for telling me. I do not feel so afraid of going to Saint Martin now. I will try to make it a good marriage, and I will try to love Comte de Lambert. Who knows, I may not have to try. It may come naturally."

"Oh, I pray it does, *ma chérie*."

Bettina stood back and smiled warmly at her mother. "So I am half-Irish. Does Papa — does André know? Is that why he never showed me love?"

"You must understand, Bettina, that André is not a demonstrative man. He believes you are his daughter, but he wanted a son badly. And the doctors said I could have only the one child because there were problems with your birth. He may have re-

14

sented you because you were not the son he wanted, but in his way he loves you. It is unfortunate that he doesn't show it, and I know he has made you unhappy."

"I've spent most of my life trying to win André's approval, and he is not my real father." Bettina mused. "I sought love from the wrong man."

"I'm sorry, Bettina. I guess I should have told you the truth when you were little, but I couldn't. It is not an easy thing to admit. But you must continue to call André papa. I was deathly afraid at the time that you might be born with Ryan's flaming red hair. But luckily you have my white-blond hair and my papa's changeable eyes. Of course, those eyes of yours can be a hindrance to you. You cannot hide your feelings with those clear, dark eyes. As they are now, dark blue, I can tell that you are happy."

"You are teasing me!"

"No, *ma chérie*. Even now your eyes are turning dark green." Jossel laughed. "I know it must be unsettling to learn that you can't hide your feelings, but your eyes always show the truth."

"But why haven't I ever noticed this? I always thought my eyes were blue."

"Because when you are angry or upset, you would hardly look at yourself in a mirror. You do as your real father did. You pace the floor; you cannot sit still. You inherited many things from Ryan."

"I've always wondered why I am taller than both you and André. Was your Ryan a tall man?"

"Yes, very tall. He was such a handsome young man! But he had a quick temper and an unrelenting Irish stubbornness, just like you. But do not worry about your eyes, *ma chérie*. Not many people notice such things, and you can always say your eyes change with the light, as a fire opal does."

"Why didn't you go away with him, Mama? Why did you stay here and give up your happiness?"

"Ryan had to go back to his ship, and I could not go aboard with him, especially since I already knew that I was carrying you. Ryan was just a common sailor, though this mattered little to me, but he wanted to make his fortune before he took me away.

15

He promised to come back for me, and I waited many years before I gave up hope. I don't like to think why he didn't come back. I would rather think that he found a new love in another land than that he might be dead."

Bettina was sad to think that her mother would probably never learn the real reason. "Did he know about me?"

"Yes. I just wish that he could have seen what a lovely child he sired."

Later, after Jossel went to bed, Bettina sat before her dressing table looking at herself in the mirror. She wondered why Comte de Lambert had chosen her as his wife. She supposed she was pretty in a way, but she didn't think she was as beautiful as her mother fondly said. She had a nose that curved slightly at the tip, an oval face, but she felt that her forehead was not high enough. Her pale skin was smooth, without a blemish, but her thick flaxen hair was straight, not fashionably curly, and she hated it.

She stood out oddly among the girls at school, who teased her for her different appearance. At five feet, six inches, she towered over the petite French girls. And instead of having full breasts and soft, round curves, she was very slim. Her breasts were nicely shaped and not too small, so she didn't find much fault there. It was her hips that she cursed. They were slim — too slim, in fact — and her long legs didn't help matters. Her tiny waist added a slight curve to her hips, but it annoyed her that she had to pad her skirts in that area. She liked to hear her mama call her beautiful, even though she knew it wasn't true. It was only through Mama's eyes that she was beautiful, because Mama loved her. She would miss Mama so.

Her mother's revelation hadn't really disturbed Bettina. In a way, it seemed that a great burden had been lifted from her. She was a — she had heard the servants use the word and knew what it meant — she was a bastard. But what did it matter? No one knew about it except her mother. Bettina wished that Ryan had come back for her mother. And now she, too, wondered what had happened to him. Could he have been shipwrecked, or killed? Or was he still roaming the seas in search of a fortune to bring back to Mama? She liked the last explanation best. He

16

could still come back for Mama after all these years, and they could come and live on Saint Martin with her.

"Oh, Bettina, you dream too much," she whispered aloud. "I must face reality. I am going to go to a stranger and live with him and be his dutiful wife. Well, maybe not so dutiful." She laughed. "But I will be his wife and I — I don't even know what he looks like! He could be fat and short, or old. I must remember to ask Mama what he looks like. Maybe he will be young and handsome. Yes, and he did want me. I must remember that."

She yawned, then looked once more at her clear blue eyes in the mirror, eyes as dark as sapphires.

"Mama must have been teasing me. How can anyone's eyes change color?"

Bettina stood up and walked to the large four-poster bed with its frilly pink-and-white canopy. She crawled under the covers and tossed her long, unbound hair over the side of the bed, where it flowed to the floor. With so many things going through her mind, it was a long time before she finally went to sleep.

17

Chapter 3

"Wake up. Wake up, Bettina."

Bettina opened her eyes quickly at the sound of her mother's voice, but then remembered regretfully what day this was. Today she would leave her home forever.

"I told those silly maids to wake you early this morning," Jossel continued. "But I should have known they wouldn't pay attention to me. This whole house has been in such confusion this last month, preparing for your journey. It is a wonder anything gets done. The servants are so excited you would think they were going with you. And oh, how they envy Madeleine. I am going to miss that bossy old woman. She has been more like a mother to me than my own, but you need her now more than I do." She paused and looked at her daughter, her eyes wet with unshed tears. "Oh, Bettina, this month has gone by too quickly. You are finally leaving me to start a life of your own."

"But you said it will not be forever, Mama," Bettina replied, edging her long, slender legs over the side of the bed.

"Yes, but that does not help the fact that you are leaving today."

"Maddy and I still have to travel to Saint-Malo, where the ship is, and you and Papa will come with us that far. You knew this day would come, Mama."

"Oh, why did André have to choose a man who lives across the sea?" Jossel asked, wringing her hands. Then she shook her head in resignation. "Well, it is done. Now you must prepare, for we leave in two hours' time. Oh, where are those maids?"

Bettina laughed. "They are probably in the kitchen discussing my journey. They seem to think Saint Martin is going to be an exciting place to live. But I can dress myself, anyway. You forget I did without servants all those years at school."

The maids finally came, and after receiving a tongue-lashing from Jossel, they rushed about the large bedroom, laying out the clothes that Bettina would wear for the journey to Saint-Malo. One of the maids left the room to get water for Bettina's bath, and for the next two hours everybody scurried about, seeing to the last details.

Soon, Bettina and Madeleine were ready to go, wearing comfortably warm traveling clothes, for it was October and the weather was quite chilly this early morning. Mama joined them at the entrance, and, surprisingly, it was André who was the last to arrive.

The large coach that André had purchased especially for the journey to Saint-Malo was impressive indeed. It was drawn by six coal-black horses and was large enough to carry all the trunks on top, including the small chest that contained Bettina's dowry in gold.

Bettina leaned back on the velvet seat, with her mother beside her, and closed her eyes. The past month had been hectic, and she and most of the household had worked day and night on her trousseau. Her wedding dress had taken the longest time to make, of course, but it was a beautiful garment, a masterpiece, and all who had worked on it were proud of the results.

The dress was creamy white satin, the same color as Bettina's hair, covered with handmade lace, except for the tight-fitting sleeves. Flowing lace sleeves fell away from the shimmering satin ones. It was a beautiful gown, caught tight about the waist, with a square neckline and flowing skirt, the lace divided in the front of the skirt to reveal the satin beneath. Bettina would wear white satin slippers with the dress, and the white pearls André had given her on her nineteenth birthday. Her veil, yards of white lace, had been worn by her mother on her own wedding day.

Madeleine had personally supervised the packing of the wedding dress in a separate trunk so it would not wrinkle too badly. She felt she was reliving the past, for twenty-two years before she'd gone through the same preparations for Jossel's marriage.

The small three-masted vessel lay at anchor for many days, waiting for the passengers who would sail to Saint Martin.

Jacques Marivaux, captain of the *Windsong*, stood on the fore-deck, a frown on his bronzed, weather-beaten face as he gazed out into the harbor. He was uneasy.

The Comte de Lambert had commissioned Jacques to go to France, pick up his intended bride and her servant, and take them back to Saint Martin. When de Lambert had first approached him, Jacques had been ready to resign from the *comte's* service rather than transport women. But de Lambert had made too tempting an offer.

This young woman must mean a great deal to the *comte*. But still, there were numerous difficulties involved. Jacques would have to isolate the women from his rough, randy crew. Also, women were supposed to be bad luck on board ship, and the superstitious would blame every mishap on them. The women themselves would expect to be pampered, with fine food and comfortable quarters. Jacques knew this was going to be the worst voyage of his twenty years at sea.

Luckily, they had been at Saint-Malo for a week, and his crew had been let loose on the town since they first docked. They should have had their fill of women to last them awhile. But during the last month at sea he would have to worry about mutiny.

Then Jacques saw a large carriage turn off a side street and rumble onto the dock. That must be the bride and her family, he thought apprehensively, seeing the many trunks piled on top. He would have to round up his crew tonight and set sail tomorrow, if the wind permitted. *Mon Dieu!* Why had he taken this commission?

Bettina looked out the small carriage window and saw the many ships at anchor in the harbor. There were so many vessels, all of different sizes, that she wondered which one could be the *Windsong*. André had said it was a small three-masted vessel, but there were many that fit that description. She would have to learn more about ships, since the *comte* owned many vessels, the *Windsong* only one of them.

The carriage pulled to a halt, and André got out and asked a passing sailor where the *Windsong* was anchored. As it turned out, they were right in front of her. André went up the gangplank and spoke with a big man standing on deck. After a few minutes, he came back and entered the carriage again.

"The *capitaine* has to get his crew together, so we will take lodgings for this night. The trunks will be unloaded and put aboard now, so there will be a short delay here."

André was being generous, for usually he didn't waste his time explaining anything to his family.

The inn where they took lodgings was fairly decent. Bettina had a small room to herself, and she enjoyed her last bath that night. Jossel had told her that, unfortunately, she would not be able to bathe properly for the duration of the voyage. So Bettina soaked in fragrant suds for two hours.

The following morning, before the sun had risen above the horizon, the captain of the *Windsong* called on Bettina personally. André quickly introduced Captain Jacques Marivaux to his daughter, and they hurriedly left for the ship.

Bettina cried, as she'd known she would, and so did Madeleine and Jossel when they said good-bye to each other. Bettina also kissed André lightly on the cheek, though he seemed embarrassed. But he was, after all, the only father she had ever known, and she couldn't help loving him, despite his strictness. It would have been nice, though, if André could have said he loved her, just this once.

So she said good-bye to André Verlaine, a small man who would never again cause her heartache. But she couldn't bear to leave her mother, and it took an impatient Captain Marivaux to separate them. He hurried them, for the ship had to clear the harbor in order to catch the morning breeze that would take her out to sea.

With a last tearful glance at her mother and her beloved France, Bettina turned and walked carefully up the gangplank. All eyes on board the ship were drawn to her. There had been no time this morning to bind her hair up, so she had just tied it back with ribbons. The snowy blond tresses streaming down her back were a sight to behold as the sun caught and lit her hair to blinding brilliance.

It was a moment of anxiety for Captain Marivaux as his crew

21

stared hypnotized at Bettina. He had not expected Comte de Lambert's intended bride to be such a beauty. *Mon Dieu,* but the *comte* was an extremely lucky man.

Captain Marivaux barked orders left and right, and reluctantly the crew dispersed. However, many still ogled the women, so the captain quickly escorted them to his cabin and left them there. He was giving up his cabin for the remainder of the voyage because it was the largest on the ship and Comte de Lambert had insisted his bride be made comfortable. The arrangement was hardly satisfactory, but it would have to do.

Besides the women, he was also transporting a fortune in gold that was Mademoiselle Verlaine's dowry. Why Monsieur Verlaine thought he needed to send so much gold was beyond Jacques. The beautiful *mademoiselle* was all the prize any man could want. She did not need a fortune to go with her.

The gold that Jacques Marivaux was carrying might make any man turn pirate. The *mademoiselle* alone was temptation enough. But the captain had given his word, and it was a matter of honor. He would see the *mademoiselle* safely to Comte de Lambert or die trying.

Chapter 4

After a week at sea, Bettina missed the luxury of her baths. The small bowl of water allotted to her each day was hardly sufficient, and she soon found that her dirty hair was to be her worst problem. But after two weeks she was able to wash it, when the *Windsong* encountered her first rainstorm on this voyage. She had to go on deck, which the captain sternly disapproved of, and let the rain caught by the slackened sails pour down on her. It meant getting soaked to the bone and having to walk across the slippery, dangerous decks, but it was worth it.

The men were ordered below decks, for the captain preferred not to take chances. But with Jacques Marivaux and his officers on guard, and Madeleine beside her, Bettina felt quite safe.

The captain joined Bettina a few times for dinner, and each time he stressed that she must remain out of sight of the crew. She was allowed on deck in the late evening, after most of the crew was below, but only if the captain or one of his officers was with her. Bettina couldn't understand why, and the captain was too embarrassed to explain. Finally, Bettina asked Madeleine why she couldn't have the freedom of the ship.

"It's not for you to concern yourself with, *ma chérie,*" Madeleine said. "You just do as the *capitaine* instructs."

"But you do know the reason, don't you, Maddy?" Bettina pressed her.

"Yes, I suppose I do."

"Then why do you hesitate to tell me? I am not a child anymore."

Madeleine shook her head. "You are innocent of life, and a child in many ways. You know nothing of men, and the less you know, the better."

"You cannot protect me forever, Maddy. I will have a husband soon. Must I be completely ignorant?"

"No — no, I suppose you are right. But do not expect this old woman to tell you everything you want to know."

"Very well, just tell me why I cannot have the freedom of the ship," Bettina replied.

"Because you must not tempt the crew with your beauty, my pet. Men have strong desires that make them want to make love to a woman, especially one as lovely as you."

"Oh!" Bettina gasped. "But surely they know that they cannot."

"Yes, but if the crew is subjected to seeing you every day, then they will begin to want you. This desire that a man has can become so overpowering that he will even risk death to make love to a woman."

"How do you know all of these things, Maddy?" Bettina asked, smiling.

"I may never have married, but I have knowledge of men. When I was young, I was not shielded from them as you have been, Bettina."

"You mean you have made love with a man?"

"Now your curiosity goes too far, young lady. Leave this old woman in peace."

"Oh, Maddy." Bettina sighed, for she knew Madeleine would tell her no more, and there were so many things that she wanted to know. Perhaps after she was married all her questions would be answered. But she couldn't help wondering what making love would be like. It must be a great pleasure if men would risk their lives to do it. But she would just have to wait until she was married; then she would learn what it was all about.

After three weeks at sea, a most unpleasant incident occurred. Bettina was alone in her cabin, for Madeleine had left her to wash some of their clothes. When the door opened, Bettina didn't even glance up, thinking it was Madeleine returning. But she screamed when two hands clamped down on her shoulders and spun her around. The man didn't seem to hear her. He just held her, his glazed eyes covering her body slowly, but he made no move to do anything else.

"Seize him!" the captain shouted.

Bettina started, and then two men hurried into the cabin and took hold of the man. She followed in confusion and watched as the man was dragged across the deck, despite his frantic struggling. He was then tied to the mainmast and the first officer ripped his tunic fiercely apart.

Captain Marivaux appeared beside Bettina, scowling. "It is most unfortunate that this has happened, *mademoiselle*. Comte de Lambert will be furious when he learns that you were nearly raped."

Bettina did not look at the captain, for she was staring as if in a daze at the poor man who was awaiting his punishment. The first officer himself stood behind the man with a short whip in his hand. The whip was made of coiled leather, about a yard long, frayed into many knotted strands.

The captain addressed his crew harshly, but Bettina was too appalled at what was about to happen to even listen to his words. Then Captain Marivaux gave the signal and the first officer cracked the whip in the air once, twice, then brought it down with brutal force across the man's back. Thin trickles of blood ran down from the red streaks across the man's quivering flesh. Then another streak appeared as the whip lashed down once more.

"No, for God's sake! Stop this!" Bettina cried.

"It must be done, Mademoiselle Verlaine. The crew was warned, so it is no fault of yours."

Again and again that horrible instrument tore into the man's back, splattering his blood across the deck and onto nearby men's clothing. Bettina didn't know when she ran to the railing. Perhaps it was when the man started screaming, but even that didn't last for long. When her retching finally stopped, she could still hear the horrible sound of the whip tearing into the man's flesh, and there was not another sound to be heard.

Finally it stopped. Thirty lashes had been given, she was told later, and the man was only barely alive. In Bettina's mind, the man had only frightened her, and for this he was writhing in pain and would be useless for the remainder of the voyage.

Bettina cried that night, and she was sick three more times, every time she thought about that horrible scene. A man had almost died because he had nearly raped her. Raped.

"What did the *capitaine* mean, Maddy, when he said that man nearly raped me?" Bettina asked late that same night. "All he did was look at me, and for that he suffered terrible pain."

Madeleine, who was lying on her small cot, was staring moodily at the ceiling of the cabin. She was as disturbed as Bettina over what had happened that day, but her concern was for her ward.

She looked at Bettina now, a worried expression on her face. "He would have done more than that if the *capitaine* had not come in time. This is my fault, Bettina. I should not have left you alone."

"But the man did nothing, and now he is marred for life because of me!"

"He disobeyed the *capitaine*'s orders, and for that he was whipped. The crew was warned not to go near you, Bettina, but this man did not heed the warning. He would have made love to you if the *capitaine* had not heard your scream," Madeleine said quietly.

"Then why didn't the capitaine say that, instead of saying he nearly raped me?"

"Did you want that man to touch you?"

"Of course not," Bettina replied.

"Well, he would not have taken your wishes into consideration. He would have forced himself on you against your will, and that is rape."

Bettina leaned back on her own cot, her mind in a whirl. So that's what rape was — making love to women who did not want to be made love to. How awful! But then, she still didn't know what making love was all about. Oh, she was so stupid! When would she learn? When would she find out what making love was like? When she was married, she reminded herself, and that would be soon enough.

Chapter 5

The *Windsong* was making rapid headway into warmer waters, but she still had a great distance to go before reaching Saint Martin. The weather had changed considerably, and the wind no longer had such an icy bite to it.

Bettina knew that she could look forward to a warm tropical climate on the small island of Saint Martin. Captain Marivaux answered many questions when he dined with her. She learned that her future husband owned a large plantation on the island and that he had gained great wealth by exporting cotton.

After the horrible time when that poor seaman was whipped so cruelly, no other such incidents occurred. The crew was careful to stay well away from Bettina when she was allowed on deck.

After a month at sea, they encountered another storm that was quite mild at first, and Bettina was able to wash her hair again. But she had barely finished when the storm increased in intensity, and she was forced to return to the safety of her cabin.

It seemed as if the heavens had opened up and were throwing their vengeance on this ship alone. It stormed all through the night, and the violent pitching of the ship made it impossible for Bettina to sleep. She tried pacing the floor nervously but was quickly thrown against the walls of the cabin. Luckily, everything was securely fastened down, and Bettina dashed back to the built-in captain's bed for protection.

Amazingly, Madeleine had fallen asleep quite easily, which annoyed Bettina, who was very frightened. She was sure that the *Windsong* would crash over into the sea and they would all drown.

But sometime in the middle of the night, with her hands braced against the sides of the little bed and her still-wet

27

hair trailing over the side, Bettina herself finally went to sleep.

The sea was calm the following morning when Bettina awoke. She chided herself for being so frightened the night before, and was sure it hadn't been such a bad storm after all.

Madeleine was already up and dressed, and pouring the allotted amount of cold water into a small bowl for Bettina's morning toilette.

"Did you sleep well, my pet?" she asked cheerfully.

"I did not," Bettina grumbled and swung her long legs off the bed. Her damp hair fell over her shoulders, and she grimaced. "Maddy, be a dear and go ask the *capitaine* if I can dry my hair on deck."

"I will do no such thing. You are not going out there in the morning," Madeleine answered adamantly.

"If I have the *capitaine's* permission, then it will be all right. And you know how long my hair took to dry last time. I nearly caught cold."

"There is worse you can catch up on deck," Madeleine replied.

"Please, Maddy, do as I ask."

"I will, but I don't like it."

Madeleine left the cabin, grumbling to herself as she closed the door. Bettina dressed quickly in a velvet dress of a dark violet that contrasted vividly with her hair. When Madeleine returned, she led Bettina to the rear deck of the ship.

"I still don't like this, young lady, so be quick about it," Madeleine said sternly.

Bettina laughed. "I cannot make the wind blow faster, Maddy. But it will not take long."

She faced the wide expanse of sea to let the wind sweep through her hair, drying it swiftly. After a few minutes she spoke again.

"Where is the *capitaine?*"

"On the gallery. I am surprised he agreed to let you on deck after what that poor sailor attempted."

Bettina turned to see the captain in a heated argument with one of his crewmen.

"Look, Bettina, a ship!" Madeleine cried.

Bettina turned and saw the other sail in the distance.

"Ladies, you must return to your cabin quickly." Bettina jumped as the captain came up behind her. "If that seadog of a lookout had been doing his job, instead of watching you, then he would have seen the vessel in time. As it is, they are coming straight for us."

"Is there anything to be alarmed about, *Capitaine?*" Bettina asked worriedly, a frown puckering her brow.

"That ship is not flying her colors. She may be a pirate vessel."

Bettina gasped. "But surely they will not attack the *Windsong*!"

"It is unlikely that they will, *mademoiselle,* but one never knows about these cutthroats. We will try to outdistance them, and I must ask that you lock the door to your cabin. Do not open it for any reason until the danger is past. And do not worry. We have succeeded in fighting off pirates before."

Bettina felt sick inside. Do not worry, the captain said! How could she *not* worry? She had heard vivid stories about pirates from other girls in the convent. Pirates were horrible, horrible men! They were the rogues of the sea, the Devil's workers, who plundered, murdered, and raped. *Mon Dieu,* this could not possibly be happening!

"Maddy, I am frightened," Bettina cried, close to tears.

"We are not going to worry. This is an able ship, my pet. The pirates will not have a chance to board her. And besides, the other vessel may be friendly. You must not fear, Bettina. The *capitaine* will protect you, as will I."

Madeleine's words were reassuring, but Bettina was still alarmed, and even more so when they heard cannonfire. Madeleine's soft gray eyes widened as she stared at Bettina, who had turned suddenly pale. A thunderous blast echoed in the small cabin, and then they heard the cracking of timber and a loud crash. They knew that one of the *Windsong*'s masts had fallen.

Soon they felt a jarring, as of one ship coming up against the other. Shouting could be heard, and gunfire, and the sickening sound of screams — men screaming as they met their deaths.

Madeleine sank to her knees to pray, and Bettina quickly joined her. After a short while, the gunfire ceased, and they heard boisterous laughter. Perhaps the crew of the *Windsong* had won.

Was it too much to hope for, that they were safe now? But then they heard English words among the laughter. The crew of the *Windsong* was entirely French, and spoke only French. The pirates had won!

Chapter 6

"Cap'n! The wench I told ye 'bout, she's got to be hidin' in the hold or in one o' them cabins."

"Blast it, man, we don't have all day! Search the whole ship, but be quick about it."

Bettina felt the sweat of fear break out all over her, and she wanted to die.

"Why, oh why didn't the *capitaine* give us a weapon?" Bettina whispered, clasping her hands to still their trembling.

"He did not expect to lose the battle," Madeleine answered quietly. "But do not worry, Bettina. I will tell their leader that he can gain a great fortune if he will deliver you unharmed to Comte de Lambert. The *comte* will surely pay the price. He is a Frenchman and honorable."

"But these men are pirates, Maddy!" Bettina cried. "They will kill us!"

"No, my pet. They won't kill us without reason. You must not worry about that, and you must not act frightened when they find us. Pretend you do not speak their English. I will speak for you. And for God's sake, do not lose your temper with these men," Madeleine warned. "If you do, they will not think you are a lady of good breeding and wealth."

"I am too frightened to lose my temper."

"Good. Now, we must pray that their leader's greed for wealth is more powerful than his lust."

"I don't understand, Maddy."

"Never mind, *ma chérie*," Madeleine replied, her voice betraying her concern. "Just remember to say nothing."

The laughter and noise became louder as men moved back and forth in front of their cabin.

"She weren't in the hold, Cap'n, an' them other cabins were empty."

"Tear down the last door," replied a deep voice very near to the cabin, and the pounding started immediately.

"Dear God!"

"Hush, now." Madeleine said quickly. "Remember to speak no English!"

Bettina was beside herself with fear. She was sure she would meet her death this day, and Madeleine could do nothing to prevent it. After a few more moments, the door crashed in, and Bettina screamed when she saw the grinning, bearded men.

"Glory, but them Frenchies sure turn out beauties!" said a short sailor with a patch over one eye.

"Aye, mate. I'd give me blessed mother to be the cap'n today."

"Where is your *capitaine?*" Madeleine asked curtly.

"Ye'll see 'im soon enough, old woman," one bearded man said, leading them out of the cabin.

Bettina avoided looking at the dead bodies of the *Windsong*'s crew as she crossed the deck and was handed down to the other vessel. Madeleine kept close by her side, with one arm around her waist for protection.

The pirate ship was three-masted, about the same size as the *Windsong*. But the crew was a rowdy, unkempt bunch. The men stopped what they were doing and stared at Bettina. Some wore no shirts, others wore only short vests to cover bare chests, and most were barefooted. Many wore golden rings in their ears, and all were heavily bearded.

"I demand to see your *capitaine*," Madeleine said to the man who had escorted them onto the pirate vessel.

Another man jumped down from the deck of the *Windsong* and came around to face them.

"So you speak English," he said. "Well, at least we will know your worth now."

He was a big bear of a man, and Bettina felt tiny and frail standing next to him. She was used to looking at men on their own eye level, and even looking down on quite a few. But this man was at least six feet tall and at least two feet wide across his chest. He was not fat, but was heavily muscled, as could be seen clearly by his huge, bare arms. His light-brown hair was cut short, coming only to his massive shoulders. But the thick, full beard that completely covered his face made him look so sinister, so dangerous. Bettina shivered.

"Well, what have you discovered, Jules?"

It was the man with the deep voice, who seemed to be in command. He jumped down onto the deck behind them.

"They speak English, Tristan, at least the old one does."

This man Tristan stood directly behind Bettina, and she turned around to face him. What she saw made her gasp, for this man was even taller than the other one. He was truly a giant! He was only a few inches from her, and Bettina had to look up past his broad chest to see his face. His eyes were a startling pale blue, and a long, thin scar started in the middle of his right cheek and cut a path into the dark gold of his beard.

Bettina stared for long moments at the thin scar, and the man's muscles tightened and his eyes grew icy. He grabbed hold of her arm, making her wince, and started to walk her across the deck.

"*Monsieur,* wait!" Madeleine cried. "Where are you taking her?"

The man turned around and smiled coldly. "To my cabin, *madame,* to talk with the young lady. Have you any objections?"

"Of course!"

"Well, save them!" he said curtly and dragged Bettina along.

"*Monsieur,* she does not speak English," Madeleine called after him.

This brought laughter from the crew, and halted the man again.

"How ye goin' to tell 'er what to do, Cap'n?"

"Fer what the cap'n 'as in mind, no words is necessary."

More laughter followed, which obviously annoyed the captain, for his grip tightened on Bettina's arm. She cried out in pain, and he released her immediately.

"Blast you scurvy dogs!" he shouted at his crew. "You've had enough amusement for one day. Get to your duties and get this ship under way." He then turned to Bettina. "I am sorry if I hurt you, *mademoiselle.*"

She had not expected an apology from this pirate captain.

33

Was he not as dangerous as he looked? She stared at him curiously, but did not speak.

"Blast!" he said, scowling, and turned to the other big man. "Jules, bring that woman here."

Madeleine hurried to them without assistance, charged with concern. "You are not to harm her, *Capitaine!*"

The captain looked at Madeleine with surprise, then suddenly burst into laughter. "Are you giving me orders, *madame?*"

"I cannot let you harm her, *monsieur.*"

Jules chuckled at this, but the captain flashed him a murderous look, then focused his attention on Madeleine again.

"Are you her mother?"

"No, I was nurse to her and her mother both. I will be nurse to her children as well," Madeleine replied proudly.

"Is she with child now?"

"*Monsieur!* You cannot ask —"

"Blast it, answer me, woman!" the captain cut her off sharply.

"No, she is not."

The captain's annoyance seemed to disappear with her answer. "Now tell me, why do you speak English and she does not?"

"I — I was born in England. I came to France as a child with my parents," Madeleine said truthfully.

"She speaks no English at all?"

"No, *Capitaine.*"

He sighed and studied Bettina, who had been watching him the whole time. "Who is she?"

"Mademoiselle Bettina Verlaine."

"And where was she being taken?"

"To Saint Martin, to be married to Comte de Lambert," Madeleine replied quickly.

"And the fortune that was found on your vessel — it was her dowry?"

"Yes."

The pirate captain smiled lazily, displaying even, white teeth. "Her family must be very rich. And her betrothed, he is also a man of wealth?"

"Yes, he will pay you well if you deliver her safely to Saint

34

Martin — unharmed."

He laughed at her last word. "I'm sure he will, but I will have to think on the matter." He turned to Jules. "Take the nurse to your cabin and lock her in. The *mademoiselle* will come with me."

Madeleine was dragged away, screaming and kicking to be free, and Bettina suddenly felt horribly afraid. She couldn't stop thinking of the stories she'd heard in the convent. Wouldn't a quick death be preferable? She looked at the railing of the ship. It was not so far to reach, and then to be engulfed in the cold blue water. . . .

"Oh, no, Bettina Verlaine, not yet, anyway," the captain said, as if reading her mind.

He took her arm and led her to his cabin. Inside the small, disorderly room, the captain sat Bettina down in a chair beside a long table. He filled two tankards with a dry red wine, handed her one, and sat down also. The long table obviously served as a desk, for it was covered with charts and nautical instruments.

He leaned back in his chair and stared at her silently. She watched his light-blue eyes nervously, and felt the color rising to her cheeks under his close examination.

"My men seem to think you are a beauty, Bettina," he remarked casually. "But frankly I don't see how they could tell with that black powder covering your face."

Bettina instinctively tried to rub away the black. But when her hand came away clean, she realized he had tricked her.

"So you understand English after all. I thought as much. Why did your servant lie?"

Bettina hesitated before answering. "She — she did not want me to talk to you. I think she was afraid I would lose my temper."

"And will you?"

"I see no reason why I should."

The captain laughed deeply. "Was the old woman lying about your betrothal also?"

"No."

"So this Comte de Lambert really is a wealthy man?"

"Yes, extremely so, *capitaine,*" Bettina replied, beginning to relax a little.

The man didn't seem half so dangerous as she had expected him to be. She had to admit he was handsome, and he appeared to be young, though his golden beard made him look older.

"You will be a rich man if you take me to my betrothed," Bettina said.

"I have no doubt of that," he replied easily. "But your dowry alone has made me a rich man, and I don't hold with carrying women on my ship."

"Then what will you do with me, *monsieur,* throw me into the sea — after you have raped me?" she asked sarcastically.

"Exactly."

She stared at him, aghast. She had expected a denial, but without one, what could she say?

"Is — is that your intention?" she asked fearfully.

He stared down at his tankard of wine for a moment, as if contemplating her question. Then he looked at her, an amused expression on his face.

"Take off your clothes."

"What?" Bettina whispered.

"I intend to make love to you, Bettina Verlaine, then I will take you to your betrothed. So take off your clothes. I would rather not have to rape you and perhaps hurt you in the process."

"*Non, monsieur, non!* Comte de Lambert will not take me if I am dishonored!"

"I assure you, *mademoiselle,* he will take you, and he will pay a high price to do so. He has seen you, hasn't he?"

"Yes, but —"

"Then there is no question about it. Your lack of virginity will not matter too much."

"No!" Bettina replied adamantly. "I will not go to him dishonored. It would shame my family. I will not do this!"

"I'm afraid you have no choice in the matter. But I'm sure the *comte* will hide the fact that you will be no virgin on your wedding night," the captain remarked calmly.

"No, you cannot do this to me!" Bettina cried, her green eyes wide with fear.

"I repeat, Bettina, I am going to make love to you. Nothing

36

will save you from that. But I don't want to have to force you. I don't like rape."

"But it is rape, *monsieur,* for I don't want to make love!"

"Call it what you like, as long as you don't fight me."

"You — you must be crazy! You cannot expect me to be submissive, to just let you — I won't!" she stormed, her fear replaced by anger. "I will fight you with all my power!"

"Let us strike a bargain, *mademoiselle.* Besides you and your servant, a few other prisoners were brought aboard for sport, including the captain of the French ship."

"For sport?"

"My men are a ruthless bunch. They seem to take pleasure in killing a man slowly. First they cut off the ears, then the fingers, then the feet — need I go on?"

Bettina felt sick. "You — you allow this?"

"Why not?"

She turned pale at his answer. He must participate in this sport also. *Mon Dieu!*

"You spoke — of a — bargain," she said weakly.

"Your submission for the lives of those men. You I will have whether you fight me or not. I will not be denied you. But I will spare the lives of the prisoners and set them free in the next port on one condition — that you don't fight me." He paused and smiled. "You have lost already, Bettina, for I will have you no matter what you decide. But the prisoners have everything to gain. They will live and not be harmed if you agree. I want your answer now."

"You are merciless!" Bettina gasped. "Why must you rape me?"

"You surprise me. You are a prize worth having, and I want you," he said.

"But I do not want you!"

"I will tell you, Bettina, that you are the only reason I captured your ship. I usually prey only on Spanish vessels. My lookout saw you on deck and described your beauty to me. You should be grateful that I don't intend to share you with my crew. But enough, I want your answer!"

"You leave me no choice," Bettina replied slowly, feeling completely helpless for the first time in her life. "I must save the lives of those men."

"You will put up no resistance?"

"No, *monsieur,* I will not fight you."

"Good. You have made a wise decision. I'm sure the prisoners will be most grateful. I will tell the men to leave them be. While I'm gone, I want you to remove your clothing and wait in my bed."

He left and closed the door after him. There was no escape. There was absolutely nothing Bettina could do now, and she wouldn't even have the satisfaction of fighting him.

Reluctantly, and very slowly, Bettina started to undress. She was finally going to find out what making love was like — or rape, anyway. Well, at least by her submission she would save the lives of a few Frenchmen. She kept that thought with her to help her endure what would follow.

When the captain came back into the cabin, Bettina was still wearing her shift. He closed the door, then frowned at her.

"You haven't changed your mind, have you?" he asked brusquely.

"No, have you?"

He laughed then, and walked across the cabin to stand before her. She felt small and helpless next to his towering frame.

"No, little one. Nothing can make me change my mind." He gathered the mass of her hair in his hands and rubbed it between his fingers, feeling its soft, silky texture. Then he laid it over her shoulders.

"Remove your shift, Bettina. I can't wait much longer."

"I hate you, *monsieur!*" she hissed through clenched teeth.

He laughed again "Although *monsieur* sounds lovely coming from your sweet lips, I would prefer you to call me Tristan. Now, finish your wine, Bettina, for it may help you somewhat. I have never lain with a virgin before, but I've been told it is painful the first time."

"It would take two barrels of wine to wipe away what you are about to do, Monsieur Tristan!"

"Just Tristan! And don't try my patience, Bettina. What will happen to you will happen, but I can still change my mind about the prisoners. Drink the wine and then remove your shift without further comment."

Bettina could not delay any longer. She drank the wine, turned her back to him, and slowly removed her last piece of clothing. She veiled her body with her knee-length flaxen hair, then turned to face him.

Tristan did not take her gesture as defiance, merely as modesty, but he would not allow even that. He parted her hair and feasted his eyes on her slender body for many moments. Then he took her face in his hands and kissed her tenderly.

Bettina had not expected this. Why did he kiss her? Why not get it over and done with?

His lips parted hers, searching, demanding a response. She wanted to pull away, but he would consider that resistance. She had to think of those poor captured men and nothing else. She must let him have his way with her.

His arms circled her and pressed her unclad body against him, and his mouth became more demanding, hard, and yet not hurting. And suddenly Bettina felt a strange sensation, something she had never experienced before. It was an unusual feeling, as if she could actually feel the blood flowing through her veins. It was an exciting feeling, and it made her relax against him and accept his kiss willingly, made her forget she was standing naked in a stranger's arms.

Then he stopped kissing her, and picked her up in his powerful arms. She stiffened as he carried her to his bed and there laid her down gently. He took off his clothing with slow deliberation, keeping his eyes on her the whole time. She in turn could not look away from him, though she wanted to. When at last he was naked, Bettina stared in amazement at his lean, muscular body; the wide shoulders that tapered to narrow hips, the hard, flat middle and long, firm legs.

Tristan came to her and lay down beside her on the narrow bed. He looked into her face for a long while and then brushed one hand across her breasts. He watched for her reaction, and it came immediately as her eyes widened in confusion.

He laughed softly and cupped one breast, squeezing it gently. "Did you expect me to be quick about it?"

"Yes. Oh, please, Tristan, please don't do this to me. I ask you once more, please spare me this shame!" she pleaded uselessly.

"No, little one, it is too late for that."

"Then be done with it!" she said sharply.

His eyes narrowed angrily. He mounted her then, his great weight pressing her into the soft mattress. He thrust into her quickly, and a searing pain followed. She screamed and dug her nails into his back, but as quickly as the pain had come, it was gone.

He moved inside her, slowly at first, then faster, much faster, and it actually felt good. Bettina relaxed and shamefully enjoyed the feeling of him inside her. But then he gave a final deep thrust and relaxed completely, crushing her with his huge body.

Bettina didn't know what to do. Was that all there was to it? She admitted it had been pleasant after the initial pain, but if that was all there was to making love, she could do without it. Where was the extreme pleasure that could make a man risk death? Perhaps only the man experienced pleasure from making love.

"I'm sorry, Bettina. I didn't mean to be so quick, but you have a sharp tongue. Next time, it will be better for you."

"Next time!" she gasped. "But I — I thought that —"

"No, little one," he cut her off with an amused smile. "Saint Martin is a long way off. And since you will be sharing my cabin with me, I will make love to you whenever I wish. This will be a most pleasant voyage."

When he got up and began to dress, Bettina quickly pulled the cover over her nakedness. What was she going to do? Lying with him once was bad enough, but he had given her no choice and she would have been able to live with that shame. But to submit to him again and again, and not be able to fight him — she would be his mistress! How could she live with that?

Tristan had been quietly scrutinizing her. Now he leaned over her and softly brushed his lips against hers.

"I must leave you now, to see my crew and change course for Saint Martin. Under no condition do I want you to leave this cabin."

"But I want to see Maddy. I want to see the prisoners and tell them they have nothing to fear."

"No," he said sharply. "Your servant can see to the prisoners, and you can see her later — not now."

With that he left the cabin. Bettina thought of locking the door against him. But he would only break it down, and then she would have to suffer his anger. She shuddered to think what that would be like. So far, this Tristan had been in a good mood and had shown only one side of his character, and yet he had taken her against her will. She wouldn't care to see his violent side.

She was at the mercy of a ruthless pirate! He could kill her if he wanted to! She was completely in his power, and she didn't know what to do about it.

She got off the bed and stared stupidly at the blood on the covers — her own blood. I hate you, *Capitaine* Tristan, she thought bitterly. You have ruined me, shamed me, dishonored me! She stamped her foot in outraged fury.

Bettina's breathing slowed. There was no point in getting so upset, when she couldn't take it out on him. But she wanted to — how she wanted to!

There was a small bowl of water on a washstand by the bed, and with this Bettina washed herself as best she could. She hurriedly dressed, then rebelliously poured more wine into the tankard on the table. She sat down and started to drink, but then she heard a soft knock on the door. A second later, it opened and Madeleine rushed in and closed the door quickly.

"Oh, Bettina, are you all right? He — he didn't — he —"

"He will take us to Saint Martin, but —"

"Then you were spared — thank God! I was afraid for you, Bettina. *Mon Dieu!* I did not know what to think when he had me locked up. The *capitaine* is such a big man — I was afraid he would hurt you."

"I was not spared," Bettina said quietly. "He was determined to take me, and he did."

"Bettina — no!" Madeleine gasped. She started to cry.

"It's all right," Bettina said, putting her arms around her old nurse. "At least we are still alive. And he has promised to

41

take us to Saint Martin."

"My God, Bettina! He didn't have to rape you. The man has no honor!"

"I tried to dissuade him, but he wanted me. He said he would have me regardless of anything. It is done now, and there is nothing I can do about it. But at least I was able to save the prisoners."

"What prisoners?"

"You have not seen them yet?" Bettina asked.

"I didn't know there were any," Madeleine replied. "That big man called Jules let me out of his cabin and told me to go help in the galley. Their cook was killed in the last battle they fought. But I came here first."

"Well, go and find the prisoners. *Capitaine* Marivaux is one of them. Tell them not to worry about their fate, that they will be set free in the next port. And if any are wounded, care for them, then come back and tell me how they are. The *capitaine* will not let me leave the cabin."

"Is there anything I can do for you first?" Madeleine asked, her gray eyes filled with concern. "I hate to leave you after what you have been through."

"No, I am fine, Maddy. I thought it would be a horrible experience, but it was not so bad," Bettina said. "He was gentle with me, and he is young and pleasant to look upon. The only thing that hurt was that he gave me no choice — he didn't care about my feelings."

"I am glad you have taken this so well."

"There is nothing else I can do," Bettina said.

Madeleine left, but returned after only a few minutes had passed. "There are no prisoners, Bettina. I asked one of the crewmen if he would take me to them, but he said no one was brought aboard but you and me. I asked another, and he said the same."

Bettina stiffened. Every nerve, every fiber in her body was filled with rage.

"He lied! He lied to me — he tricked me! Damn his soul to hell!"

"Bettina!" Madeleine gasped. "What is the matter with you?"

"He — he lied to me! He told me there were prisoners, that he would spare their lives if — if I would not fight him!" Bettina stormed, her green eyes alight with a raging fire.

"Oh, Bettina!"

"So I submitted. God knows, I wanted to fight, but I did not. I could endure it because I thought I was saving the lives of those men. *Mon Dieu!* I will kill him!"

"No, Bettina, you must not talk like that! What has happened cannot be undone. And you said it was not so bad," Madeleine said.

"That is not the point! He tricked me. This *Capitaine* Tristan will find out what I think of deception! He will be sorry he ever brought me onto this ship. I will have revenge! I swear it—Tristan will pay for this!"

"For God's sake, Bettina, be sensible! You will only succeed in getting us killed."

But Madeleine might as well have kept silent, for Bettina was pacing the floor with angry strides, and her old servant's warning didn't even interrupt her murderous thoughts.

Chapter 7

"So, Tristan, what have you decided to do with the woman?" Jules asked when he joined his friend on deck.

"I will take her to Saint Martin. This Comte de Lambert will pay handsomely for her," Tristan replied. "And the ransom will be worth the delay in returning home."

"I agree, though the men may not. But don't you think this man will mind that his intended bride is no longer a virgin?"

"He won't know about it until after he has paid the ransom, and then it won't matter to us. But I doubt it will matter to her, either. He will still want her."

"You are a devil, Tristan," Jules laughed. "So the blond wench was as good as she looked, eh?"

"Better! But it is dangerous for a woman to be that lovely. She could have the world at her feet if she wanted, but I don't think she realizes her own worth. That one will wreck many lives before she is through."

"But not yours, eh?"

"No. I would consider keeping the wench for myself, but she might distract me, and I cannot rest until I find Bastida and put an end to his miserable life!" Tristan replied heatedly.

"I know what eats at you, Tristan, but let's not think of it now. There is time and enough to find Bastida."

"You're right, old friend. There are much more pleasant things to think of now."

Jules grinned mischievously. "I thought you liked your women willing."

"What I don't like is using force and facing a woman's wrath. But as usual, logic won out over force."

"The men, they envy you this one. I don't think any of them

have ever seen such a one as her," said Jules.

"Nor have I ever seen one so lovely before. She is a lady, but one with a temper."

"Well, after seeing her, the men have only one thing on their minds. I think it would be wise to drop anchor in the nearest port. Let the men have a day or two carousing in the brothels. That should help them forget the one tucked away in your cabin, and satisfy them until we return home."

"I agree," Tristan replied. "We can head for the Virgin Islands and make Tortola by nightfall. The men —" Tristan stopped short when he saw Bettina's servant talking to one of his men. "What is she doing out of your cabin?"

Jules looked in the same direction as Tristan, then answered, "I released her to work in the galley. We haven't had a decent meal since old Angus died."

"You trust the old woman not to poison us?" Tristan asked with a grin.

"No. I will see that she tastes the food herself before it is served."

Tristan frowned as he watched the servant slip into his cabin. "What the devil? My cabin is not the galley. Go ask Joco what the old woman spoke to him about."

Jules did as he was asked and came back to Tristan's side a few minutes later. "She asked to be taken to the prisoners. What would make —"

"Blast!" Tristan cut him off sharply. "I suppose Joco told her there were no prisoners?"

"Of course."

"Mother of God! You should have asked me before you released that old woman. Now I can expect the wrath of hell to fall on my head when I walk through that door!" Tristan exclaimed, nodding at his cabin.

"What are you talking about?"

"I told the girl we took prisoners. I told her I would spare their lives if she did not fight me. She agreed. But now she must know I tricked her. She is probably plotting right now how to tear my heart out!"

Jules burst out laughing. "You give the girl too much credit.

She's probably too frightened of you to do anything."

"I have doubts about that."

"Why did you tell the girl we had prisoners when we have never taken any before? Why didn't you just threaten the servant's life? That would surely have done the trick."

"I did not want the girl to think me monstrous enough to kill old women," Tristan answered irritably.

"Why should you care what she thinks of you?"

"Never mind," Tristan replied in a gruff voice. Then he saw the servant leaving his cabin. "Go speak with her. I would know what to expect before I enter my cabin and find my pate split open."

Jules left and returned with a halfhearted grin on his lips. "The old woman said the girl has vowed revenge and might do something foolish. Do you want me to go in first — to make sure she is not waiting to slit your throat?"

"I have been a fool! I didn't think to remove the daggers from my cabin."

"For the love of God, Tristan! You don't think she would —"

Tristan cut him off. "Yes, I do. I told you the girl has a temper. But since the daggers are in a box on the bookshelf, maybe she hasn't found them. At any rate, I can manage her."

"Tristan?"

"Do you think I can't handle a mere wisp of a girl?" Tristan laughed. "Come now, Jules. If I can take on six Spaniards in a single bout, what chance has that little French flower?"

"Women don't fight like men — just be careful," Jules replied.

"You have been with me a long time, Jules. When have you known me not to be careful?"

Jules could only sigh as Tristan walked away. His young friend knew nothing of women. Tristan had spent most of his life with only hatred in his heart and little time for anything else. How could he know that one woman's fury could match that of twenty Spaniards in a single bout?

Deciding on a surprise attack, Tristan opened the door to his cabin very quickly. Bettina stood on the far side of the room, giving no outward sign of the fury she felt. But he guessed she had found the daggers, for her hands were hidden in the folds

46

of her skirt. He didn't notice that her hair was braided so it would not hinder her attack, and that her eyes were a deep, smoldering green. Tristan just hoped that she didn't know how to handle a dagger, and especially that she wouldn't know how to throw one.

He crossed the room slowly, watching her arms. She wouldn't suspect him of knowing what she was about to do, so he had that advantage. When he reached the table, he turned his back on her, giving her a chance to attack. She did so immediately, and Tristan turned just in time to catch her uplifted wrist holding the long dagger.

He stared at her in disbelief as he twisted her wrist until she dropped the weapon. Tristan hadn't believed she would actually try to kill him. Threaten him, or fend him off, yes. But to raise the blade and try to spill his blood, no.

Mother of God! Did she have no care for her own life? Did she think that she could kill him and that his crew would do nothing about it? Perhaps she didn't care what happened to her. If that was so, this woman was more dangerous than he thought. If she could put her hatred for him above her own life, then — but wasn't that the way he felt about Bastida? He would have to take precautions with this little flaxen-haired beauty.

"What did you hope to gain?" he asked her quietly.

"I wanted to see you dead — by my hand!" she screamed, her eyes like flashing emeralds.

"You don't care about your own life?"

"I care only about the end of yours!" she fumed, struggling to pull her wrist free from his iron grip. "I will find a way, Tristan. I will kill you yet! You tricked me! You — you merciless pirate!" She struck out at him with her free hand, but he grabbed it in time. "You will pay for lying to me!"

"I lied to you — I admit it. But it was only to save a lot of trouble and pain. Would you have preferred me to rape you forcibly? It would have been quite easy, I assure you. You may be tall for a female, Bettina, and stronger than most, but as you can see now, you are no match for my strength. You are merely angry because I didn't allow you to fight for your virginity when you wanted to."

47

"And I would have fought you. You —"

"Yes, of that I am sure. So where is the harm? I saved you from hurt, for who knows what I might have done in the heat of passion to still your struggling. I have never been faced with the situation before, so I can't say for sure, but I might have beaten you or — killed you," he added, just to test her reaction.

"But you would not have been unharmed yourself, *monsieur,*" she spat at him.

"Really, Bettina?" He laughed deeply now. Never having been faced with a woman's anger, he began to find it amusing. "How would you have done that, when you can't escape my grip now?"

She stamped down hard on his foot in its soft boot, and his amused expression turned to one of pain. He released her immediately. She dashed to the opposite side of the table while he clasped his throbbing foot.

"Ha! You would not need all your strength, eh, *Capitaine?* You underestimate me! I will hurt you again, with great pleasure, if you so much as come near me!" Bettina raged.

She felt safe with the long table between them, for this Tristan was nothing but a big, clumsy ox. With her lithe form, which for once she was glad of, she would have no trouble at all staying out of his reach.

"You little she-devil!" he growled. "I will do more than come near you, vixen. I will take you again — now! And this time you can fight all you want, but don't be surprised if I give you the same."

She had expected him to circle the table, but when he started to climb over it, Bettina became alarmed. She picked up the first object within her reach, one of the heavy instruments lying on the table. He backed off when he saw her intent, but Bettina was not merely threatening him, she was out to do damage. She threw the object at him, then quickly reached for another and another, but he knocked the objects aside with his huge arms.

When the supply of weapons dwindled, Bettina picked up the last two that would be of any use, the two heavy tankards that they had drunk from earlier. She hurled them in quick succession, and, luckily, the second one struck Tristan's head. He fell forward and lay completely still on the floor of the cabin.

Bettina stared disbelievingly at his motionless body, but when she noticed the blood mingling with his dark-gold hair, panic began to rise in her. She carefully skirted his long, muscular body, and when she was out of his reach, she ran for the door. Swinging it wide open, she ran out onto the deck of the ship.

She knew only that she had to escape the cabin, escape from the sight of the murder she'd done. Perhaps she could hide, somehow find a weapon and force the crew to put her ashore. But before Bettina had run ten feet from the captain's cabin, a crewman caught her and pinned her against his foul-smelling body.

"What's this?" he laughed, enjoying the feel of her next to him. "The cap'n's wench out for a little walk?"

"Yes, and you will pay dearly if you do not let me go!" Bettina said angrily. Perhaps she could use the captain's power to gain what she needed, as long as the crew didn't discover that he was dead.

"Oh, will I now?" the man asked, but he released her just the same. "Do the cap'n know ye be on deck?"

"Yes. He's — he's sleeping." She realized her mistake too late.

"Sleepin'! The cap'n don't sleep in the middle o' the day. What lies be ye tellin' me, girl?" the man asked gruffly; then he looked up and called out. "Mr. Band'lar'. This wench says the cap'n be sleepin'."

"Go and see if she speaks the truth, Davey."

Bettina looked up and saw the big bulk of the first officer, who was standing on the gallery above her, as another seaman ran toward the captain's cabin.

"The *capitaine* said he did not wish to be disturbed!" Bettina said quickly, hearing the fear in her own voice.

"Do as I say, Davey!" Jules Bandelaire barked.

What could she do now? The man who had grabbed her was also moving swiftly toward the open door of the captain's cabin. Bettina looked about frantically, but she was suddenly surrounded by members of the crew, who had come to gaze at her and see what they were missing.

The man called Davey had entered the cabin, but now he appeared in the doorway, his face pale and disbelieving. "She's killed 'im! She's killed Cap'n Tristan!"

49

"Mother of God!" Jules bellowed and slammed his fist down on the railing, causing it to crack sickeningly.

Bettina dashed through the men who stood around her, but they were too shocked to notice — shocked that a mere wisp of a girl could kill their captain. But escape was hopeless. Jules jumped down from the gallery and grabbed Bettina's long braid, jerking her to a painful stop. Slowly, he pulled her back until his huge hand held her braid at the nape of her neck.

"I want you to know, bitch, that you have killed the only man I could call my friend. And for this you will die the worst of deaths, by my hands and mine alone!" He shoved her forward, and Bettina fell into the arms of two crewmen. "Tie her to the mainmast and stand by with water. This bitch will feel the full weight of the cat — until she is dead!" Jules stormed. His dark-brown eyes showed no mercy.

"Mon Dieu!" Bettina gasped. Her face turned ashen. Aboard the *Windsong*, the man had mercifully passed out soon after the whipping had begun, and had not regained consciousness. But she would be revived with water again and again. The captain's friend would make sure she felt every bite of the lash until she died. "Please, *monsieur!* Shoot me instead, I beg you!"

"You have killed the captain of this ship, who was also my friend. Shooting is too good for the likes of you," Jules said, his voice filled with hate.

Bettina struggled to break loose from the men who held her, but there was no escape. She was dragged to the mainmast and tied securely, embracing it. A moment later, someone ripped her beautiful velvet dress down the back. Then he ripped her shift and pulled it wide apart to reveal her entire soft-fleshed, white back to the gaping sailors.

Jules Bandelaire cracked the whip once in the air. Bettina jerked with fear, and before he could crack it a second time, she fainted. But without noticing this, Jules lifted the whip high above the tender flesh of her back to begin her slow and painful death.

Chapter 8

What Tristan witnessed when he staggered from his cabin brought instant clarity to his jumbled thoughts, and his familiar bellow could be heard in every corner of the ship.

"Hold!"

Jules was stopped barely in time, and he turned to see Tristan coming toward him, holding one hand to his aching head.

"Mother of God! Have you gone mad, Jules," Tristan asked when he reached them, an angry scowl on his face at the sight of Bettina's bared back.

"God's truth, Tristan, I have never been more pleased to see you! Davey, that fool of fools, said you were dead — that the wench killed you!"

Tristan grinned now, but only slightly, for his head was throbbing painfully. "Didn't it occur to you, old friend, to check for yourself? If you had done so, you would have found that the vixen merely rendered me unconscious. Thank God I came to in time! There would have been hell to pay had you marred that lovely back, for I'm not finished with this hellcat yet!" He turned to Davey. "Untie her! And the next time you pronounce a man dead, make sure that he is. Had the lady come to harm, Davey, you would have received the same punishment that my good friend here was going to give her."

"Aye, Cap'n," Davey replied weakly.

When Bettina was released, Tristan lifted her limp body in his arms and looked down at her serene face. She would not be so still if she were awake, he mused thoughtfully.

"Tristan, you can't mean to keep her in your cabin after what she has done. You vowed to be careful, and yet she got the better of you. I warned you that women don't fight as men do. Next

51

time, she may succeed in killing you," Jules said worriedly.

"Aye, she has vowed to do just that. I underestimated this one. I compared her to the meek, timid ladies I have known in the past. But I won't make that mistake again."

"What will you do, tie her up at night, or let her cut your throat while you sleep?" Jules asked.

"I don't think she will try to kill me again, at least not while she's on my ship. She had the chance to end my life when I was unconscious and at her mercy — but she didn't."

"No, because she thought you were dead already!"

"How do you know that?"

"When I told her I would take her life for taking yours, she only begged me to shoot her instead of using the whip on her."

"Very well, so she thought she had accomplished what she set out to do. But she has learned now what the consequences would be. Thanks to you, old friend, I know that she has a deathly fear of the whip. Didn't she faint before you laid one stroke?"

"Aye."

"Well, that's just the kind of information I need to put her where I want her."

"You underestimated her once, Tristan. Don't do it again. I love you as a son — as a brother. Don't make a mistake with this wench."

"She intrigues me, Jules. It would give me great pleasure to tame this particular lady."

"Lady! That vixen is no lady!"

"Aye, she is a lady, gently reared. Where the hellcat part comes from is a mystery I would like to solve. She has a devil of a temper. Now find something for my head, for it's pounding like native drums. And get those men back to work."

Tristan made his way back to his cabin with Bettina still sleeping in his arms. He laid her gently on his bed, then stood looking down at her for a few moments.

Would she awaken still frightened, or with renewed fury at finding him alive? He hoped for the fury. He wouldn't care to see this beauty cower before any man, not even himself. He would enjoy trying to break her in what little time he would have her, but somehow he knew that Bettina Verlaine could not be broken, not as long as there was life in her. She could be made to submit to him, but no one could break her will.

Jules came into the room and surveyed the damaged instruments on the floor with a shake of his head. He picked up the two tankards, brought them to the table, and filled them with wine, wishing for something stronger.

Madeleine appeared in the doorway and looked anxiously from the captain to her charge lying in his bed, then back to the captain again. Jules cleared his throat and beckoned her to enter.

"She said she is learned in ways of healing. I didn't think you would mind having her tend to your wound. Her hands are delicate compared to my clumsy ones," Jules said to Tristan, who had sat down by the table.

"Very well, as long as this one doesn't wish to cut my throat, too."

"That I would like to do, *monsieur,* but I will not," Madeleine replied.

Tristan chuckled softly. "At least you are honest, old woman. What is your name?"

"Madeleine Daudet."

"Well, Madeleine, did you witness what almost happened to your lady?" Tristan asked quietly.

"Yes, *monsieur.* I came on deck just before — before she fainted."

"It is fortunate for her that you didn't cry out," Tristan remarked, noting the woman's swollen lip that she had bitten to still her screams. "Had you done so, Jules wouldn't have heard me stop the whipping, and Bettina would have received at least two lashes before I could have reached her."

"Thank God you awoke when you did, *monsieur,*" Madeleine said. She bent over him and began to clean the wound.

"Then you know why my friend here was going to whip Bettina — in fact, to whip her to death?"

"Yes, because the crew thought she had killed you. I tried to dissuade Bettina from trying to do you harm, but she would not listen to me. Bettina has always been headstrong and determined, but never so much as today."

Tristan laughed, and glanced at the senseless girl in his bed. Then he turned back to Madeleine, his brows knitted in thought.

"Tell me about her. Where does this furious temper of hers come from? I would expect as much from a street whore or a barmaid, but not a lady."

"She *is* a lady, *monsieur*," Madeleine replied indignantly. "But as a child she was denied what she most wanted — her papa's love. This led to bursts of temper and defiance, and her papa sent her to a convent. She spent most of her life there."

"Was she to be a nun?"

"No, it was a school for girls."

"And what did she learn at this convent — how to pray?" he asked, with humor in his voice.

"Of course she learned of God and His ways, but she was also taught to read and write, to tend the sick and wounded, to be gentle and loving, to control her —" She stopped, realizing how ridiculous it would be to finish.

Tristan laughed softly. "You were going to say temper, were you not? So Bettina wasn't a very good student, eh?"

"She was an excellent pupil," Madeleine said in defense of Bettina. "It is just that when she feels intensely about something, she is blind to everything else. But I have not seen that happen since she was a child. It was only her papa who could make her temper rise, but when she came home from school, she was able to control her emotions. In fact, *monsieur,* I have never seen her so angry as she was today. Bettina is kind and gentle by nature, just like her mama. When she finally gave up trying to win the love of her papa, she was quite happy with life. Just her smile can make others feel as she does."

"I have yet to see this smile or this kind and gentle nature," Tristan remarked.

"You alone would know why, *Capitaine*. You have — have —"

"Dishonored her? Yes, so I've been told."

"You should not have touched her!" Madeleine snapped angrily. "You had no right. But since you were determined to have her, it would have been better if you had not tricked her. She accepted her fate until she learned you had deceived her."

"I only wanted to avoid hurting her, *madame*. But tell me,

does she want to marry this *comte?* Is she in love with him?" Tristan asked.

"Her papa arranged the marriage. Bettina had no say in the matter, but she must do what is expected of her. She knows this. As for love, you cannot love a man you have never seen."

"So she doesn't even know what her betrothed looks like. Would I be safe in saying that I might be delivering her to some fat old goat whom she would prefer not to marry?"

"No, *Capitaine,*" Madeleine smiled. "The Comte de Lambert is young and handsome. I have seen him."

For some reason, this bothered Tristan. "Enough of this now," he said. "I need some quiet to rid me of this headache. See to the ship, Jules. If you need me, I'll be here — ah, resting."

"Resting! If you want rest, you had better hope the wench doesn't wake."

Jules chuckled at his own words, then escorted Madeleine to the galley, where she should have gone to begin with. If she had done as Jules had instructed her, none of this would have happened, Tristan mused, and Bettina would still believe his lie. But there was no point in thinking about that now.

Tristan poured more of the wine into his tankard, leaned back in the chair, and fixed his gaze on Bettina. It would not take very long to reach Saint Martin, probably less than a week if the winds were favorable. That wouldn't give him very much time to enjoy this beauty. In all his twenty-six years, he had never met a woman as beautiful as Bettina Verlaine, nor one with such a maddening temper.

Chapter 9

Bettina's eyes fluttered open slowly, then widened to enormous dimensions when she remembered everything that had happened. She sat up quickly and arched her back, but she could feel no pain, just a slight draft on her bare flesh. What had happened? Why was she still alive?

She trembled violently for a moment, remembering the awful sound of the whip cracking in the air. My God! How had she possibly escaped that horrible death? She must have fainted. Were they just waiting for her to awaken before continuing? She had never anticipated that they would whip her to death for killing the captain. She could endure anything — yes, anything — except that excruciating torture.

Why did I have to kill him? she thought miserably, covering her face with her hands. I would only have had to endure a short time with the *capitaine;* then I would have been free — free to enjoy a long life. It would not have taken too long to forget about this experience, to be happy once again. Why did I jeopardize my whole life just for revenge? After all, the man was a pirate. I should have expected no more than deceit and lies from him. Bettina moaned softly in her misery. What was going to happen now? Was the first officer preparing an even more terrifying death for her? She must escape this cabin, she decided. She would jump ship and end her life in the sea. She could swim, but being so far from land, exhaustion or sharks would soon claim her. Not exactly the way she would choose to die, but a kinder death by far than the lash.

Without a second thought, Bettina pulled her legs over the side of the narrow bed and stood up. Then she froze, and a small gasp escaped her soft lips. He must be a ghost, was her first

56

thought. But as she stared fearfully at him, she saw that his eyes were gleaming with merriment, with devilry. His eyes were clear, clear as the bright sky — hardly the eyes of a dead man.

The blood rushed to her face. She had failed! He was alive, and that was why she was here, unharmed. He had been watching her without speaking since she awoke, letting her suffer with doubt and anxiety. Now he sat there facing her, his legs spread out before him, holding a tankard of wine on his hard, flat middle. He was smiling. Smiling!

Bettina stiffened as rage filled her. "You!" she managed to scream at him. "You should be dead! But I will yet succeed, Tristan!"

"Do you really long to feel the lash across your tender flesh, Bettina?" he asked quietly. He set the tankard back on the table.

She paled visibly. Hadn't she just asked herself why she had killed him? He was not worth that kind of death.

"I would know the answer, Bettina," Tristan said more loudly. "Are you willing to go through what would have happened to you had I not come awake in time to stop it?"

Her eyes were dark and fiery emeralds, caressing him with her hatred. There were other ways to take revenge, and she would find one. But she would wait until she was safe.

"Answer me, blast it!" He slammed his huge fist on the table, making her jump.

"I have no wish to feel the lash, as you must know!" she said heatedly.

He smiled at her reply. "Then I can be safe in sharing my cabin with you?"

"I do not want to stay here! Surely you don't wish to keep me after what I attempted."

"On the contrary, little one, I will enjoy your company." He chuckled wickedly.

"Then you will be safe from death, *monsieur,* but not from harm!" she retorted angrily.

"I think not, Bettina. Do you see this?" He picked up the coiled whip he had placed on the table earlier. "I am not opposed to using it."

"You wouldn't!"

"Do you doubt it? Would you like a demonstration?"

"I am not your slave, *monsieur*. I will not obey you!" Bettina replied furiously.

"Won't you? Come here, Bettina," he commanded, clearly enjoying the game.

"No, no, no!" She stamped her foot in defiance. "I will not come near —"

Before she could say more, the coiled leather sailed through the air and bit into the thick folds of her velvet skirt. Bettina jumped, and stared stupidly at the long slash that revealed the white material of her shift beneath the velvet. She looked up at Tristan slowly, her eyes wide and filled with terror. Did he miss touching her skin on purpose, or was his aim bad? She would not tempt him to try again.

Gathering her courage, Bettina moved to stand before him. "What do you wish, *monsieur?*" she asked haughtily.

He burst out laughing. "What I want can wait. Are you hungry?"

She nodded reluctantly, and for the first time noticed the platter of food at the far end of the table. She was famished.

Walking past him to the other chair, Bettina sat down and started to eat. After a few moments, she looked up slowly and saw that Tristan was still watching her intently, an amused expression on his bearded face.

"Is it all right if I eat, *monsieur,* or do you wish to starve me?" she asked sarcastically.

He frowned. "Eat your fill, and then you will find out what I wish to do."

Bettina ate with deliberate slowness, irritating Tristan further. But if she could annoy him in any way, any way whatsoever, then she would do so. Just as long as she could get away with it.

As she continued eating, she noticed that candles had been lit in the room, and that it was dark outside the small window at the foot of the bed. Well, now that night had fallen, she could at least insist that it be dark in the room if he was going to rape her again. She couldn't bear the indignity of him staring at her unclad body as he had earlier. She wondered briefly where she would sleep, for no doubt the beast would not give up his bed when he finished with her. But what was she thinking about? She would not let him rape her again.

"Finish your meal now, Bettina, or you can go without it, for I'm tired of waiting."

"Waiting for what, *monsieur?*" Bettina feigned innocence. "You raped me once. Surely you do not intend to do so twice in the same day?"

His devilish grin was her answer. Bettina jumped up and ran for the door, but the crack of the whip in the air halted her.

"Come here, Bettina!"

She felt panic rising in her again, but fear of what he might do made her obey. She turned and walked toward him slowly. When she reached him, he took her hand and pulled her closer until she stood between his knees. Then, without warning, Tristan reached up, grabbed her dress at the shoulders, and yanked it down to her waist.

Bettina gasped and drew back her hand to strike him, but he caught both her hands and twisted them behind her back, bringing her unclad breasts close to his face.

"You are hurting me!" she cried, trying to pull free.

"Don't you want to hurt me?" he asked, but he released her arms. "I know that you wish to fight me, Bettina, but know now that I will not allow it. For every time you strike me, you will receive ten lashes. For the slightest resistance, you will receive five lashes. Do you understand me?"

Damn him! Again he would deny her the satisfaction of opposing him. If she was to be raped, why couldn't she at least fight for her honor like other women? But he would not allow her to. It was unbearable, for she would have to submit to this man as if she were willing.

"Will you fight me, Bettina?" he asked her quietly, his soft blue eyes looking into her deep green ones.

"You must fear that you are no match for me if you have to threaten me to ensure your own safety. Are you afraid of me, *Capitaine*, because I was able to best you this afternoon?" she asked sarcastically, pleased to note the narrowing of his eyes. "What would your crew think if they knew you

59

couldn't handle a mere girl?"

"Your ploy has not worked, Bettina, though it was a good try. When I can avoid conflict, I do so. I avoid possible injuries and pain, and leave room only for pleasure."

"And what of the anguish of my mind? I would rather suffer a bruised and swollen face, even broken bones, than let you rape me without resistance. It is you who are afraid of the injuries that I might inflict on you if you were to remove your threats."

"Again a good try, little one, but the threats will remain. Now, you have wasted enough time trying to bait me. Remove the rest of your clothing and be quick about it."

"I will not! I won't make this easy for you!" she cried indignantly.

"Do you want me to rip your dress completely apart?" Tristan asked.

"Oh, I hate you!" she fumed, but she removed her garments just the same. She reddened as she stood before him, completely unprotected from his lustful gaze. "If I must suffer this indignity, Tristan, at least let me do so in the dark."

"You have nothing worth hiding, little one."

"Please!"

"No!" he replied sharply.

"You are cruel beyond reason, *monsieur*."

"You may think so now, but were I to keep you for my own, then you would change your opinion of me," he said. "You would look forward to my taking you in my arms. Although you didn't reach fulfillment when we made love the first time, you can't deny you enjoyed the feeling I gave you."

"You — you are insane! Your touch sickens me!"

"You wanted to kill me for lying to you, Bettina, but now you are not speaking the truth. Shall I prove it to you?"

Without waiting for her to answer, Tristan grabbed her around the waist and pulled her forward until his parted lips covered the tip of one rounded breast. Bettina gasped instantly and put her hands on his shoulders to push him away. But he tightened the grip on her waist until she stopped. His mouth, now moving from one breast to the other, was like wildfire, searing her to her very soul. Tristan continued with his play, sucking, teasing, nibbling softly at her breasts, until Bettina thought she would cry out with the pleasure she felt. Her entire body was aware of his lips, branding her with the truth of his words. But then he stopped.

Bettina knew what this was leading to. She began to panic again as Tristan stood up and removed his clothing. He had said that she didn't reach fulfillment before. Was there a greater pleasure to making love? And if there was, would she experience it this time — would he know if she did? No! It couldn't happen — she couldn't bear it. It would be too humiliating if he knew he gave her pleasure. If she couldn't fight him physically, she must at least fight the pleasure he could give her.

Tristan picked her up and carried her to the bed, then lay down beside her. His lips found hers, and he kissed her hungrily, demanding a response that she wouldn't give. She searched her mind to find something — anything — to make him angry and make him finish with her quickly.

His hand brushed across her breasts, caressed her belly, and moved lower.

"Tristan!" she cried out, shocked. "I am not a woman of easy virtue who longs to have your fingers explore her body. I am a lady, *monsieur,* and you disgust me!" she hissed, her voice filled with contempt.

"By the saints, vixen, you tempt me to throw you to the sharks!" he growled angrily.

"Better that they feed on my body than you!"

"Your sharp tongue will deny you much, Bettina."

With that, he climbed on top of her and entered her quickly, and a bit painfully. He rode her hard, with deep, penetrating thrusts, and despite Bettina's desire to resist, a growing, unbelievable pleasure began to spread through her body, until it was cut short by Tristan's final deep thrust.

Bettina felt like screaming when he relaxed on her, exhausted. A minute passed, then two, but Tristan didn't move.

"I wish to get up," she said coldly.

He leaned on his elbows and stared down at her. "Why?" he inquired softly.

"I would like to go to sleep, if you don't mind. So will you please let me up?"

"You don't make sense, Bettina. If you wish to sleep, then do so."

"I realize that you are no gentleman, and that you would not give up your bed for a lady, so —"

"On that count you are right," he interrupted her. "But I need not give up my bed when I intend to share it."

"No!" she cried, trying to push him from her, but it was like trying to move an iron man. "I refuse to share this bed with you, Tristan. It is bad enough that I have to suffer your — your mauling and raping my body, but I will not share your bed!"

"And if I insist?"

"You will not!" she fumed.

"Ah, but I do insist, little one," he returned, with an amused smile curling his lips.

"Don't you know how much I detest you?" she hissed as she squirmed to get out from beneath him. "I cannot stand to be near you. Now release me!"

"If you don't stop wiggling, you will be raped a third time this day. Would you prefer that to sharing my bed?" he asked, his eyes gleaming with devilry.

Bettina froze, fearing even to breathe. She could feel him growing inside her, and her eyes widened. They were deep pools of green, pleading silently with him for mercy.

"What is your answer? Will you share my bed?"

"As with everything else, you leave me no choice. But your weight is unbearable, Tristan. I cannot possibly sleep this way."

"I will concede you that, but nothing more."

With that, he rolled to her side, and Bettina quickly yanked the covers over her and faced the wall, getting as close to it as she possibly could. She heard him laugh softly, but he soon fell asleep.

Oh God, how she hated him! He could just fall asleep as if this day had been no different from any other. While she — she wanted to scream. If someone had told her yesterday that she would fall into the hands of a ruthless pirate, she would have laughed hysterically. But now — now that she had been raped, not once but twice in the same day by this giant of a man, now that she was no longer innocent and suitable for marriage, she couldn't even cry. Tears would free her of some of this anguish. But she was too angry to cry.

Tristan, beast that he was, enjoyed having her in his power. Well, it would not be for too long. Once he set her free and she was no longer at his mercy, she would find a way to take revenge against him.

She could hire a ship, a mightier ship than his, and blow him off the seas. Yes, even if she couldn't cut his throat with her own hands, she would still bring about his death. The Comte de Lambert would help her. Of course, the *comte* might not want to marry her anymore. Well, if he didn't, then she would just have to find another way. But she would not rest until she had sent Tristan to hell. And with that thought, Bettina finally slept.

Chapter 10

Bettina awoke suddenly. She had been dreaming about Tristan, and her first thought was what a horrible nightmare she'd had. But when she looked around her and saw where she was, she knew it hadn't been a nightmare.

It was all true. She was actually on a pirate ship. She was actually at the mercy of a man she knew nothing about, a man who enjoyed having her in his power. And he did enjoy it. She had seen it in his eyes, heard it in his tone of voice. He was a man who cared only about his own desires, and nothing about her feelings.

With a sigh of hopelessness, Bettina threw off the covers and sat on the edge of the narrow bed. She saw her violet dress lying in a heap by the table, and realized that she had slept without any clothes. In all her nineteen years, she could not remember once going to bed without a nightdress on.

She looked about the small room, hoping to find something to wear besides her torn shift and dress, and saw a beautiful, handcarved wooden chest standing against one wall. She went to this, instinctively knowing that it contained the captain's clothes, and opened it. Her first impulse was to rip the contents to shreds, but she quickly shook off that notion. She could well guess what the consequences would be. She carefully sorted through the clothes, hoping to find a robe of some kind, but had to settle for a light-blue silk shirt.

Bettina slipped it on over her head, and found that the deep, open collar partially revealed her taut young breasts. The hem of the shirt did not reach her knees, but she decided against wearing any of Tristan's breeches. The man was just too big. She would have to find a needle and thread to repair her dress before Tristan returned.

As Bettina started to rummage through the rest of the cabin, she was stopped short by a knock at the door. Her first thought was to find something to cover her exposed legs, for she feared it was Tristan or one of his crewmen, but she relaxed when Madeleine came into the room. She was carrying a small tray of food that she set down on the table.

"Are you all right, Bettina?" Madeleine asked. "I was so worried that the *capitaine* might do you harm."

"He didn't beat me, as you can see," Bettina answered, feeling her temper rise once again. "This Tristan exacts his revenge in a much more subtle way."

"I don't understand."

"Of course you do!" Bettina snapped angrily, but felt ashamed when she saw the stricken look on her servant's face. "I'm sorry. You see, the *capitaine* has threatened to whip me if I resist or disobey him in any way. He gives me no choice but to submit as if I were willing. I cannot stand it! I want to fight him, but I fear the whip more than anything else."

"Oh, I am relieved to hear this, my pet."

"How can you say that, Maddy?" Bettina asked, startled. "How can you be relieved that I must submit to that — that *monster?*"

"I simply don't want you injured," Madeleine said in a hurt voice. "I would do anything to prevent that man from taking you, Bettina, but there is nothing I can do. There is nothing you can do, either."

"I could do something if he had not threatened to whip me."

"Yes, and that is why I'm relieved, Bettina. I know your temper. I remember the time you fought the stableboy when you were a little girl playing at being the boy your papa wanted. The boy teased you, and you would not give up until you had thrown him to the ground. I know you well, my pet, but neither of us knows this *Capitaine* Tristan. I have no doubt that he would harm you if you tried to fight him."

"I do not care about that!" Bettina snapped.

Madeleine sighed. "I wish your first time with a man could have been happier. But the damage is done, Bettina. The scars

65

of the mind will eventually heal and be forgotten. But scars on your body would be there forever to remind you of this unpleasant experience."

"Unpleasant! You are too kind," Bettina declared. "Terror-filled or nightmarish, yes, but unpleasant — this could hardly be called just an unpleasant experience."

"But that is all it is, an experience that you are going through. It will all be over soon, and then you will marry the *comte*, and —"

"Will I?" Bettina said skeptically.

"But of course you will."

"What if the Comte de Lambert doesn't want to marry me when he learns that I have been dishonored? And worse, what if he will not pay the ransom? What will happen to us then?"

"You must stop thinking like this, Bettina. The *comte* is a Frenchman. It is a matter of honor. He will pay the ransom, and he will also marry you. Now come and eat your food before it is cold."

Bettina supposed Madeleine was right. There would be time to worry about the *comte* later. Her main concern now was the captain, and how to avoid a repetition of his lovemaking.

Madeleine had brought two bowls of thick bean soup, and they ate in silence. Bettina finished first and leaned back in her chair to study Madeleine's face. Her old nurse looked tired.

"You must forgive me, Maddy. I have been so caught up in my own self-pity, I did not even think to ask how you fared. Are you being taken care of? Do you have a place to sleep?"

Madeleine looked up and smiled. "You have no need to worry about me, my pet. I have nothing to fear from these men as long as they appreciate my cooking."

"Your cooking? Did you prepare this soup?"

"I did." Madeleine chuckled. "They have made me their temporary cook. I do not mind, for it gives me something to do. There is not much to work with in the galley, but I can turn out a better meal than that fool of a lad I replaced."

"I am sure you can, Maddy."

"And the first officer vacated his cabin for me, so I have a place to sleep."

Bettina shivered at the mention of the big man who had

66

wanted to whip her to death.

"You must not judge Jules by what happened yesterday," Madeleine said. "I dined with him last night, and he does not seem to be such a bad man."

"But he wanted to kill me. And he would have if —" Bettina stopped. She hated to admit that Tristan had saved her from that horrible fate.

"Yes, he would have killed you," Madeleine said. "And if he had, then I would have tried to kill him. Don't you see, Bettina? Given the same circumstances, you or I would have reacted the same way. Jules thought you had killed his friend. He told me last night that Tristan is like a son to him, or more like a brother, for they are only ten years apart in age. Tristan lost his parents when he was but a boy, and Jules took him in and raised him. They have been together ever since. They are close, very close. Would you not have acted the same way as Jules if you thought someone you cared for had been killed?"

"I suppose so," Bettina answered grudgingly. She knew Madeleine was right, but this Jules still frightened her.

"Fate put us at the mercy of these men," Madeleine continued. "And that is what we must remember — we *are* at their mercy. I still fear that you will do this Tristan harm, and then Jules will —"

"No, I will not try to kill him again. At least, not until we are safe."

"What do you mean?"

"I will still have revenge. Tristan dishonored me, lied to me — tricked me!"

"But Bettina, he is a pirate. A battle was fought, and our ship lost. The *capitaine* wants you, and to his way of thinking, he has a right to you as the spoils of that battle. These pirates could still kill us if they chose to, and they probably would if it were not for the ransom," Madeleine said.

"I suppose you are right."

"So you must not antagonize the *capitaine*, for he alone holds your life in his hands."

"But I hate him! I will see him dead!" Bettina replied heatedly.

"Bettina, what is the matter with you? You usually accept a

situation when it is inevitable. Why don't you try to make the best of it? It will not be for very long."

"One day is too long to be in that man's power. He is an arrogant beast! He enjoys humiliating me."

"Bettina, please! You have much to live for when this is over. Do not jeopardize your life!"

"Don't worry about me, Maddy."

"How can I not worry about you when you talk like that! This Tristan spared the crew of the *Windsong*, which was merciful indeed, but he might kill you yet if you anger him. You don't know —"

"What do you mean he spared the crew?" Bettina interrupted. "He killed them, murdered them all!"

"You must have seen that was not so, Bettina," Madeleine said.

"I saw — I saw nothing," she admitted reluctantly. "I could not bear to look as I was led across the deck, I assumed they were all dead."

"They were not. I saw them breathing. Many were unconscious, and most were wounded, but I don't think any were actually dead."

"Why would he allow them to live?"

"I don't know, love. I thought it strange at the time. Pirates are supposed to be cutthroats who kill easily for pleasure or gain."

"They are still robbers, and they attacked the *Windsong*, didn't they? Maybe Tristan was in a lenient mood yesterday, but he is still a pirate, and I will see him dead for what he has done to me."

"Ah, Bettina," Madeleine sighed. "Why could you not be more like your gentle mama? Accept the truth that men rule this world and we women have no say. It would be much easier for you if you did. Just as you had to obey your papa's orders at home, now you must obey this Tristan. And when you marry, you must obey the *comte*. Men have a way of punishing us women when we do not comply with their wishes. Did you not learn that when you were young and defiant? You were sent away to school when it was your mama's wish to keep you at home. Your papa punished you both by sending you away. Have you not learned from your mistakes?"

"But that was different."

"Yes, I suppose it was. A male relative legally rules your life. This Tristan is not a relative, but you are under his power now, and the laws of society are not here to prevent his harming you. Just remember that, my pet, for your own sake. Give up this revenge you speak of."

"I have said I will not kill him until we are safe, but then I will find a way."

Madeleine let it go at that. There was no point in trying to talk sense into Bettina when she felt this strongly.

"I must go now to prepare the noon meal." Madeleine reached into her pocket and pulled out a needle and thread. "I obtained these so you could repair your dress. I would do it for you, but I think you need something to do."

"Yes. And thank you, Maddy. You always think of everything."

"Not everything, or I would have thought of a way to keep that man from you."

"I will think of a way myself," Bettina returned.

Madeleine shook her head and got up to leave. "I will return later, Bettina, if I can. I may be too busy, though, if the new supplies the *capitaine* promised arrive this afternoon."

"What new supplies?" Bettina asked in surprise.

"The ones Jules went ashore to purchase. He left this morning."

"He went ashore!" Bettina exclaimed. "Then we are near land?"

"I thought you knew. The ship dropped anchor in the middle of the night. We are in the port of Tortola."

Bettina finally noticed the stillness of the ship. After being at sea for so long, she should have known immediately upon waking that the ship was not moving, but her tumultuous thoughts had kept her from noticing.

"Now we can escape!" Bettina said quickly, excitement rising in her voice.

"That is impossible, Bettina. We would need a boat, for the ship is far from shore. And the crew has taken them all."

"We can swim!"

"I — I do not know how," Madeleine admitted reluctantly.

"Oh Maddy," Bettina nearly cried. Then her hopes rose again. "I will go alone. I will bring back the authorities, and these pirates will be arrested and hanged. We will be free!"

"It is a good thought, my pet, but it would never work. The *capitaine* is still on the ship. He would never let you escape."

Bettina's hopes were shattered with those few simple words.

Chapter 11

It was a decidedly long day, or so it seemed to Bettina. After she finished repairing her dress and shift, she busied herself with putting the cabin in order. She noticed that the daggers and the whip were gone, but she had expected that. She stacked the captain's books, all of them dealing with the sea and of no interest to her. Then she found places to put all the odds and ends, so that when she was finished, it looked like a completely different room. But this didn't take very long, and soon she was pacing the floor in want of something to do.

She decided to leave the cabin for a breath of fresh air and to have a look at the island where they were anchored. But as soon as she stepped out of the room, a burly fellow shouted that she was not allowed on deck. The man looked too mean to argue with, so she went back into her temporary prison and slammed the door shut.

With nothing to do, Bettina tried to sleep, but the room was too stuffy. She tried to open the small window, but it was stuck and wouldn't budge. She longed to stand on the deck and let the cool breeze whisk through her hair. But no, this was not allowed, by the captain's order, she was sure. The idea that she might try to escape must have crossed Tristan's mind.

Bettina still intended to escape, though, and as she moved restlessly about the cabin during the day, an idea slowly formed in her mind, giving her new hope.

Bettina got up to light the candles when the cabin darkened with the approach of night. The cool night air caressed her cheek, and she turned to see Tristan standing in the open doorway.

"Did you miss me, little one?" he asked, a hint of laughter in his voice.

She backed away from him when he closed the door and started unwinding the whip that was wrapped about his chest, the handle hanging over one shoulder.

"You haven't answered me."

"If I never laid eyes on you again, I would be the happiest woman alive."

"I'm glad to see you are still your sweet self," he said sarcastically.

"And you, I see, are still a coward. You are afraid to be in the same room with me unless you have your whip for protection!" Bettina snapped, gaining courage from her mounting anger.

Tristan smiled at her and dropped the whip on the table. "I will soon prove that I don't need this whip to tame you."

Bettina did not understand him. But when the knock came at the door, she soon forgot about it. A young cabinboy brought in a large platter of food and put it on the table. He glanced shyly at Bettina before quickly departing, leaving her alone with the captain once again.

They ate in silence, and Bettina kept her eyes on her food. She knew that Tristan was watching her. She again took as much time as possible to finish the meal, but he did not seem to mind this time. Perhaps he was tired, she thought hopefully, and he would not demand anything of her tonight.

"Would you like to go for a walk?"

Bettina looked up at him, and met his smiling blue eyes.

"I wanted to go out today, when it was so hot in here. Why was I not allowed to do so?" Bettina asked, trying to keep her voice calm.

"Because I don't want you on deck during the day," he returned.

"But why? On the *Windsong* I had to stay below to avoid tempting the crew. But your crew has gone ashore and there would be no one to see me if I ventured on deck. Are you afraid

I will escape, *Capitaine?*" she asked saucily.

"No, you will not escape, Bettina, so put the thought from your mind. Even if you managed to reach the shore, you would have nowhere to go. I would find you."

"Then why must I stay in your cabin? At least let me have the freedom of your ship while your crew is gone. There can be no harm in that."

"Not all of my crew has gone ashore, Bettina. And there are many ships in the harbor. The docks are swarming with men. I would prefer it if you were not seen aboard my ship."

"Are you afraid I will be rescued and you will be hanged for the pirate you are?" she asked.

"Hardly that, little one," he smiled. "But some lowlife slave trader could sneak aboard my ship at night and steal you away. Your fate would be much worse than it is now."

"I doubt it could be worse, *Capitaine,*" she replied, throwing him a contemptuous glance. "Very well, then. How long will you be in this port?"

"Not long. Another day or so."

"And from here you sail to Saint Martin?"

"Yes."

"Then, once you sail, can I have —"

"No!" He cut her off, anticipating her question. "You are too much of a temptation, Bettina."

"That is ridiculous. I am no different from any other woman, and your men will surely have had their fill by the time they return."

"Yes, they will be sated and quite content with themselves. But if you were allowed on deck each day, trouble would arise. You are very desirable, Bettina, and I will not have my men tempted by the sight of you."

"Your men have already seen me."

"Yes, and they know that you are mine. They will remember that you are beautiful, and they will say the captain is a lucky man. But if they were to see you every day, some might risk death to have you."

"What death?"

"I do not share my women, Bettina. I will kill any man

73

who touches you," he said.

Bettina shivered, remembering the man who had almost died on the *Windsong* because of her. But it didn't matter, because she wouldn't be on this ship tomorrow. She was just stalling for time, for she still had to contend with Tristan this night.

"You are being unreasonable, *Capitaine*. I have nothing to do in your cabin. Your books do not interest me, I have nothing to do with my hands, and it is unbearably hot in this room. Could I at least leave the cabin for a little while during the day? You could watch me."

Tristan sighed and leaned back in his chair. "I have a ship to run. I can't concentrate on my ship and worry about you at the same time. If you are in my cabin, I know you are safe. Besides, whether I watch you or not does not keep you from the sight of my crew. As for the heat, you need only open the window."

"Your window, *Capitaine*, is stuck," she replied flippantly.

Tristan got up, walked to the window, and opened it quite easily. "It seems you are not as strong as you like to think, little one. Now, would you like that walk?"

Without answering him, Bettina rose and left the cabin. She didn't wait for Tristan, but walked ahead of him until she reached the railings on the foredeck. She stood there, mesmerized by the beauty of the full, brilliant, tropical moon hanging above the horizon, lighting the black water. The sea was calm, and a cool breeze ruffled Bettina's hair, relaxing her.

The island in the near distance was bathed in moonlight. Bettina could see the outline of tall, exotic mountains in the background, but the town in front of her could have been a port anywhere in the world. She saw none of the tropical beauty she had expected to find in the New World. But of course it was night, and all she could see were the buildings that lined the dock.

It was a beautiful, warm night — a night made for love. She knew that she could look forward to many such nights when she reached Saint Martin, and she hoped that she would find love there — love that could make her forget this nightmare she was living.

She felt Tristan's presence behind her. Looking down, she saw his hands clutching the railing on both sides of her, leaving her no way to escape. He was standing so close that his body was touching hers, and then she felt his lips brush against her neck. Gooseflesh spread down her back, making her whole body tingle, and she realized that she must break this mood before he went any further.

"Why did you let me believe that you had killed all of the *Windsong*'s crew?"

He laughed softly and wrapped his arms about her waist, pressing her even closer to him.

"You wanted to believe the worst about me, and I saw no reason to deny you that satisfaction, since it was all you had. I'm sorry to disappoint you, but I'm not the cutthroat you thought I was."

"But you are a pirate!" she exclaimed, turning around to face him.

"Not exactly. Again I must disappoint you. I am a privateer under the sanction of England. I prey only on Spanish vessels, as I told you — plate ships carrying gold back to Spain. Do you know how the Spanish get their gold, Bettina?" Tristan asked, his voice suddenly cold. "By the death of men, women, and children. The Spanish enslaved the natives of the conquered Caribbean islands, and they starved and beat them to death because they didn't work fast enough. And when the native Indians were exterminated, the Spanish brought in black slaves and treated them no better. I have no love for Spain, and I enjoy taking her gold and giving it to England. You may be surprised to learn that there are French buccaneers who do the same thing, and give the gold to France."

"You lie! All you ever do is lie. If you prey only on the Spanish, why did you attack the *Windsong*?"

"I intended to board her and speak with you, or bargain with the captain to learn where you were being taken. The *Windsong* fired first, and I have never run from a fight, Bettina. However, since the battle was on, I gave the order to avoid killing. I boarded the ship, took you, and left."

"But that is piracy!"

"That is the result of a battle."

"You didn't have to rape me, *Capitaine!*"

"No, I didn't. But you are just too tempting, little one. I'm afraid I don't have the will to resist you." He sounded as if he were teasing her. Then he pulled her to him and his lips crushed down on hers. When she tried to push him away, he only pressed her closer, molding her body against his. She could feel his desire, and she knew what this kiss would lead to. What could she do this time? How could she fight the pleasure that was already creeping through her body?

Tristan released her suddenly, and Bettina fell back against the rail, breathing heavily. She stared at his amused expression, clearly illuminated by the moonlight, and became furious that he could play on her senses so easily.

"Come," he said, taking her hand and pulling her behind him as he walked back to his cabin.

Inside the privacy of the small cabin, Tristan closed the door, and Bettina ran to the opposite side of the long table. Seeing the accursed whip lying there, she picked it up and threw it out the open window. With this done, she turned to face Tristan defiantly.

But he was obviously amused. "You're not planning on resisting me, are you, little one? I have thought about this moment all day." His soft blue eyes met and held her dark-green ones. "Remove your dress, Bettina. The time has come."

What can I do? Bettina thought wretchedly. I am such a coward! I fear the whip more than death itself. I should have jumped ship today, but it is too late now.

"Now," Tristan bellowed.

She screamed her anger and frustration at him. She ripped her mended dress open again, then yanked the sleeves off, tearing the dress further. She pulled her shift over her head and threw it at Tristan. Then she went to the bed and waited.

Tristan undressed quickly and came to her. When he lay down beside her, she looked at him wildly, her green eyes wide and filled with flame.

"I hate you, Tristan, with all my being. I loathe your touch, so if you must rape me, then be quick about it," Bettina hissed.

76

But he paid her no mind. "Not tonight, Bettina. Tonight you will discover the joys of being a woman."

"Your pride is great, *monsieur*." She laughed bitterly. "It would take a better man than you to teach me those joys."

When his face darkened, she knew that her gibe had worked. He spread her legs and entered her cruelly, but she welcomed the pain. This time she was too distraught to feel any pleasure, and only when he finished with her did she relax.

"Why do you do this to yourself, Bettina? Why do you deny yourself the pleasure I can give you?"

She opened her eyes to see him staring down at her, and she realized that the danger was not yet over.

"I deny myself nothing. I merely spoke the truth," she returned, her tone full of contempt.

"You're a witch."

"And you, *monsieur,* are the Devil incarnate."

The room filled with his laughter. "If I am, then we make a good pair, you and I."

He left the bed and put on his breeches, then poured wine into his tankard. Before he drank, he bent down, picked up her dress, and laid it over the chair.

"You will have to take better care of your clothes, little one. You would not look so appealing wearing mine."

"I have other dresses," she replied tartly.

"Do you? And where might they be?"

"In my trunks, of course."

"No trunks were brought aboard my ship, Bettina. Only you, your servant, and your dowry."

Her eyes opened wide. "You are lying to me again!"

"Why should I lie about this?"

"But my trousseau was in one of those trunks!" she yelled at him.

"I'm sure your future husband will purchase you another trousseau."

"But I don't want another one!" She felt the tears coming, but she couldn't stop them. "I worked for a month on my wedding dress. It was a beautiful gown and you — you —" She burst into tears, hiding her face in the pillow.

"Mother of God! You don't cry over your loss of virginity, but you cry over a lost dress. Blast all women and their tears!" Tristan grabbed his shirt and stalked from the cabin, slamming the door as he left.

Chapter 12

Bettina lay on the narrow bed, silently counting the minutes as they passed. At least three hours had gone by since she stopped crying. Crying was such a foolish thing to do. Only weak women spilled tears, or those who would play on another's sympathy. But she was not weak, and she vowed she would never let a man see her cry again.

Her tears had ruined her plans and made Tristan storm from the cabin. He had not yet returned, and she had no way of knowing if he would or not. He could have gone ashore, he could be sleeping elsewhere, but she couldn't leave until she knew exactly where he was. He must return to the cabin!

Another hour passed, and then two more, but she was still alone. It was well after midnight now, and Bettina was finding it increasingly hard to keep her eyes open, but couldn't get up and pace to ward off the drowsiness. She had to appear to be sleeping when and if Tristan did return.

When the door to the cabin finally opened, Bettina closed her eyes and lay perfectly still. The room was in darkness, with only a tiny sliver of moonlight spilling in through the window. She couldn't see Tristan, but she could hear him as he stumbled toward the bed, mumbling a curse when he bumped into the table. A moment later, he dropped down on the bed beside her, his arm feeling like a heavy board as it fell across her chest, making her gasp. But he didn't seem to hear her.

The fumes of liquor hit Bettina in the face, and she smiled to herself. This was better than she had hoped for. He was already asleep, would sleep like a log for what remained of the night, and would probably still be sleeping when she brought the authorities back to arrest him.

Bettina carefully lifted his arm off her, then quickly scooted to the end of the bed, rather than risk crawling over him. She went straight to Tristan's chest of clothes and took out the two articles she had laid on top of the others.

She had decided earlier that she would have to wear his clothes, for her velvet dress would be too heavy and cumbersome to swim in. She had picked out the darkest colors he had, so it would be less easy to see her.

She braided and tucked her pale hair underneath the bulky blue shirt. And to hide the top of her head, she was forced to take the one hat Tristan had. It was wide-brimmed, with a sweeping plume, a hat that was definitely in fashion but that she could hardly picture Tristan wearing. This sort of hat was worn by gentlemen with long, fashionable curls, and short-haired Tristan was no gentleman.

She secured the baggy black breeches about her waist with a strip of material she had torn from her shift, and she was ready to go.

She knew she must look utterly ridiculous, but there was nothing else she could do. She opened the door, carefully closed it behind her, and nearly despaired when she saw how light it was outside. The moon lit everything as plainly as if it were only late afternoon.

She hated to leave the shadow of the wall behind her, but she had to find a way to climb down the ship's side and escape quietly. It would be easier to run for the railing and jump, but someone would surely hear her hit the water, and that wouldn't do.

Scanning the deck, Bettina could see no one. All was silent. Someone was probably standing watch, but she could only pray they wouldn't see her. She moved away from the wall very slowly, but then a sudden panic gripped her and she darted to the railing. She looked about frantically, and saw a rope ladder strung over the side of the ship, which must have been left there by the shore parties. A few moments later, she slid easily into the warm black water.

It took her over thirty minutes to swim to the piers, what with circling around the other ships in the harbor and continually having to retrieve Tristan's hat. By the time she found a wooden ladder that climbed to the dock, she was exhausted. Her arms felt like dead weights, and she knew she would be aching all over in a few hours. But it was all worth it just to see Tristan hang, and she wouldn't budge from this island until the governing authorities sent him on his way to hell.

Bettina wanted to laugh aloud at that thought, but instead she stared out into the harbor at Tristan's ship. She could see the deck clearly, even from this distance, but no shadow moved, all was still, and she was still safe. She turned and faced the town, then shivered slightly. It was just as still, and she stood alone on the dock. But floating through the air came the faint sound of music to mix with the quiet lapping of the waves behind her. She walked toward the music, hoping to find people who could direct her to the authorities.

As the music became louder, Bettina could hear the sounds of drunken revelry accompanying it, and she stopped short when she saw the lighted tavern. A puddle of water from her sodden clothing formed around her bare feet while she weighed her problem. It was possible that some of Tristan's crew would be in that tavern. If she walked in, they might not recognize her, dressed as she was, but she couldn't take that risk. Then again, she had to find help, and there was no one on the street except herself. If she went into the tavern and was recognized, she could always run.

Bettina walked up and down the street, trying to come to a definite decision. She kept hoping someone would come out of the tavern, or that she would run into someone on the street, anyone she could seek help from. But no one appeared. She could find herself an alley to hide in and wait until morning, when the streets would be crowded with people, but by then Tristan might have his whole crew out looking for her. And besides, she wanted to take the law back to the ship before Madeleine awoke and started to worry about her.

Slowly, Bettina edged over to the open door of the tavern. She stood to one side and scanned the room nervously to see if she recognized any of Tristan's crew. But it was impossible to tell. There were so many men with their backs to her, and others were sleeping with their heads on the tables. There were women in the room also, barmaids serving drinks, whom the men apparently regarded as fair game for fondling and pinching.

Bettina was repelled by the foul odor that was heavy in the air, even outside the door, but she knew she had to walk into the tavern if she were going to find help. She walked quickly to the nearest table, where three men were avidly playing some sort of game with small sticks.

"Monsieur," she ventured, but not one of the men looked up at her. *"Monsieur,* I seek a *gendarme."*

"Speak English, will ye?" one of them said. He glanced at her, and then his eyes opened wide. "Blimy! Will ye look at that!"

The other two men looked at her with greedy eyes, and Bettina looked down at herself. She gasped when she saw that the thin, wet shirt clung tightly to her breasts and was nearly transparent. She quickly pulled the material away from her skin, but it was too late, for at least half a dozen men had already seen the clear outline of her perfectly formed breasts.

"What's yer price, wench? I'll pay it, no matter what," one man said. He rose from his chair.

"Sit down, mate," another said. "I saw 'er first."

"Get the hell out of here!" a huge man behind the bar yelled at her. "Ye're gonna start a bloody fight, blast ye!"

But the fight had already started between the two men who had spoken first. Others joined in, just for the love of a good fight, and in seconds the room was full of drunken, brawling men. Bettina started backing away to escape, but then a huge hand clamped down on her shoulder.

"Ye're gonna pay fer this!" the barkeeper shouted in her ear. "Ye're gonna pay fer the damages!"

Bettina quickly jerked free and ran for the door, but the fat barkeeper followed close behind her. She ran frantically down the street, ducked into the first alley she came to and stumbled over piles of garbage as she made her way to the other end. She came out into a lighted square, saw a uniformed guard on the other side, and ran toward him. She could hear the fat man shouting behind her.

"*Monsieur,* are you a *gendarme?*" she asked, when she reached the man.

"What?"

She didn't know why she had assumed this town would be a French settlement. "Are you an official of the law?" she asked in English.

But the man in uniform was distracted as the fat man came running across the square toward them. "What have you done, girl?" he asked.

"I have done nothing," she replied. "I was seeking the law when —"

"Arrest her!" the barkeeper shouted as he panted up to them.

"What has she done?"

"She — she came into my place like that," he answered, motioning to her. "And she caused a bloody fight. There's damages!"

"Is this true, girl?" the officer asked sternly.

"I was only seeking help. I could find no one on the street to ask," Bettina replied.

"Help for what?" the officer asked.

"There are pirates in the harbor. They were keeping me prisoner. I escaped to find the authorities, and —"

She stopped when both men laughed at her answer. What was so amusing about her story?

"Telling lies won't help you out of this," the officer said. "Now, can you pay for the damages you caused, or do I arrest you?"

"But I'm speaking the truth!" Bettina exclaimed.

"Can you pay for the damages?" he asked again, impatience creeping into his voice.

"No."

"Then come along." He took her arm and started to escort her down the street.

"What about the damages?" the barkeeper called out.

"You'll be paid, citizen, as soon as the girl's sold into service."

"You must listen to me," Bettina pleaded.

"You can save it for the magistrate," the officer said gruffly as he took her into a very old building at the end of the square.

"When can I see him?"

"In a week or so. There are others before you."

"But the pirates will be gone by then!"

He pulled her around to face him, his eyes without compassion. "We have no pirate ships in our harbor, wench. And if you tell the magistrate such a ridiculous story, he'll probably sell you into service for at least seven years. If you tell the truth, he may go easy on you."

"Easy?"

"Let you serve in his house for a few years. The old magistrate likes a pretty wench to warm his bed."

He led Bettina into a large courtyard, lined on three sides with barred cells. She gagged at the stench of the place and fought down nausea. He opened an empty cell and shoved her in, then slammed the iron bars shut.

"Please, you must believe me!" she pleaded, but he walked away, leaving her alone in the dark, stinking cell.

He returned a moment later and tossed a coarse blanket through the bars at her.

"You had best get out of those wet clothes. You won't be worth anything dead."

She was alone again. She couldn't see into the dark cells across from her, but she could hear moaning and crying all around. She fought back tears of self-pity, but the salty drops spilled down her cheeks, anyway. Why hadn't they believed her?

Bettina threw Tristan's hat on the floor and stamped on it. This was all his fault! By escaping him, she'd just gotten into worse trouble. She could tell the truth and spend seven years in servitude, or she could make up a believable lie and end up being an old man's bedmate. And in the meantime she must spend a week in this filthy cell, without even a cot to sleep on.

With an overpowering sense of hopelessness, Bettina slipped out of her wet clothes and wrapped the rough blanket around her shivering body. She then curled up in the corner of the cell and let sleep wipe away her misery.

Chapter 13

The night was clear, and a full moon shone above the peaceful little village by the sea. A young boy of twelve was asleep in his parents' one-room house. His father had not gone out in the fishing boats with the other men of the village that night because of a fevered cold, so both the boy's parents slept in there big bed in the corner of the cottage.

Three hours after the fishing boats had left the little village, the Spaniards came. They came not for riches, for the village was a poor one. They came for sport, to destroy, and rape, and kill.

The young blond boy was the first to wake when the screams started in the streets. He watched as his father jumped from his bed and grabbed a kitchen knife, the only weapon he could find, then started to run outside, with the boy's mother begging him not to go. But the tall man with golden hair did go, and he was one of the last to die by the dark Spaniard's blade. The boy watched from the window, with his mother beside him, as the Spaniard wiped his sword on his father's blood-soaked body.

The boy's mother screamed, and this brought her to the attention of the Spaniard, who started for their house. The woman forced her son to hide under his bed in the single room, and ordered him to remain quiet no matter what he heard or saw. Then she grabbed one of the kitchen knives, spilling the rest on the floor, and waited for her husband's murderer to enter the house.

All the boy could see in the next minutes from where he lay under the bed was the Spaniard coming through the door and then shuffling of feet as his mother struggled with the man. The woman was tall, and her strength was increased by blind rage.

It was a long time before the knife she held fell to the floor, but still the man could not bring her down. Then one of the Spaniard's friends came to the door and spoke to him in Spanish, calling him by name — Don Miguel de Bastida.

By himself, Bastida had been unable to overcome the boy's mother, but with the help of his noble friends, she was brought quickly to the floor. Bastida was the first to rape her, while four men held her down and others stood by watching and laughing. When Don Miguel de Bastida finished with her, he sat at the table and watched as one man after another climbed on top of the woman, laughing all the while. Unfortunately, the boy's mother was the most beautiful of the village women, and even those men who had already raped other women wanted their turn with her.

The boy watched all of this as he cowered beneath the bed, not really understanding why his mother was screaming. But he remembered his mother's warning and remained silent, never having disobeyed her. The screams stopped after the fourth man, and she lay moaning while five more had their way with her, some of them finding pleasure in beating her.

Bastida stayed until the end, laughing and encouraging even the last man. When it was over, when only Bastida was left in the room, the woman slowly struggled to her knees, half-demented now, blood oozing from cuts on her face. With a parting comment, Bastida turned to leave also, but the woman found strength to grab one of the knives on the floor and lunge at the Spaniard.

Then the boy heard his mother's last cry, and she fell in a heap to the floor. Bastida spit on her lifeless body and continued out the door, and it was only then that the young boy crawled from his hiding place. He ran after the Spaniard, nearly blinded by his silent tears. He attacked the Spaniard with his bare fists, but Bastida only laughed and laid open the boy's cheek with the point of his sword. Then he kicked him to the ground only a few feet from where his father lay, and told him he was no match for — no match for. . . .

Tristan bolted upright in bed, covered with a cold, clammy sweat. It had been so real, exactly the way it happened fourteen years ago. Mother of God, why must the past still haunt his dreams? He would never forget that night the Spaniards came to his village, but why did he have to see his parents murdered over and over again in these nightmares? Would he never find peace?

Tristan got up and splashed cold water on his face, and only then did he see he was alone. He dashed from his cabin, his face as dark as a stormy sea, and in less than five minutes, he was certain Bettina was not on his ship.

"Is this the one, Captain?"

Bettina opened her eyes and saw the man who had brought her here last night. She blinked twice before she could believe that the tall man with him was Tristan. They were standing inside her cell, casually observing her.

"Yes, this is the girl. I should leave her in your care. It would serve her right for all the trouble she's caused me," Tristan said in a steely voice.

"That could be arranged, Captain. She can still be brought up on charges of disturbing the peace. The magistrate would like to get his hands on this one."

"Well, I promised the girl's father I would bring her to him. Otherwise, I would wash my hands of her."

Bettina was confused. She stood up, careful to keep the blanket wrapped tightly about her, and pointed an accusing finger at Tristan.

"He lies! He is the one I told you about — the pirate. You cannot let him take me!"

"Do you really prefer what awaits you here to the comfort of my ship, little one?" Tristan asked.

What could she say? Her options were all equally loathsome. Seven years' service, a few years with an old lecher, or a week on Tristan's ship and then freedom. Thankfully, Tristan did not wait for her to answer.

"You see, she is such a troublesome creature that her father has decided to put her in a convent. She hates the idea, so will do or say anything to avoid being taken home."

"It is a shame such a pretty girl should be given to the church.

I give her into your care, Captain, but please keep her confined to your ship for the duration of your stay."

"She will give you no more trouble. You have my word," Tristan replied coldly.

He opened the long cape he had draped over one arm, and wrapped it around Bettina. He then picked up the wet clothes that she had dropped on the floor the night before. When he saw his hat, he scowled at her, but he said nothing as he picked it up and escorted her from the cell.

"You put on quite a show last night, displaying your body to half the men on the dock," Tristan growled as they stepped out into the square. "Just what the hell did you think you were doing?"

"I — I —"

"Never mind!" Tristan cut her off brusquely, tightening his grip on her arm. "Anything is preferable to sharing my bed, isn't it? Even getting yourself arrested!"

"Yes, anything!" Bettina snapped in defiance.

He turned her around to face him, and his eyes were like blue ice crystals. Bettina feared for a moment that he was going to kill her right there on the street.

"There is only one thing that prevents me from throwing you back into that jail, and that is the pleasure I'm going to have in breaking you," he said in a harsh whisper. "I have yet to teach you something, my willful wench. And knowing how you feel about me, you won't enjoy the lesson."

"What do you mean?"

"In good time," he snarled cruelly, and started across the square. "And kindly keep that cape tightly closed, Bettina, or I will wring your pretty neck."

She was completely naked beneath the cape, but now she had half a mind to throw it open just to spite him, despite her modesty.

Tristan was seething with anger. He probably had had to pay damages to the tavern in order to get her released. She wondered what he would do to her. What was this lesson he was going to teach her? She shivered slightly, despite the hot sun.

As they passed through the town, Bettina's face grew red

when she realized how stupid she had been. If only she had asked what country claimed this island, she could have saved herself much trouble. This settlement was English, and Tristan had said he had England's sanction. No wonder those men had laughed at her when she told them a pirate ship was in the harbor. To the English, Tristan wasn't a pirate.

In less than an hour, Bettina was back in Tristan's cabin, but this time, he locked the door after he shoved her inside. He hadn't said another word to her, so she still didn't know what to expect. She was left alone for the rest of the day, and spent the time repairing her dress again. Madeleine came to see her that evening and spent more than an hour scolding her for her escape attempt. But when Madeleine left, Bettina was alone again, and she was still alone when she finally fell asleep.

Chapter 14

A soft, gentle pressure on her lips awoke Bettina from a sound sleep. She opened her eyes to find Tristan kissing her. It was a tender sort of kiss — the kind a husband would give his wife upon waking. She tried to rise, but Tristan held her firmly against the mattress.

"I wish to get up, Tristan."

"I am well aware of your wishes, Bettina, but unfortunately for you, I have something else in mind."

He spoke bitterly and the smile on his lips did not reach his cloudy blue eyes. He was still furious about what had happened yesterday, she could see that. So why had he kissed her so tenderly just a moment ago?

"Let me up!" she demanded sharply. "You know I can't stand to be near you!"

"Yes, I know," he said. "And that is why I'm going to enjoy giving you your final lesson."

"Surely you do not intend to —" She stopped when he reached beneath her shift and caressed her breast, giving her the answer. "At least have the decency to wait until night before you torture me!" she snapped.

"Torture? Is that what you call this?" he asked, teasing her nipple with his fingers.

"Yes! It is torture for me because I hate you!"

"You may hate me, my little French vixen, but your body will love what I'm going to do to it."

Before she could protest, Tristan had slid her shift up, pulled it over her head, and tossed it on the floor. He parted her legs with his knees and began to stroke the soft flesh between her thighs.

"No!" she screamed. She tried desperately to pull his arm away, but it would not be budged.

Pleasure was spreading through her body, and she could not stop it. His fingers were working magic, bringing her body to life against her will. He buried his face in her neck, searing her tender skin with his lips, and she knew she would be lost if she didn't stop him now. She had to stop him!

"Your — your beard," she finally managed to say. "It annoys me. It tickles."

He raised his head to look at her, but his eyes held no mercy. "You did not complain of this before."

"You were quick before," she snapped. "The tickling will make me laugh, and you might think I am laughing at your love-making."

"With whom do you compare my lovemaking, Bettina, when you have had no man before me?"

"The fact that you sicken me is enough," she retorted, but she could see the futility of her efforts. How could she make him angry enough to rape her quickly?

"Your biting tongue will go unheard this time, Bettina. Once and for all you will learn what it is to be a woman." His words were deliberately cold.

He rolled on top of her and covered her lips with his, stilling further protest. He entered her slowly, gently, and this time there was no pain. His actions did not match his emotions, for he was being tender, while his mood seemed cruel. He was taking revenge against her with his patience, but she had no way to fight it.

He went deep inside her and remained still as he covered her face and neck with kisses. His lips found hers again, branding her with the passion of his kiss. He started to move inside her, slowly at first, then faster. A feeling was building, spreading through her loins like liquid fire. And soon Bettina clung to Tristan as ecstasy exploded inside her.

Bettina heard Tristan laugh deeply, triumphantly, and she felt more humiliated by this than by anything she had gone through so far. So this was his revenge — to give her that wonderful, that unbelievable pleasure. And at the height of the moment, she had clung to him as if she couldn't bear to let him go.

"Do you still criticize my loving, little one?"

She looked up into his smug, smiling face and suddenly felt angry beyond endurance. At him, for he would never let her forget his power — and with herself, for losing control of her body in passion.

"Damn you, Tristan!" she screamed and pushed him off her body.

He watched with amusement as she scrambled out of bed and grabbed her shift from the floor. She put this on quickly, then faced him with her hands on her hips. Her long, silky hair tumbled all about her.

"Nothing has changed! Do you hear me? Nothing! I still hate you — more now than ever!"

"Why? Because I made love to you and you enjoyed it?" Tristan asked. He rose from the bed and began putting his clothes on.

"My body may have betrayed me, but it was only because I couldn't fight you. Your accursed threats stopped me! And —"
She stopped suddenly, and her eyes flew open.

Oh no! How could she have been so stupid? He would not whip her! He had been bluffing! He hated the Spanish for beating their slaves, he'd said, and he'd never harmed her yet, despite all the trouble she'd given him. Why hadn't she seen through his game sooner?

"Bettina, what is the matter with you?" he asked.

"Damn your blackhearted soul to hell, Tristan!" she stormed.

"Where the devil did you pick up such language? Not in the convent, I'm sure."

"From your crew! They don't have the decency to watch what they say with ladies aboard."

"And you think this language befits a lady?" he mocked her.

"I no longer feel like a lady. You have taken that from me — but no more!"

"And what is that supposed to mean?"

"Oh, nothing — nothing at all."

She decided to wait before calling his bluff until it would be to her advantage. She suddenly smiled, and then she began to laugh at the bewildered look on Tristan's face. How happy she was! Happy that she would no longer have to submit to this giant, this beast of a man, happy that she would no longer have to cower before him or endure his caresses. She could fight him now. And if his strength should prevail over hers, well, there was no humiliation in that. She would at least go down fighting. She continued to laugh.

"Have you taken leave of your senses?" Tristan demanded.

He suddenly feared that he had pushed her too far. He came over to her and shook her by the shoulders until she stopped laughing. But she still smiled up at him. And then he became even more confused as he stared down into her dark-blue eyes.

"What color are your eyes, Bettina?" he asked wonderingly.

She stopped smiling and pulled away from his grip. "You have seen my eyes enough to know what color they are," she snapped, turning her back on him.

"Your eyes were blue just now, blue as sapphires. Yet ever since you have been on the *Spirited Lady*, they have been green — until now."

"Don't be absurd. Eyes do not change color. It was merely the light."

"Look at me now!" he commanded. And when she refused, he swung her around, only to find that her eyes were green again.

"I told you it was merely the light," she said. But she turned away from him quickly, for the confusion on his face made her want to laugh again.

Tristan had the uneasy feeling that Bettina was making a fool of him. It was not the light. He knew damn well what he'd seen. Her eyes had been as blue as the depths of the sea. Did her eyes change with her moods? Green when she was angry or afraid, and blue when she was happy? She had been happy for a moment. But why? What did she have to be happy about in her present situation? Well, he was sure it would take coaxing to find out, and he didn't have the time now.

"Is that the name of your ship? The *Spirited Lady*?" she asked.

"What? Oh, yes," he said, and grinned at her. "The name rather suits you, too, doesn't it?"

"Do you think so?" she asked coquettishly. "You have hardly

allowed me to be very spirited."

"And what of your outburst just a few moments ago?"

"Did it hurt you very much, *Capitaine?* I do not see your wounds," she teased.

He smiled and changed the subject, for she was obviously playing a game with him. "I will see if there is any material in the hold. If so, you can make yourself some cooler dresses. It will also give you something to do."

"Thank you."

He looked at her quizzically, for he did not expect her gratitude. She had changed toward him, and it baffled him. He would soon find out what she was up to. With that thought, he left the cabin.

Shortly after the captain left, Madeleine came to the cabin with a platter of food, and she and Bettina ate together. She immediately noticed Bettina's gaiety, but she believed that Bettina had finally decided to accept things the way they were.

They had left Tortola at dawn, but Bettina didn't know this until Madeleine informed her. It annoyed her that the captain could distract her so that she didn't notice anything but him.

Tristan returned before noon with two bolts of pastel silks. He placed these on the table, along with a ball of lace and threads, then produced a pair of gold scissors that he had tucked in his belt. But he hesitated before placing these with the rest.

"Can I trust you not to use these scissors as a weapon?" he asked curtly.

"I have said I will not try to kill you again, Tristan," Bettina replied as she stood up to examine the silks. "My word is good, even if yours is not."

He smiled, but he was still reluctant to hand over the possible weapon.

"If you still do not trust me, then Maddy can take the scissors with her when she leaves, and return them to you. Would that be satisfactory?" When he still appeared to be reluctant, she laughed softly. "I will make it easy for you, *Capitaine*. You need not admit that you fear me. Maddy will bring you the scissors when she leaves."

94

Madeleine nodded her head to say she would do this. She wondered why Bettina was playing this game with the captain, but thank God, he did not seem to mind. But she held her breath as Bettina continued.

"How is it, Tristan, that you have this material, when you say you only attack ships carrying gold?"

He grinned now as he noticed her blue eyes. "The material was on a plate ship, along with many other goods that were being delivered to a Spanish *condesa*. If these colors do not suit you, there are others to choose from."

"Then you will not mind if Maddy replaces her wardrobe also?" she ventured sweetly.

"The material could be sold in Tortuga for a handsome sum. It is enough that I have put it at your disposal."

"It is not enough! Need I remind you that it was you who saw fit to leave our trunks behind, leaving us with only the clothes on our backs?"

"Very well!" Tristan replied harshly. "Is there anything else you wish, my lady?"

"Only never to lay eyes on you again," she answered tartly, a half-smile on her rosy lips.

"That, I am afraid, I will not grant."

With that, Tristan turned and left the cabin. Bettina sighed and turned to look at her servant, who was somewhat pale.

"Bettina, you must be careful what you say to the *capitaine*. You must not make him angry!" Madeleine warned urgently.

"And *you* must not worry," Bettina returned. "The *capitaine* will not harm us."

"But you said he will whip you if you resist him."

"Yes, but I was not resisting him. I was merely taunting him. And as you can see, he did nothing," Bettina said.

"But why were you mocking him? It was as if you were trying to make him lose his temper. You have known this man for only four days. It is impossible to judge how he will react to your taunts."

Bettina decided not to tell Madeleine of what she planned for tonight, for this would really alarm her.

"Do not worry. I can hold my own where Tristan is concerned.

Now, come, let us begin," Bettina said, taking the lime-green silk for herself.

Madeleine shook her head with a weak smile. "I will ask the *capitaine* for plain cotton. Never in my life have I worn silk, and I do not intend to start now."

Chapter 15

"I took the old one into the hold."

Bettina started at Tristan's words, for she was so busy working on her new dress that she hadn't heard him enter the room.

"What?"

"Your servant. I took her into the hold to get the cotton she requested, and when she saw this, she said you would need it," Tristan replied, laying the silver comb on the table before Bettina. "Are you satisfied now?"

"Satisfied? I did not ask you for the material, *Capitaine*. You offered it. I merely suggested that you do the same for my servant. I have thanked you for this already — I will not do so again. As for the comb, it is indeed beautiful, but I had a comb, Tristan. It was not as nice as this one, and only made of wood, but I cherished it because it was a gift from my mama. The comb is needed, but it does not replace my own."

"Would you have me go back to recover your trunks?" Tristan asked sarcastically.

"Yes."

He sighed, for he should have known what her answer would be. "The crew of the *Windsong* will have recovered sufficiently from their wounds by now. It would mean another battle."

"I forget that you are a coward," Bettina replied.

"I have never run from a battle — I've told you this already."

"No, it is only women you are afraid to fight."

"Fighting you would gain you nothing, Bettina. Though you think you would do me damage, you would not. I don't want to hurt you in the struggle, that is all."

"But I would love to hurt you, Tristan — to see you in pain for what you have done to me."

"Well, my bloodthirsty little vixen, that you will not do."

Bettina smiled and said no more. She continued her sewing as Tristan sat down and poured himself a tot of rum.

"Have you eaten?" he asked, leaning back in the chair to study her.

"Yes," Bettina replied. "That young boy brought the meal some time ago. I was beginning to hope you would not return this night — since it is already so late. Did Maddy return the scissors to you?"

"What sort of game were you playing this morning, Bettina?" he asked, ignoring her taunt. "Why has your attitude changed so suddenly?"

"My attitude has not changed," she replied softly. "I still hate you, Tristan."

With her unbound hair falling over her shoulders, and her head bent over the dress she was making, Tristan could not see Bettina's expression. What he wanted to see were her eyes. Were they dark sea-blue or turbulent green? Her tone of voice revealed nothing of the hatred she spoke of, yet he knew she spoke the truth. There was no doubt that she hated him, but where was the fire and ice of the day before? Where was the fiery temper of early this morning, before this change came over her?

"Would you care for a walk before we retire?" Tristan asked.

"Not if you intend to kiss me in the moonlight again."

"I plead guilty to the intention. So if you wish to remain stubborn, we will retire now."

"I will walk alone," she ventured.

"No, you will not!"

"Then you may retire."

"So will you, little one," Tristan replied. He stood up and drained the last of the rum.

"Not until you have removed your beard."

"What?" he exclaimed, sure that he had heard her incorrectly.

"You will cut away that beard — until your face is smooth. I was not jesting when I said that your beard annoys me. So remove it!" Bettina demanded, looking at him now with eyes like emeralds.

"I will do no such thing, woman!"

Any delay was worth gaining, even if it was pointless, thought Bettina. His beard did not really bother her, but it was worth the argument just to see if she could win.

"I insist that you shave it off, Tristan. I will not move from this chair until you do so."

"You are in no position to insist upon anything," he grunted.

"Would you have me resist you over such a trifling matter?" Bettina asked, mockery in her soft voice. "Why won't you do this small thing for me?"

"I like my face the way it is!"

"Well, I do not!" she snapped. "Are you afraid to get rid of your beard because then your scar would be more pronounced? Again the coward, eh, *Capitaine?*"

His body became rigid at the mention of his scar, and his eyes were cold as he glared at her.

"You go too far, Bettina!"

She could see that she had. He was obviously very sensitive about the scar on his face. She reminded herself that she didn't really know this man, that she wasn't qualified to judge his reactions. But she wouldn't back down now.

"Why do you hide the scar? Many men have marks on them. It is nothing to be ashamed of."

"I do not hide it! Would you have me smooth-faced when my crew is not?"

"Yes. I told you your beard annoys me. Remove it and prove to me you are not a coward."

"No!"

"Then go to bed, Tristan, but you go alone. I will not yield on this matter."

"Blast you, woman!" he stormed, but Bettina remained calm and returned to her sewing.

She intended to stand firm on this, he could see that. She just might call his bluff, and he didn't want to lose the hold his threats had on her for such nonsense. Women and their idiosyncrasies!

"I will be back shortly, and when I am, I want you in that bed with your clothes removed! Do you understand? Undressed and waiting!"

99

Tristan turned on his heel and stalked from the room. It was not far to the cabin that Jules was presently sharing with Joco Martel, and, seeing the light under the door, Tristan knocked loudly. After a moment, the door opened and Jules stood there, a bemused expression on his face.

"I was of the impression you had retired for the night," Jules remarked.

"I did, but I need your help."

"Can't it wait until morning, Tristan?"

"No!" Tristan shouted. "I need you to remove my beard — now!"

"What kind of joke is this? Why the devil would you want your face shaved, and why now?"

"Blast it, Jules! Don't ask so many questions — just do it! If I had a looking glass, I would do it myself."

Jules started to laugh boisterously. He turned his head and looked at Joco, who was sitting at the table.

"It seems the hot-tempered *mademoiselle* has won a bout with my friend here," Jules remarked to Joco, then turned back to Tristan. "This *is* her idea, isn't it? Since when do you do what the wench asks? What's happened to your logic?"

"It wouldn't work on this matter, so get it done with," Tristan growled.

Later, when he returned to his cabin, Tristan felt like an utter fool. He could still hear Jules's laughter and his biting words: "Now you look like the young lad that you are." And indeed he did look younger than his years now. Blast it! No other woman had ever complained about his beard, and most men wore one. Bettina had complained just to annoy him — he was sure of that now. Well, it would not take long for the beard to grow back. And with that thought, Tristan opened the door to his cabin and walked inside.

Bettina had been pacing the floor, dreading the moment when Tristan would return and the battle would begin. But now she was taken aback by the sight of him.

Tristan's full golden beard had hidden much, and without it she could see how very handsome and young he was. She could not take her eyes away from his face, and stood motionless in the middle of the room.

A fleeting thought came to her mind, that she could fall in love with this man if she did not hate him so. But the thought was absurd.

"When I give an order, I expect it to be obeyed!" Tristan said harshly.

But Bettina paid no attention to his tone of voice. Without the beard, he no longer looked like a dangerous pirate and she couldn't fear him. He was still a giant compared to her, but with such a handsome face, she could not take his harshness seriously.

"I no longer obey your orders," she stated finally.

His jaw tightened.

"What the devil does that mean?"

"I mean, Tristan, that you do not own me and you are not my husband. Therefore, I will not obey you."

Tristan crossed the short distance between them and stood towering before her. Gently he lifted her face up to his, but she avoided his eyes.

"Have you forgotten that you are on my ship — that you are in my power?" Tristan reminded her, the harshness gone from his voice.

"I may be on your ship, but it was not by my choice. And in your power? Perhaps. But as I said, Tristan, you do not own me. I am not your slave."

"You are my prisoner."

"Oh, yes, of course," she said dryly. "And prisoners who do not obey orders are whipped. Is that not right, *Capitaine?*"

"Is that what you want?"

Bettina took a step backward and looked at him oddly, as if she were thinking of an answer to his question. And then, unexpectedly, she swung her arm sideways and cracked her closed fist against his cheek, knocking him off balance.

Tristan's first impulse was to strike back, and he raised his hand, but stopped when he met her cold defiance. She stood there without flinching, rubbing her throbbing fist with her other hand and waiting for him to strike her. When he didn't, she laughed bitterly.

"Where is your whip, Tristan? Produce it and carry out your

threats. I believe it was ten lashes for every strike, was it not? Or perhaps you would rather wait until the count increases? I am sure it will before the night is through."

Tristan sighed heavily and moved away from her. He sank into the chair facing Bettina and spread his legs out before him.

"So it has come to this," he said in a level voice. "Is that why your disposition changed, because you think I will not carry out my threats?"

"You deal only in trickery! You are a liar, and I will no longer believe a word you speak!" she returned heatedly.

"What makes you so sure I was bluffing?"

"By your own words, that you hate the Spanish for beating their slaves. You would not do the same," she said triumphantly.

"Those were not my exact words, Bettina. It is not for beating their slaves that I hate the Spanish, but for another reason that runs much deeper."

Bettina faltered. The sudden anger in his eyes at the mention of the Spanish made her shiver slightly.

"If you whipped me, you could not — could not —"

"Make love to you?" Tristan finished for her. "Why? It would indeed be painful for you, but how would that stop me?"

Her anger flared. "You wouldn't!" she stormed.

"Why not? It would cause me no discomfort. Your reasoning is only from your point of view, not mine."

"You could not turn me over to my betrothed if my body were marred."

"You amaze me, Bettina. According to your logic, you would have me turn you over without a stitch on. I can assure you that you will be clothed. There will be no evidence to view."

"I have a voice, Tristan!"

"You will be gagged," he said matter-of-factly. "The exchange will take place on the *Spirited Lady*, with the Comte de Lambert brought here by my men. I will be far at sea before the *comte* can give chase."

Bettina felt sick inside. She had called his bluff and lost. She had been fooled into thinking that he was not a cold-blooded pirate, fooled by his handsome face. But what was he waiting for? Why hadn't he struck her in return?

102

"What — what do you intend to do?" she asked, her eyes dark with fear.

"Nothing."

"But I —"

"You were right, that is all," he said.

She stared at him, aghast. "Then why did you deny my reasoning?"

"Because your reasoning is not mine."

"But I do not understand," Bettina returned.

Tristan leaned forward in the chair and rested his hands on his knees. His expression was void of anger, nor did it show compassion.

"Have no doubt, I will use the whip if I have to, Bettina. So do not underestimate me in the future. But I would not whip you simply because you choose to fight rather than submit to me. That is your rightful choice."

Bettina's eyes flamed. "Why did you trick me if you feel this way? Why didn't you let me fight for my honor in the first place?"

"Understand this, Bettina. You mean nothing to me, except as a pleasure in my bed. I admit that you are the loveliest woman I have ever come across, but there is no room in my life for you or any other woman. I chose to enjoy you and to avoid conflict if possible — it didn't matter by what means. But since you are determined to fight me, Bettina, so be it. This is your right, and I will not whip you for it."

"Oh!" Bettina swung around so she wouldn't have to look at his arrogant face. More than anything, she wanted to kill him! But she couldn't. She had sworn to wait until she and Madeleine were safe. But then — yes, then . . .

"You still need not fight me, Bettina," Tristan said, breaking into her murderous thoughts. "The damage has been done, and you could gain nothing but frustration."

"I would gain satisfaction!" Bettina faced him again, prepared for battle.

"Then it is to be rape?"

"It has always been rape!" she snapped.

"You won't like it, Bettina."

"Nor will you!"

"Again the test of strength, eh? Well, at least I will prove once and for all that your strength is no match for mine."

He stood up, and Bettina ran for the door. But before she could open it, Tristan had picked her up and thrown her over his shoulder. She kicked her feet, but they struck only air. She pounded on his back with her fists, but it was like beating on solid rock. When Tristan reached his bed, he tossed her down, stunning her for a moment. Bettina fought to untangle herself from the web of her unbound hair, and Tristan quickly removed his breeches and tunic. When she finally looked up at him, he was standing naked and ready, a devilish grin on his firm lips.

"This will be easier than I expected," he laughed.

"No!" she screamed, and started to scramble from the bed, but he was on her in a second.

"Will you be sensible, or will you repair your dress for a third time come morning?" he asked.

"You go to the devil!" she cried furiously.

She began to struggle, only to find Tristan's hands locked on her wrists. He pulled them above her head, leaving her defenseless except for her legs, and these were hampered by her skirt. His weight pressed down on her, and Bettina suddenly felt suffocated. She continued her panting efforts to free herself, but she could hear Tristan laughing. Laughing!

Bettina screamed then, a deafening scream of rage, but Tristan covered her mouth with his. When she thrashed her head from side to side to avoid his lips, he released her hands and held her face still, bruising her soft lips with his brutal kiss. He stopped, however, and cried out in pain when she raked her nails down his back.

"Damn you, she-cat!" he growled. He secured her wrists with one hand and ripped her dress down to her waist with the other. He looked at her coldly and continued to watch her terror-filled expression as he finished tearing her dress apart. Then he tore the soft material of her shift away until her young flesh was open to his view. Tristan hoisted her legs over his shoulders and held them there with his massive arms. He entered her cruelly and raped her body with his anger.

When he had finished with her, his anger subsided. He released her and rolled to her side, not caring whether she resumed her attacks. But she just lay there, staring at the ceiling. She didn't even move when he pulled the cover over her.

"Bettina, why do you insist on pain? You experienced the ultimate in pleasure this morning, and I would gladly take you to those heights again," he said quietly.

"You have no right to give me this pleasure!" she snapped, coming to life again and surprising him with her quick reply. "Only my husband will have that right. And you are not my husband!"

"And you will give yourself freely to this *comte* when you marry?"

"Of course."

"But he is a man you have never seen. What if you hate him, even as you hate me? What then, Bettina?"

"That is of no concern to you."

Bettina suddenly remembered the talk she had had with her mother about her forthcoming marriage, and her mother's wish that she find happiness at all cost. What if the Comte de Lambert was a cruel man — a man like Tristan?

No! She must not hate her future husband. She would need him to fulfill her revenge against Tristan.

"Since I will take you again, anyway, why not enjoy it, Bettina?" Tristan asked quietly. "No one need know that you abandoned yourself to me."

"I would know!" she cried indignantly. "Now leave me be!"

She turned her back on him and let the silent tears caress her cheeks. It was a long while before Bettina could sleep. But Tristan's thoughts were equally troubled, and late in the night he quietly left the cabin.

105

Chapter 16

The morning was well under way, and Tristan tried to control the urge to knock a few heads together. The surprised looks and hushed snickering from his crew, as if they could hardly recognize him without his beard, were wearing down his nerves. He had a mind to shave the whole lot of them; then he would see who would laugh!

It was in this angry mood that Tristan pounded on Jules's door. Madeleine Daudet opened it, then shrank back from him, fear in her eyes. With a scowl on his face, Tristan stepped into the cabin to find Jules sitting at the table over a cup of steaming black coffee.

"What the hell is keeping you, Jules?"

"I've been trying to reassure this one that you didn't beat her lady last night. Can't you keep that blasted wench from screaming her head off?"

"Would you have me gag her? That would just increase her low opinion of me, although why that should bother me, I don't know," Tristan said. He turned to Madeleine with a look of annoyance. "Go to your lady. You will find her no worse off than she was yesterday. In fact, she should be quite pleased with herself."

Tristan watched the old woman leave the cabin; then he closed the door and faced his friend. Jules laughed boisterously.

"Blast it, Jules!" Tristan stormed. "Your amusement at my expense has gone far enough. Perhaps if I shaved off your beard, you would not find it so humorous!"

"It is not your smooth face that I find amusing, 'tis your black eye," Jules chuckled.

Tristan felt the tender area below his eye and winced. So,

he had a black eye to go with the raw scratches on his back. He had forgotten about the blow Bettina had dealt to his cheek.

"Why do you let the wench get the better of you?" Jules asked soberly. "A good beating would put her in her place. I had to lock the old servant up last night when the girl started screaming. She was going to race to her lady's rescue."

"I'll handle the girl the way I see fit. I'll tame her yet, and I've decided to keep her for a while," Tristan said, grinning.

"What the devil are you talking about?"

"Just that I've a mind to enjoy Bettina Verlaine's company for a bit longer than planned. I changed course for our home island last night," Tristan replied.

"But what of the ransom?"

"I will still collect the ransom — but not yet. The *comte* can wait to enjoy his bride. And can you honestly tell me you're not impatient to return to your little Maloma?"

"No, that I can't. But Bettina and Madeleine think they are going to Saint Martin. What's going to happen when they find their destination has been changed?" Jules asked.

"They needn't know until we reach home. Bettina will be the only one who will raise hell, but there won't be anything she can do about it." Tristan paused thoughtfully. "Why don't you sound out the crew today and see what they have to say. These last two years at sea have yielded much booty. They shouldn't mind losing their shares of the ransom for the moment."

"No, I'm sure they will gladly go along with your decision," said Jules. "They are anxious to get back to their women."

"One more thing. Whatever you do, don't let the old woman know of this. Warn the crew not to speak of it in front of her."

"Bettina, are you all right?" Madeleine asked. She closed the door and sat down across from her ward.

"Yes, why do you ask?"

"I heard your screams last night. I thought that he —"

"It was nothing," Bettina said quickly. "Just screams of frustration, no more."

Madeleine was perplexed. Bettina's lips were tight, her knuckles taut as she took careless stitches in her violet dress. She was wearing only her white shift, and Madeleine noticed the uneven seam in the front where it had been repaired. It was not like Bettina to sew unskillfully.

"I saw the *capitaine*," Madeleine ventured. "He said that you would be pleased with yourself, but you do not seem so."

Bettina looked up, her eyes like glittering emeralds. "So the *capitaine* thinks he can predict my feeling now. He is indeed a fool!"

She, too, had thought she would be pleased at being able to fight Tristan. But losing to him had meant utter humiliation. She couldn't stop thinking about the degrading way he had raped her — raising her legs over his shoulders.

She had awakened quite early, relieved to find herself alone. She had sponged herself with cold water from the washstand, then began to repair her shift. But with each stitch she took, scenes from the night before flashed before her eyes. Her lips were still tender and slightly swollen from Tristan's hard, angry kisses. And there were tiny blue marks on her wrists, testimony to his superior strength.

She decided to stop repairing her clothes every morning. She would wear Tristan's clothes, and if he insisted on ripping them off her every night, it would be his problem.

Bettina smiled now at her servant. "I must remember to ask Tristan if there is any white satin in the hold. I should begin making a new wedding dress as soon as possible." There was a sparkle in her deep-blue eyes.

"But you have yet to finish the silk dress you started yesterday," Madeleine reminded her, glad to see Bettina smiling again.

"The green dress will not take long to complete. And the sooner I make my wedding dress, the sooner I will be able to marry the *comte*."

Chapter 17

Bettina had spent eleven days aboard the *Spirited Lady*, and had decided it was amazing how time seemed to stand still just when one willed it to fly on swift wings. Tristan stayed away from his cabin during the day, but every night he spent with her added to her fury and outrage.

She recalled clearly the first night, a week ago, that Tristan had come into the cabin and found her wearing a pair of his breeches and a soft gold shirt. She could still hear the sound of his laughter ringing in her ears. And it didn't take long to learn what he found so amusing when he yanked the clothes from her body with hardly any effort at all, the large articles sliding off quite easily. But she continued to change into Tristan's apparel each evening to save her dresses from further ruin.

One night in particular haunted her thoughts. Tristan had taken his time with her, coaxing her body to life, holding her immobile while he worked his magic. And then afterward, instead of laughing triumphantly, he had gently kissed the tears that slid from the corners of her eyes. She hated his gentleness more than his cruelty.

Bettina cut the thread on the hem and held the dress out in front of her. It was a simple dress, sleeveless and untrimmed, made of soft lilac cotton. It was definitely not in fashion, but it would keep her cool during the heat of the day. Tristan had agreed to bring her some white satin, then had turned around and refused her when he learned she wanted it for a new wedding dress. It still didn't make any sense to her.

"Bettina, we're there!"

Bettina started violently when Madeleine rushed into the room, leaving the door open behind her. Her face was flushed and her gray-brown hair was matted and wet about her temples from working in the galley.

"You scared the wits out of me. What —"

"We're there, my pet!" Madeleine answered. "I saw the island when I went up on deck for a breath of fresh air. We have reached —"

Before she could finish, Bettina had run from the room, across the deck, and up to the ship's railing. She didn't even hear Madeleine come up behind her.

"It is not what I expected Saint Martin to look like," Madeleine said quietly. "I mean, it looks deserted. But it is beautiful, is it not?"

Beautiful was hardly the word. A gleaming white beach surrounded them, for the ship was in a small turquoise cove, completely hidden from the vast sea beyond. Swaying palms lined the beach, and a dense green jungle flourished beyond. A magnificent two-horned mountain towered over the island, covered with smooth, gray-green foliage and surrounded by dark-gray clouds. A deep gorge between the two peaks cut to the heart of the mountain, where the rays of the late morning sun found and brilliantly lit a white cloud formation.

Bettina turned to her servant, her blue eyes alight with pleasure.

"I never dreamed Saint Martin would be this beautiful — it is a paradise!" Bettina exclaimed. "Oh, I am going to love it here."

"I think I will, too." Madeleine smiled. "Though it seems strange to see all this greenery in the middle of winter."

"Yes. Imagine what it will look like in spring and summer!"

"I could not even begin to," Madeleine laughed.

"I wonder where all the natives are?" said Bettina. "I can't see any buildings, either."

"This is probably just a deserted side of the island."

"Of course," Bettina replied. "It would be dangerous to sail a pirate ship into a crowded enemy harbor."

"Yes. But there is another ship in the cove. Come and see it."

"What ship?" Bettina asked.

"It was already here when we came. But there is no crew aboard her."

They crossed the deck to see the other vessel. It had three bare masts and looked like a sister to the *Spirited Lady.*

"I wonder where the crew is," said Bettina.

"They must be on the island," Madeleine said. "Perhaps the town is not so far away after all. It is probably just hidden by the jungle."

"Do you think so?"

"Of course. It should not take long to contact the Comte de Lambert. We will probably be at his plantation before the day is through."

Bettina rejoiced. Freedom at last! No more Tristan, no more rape and humiliation. And soon, revenge.

"Oh, Maddy, this nightmare is finally over!"

"Yes, my pet, finally."

Bettina turned to walk back to her cabin, and ran into Jules's massive chest. She gasped and stepped back with wide, terror-filled eyes.

"If you ladies will return to your cabins and collect your belongings, you will be taken ashore presently," he said politely. Then he looked to Madeleine and his voice softened. "If you will hurry, please. The first boat has already been lowered, *madame.*"

"Where — where is the *capitaine?*" Bettina ventured. It was the first time she had seen Jules since the day he had tried to whip her, and no matter how much Madeleine spoke in his defense, Bettina still feared him.

"Tristan is busy."

"But he said the exchange would take place aboard this ship. Why are we going ashore?" Bettina asked.

"The plan has been changed."

He turned and walked away, leaving Bettina bewildered. Why would Tristan change his mind about the exchange?

Bettina left Madeleine and went back to Tristan's cabin. It took her only a minute to fold her two dresses. She decided to leave the silver comb that Tristan had given her, for the Comte de Lambert would surely give her anything she needed. But then she changed her mind. It was a costly item, and she would take it if only to keep Tristan from selling it. She would throw it away

111

later, as she planned to do with the two dresses she had made aboard the *Spirited Lady*.

Without a final glance at Tristan's hated cabin, Bettina walked back on deck, the soft green silk of her skirt swaying gently. She crossed to the railing and was disappointed to find that clouds now blocked her view of the beautiful, horned mountain. She might never see that trick of light again, where only the heart of the mountain had been lit, deep inside the gorge. But perhaps it had been a good omen welcoming her to her new home, a promise of the many wondrous things she had yet to see, and of the happy life she would have here with the *comte*.

A surge of happiness lifted her spirits, and the sun touched her face as it broke through the clouds to light the small cove.

"Are you ready to leave, little one?"

She turned abruptly at the sound of Tristan's deep voice. He stood on deck with his legs apart, his hands clasped behind his back and a warm smile upon his lips. He looked very handsome, and was elegantly dressed in a white silk shirt, ruffled at the neck and cuffs, white breeches, a black leather vest belted closed, and black knee-high leather boots.

"I was ready to leave you eleven days ago," she told him haughtily. "How long will it be before the exchange takes place?"

"Are you so anxious to part from me?"

"That is a ridiculous question to ask, Tristan. I pray for the day when you will be wiped from my memory," she said icily.

"Your hair is stunning when the sun shines on it," he said playfully.

"Why do you change the subject?"

"Would you prefer to go to my cabin, where we can discuss the subject more privately?" he ventured, his eyes twinkling.

"No!" she said. "I am ready to leave."

"Then come, my love," he replied, taking her arm and leading her across the deck to where Madeleine and Jules were waiting. "You can leave your belongings on board if you like. My men will bring them ashore later," Tristan said.

"No, I want to leave now, with everything."

"As you wish."

Tristan helped Bettina into one of the two small landing boats.

Madeleine sat beside her, with Tristan behind them at the rudder and six crewmen in front. Jules went in the other boat. The crewmen pulled strongly on the oars, and they surged over the short stretch of water toward the beach.

As Bettina watched the small waves lapping at the sides of the boat, she wondered idly why Tristan hadn't tried to bed her one last time this morning. If she had learned anything about him these past eleven days, it was that he was a very demanding man, so why would he pass up this last chance?

But, she told herself, she should just be thankful that he had been occupied elsewhere and that this nightmare was at an end.

They reached the shore, and the man called Davey jumped into the water to pull the small boat up to the sand. Tristan helped, and then insisted on carrying Bettina up to dry sand, where Madeleine joined her.

Bettina started to stroll down the beach, thinking that it would take some time to ferry the whole crew ashore. But Tristan stopped her before she had walked three yards.

"We go now."

She turned back at his command, to see that both boats were heading back to the ship. Jules had remained behind and was leading Madeleine and ten crewmen to the edge of the beach. Tristan took Bettina's arm.

"Aren't we going to wait for the rest of your crew?" she asked, looking out to the ship. "Or don't you need them?"

"They will come later," he said, and led her to join the others.

"But where are we going?"

"It is not far."

Bettina stopped walking. "Why are you being so evasive? I want to know where you are taking us!"

"There is a house not far from here. You would like a bath, wouldn't you?"

She smiled. She hadn't had a real bath, in a tub, for far too long. And she definitely wanted to be clean when she met the *comte* for the first time.

Tristan took her hand and led the way into the forest along a man-made path. The forest was not so dense here as she had thought. The trees were widely spaced, and there was hardly any undergrowth, mostly bare sandy earth, with short, stubby grass growing here and there.

They soon reached the house that Tristan had mentioned, which looked more like some kind of fortress. The building was large and built of heavy white stones. The first floor was square, and a royal palm tree stood on either side of the small front door. The second floor was U-shaped, forming a courtyard open to the front above the door. A small jungle of beautiful flowers and plants grew in pots in this courtyard, some reaching above the second-floor roof, and some trailing over the edge of the courtyard. The front-door palm trees framed the potted jungle and towered above the house. Beautiful rolling lawns, immaculately cared for, surrounded the house on all sides. The most beautiful flowers, with red, yellow, orange, even purple and blue blossoms, grew at the edge of the lawns and against every wall. The house seemed sturdy and welcoming, and she almost wished that it belonged to the Comte de Lambert, for she would have liked to live here.

Suddenly, the front door was opened by a tall man. The single door was small, out of proportion to the rest of the house, and the man's frame completely blocked it. He stood with his legs astride, his hands on his hips, and looked very angry.

Tristan stopped, and Jules came up from the rear to join him. They stood only a few feet from the man in the doorway, and Bettina sensed tension in the air.

"I would hardly be recognizin' you, Tristan, were it not for your watchdog Bandelaire," the man challenged.

"I can see you haven't changed, Casey," Tristan replied harshly.

"That I haven't. And I'm still young enough to take you on, lad."

"But you'll still have to fight me first, Casey," Jules growled.

"Enough!" Tristan said. "It's time this old seadog and I had it out."

Bettina gasped as the two men charged at one another, but then they embraced each other and started laughing. These men were like children playing a stupid game, Bettina thought angrily. They were friends!

The man they called Casey now had a genuinely warm smile

on his lips. He stood beside Tristan and greeted Jules with a tight clasp of hands.

"It was a foolish thing to do!"

"What?" Bettina asked Madeleine.

"I thought my heart would stop!" Madeleine answered. "I am too old to witness such foolishness."

"Why are you upset?" Bettina asked, forgetting her own annoyance.

"Jules —"

"Jules!" Bettina exclaimed, and suddenly she remembered how the big man's voice had softened when he spoke to Madeleine. "What is he to you?"

"Nothing," Madeleine replied. "But he told me I remind him of his mother. I thought it was touching. He treats me kindly, and you should hear how he raves over my cooking."

"Honestly, Maddy, you sound as if you have adopted him!"

"I was only concerned for him. That man they called Casey looked so mean."

"Jules is the same height, younger, and nearly twice the weight of the other man," Bettina replied, irritated. "There was no reason for you to be afraid for him. And —"

"Be this another one to add to your harem, lad?" a man's voice asked.

Bettina turned and saw that Casey was staring directly at her. She felt the blood rush to her cheeks.

"I have no harem, Casey, as you're well aware," Tristan smiled. "One spirited lady is all I can handle at a time."

Jules laughed, understanding which spirited lady Tristan was talking about. But Casey was perplexed, thinking of Tristan's ship.

"Is this woman married, then?" Casey asked.

"No, but she's spoken for, so cast your eyes elsewhere," said Tristan.

"And here I thought I was in for a change in me luck. Be there no room for bargainin'?"

"None at all," Tristan answered. "So warn your crew that she is not to be approached."

Bettina was ready to spit fire, and she stiffened when

Tristan approached her.

"Would you like to have that bath now, or would you prefer something to eat first?" he asked.

"Neither, if the house belongs to that crude man!" Bettina replied heatedly, her dark-green eyes flashing.

Tristan laughed. "It's not Casey's house, but you have misjudged him. He's a good man, and was merely jesting about you. His crew is off carousing in the village, but he rarely goes there."

"How far is this village?"

"About a mile inland."

"Is that where the Comte de Lambert has his plantation?" she asked hopefully.

"No."

"Then where —"

"Come," he said, cutting her off. "I'll show you to a room where you can bathe."

"How long will we be here?"

"A while," he replied curtly, and led Bettina into the house. Jules had already taken Madeleine inside, and Casey had disappeared.

The entire square bottom floor formed one cool, dark room. There were only a few windows on three of the walls, and these were small and high, above eye level, letting in very little light. The wall to the right held a stone fireplace, very sooty, which seemed to be used for cooking. A few wooden chairs stood beside the fireplace and a plain sideboard with pots and dishes.

A huge table stood in the center of the room, made of rough, uneven wood, with twenty or more chairs about it. Above the table, and oddly out of place in this big room, was a large crystal chandelier with half-burnt candles. There was no other furniture in the room, and nothing adorning the stone walls. A sturdy wooden staircase without railings led up to the second floor.

"There are six rooms upstairs, three on each side of the house. You may use the first room on the right side," Tristan told Bettina.

"After I bathe, will we be leaving?"

"We will eat first. But you can take your time, for I have to see about the provisions."

Tristan ordered a caldron of water to be heated over the fire, and left. Bettina put aside her annoyance at Tristan's evasiveness and turned to Madeleine.

"The *capitaine* said we could use the first room on the right. It will be good to have a bath after being so long at sea."

"It certainly will," Madeleine replied. "But I want to see to the meal first."

"Very well," Bettina said and started for the stairs.

At the top of the stairs was a short corridor brightly illuminated by windows on both sides, one side looking out on the beautiful courtyard garden on the roof, and the other side looking down on the green lawns behind the house. The corridor continued into both wings, with bedroom doors on one side of the passage and windows looking out on the garden on the other side.

Bettina walked into the large bedroom Tristan had said she might use. It looked comfortable, but there was dust on everything, including the thick green-and-yellow quilted bedspread. There was a very large black-green-and-yellow Oriental rug that almost completely covered the floor. A large sea chest was at the foot of the big four-poster bed, and two chairs, covered in light-green velvet, stood against a wall.

The room had no fireplace, but Bettina supposed there would be no need for one in such a warm climate. The window overlooking the lawn had a wonderful view of the horned mountain in the far distance. But Bettina was disappointed to see that the mountain was still dark and brooding.

She went to the large chest at the foot of the bed and opened it, but it was empty. There was an intricately carved folding screen in one corner that hid a fairly large tub. Bettina ran her finger along the rounded top edge of the screen to remove the dust, then laid her dresses over it. She set her silver comb on the table beside the bed, then stripped the heavy cover off the bed and shook it out, watching the dust particles float in the air. She put the spread back and dusted the rest of the furniture with her hands until young Joey, the cabin boy, entered the room with the first buckets of warm water, Madeleine following him with towels and soap.

With the door open, Bettina could hear the sound of female

giggling coming from the first floor. "Are there other women here?" she asked in surprise.

"Yes. A couple of girls from the village just came," Madeleine replied, "to help in the kitchen. They're pretty girls, golden-skinned, dark-haired. They speak Spanish."

"Really?" Bettina said. "I thought Saint Martin was occupied only by the French and Dutch."

"Apparently not, my pet."

Chapter 18

The water was pleasantly warm, and Bettina lazily watched the floating soap bubbles, intending to soak for hours. She didn't hear the door open, and she started when Tristan folded the screen and set it against the wall. He stood looking down at her for a moment, but her hair floated in the water around her, hiding what he had hoped to see.

"Get out of here!" Bettina snapped. But he walked to the bed and sat down facing her. She wished now that she hadn't dusted the spread. "Leave now or I — I will scream!"

Tristan laughed heartily. "You should know by now that your screams will not bring help. But I came here to talk — nothing else."

"We have nothing more to talk about," she said, "except returning me to my betrothed. And that can wait until I have finished my bath. So please leave."

"This is my room, and I choose to stay."

"Your room!"

"Yes. And I would prefer you remained where you are."

"Why?" she demanded.

"Because you're at a disadvantage, and that is the way I want you."

"I do not understand."

"You see, Bettina, this is not only my room. This is my house. And we will be staying here for a while."

"But you — you must be mad to tell me this! You know I will inform the *comte,* and he will come after you."

"How so?" Tristan asked, amused.

"You live on the same island. It will not be hard to find this house again."

"Ah, Bettina." He sighed heavily. "Is it so hard for you to accept the obvious? No one will ever be able to find my house. This is not Saint Martin, but only one small, uncivilized island among many."

"No! You are lying to me again!"

"I speak the truth — you have my word. I changed course a week ago. I know that you don't like it, but you might as well accept it. We will stay here a month — perhaps two."

"No — no! I will not stay here with you! Why did you change course? Or did you never intend to take me to Saint Martin?"

"I didn't lie to you at first. I simply changed my mind and decided to come home for a while. We were headed here when your ship was sighted. We have been at sea for two years, and my crew needs a rest. I will still take you to your betrothed if you wish. But you must consider this your home for the time being."

"No — I will not stay here!"

"Where will you go, little one?"

"You spoke of a village — I will go there," she said haughtily.

"You won't find any help in the village, Bettina. The Awawaks are peaceful farmers, but they distrust the white man. A hundred and fifty years ago, the Spanish used them mercilessly to mine for silver, and none survived but a dozen families who had escaped to hide in the foothills. When the island was drained of its worth, the Spaniards left, and the runaways returned to the deserted village. When I first found this island, I claimed this house as my own and decided to make it my home. We deal fairly with the Indians and trade for what we want. They speak some Spanish and have learned a little English since my coming, but they won't help you. And even if they did, I would find you and bring you back here."

"Why did you decide to bring me here, Tristan?" Bettina asked, trying to stay calm. "You would have delayed only two weeks by taking me to Saint Martin, and would have gained much gold. *Mon Dieu,* I was so happy — thinking I would never have to look upon you again. Why did you change your mind?"

"We were coming home for pleasure and relaxation, and you are my greatest pleasure," he replied softly, then stood up to leave. "Finish your bath, little one, and then come downstairs. The food should be ready."

"Tristan, you will have no more pleasure at my expense," she said, her eyes dark with loathing.

"We shall see," he returned.

"No, we shall *not* see! If you insist upon raping me again, I will find the means to escape you again. I give you my word!"

"And I give you *my* word that I will keep you prisoner here if I have to!" Tristan shouted, finally losing his patience. He left the room and slammed the door behind him.

Bettina's hair was still damp when she came down the stairs an hour later. She had braided her hair into a long plait and wore her dress of lilac cotton. Madeleine left the table and met her at the foot of the stairs.

"Jules told me we will be staying here for some time," she whispered. "I am so sorry, Bettina. You must be terribly upset."

"I have nothing to be upset about," Bettina said calmly. "I don't have to stay here."

"What do you mean?"

"I mean that if that arrogant fool touches me again, I will run away." She glanced at Tristan, who was sitting at the table staring at her, and smiled coquettishly at him.

"Bettina, you must not do anything rash," Madeleine said fearfully.

"I do not intend to!" Bettina snapped, but stopped at the sight of her servant's stricken face. "I'm sorry, Maddy. I am forever taking my anger out on you. You must forgive me."

"I know," said Madeleine. "You have changed much since you have been with the *capitaine,* and I understand why. I would rather you took your anger out on me. If you show anger to him, it could endanger your life."

"Have no fear, Maddy. He will not kill me. It is just that he inflames me so with rage, and he has yet to pay the price. Sometimes my emotions are so strong that they scare me."

"But Bettina, *why* do you hate him so?"

"Why? I — never mind. Come, he grows impatient."

They walked to the long table, and Bettina took the empty

121

chair beside Tristan. Madeleine went to the kitchen area, leaving Bettina with Tristan, the man called Casey on her right, and Jules, who was sitting across from her.

"Bettina, I'd like you to meet my good friend, Captain O'Casey."

She glanced at Tristan, turned to the tall man sitting beside her, and was met by a friendly smile. Casey was still a handsome man, though he seemed twice her age, she thought. His red hair was graying slightly at the temples, but his body was healthy and muscular.

"I've been talking with your servant, *mademoiselle,* and she tells me you are French," Casey said in that language.

Bettina was delighted to hear her native language, though he spoke it with an odd, Irish accent. She smiled beguilingly at him as an idea came to her.

"Is it your ship I saw in the cove, *Capitaine* O'Casey?" she asked.

"That it is, lass. But please call me Casey, as my friends do."

"I would be happy to, Casey. Will you be staying here long?" she continued.

"Perhaps another day or so. I was on my way to Tortuga, when I encountered a Spanish galleon. I stopped here to make a few repairs."

"When you leave, could you take me with you?" Bettina asked, still in French.

"But why do you want to leave?" Casey asked, frowning.

"Please — I cannot stay here!" Bettina pleaded. "If you will take me to my betrothed, he will pay you handsomely."

"And what is this lucky man's name?"

"Enough!" Tristan bellowed, making Bettina jump.

She turned, noticing Madeleine's pale face and Jules's amused one, but Tristan was decidedly angry.

"If you wish to continue your conversation, you will do so in English," he said.

"But why?" Bettina asked innocently.

"Because, my little one, I don't trust you!"

Jules's laughter shook the table.

Tristan glared at him and said, "What, may I ask, do you

find so amusing, Bandelaire?"

Ignoring Tristan, Jules turned to Casey. "My young friend here has good reason not to trust the wench," he said. "She tried to kill him once, and he probably thought that she was conniving with you to try again."

"Not exactly," said Tristan, his anger gone. "She has thoughts of escape, and I have no doubt that she will try to enlist your aid, Casey. For reasons of her own, the lady doesn't care for my company. I, on the other hand, enjoy hers extremely. I tell you now that she is mine by right of capture. The spoils of war, more or less."

"I am not!" Bettina stormed, coming to her feet.

"Sit down, Bettina!" Tristan ordered harshly. "Would you prefer I explained the situation in simpler terms?"

"No!"

"As I said, Casey, she is mine," Tristan continued. "No one touches her, and no one takes her from me."

"Have you marriage in mind, lad?" Casey inquired.

"No. You should know there is no room in my life for marriage," Tristan replied.

"That I know. So you've not yet found Don Miguel de Bastida, then?" Casey asked.

"No."

"How many years have you been searching now?"

"Twelve. Not that I'm counting. I'm beginning to think that someone might have reached him before me. He has many enemies."

"True, but I think he's still alive," Casey replied. "I talked with a sailor in Port Royal, who escaped a Spanish prison by the grace of God. He had a horrid tale to relate, but the man who sent him to that death hole was the same man you seek."

"Did the sailor say more?" Tristan asked, excitement in his voice. "Where was Bastida last seen?"

"The trial took place in Cartagena three years ago. And the man had not seen Bastida since."

"Blast it! When will I find that murderer? When?" Tristan stormed.

"You won't be findin' him here, lad. Of that I am sure," Casey said, looking at Bettina.

"No, you're right, I won't find him here," Tristan replied softly. He gazed at Bettina for a long moment, an odd mixture of emotions crossing his face. "But the search can wait for a few months."

The conversation died when the two Indian serving girls carried large platters of food to the table. They were as pretty as Madeleine had said, with long, silky black hair and brilliant black eyes. They wore brightly colored full skirts and low-cut blouses, but no shoes. They looked much alike, probably sisters, she thought, and they both shot Bettina curious glances as they put the food on the table.

Bettina turned her attention to the food. She passed up the ship's fare of dried beans and salted meat, but gorged on fresh, exotic fruit that she had never tasted before.

The crew drifted in, one by one, to eat also. Bettina wondered who this Bastida was, and reminded herself to ask Tristan about him later.

Chapter 19

Bettina asked Tristan if she could walk on the grounds and was a bit surprised when he nodded his assent. She left by the front door, walked to the side of the house and around it. As she scanned the edge of the forest, she saw a corral just inside a clearing beyond the trees. She walked there slowly, unbraiding her hair as she went to let it dry in the breeze.

At the edge of the forest, a path led the few feet to the corral. There were seven horses inside, and one beautiful white stallion that caught her eye. She beckoned to him, but he shied away from her as the others did.

Bettina wished that she knew how to ride. Her father, André, had insisted it was not proper for women. But it shouldn't be too difficult to learn, she thought, if the horses were tame.

A soft crackling of twigs made Bettina tense, and she turned abruptly, thinking to find Tristan. But a man with coal-black hair was coming quickly down the forest path. He edged his way around her, blocking the path to the house.

"If this ain't my day of days," the man smirked. "Where'd you come from, girl?"

"I — I came from the —"

"Never you mind," he chuckled. "I should've known better than to question a gift from heaven."

He started to approach her with his hands outstretched, and Bettina panicked. He was stocky in build, with bulging arms, and was a bit taller than she. It was not hard to guess his intent, and she was able to scream once before he reached her and clasped his hand over her mouth.

"What're you scared of, wench? I'll not hurt you. What I've in mind don't hurt none," he laughed, holding her to him tightly.

"We'll just go a little farther into the trees, just in case someone happens to come this way."

Bettina was desperate now. She could think of only one thing that might protect her, and she prayed that it would work. She jerked her head away from his chest.

"You do not understand, *monsieur* — I am Tristan's woman!"

The man released her and backed away warily, his eyes filled with uncertainty. "Captain Tristan ain't on the island," he said nervously; then he looked her up and down and grinned.

"He — he is at the house. We came this morning," Bettina said hastily.

"I think perhaps you're lying to me, girl."

"Please, *monsieur!* I would not want to see you die because of me."

"Die? How so?"

"Tristan has sworn to kill any man who touches me."

"That don't sound like Captain Tristan. He don't give a damn about women, and that proves you're lying, girl. Even so, you might just be worth dying for."

He grabbed her again before she had a chance to run. Bettina struggled fiercely, pounding the man with her fists while he sought her lips. And then, suddenly, he was lifted away from her and thrown forcefully to the ground.

"You blasted whoreson! I'll —" the man shouted, but stopped short when he turned over and saw Tristan standing above him, dark with rage.

"He did no harm, Tristan," Bettina said quickly. "You cannot kill him for no reason!"

"He tried to rape you! You call that no reason?" Tristan bellowed.

"But he did not," she replied weakly.

"What have you to say, Brown?"

"She said you came in this morning, Captain, but I didn't believe her. None of your crew has been to the village. I thought she was lying when she said she was your woman. Honest, Captain Tristan, if I had known she was yours, I wouldn't have touched her."

"You haven't seen your captain, then?"

126

"No. I just came from the village now."

"Very well. Since you're Casey's first mate, I'll let it go at that. But I give you warning now, Brown. Don't ever come near this one again," Tristan said, nodding to Bettina. "Now go and find your captain. I believe he's taken the other path to the village."

"Thank you, Captain Tristan," Brown said. He left quickly, without another glance at Bettina.

"I would also like to thank you, Tristan, for coming in time," Bettina said quietly.

He walked to her slowly, forcing her back against the fence with his nearness. He took her in his arms, and his lips found hers in a hard, forceful kiss. Bettina melted in his arms for a moment, letting him have his way with her. But then she regained control and pushed him away.

"I did not escape one rape, Tristan, only to be in danger of another!" Bettina snapped, angry at herself for responding to him.

"You didn't escape rape, little one; you were rescued from it. I only thought you would wish to thank me properly."

"I have thanked you already."

"So you have. Now tell me, why did you defend Brown when he nearly raped you, when you would kill me for doing the same?" Tristan asked.

"Because he did not rape me. But *you* have — many times! You have tricked me, lied to me, and used me. I hate you, Tristan, with all my being, and I will yet have revenge!" she stormed, her eyes flashing dangerously.

"Must I again fear for my life, little one?" Tristan asked, smiling at her.

"You do not take me seriously, Tristan, but you will one day. As for my revenge, it will wait until I escape you."

He laughed derisively. "And how do you propose to take this revenge you speak of?"

"I will find a way."

"Such hate from my woman. And by your own words — you *are* my woman," he reminded her.

"I am not!"

127

"What? Do you deny it now? Do you admit it to everyone but me?"

"You know why I told him that! But it seems you are not as feared as you like to think, *Capitaine* Tristan, for the man still persisted," Bettina said. She turned and walked away from him toward the house.

"Maddy, will you stay with me tonight?" Bettina asked nervously. She was sitting in the middle of the big brass bed, with her hands clasped tightly in her lap. "If he forces me to sleep with him again, I swear I will run away."

Bettina had moved her things into the room at the end of the hall. They had cleaned this room in the afternoon, while the two Indian girls had cleaned the rest of the house. Bettina would have preferred to move to the opposite wing, but Jules had taken one room, and Captain O'Casey and Madeleine had the others. Tristan wanted privacy on his side of the house.

"I will stay with you if I can, Bettina, but I do not think the *capitaine* will allow it."

"You could say that I am sick," Bettina ventured. "That something I ate disagreed with me."

"I could say that, but Tristan would be suspicious. You do not look sick," said Madeleine.

"Then you must not let him in the room."

"Bettina, he is the *capitaine,* and although I don't fear him as much as before, you forget that he is the one who rules here. He holds our lives in his hands."

"How many times must I tell you — he will not kill us!" Bettina said with exasperation. "He has given his word to me that eventually he will take us to Saint Martin."

"Why do you still resist him, Bettina?" Madeleine asked, changing the subject. "He is a handsome young man. Even the Comte de Lambert is not so handsome and virile as this one. It would be much easier on you if you gave in. And it would be no disgrace, my pet, since he gives you no choice."

Bettina was astonished. "He uses my body, even though he knows I detest him! I would prefer any other man to him!"

"He rapes you because you resist him. He wants you, that

is all. I thought you would have accepted your situation by now," Madeleine said, ignoring Bettina's anger. "Tristan treats you better than a husband would — he gives you much. He even continues to shave his beard for you. Jules told me how furious Tristan was when he cut his beard."

Bettina smiled despite herself, for that was one battle she had won without even trying. She remembered the night after Tristan had shaved his beard, and the angry scowl on his face when he saw the bright red marks his stubble left on her face. The red marks disappeared after a short time, and they didn't hurt, but Tristan didn't know this. He stormed at her for making him shave his beard in the first place, mumbling that now he would have to continue to do so. It was either that or abstain from making love to her until his beard was soft again.

Now he shaved late in the day, whenever he was of a mind to take her, which gave Bettina warning well in advance. And Tristan had shaved before dinner this day.

"Please, Maddy, you have to stay with me tonight," Bettina pleaded, going back to the subject at hand.

"Even if Tristan allows it tonight, what of tomorrow?"

"I will think of something else tomorrow. It is this night that I fear," Bettina replied. "Go now, and tell Tristan that I am ill. Tell him I want you to stay with me. But go before he comes to find me."

"Very well," Madeleine sighed. "I will try. You had better get into bed while I am gone."

Madeleine closed the door and took a deep breath before she started down the dimly lit corridor. She just couldn't understand why Bettina hated Tristan so much. She seemed to find a distinct pleasure in hating him — she came to life whenever they argued, as if she thrived on their battles.

Madeleine would help Bettina if she could, but she doubted whether she would succeed. Bettina had become an obsession with the young captain, and the more she resisted him, the more he wanted her.

She descended the stairs and slowly approached the table where the men were drinking. A couple of Tristan's men were downing large tankards of rum, and the man Jake Brown, whom she had met earlier, was seated with Captain O'Casey.

"Where is Bettina?" Tristan asked when he saw Madeleine standing beside his chair.

"She is in bed — she does not feel well," Madeleine said, wiping her hands on her skirt.

"What's the matter with her?" Tristan inquired, raising an eyebrow.

"I think it is perhaps something she has eaten, *Capitaine*. But I insist you let me stay with her this night. She needs me."

"She does, eh? Well, that won't be necessary," Tristan replied. He left his chair and started for the stairs.

"But, *Capitaine* —"

"Sit down, *madame!*" Jules cut her off sharply. "Your lady is Tristan's responsibility. If she needs looking after he can do it. Although I don't think that's what she needs."

"You keep insinuating that Bettina needs a beating," Madeleine said angrily. "I suppose you would like to be the one to inflict it!"

"Now, now, settle down," Jules said, surprised at Madeleine's sudden outburst. "I wouldn't touch your lady. Tristan would have my head if I did. It is just that he is too soft with her. He's let her have her way too much, and now she thinks she can get away with anything."

"You forget that Tristan still has to rape her," Madeleine whispered so no one else would hear.

"Exactly. That's why I say she needs a good beating."

Tristan opened the door to his room, but when he found it empty, he guessed Bettina's game. He crossed to the room next to his and found it empty also; then he went to the last door and opened it slowly. She was curled up under the covers on the far side of the bed, with her head resting on one hand. But she sat up when she heard him, her hair falling gloriously about her shoulders.

"This is not your room, little one," he said quietly. He closed the door and leaned against it.

"Then I have no room," she returned icily. "Would you prefer me to sleep outside?"

130

"No, I prefer you to sleep with me," he replied with a slow curling of his lips.

"Well, *that*, Tristan, I will not do!" Bettina snapped, her green eyes dark with fury.

"Your servant tells me you don't feel well," said Tristan. "You seem rather spirited to be ill." His grin widened, and he crossed to the bed, sitting down on the edge. "*Are* you ill, Bettina?"

"Yes!" she hissed angrily. "But I will not discuss my complaint with you."

"I think perhaps you're lying to me. But on the slight chance that you're not, I will get you some sour milk. It should relieve your stomach of its contents in no time at all."

"Thank you, but no," she returned, her chin tilted defiantly. "I would prefer to sleep if you don't mind — undisturbed."

"But I insist that you have a cure, Bettina."

"You can save your insisting for your crew," she said, edging to the opposite side of the bed. "I told you before, Tristan, that I will not take orders from you. Now where is Maddy? I want her to stay with me tonight."

"She is downstairs, but she won't be staying with you this night. Or any other night, for that matter. It would be rather uncomfortable to fit the three of us in my bed," Tristan chuckled.

"I am staying here!"

"You should have learned by now that it is pointless to argue with me. Now, will you come peaceably, or do I carry you to my room?"

"You must know better than to ask that question. I will never go peaceably to your bed! Never!" she cried. She tried to scramble from the covers.

But Tristan reached out, grabbed a handful of her flowing white-blond hair, and pulled her back across the bed. With a quick sweep of his arms, he picked her up and carried her swiftly back to his room. He dropped her on his bed, then went back to close the door. When he turned around, he saw Bettina jump from the bed, looking frantically about the room for a place to hide.

For a moment, she seemed like a frightened little rabbit, and Tristan was tempted to forget his need for her this night. But the murderous glint in her eyes struck him like a slap in the face and renewed his determination to have her.

"There is no escape, Bettina," he said, and began to remove his clothing.

She ran to the window, then looked back at him, her face a mask of fury. "I will jump!"

"No, you won't. You have everything to live for, including taking your revenge against me." He sighed, shaking his head. "Why do you fight me so, Bettina?"

"Because of your deceit, your lies, and because you continue to rape me!"

"You have just lied to me about being ill, yet I don't seek revenge against you."

"No? Then why are you keeping me here, Tristan?" she asked.

"Certainly not for revenge," he replied. "If I were to offer you marriage — what, then?"

"I would not marry you for all the riches in the world!" she said heatedly, then added in a curiously level voice, "But you do not offer marriage, Tristan."

"No, I don't. But I don't beat you, Bettina, and I give you anything you need. I ask only that you let me make love to you. De Lambert would not treat you better than I." His voice held a surprising note of tenderness.

"Perhaps not. But at least *he* will not have to rape me," she taunted.

Tristan's eyes narrowed, and he scowled darkly. "He doesn't have you yet, Bettina."

Chapter 20

Pale moonlight touched the rug by the window and filled the room with a gray light when Tristan blew out the candles. It was a long time before he finally went to sleep. Bettina was grateful that he slept on his back, for the sound of his snoring covered up her movements about the room. She eased herself from the bed without disturbing him, and quickly donned her dark violet dress, keeping her eyes on Tristan all the while.

I told you I would run away if you raped me again, Bettina thought. But you did not believe me. No, you had to force your lust on me again. Well, you will awake in the morning and I will be gone. And you will never find me, Tristan.

Bettina closed the door without a sound and cautiously made her way downstairs. She had assumed she would have to step over the sleeping bodies of the crew in the big dining hall, but there was no one about. She supposed they were either in the village or sleeping on the ship.

Bettina set out across the lawn, with only single-minded determination and outrage spurring her on. She was surprised by the brightness of the moonlight. But sudden apprehension came over her when she saw the black mass of trees before her, knowing that was the direction she must take.

The moon was slightly behind her, making it easy for her to find the wide path leading into the forest, but once she was inside, only a few pale rays of moonlight lit the ground with speckled patches of gray. It was barely enough light for her to see the corral and the seven horses within.

Bettina had to stop and think. She had to have some kind of plan. She glanced back through the trees and could see the large house quite clearly. She could see no light from any of the

133

windows, and all was quiet.

Tristan was obviously still sleeping soundly, and he probably would until morning, but she needed a lot of time to put enough distance between them. He would take one of the horses to come after her, and would catch her quickly if she were on foot. So she must take one of the horses for herself.

Bettina braided her hair quickly in two long plaits and tied them into a knot at the back of her neck. Then she crossed to the corral fence and looked for a gate. The fence was made of long wooden planks nailed to wooden posts, and formed a large, clumsy circle, but she could see no gate. She tried lifting the top plank, but it wouldn't budge. Taking a deep breath, Bettina moved to the next pair of planks, and this time the top one moved. It was quite heavy, and she had to use both her arms to lift the board from its supporting brackets and lower it to the ground.

One of the horses neighed, and then another, and Bettina gasped. The sound seemed to her like a blast of trumpets in the still night. She glanced about nervously, trying to see into the black shadows of the forest; then she looked back toward the house but there was still no sign of life there. She was aware of other sounds now: leaves rustling, mosquitoes buzzing, crickets singing, and other sounds she couldn't identify.

Take courage, Bettina. Tristan will continue to sleep — he must, she thought. She stepped over the lower plank and into the corral.

The white stallion was a soft gray in the darkness, and Bettina edged very slowly toward him. He shied away from her, and all the horses moved dangerously close to the opening in the fence. She feared for a moment that they would all escape, but then they settled down again.

This was not going to be easy, Bettina thought, almost ready to give up. She had no saddle, no bridle, not even a rope. She would have to catch the horse by his mane, then pull herself up and hope she could stay on his back. Luckily, he wasn't such a big animal, but how was she going to catch him if he kept shying away from her?

She tried again, moving more slowly this time, beckoning

to him sweetly. She reached her hand out slowly and gently touched the stallion's neck, talking to him all the while. Then she moved closer and rubbed his velvety nose, letting him smell her.

Bettina continued to talk to him for a while as she stroked his neck, hoping that he would relax and not rear up when she tried to mount him. She coaxed him the few feet to the opening in the fence. The other horses shied away as she passed them, and she prayed her stallion wouldn't move away when she lowered the remaining plank to the ground. But he stayed behind her, and even remained perfectly still when she took hold of his mane. With a jump, she hoisted herself up, lifted one leg over his back, and sat up straight.

Bettina had already decided against closing the fence, hoping that the other horses would escape during the night. Then Tristan would have no horse to follow her with.

With a feeling of accomplishment, Bettina gathered her skirt up and tucked it under her legs, then urged the stallion forward. She nearly fell when he took his first step, and she grabbed his mane quickly, almost deciding again to escape on foot instead. But the horse continued to walk slowly down the path, and she saw that it was not too difficult to stay on his back.

Looking back, Bettina saw the rest of the horses leaving the corral and following behind her. She was sure now that her escape was possible, and thought where she should go next. The obvious place would be the opposite side of the island, but Tristan would also think of this. So that left her with two choices — either the left or the right side of the island.

But first she had to locate the village. There was no point in trying to find help there, and besides, the village would probably be the first place Tristan would look. But it could take a week or even longer before she could hail a passing ship, and she needed to be far away from anyone who might see her and inform Tristan of her whereabouts.

The path turned sharply to the left, but it was still wide enough to allow moonlight to break through openings in the trees. Bettina looked back. She could no longer see the house or the corral, only thick black darkness threatening her on all sides. The other horses no longer trailed after her, but had wandered off into the forest.

Bettina felt as if she were the only person on the entire island. She fought down panic, reminding herself why she was escaping. Then she realized that she was leaving Madeleine behind.

Bettina immediately tried to turn the horse around, but then changed her mind and let the stallion continue forward along the path. She couldn't take Madeleine with her. Her only possible chance for success was to remain perfectly alone in this venture. Madeleine wouldn't have the courage to escape. She was terrified of horses, for one thing. She would try to dissuade Bettina from leaving and might even tell Tristan of her plans.

Bettina decided to get safely away and tell her tale to the Comte de Lambert. Then he would come and rescue Madeleine, and Bettina would have her revenge at the same time. Madeleine would be safe on this island for a while. Despite Tristan's anger, he wouldn't punish Madeleine.

The fifteen or twenty minutes that the horse plodded along the path seemed like hours. Bettina strained her eyes to see what lay ahead, but the forest was too dense. Then the path turned slightly to the right. There was a large clearing, bathed in silver moonlight, and Bettina could see a dozen thatched huts crowded closely together.

She quickly turned the horse around and urged him into a slow canter, straight into the dark gloom of the forest.

Bettina had her direction now: the right side of the island. There was no longer a path to follow, and the trees were so dense in this part of the forest that the stallion was forced to walk. Bettina hoped the horse had better eyes than she did, for she could barely see two feet in front of her.

The horse walked around trees and thick shrubs, never keeping to a straight line, but Bettina kept him headed slightly to the left. This would take her to the right side of the island, but farther away from Tristan.

An hour passed and then several more. Bettina had no idea how much time she had before dawn, but she knew she had to gain more distance than this before Tristan awoke. She hoped he would sleep late. No one would disturb him, and anyone who was up and about would assume that she was in Tristan's room.

Two more hours passed, and Bettina came upon a thick stand of banana trees that were too dense for her to pass through. The moon was on the other side of the island now, but Bettina could see the sky here, and it was definitely becoming lighter. She urged the stallion into a canter to circle around the banana trees. But then she had to slow down again when she entered forest land again.

She hoped that Tristan wouldn't be able to travel any faster than she. He might travel along the shoreline, but there he would have no idea where to stop and search for her. When she reached the shore, she would hide in the forest and wait for a passing ship. Tristan would never find her, no matter how long he searched.

She could distinguish color now. Dark reds and yellows — flowers that she could smell before but couldn't see. Bettina looked up and saw patches of soft blue sky, tinted with pink and orange now. Birds began to awaken, and soon the forest was alive with their sweet songs. It was going to be a beautiful day.

Then, unexpectedly, a small brown animal ran in front of the stallion. He reared up, sending Bettina tumbling to the ground and knocking the wind out of her. When she finally sat up, the horse was gone.

Bettina felt close to tears. She stood up and brushed the leaves and twigs from her dress. She was at a loss for direction until she sighted the horned mountain through an opening in the trees. She continued toward the beach, and soon found that she could make better time on foot, now that she could see where she was going.

After an hour of half-running, half-walking, Bettina could hear surf in the near distance. She ran as fast as she could, dodging trees and low bushes. And then the sun blinded her as she broke out of the forest. She fell to her knees in the cold sand.

Bettina lowered her head and after a few moments was able to still her heavy breathing. When she looked up again, she couldn't believe what she saw. To the left of the rising sun was a ship, only a mile or so offshore.

Without a second thought, Bettina jumped to her feet and started waving her arms frantically. She called out, but then thought better of this, for they couldn't hear her, anyway. The ship moved across the sun and then sailed toward another point on the island.

Bettina continued to wave, beginning to fear that no one on the ship would see her. Then the vessel turned about and started coming toward her. Bettina sank down in the sand and started crying.

She watched impatiently as a small boat was lowered. Scanning the glittering white beach, Bettina feared that Tristan might appear before the boat had been rowed ashore. But after fifteen agonizingly slow minutes, Bettina was safely in the care of Captain William Rawlinsen and on her way to his ship.

Chapter 21

"I'd take you ashore myself, Mademoiselle Verlaine, but picking you up and dropping you here has put me slightly off my schedule," Captain Rawlinsen said. "And it's good business to keep on schedule."

"It is not necessary, *Capitaine.* You have been more than kind already. I am sure I will have no trouble finding the Comte de Lambert's plantation."

"No, I don't doubt you will. His is one of the biggest plantations on the island, or so I've been told."

They stood on the deck as the small boat was lowered that would take Bettina ashore. She had grown fond of Captain Rawlinsen in the two weeks it had taken to reach Saint Martin. He was an amiable man in his early fifties, a merchant captain who transported rum and tobacco to the American colonies and brought back necessary items unobtainable in the islands.

Bettina had lied to him about how she had come to be on Tristan's island. She had said she had fallen overboard from the ship taking her to Saint Martin and had swum ashore. He had marveled that she made it to the shore alive, since there were many sharks and barracudas in those waters.

Bettina had asked Captain Rawlinsen to draw her a small map showing how to get back to the island. She had explained that it was a beautiful place and she might one day wish to show it to the Comte de Lambert. She had the small map tucked safely in the hem of her dress, which she held in her arms along with her shift and shoes.

"I still do not see why you insist upon my wearing these clothes," Bettina said, pointing to the knee-length breeches and the baggy white shirt the captain had given her that morning.

139

Captain Rawlinsen smiled. "Billy's clothes fit you nicely, child."

"Nicely? They are huge."

"That was the idea. They're loose enough to hide your beauty. Dressed like this, you shouldn't have any trouble with the sailors who roam the docks." He paused, looking at her quizzically. "How on earth did you manage to hide all your lovely hair under that red scarf?"

"I was not able to." Bettina laughed. "I have it loose beneath this shirt and — ah — tucked into these breeches." She had hoped she would never have to wear a man's clothes again.

The captain laughed now. "Well, at least it's not visible."

"But it is quite uncomfortable."

"It shouldn't take you long to find your betrothed, and then you can change back to your dress. Well, the boat's down. Rask will take you ashore. And — uh — don't forget to slump over when you walk. No use showing what we've tried to hide."

Bettina smiled and kissed the captain on the cheek, causing him to blush considerably. He helped her over the side and stood by the rail, watching the small boat row ashore.

Bettina walked slowly down the crowded dock, amazed at the bustle and activity. Many ships were being unloaded. Wagons pulled by stout horses moved back and forth. Four small children were chasing a scrawny cat around a rubbish pile. This dock was much more crowded than Tortola's.

Bettina tried stopping a sailor, but he didn't even glance in her direction. She tried again and failed. No one would pay her any attention at all.

Stopping to consider what to do next, Bettina scanned the docks. She noticed two men who were closely observing three youths begging in front of a store, accosting the customers as they came and went. She walked over to the two men, for at least they weren't in any hurry to go somewhere.

"Excuse me," she ventured.

They both turned around to look at her. The taller of the two men was Bettina's height, and he had light-brown eyes that lit up when he saw her. The other man was a few inches shorter, with beady little eyes and a hooked nose that was out of proportion to his face.

"If you ain't just what me captain ordered," the taller man said enthusiastically.

"That he is, Shawn," the other said, eyeing Bettina from head to foot.

Bettina started to back away. She looked from one man to the other.

"Wait up, me lad," the man called Shawn said quickly. "I be offerin' you the job of cabin boy to me captain."

"You don't understand," Bettina started, but the man grabbed her arm.

"Now, don't be tellin' me you wouldn't like to sail the seas. 'Tis a fine life, it be."

"No," Bettina said flatly. She tried to pull her arm away, but the man's grip was like iron.

"Where's your sense of adventure, lad? You're perfect for the task. We've seen nothin' but scrawny youths so far, who'd not last a single voyage. What say you?"

"No!" she replied again with growing alarm. "Now release me!"

But he turned her around, pulling her arm behind her back painfully. She couldn't believe that this was happening with people all around her.

" 'Tis too bad you've decided to be reluctant, lad, but it makes no difference."

"You don't —"

"Say another word and I'll run me blade through your back," he growled and bent her arm back farther. She thought she would faint with the pain. "Captain Mike sent us to find a likely lad, and you're the only one we've seen. You'll get used to the task soon enough, for Captain Mike ain't hard to please. You'll even thank me one day, for the sea's a good life."

They started forward then, with one man on each side of her, holding onto her arms. Bettina could feel the point of a knife pressed into the small of her back.

They took her to a ship that was loading cargo and preparing to set sail. The crew was too busy to notice her as the two men brought her aboard, and fear began to take root in her. What if she couldn't get out of this?

She was taken to the captain's cabin. The man called Shawn shoved her inside but halted before he closed the door. His face was dark as he sheathed his dagger.

"Old Mike wouldn't like to hear you're reluctant. I give you warnin'," he said in a dangerously even voice. "If you tell him you don't want to sail, I'll cut your throat. I hope you understand me, lad, for I'll be watchin' you."

When the door closed and she was left alone, she ran for the door. She opened it, but Shawn and his short friend were standing just outside the cabin, so she closed the door quickly. This was ridiculous. She had been kidnapped again, but this time because they thought she was a young boy. Why did she end up in even worse trouble every time she escaped Tristan?

Bettina started to pace the floor. She wished this Captain Mike would hurry up. Her only hope was to explain everything and hope that he would let her go. But what if the ship sailed before he returned to his cabin?

The minutes passed and dragged into hours. Bettina tried the door again, but Shawn was still outside, watching as he said he would. Would he really kill her if she told the captain he'd brought her here by force? But she couldn't very well become a cabin boy. The captain would soon discover she was a woman.

Why was she drawn to misfortune like a moth to fire? First Tristan, then jail, then Tristan again, and now this. And her betrothed was right here on this very island, but she couldn't even seek his help. What if this captain were another man like Tristan?

The door opened suddenly, and a tall man with flaming red hair came into the cabin. He eyed her speculatively as he crossed the room and sank into a chair behind a littered desk. He was a handsome man of middle age, but seemed bone-weary.

"So you're me new cabin boy," he sighed. Even his voice sounded tired.

"No, *monsieur*," Bettina answered weakly, not knowing whether to be afraid of him or not.

"Then what're you doing here?"

"Two of your men brought me here."

142

"What for?" he asked, his green eyes staring at her intently.

"They brought me here to be your cabin boy, but —"

"But you've changed your mind," he answered for her. "Can I persuade you to reconsider? Me last boy was washed overboard in a storm, but he was a sickly youth. Now you — you look to be a sturdy lad, and there's not time to find another boy as able as you, since we sail tonight. What say you?"

"It is impossible, *Capitaine*."

"If you're worried because you're French, there be no need," he said with a touch of impatience in his voice. "I have other Frenchies on me ship, so you'll not be alone. And you speak English well enough. There'll be a share in the profits for you, and a chance for advancement."

"If I were a boy, *Capitaine,* then I would probably be tempted by your offer."

"If you were a boy? What nonsense be this, lad?"

"I'm not a lad," Bettina replied quickly. "When your men brought me here, they did not give me a chance to explain, *Capitaine*. I am a girl."

"A girl?" he asked disbelievingly.

Bettina became irritated by his doubt, and slowly removed the red scarf, then pulled her hair out from beneath her shirt. "Yes — a girl."

Captain Mike's sudden laughter startled Bettina, and she stared at him in confusion. "I thought your face a bit too pretty for a lad, but I've seen others with such faces, so I let it pass. You should dress in the clothes of your sex, lass, to avoid confusion." Green lights seemed to dance in his eyes as he spoke.

"I am not in the habit of wearing men's clothes, *Capitaine*. I was advised to dress this way so I would not attract attention."

"But attract attention you did. So me men have resorted to impressing young lasses! I am sorry for your inconvenience, lass."

"Then I can go?"

"Yes, and go quickly, before I forget how tired I am. But hide your lovely hair again, me dear. You had best leave the same as you came."

Bettina did as he asked, relief flooding her as she tied the

143

scarf behind her head. The captain stood up and walked her to the door; then he lifted her hand and kissed it very tenderly.

"It has been a pleasure I will long remember, lass. Godspeed."

When Bettina stepped back into the blinding light, she suddenly remembered the man Shawn and the warning he had given her. She looked about the deck quickly and saw him standing only a few feet from her. Her green eyes widened at his angry glare, and she glanced back at the captain's cabin, but he had already closed the door.

"So you told him, did you!" Shawn growled.

He drew his dagger and held it rigidly in his right hand as he started to approach her. "I warned you, lad, that I did."

Bettina gasped, and her face turned a snowy white. The men on deck stopped what they were doing, thinking to witness a bloody fight, but Bettina didn't notice this. No words would come from her mouth, not even a scream, as she stood paralyzed. The man Shawn seemed to be moving in slow motion.

Run, Bettina screamed in her mind. Run, for God's sake, run! And then her legs finally moved and continued to move in a blind panic, as if they were no longer a part of her body. She ran down the gangplank and halfway down the dock, but she could hear the man right behind her.

She stumbled then and fell flat on her face, but the man had been so close to her that he tumbled over her and went sprawling yards away. Bettina jumped to her feet with lightning speed and ran toward the town, bumping into people in her flight. She couldn't even stop to seek help, for she was sure the man would knife her before she could utter a word. She had to outrun him. She had to find a place to hide.

She ran down streets, going deeper into town, but the farther she ran, the more deserted the streets became, and she could still hear the man panting and grunting behind her. Why didn't he give up?

Then Bettina ran straight into the arms of another man.

"Release me!" she screamed and struggled frantically, but this new man held her firmly against him.

"You," the man who held her whispered with amazement. Bettina looked up at him, and her eyes widened in recog-

144

nition. This was the French sailor who had been whipped because of her on the *Windsong*. Before she could speak, he had shoved her behind him and pulled a glittering knife. Shawn had reached them, and in his anger he immediately slashed at the Frenchman with his dagger.

Bettina knew she should make her escape, but she stood frozen against the front of a building, hypnotized by the flashing blades in the sunlight. The sailor who had suffered so cruelly because of her was now protecting her, and she couldn't bring herself to leave him.

The Frenchman was taller than Shawn, stockier in build, and Shawn was exhausted from the chase. But the smaller man had anger on his side, and he was determined to win. Blood appeared on both men, then more of it as the blades struck flesh and did their damage. And then the Frenchman's blade sank into Shawn's shoulder, rendering his right arm useless. A closed fist to Shawn's jaw sent him crashing against the building, where he fell in a heap to the ground.

"Come." The Frenchman took Bettina's hand and pulled her behind him down the street until he came to an old building. He took her inside, and, without encountering anyone, he marched her up a flight of stairs to a room on the second floor.

Bettina couldn't believe that she was safe. She had come so close to dying, so very close, and she began to tremble as relief flooded her. She collapsed into the only chair in the room.

When her breathing returned to normal and her heart slowed to a regular beat, Bettina took note of her surroundings. The room was very small and dark, and besides the wooden chair she was sitting in, there was only a washstand and a single bed with rumpled covers. The window looked out over a narrow alley, but the next building blocked all sunlight.

The French sailor lit a candle on the washstand. There were many small cuts on his arms and chest, and blood was dripping to the floor from his right hand, where one finger was nearly severed. Bettina was appalled and quickly stood up to offer help. The bundle in her lap fell to the floor, and she was amazed to find that she still had her clothes with her. She picked up the bundle and set it on the chair, then approached the Frenchman.

"Your hand, *monsieur,* needs bandaging."

He focused his dark-brown eyes on her, and she was taken aback by the hatred she saw in them.

"Because of you my back is forever scarred. What matters a finger also? It will be adequately paid for," he said in a brittle voice. "I am Antoine Gautier, *mademoiselle,* in case you would like to know the name of the man who is going to kill you."

Bettina felt stark terror when she grasped the meaning of his words. She ran for the door, but the man made no move to stop her. The door was locked. She turned back around to face him, her eyes wide.

"Unlock this door!" she screamed in panic.

He laughed at her, a contemptuous, cruel laugh. "Now you know how I felt when they tied me to the mast. Not a pleasant feeling, is it, *mademoiselle?*"

"Why are you doing this? Why?"

"That is a foolish question to ask, my fine lady, but I will gladly answer it. You see, I have dreamed of killing you. I have prayed to have you delivered into my hands, and now you will suffer tenfold what I did. I will not kill you immediately, Mademoiselle Verlaine, for that would be too merciful, and I feel no mercy. You will beg me to end your life before I am through, but your death will come by slow degrees by starvation and torture. But first I will have what I was whipped for desiring, many times."

Bettina's mind refused to accept his words. This was a nightmare.

"What were you whipped for, Monsieur Gautier?"

He looked at her in surprise. "You are a calm one, but not for long. I was whipped for my intentions, for something I never got to do. But I will have payment now, and then some."

"But why must you kill me also?"

"Because you could have stopped them from whipping me, but you did not!" he growled at her.

"But I did try to stop them. I pleaded with the *capitaine!*"

"Lies come easily when your life is threatened. Do not mistake me for a fool, *mademoiselle!*" he snarled, and started to unfasten his thin belt.

146

Bettina watched him with disbelieving eyes, and something snapped in her.

"Go ahead — rape me!" she screamed, her eyes wild and glazed. "Kill me! I should have died in the street by Shawn's blade, anyway! I don't care anymore. Do you hear? I don't care!"

Bettina started to laugh, an hysterical, unearthly, shrill sound that resounded in the small room. Antoine Gautier backed away from her warily.

"You are a crazy woman!" he said in a ragged voice as he edged toward the door. "You have suffered nothing yet, but already your mind snaps. There can be no pleasure in starting now. I will wait until you have regained your senses, so you will be aware of everything I intend to do. I will be back!" he hissed through clenched teeth. He left the room and locked the door behind him.

Bettina fell to her knees on the floor. Violent sobs racked her body. It was a long while before she quieted to soft whimpering. She was a child again, and imagined she was in a large room at the convent, filled with many beds. She lay on one of those beds in the dark, crying silently for loneliness because her mother had been powerless to prevent her being sent to the convent. A sister came and talked quietly to her, words that were gentle and understanding. And they finally lulled her to sleep.

Chapter 22

Thousands of stars were like flickering candles against a velvet curtain of black. Somewhere on Saint Martin, the sailor Antoine Gautier was drinking himself into forgetfulness, but in his lodgings in the trashiest part of town, Bettina slept on, undisturbed by the bugs and mice in the room.

It was well after sunrise when Bettina's eyes opened. She stared in confusion at her strange surroundings. Was this a room in that old fortress that Tristan had taken her to? But she had escaped that beautiful island, hadn't she? Yes, she had escaped and been brought to Saint Martin. She had gone in search of her betrothed, but then . . . then. . . .

"No!" she gasped as she remembered everything. "My God, no!"

Why did she have to remember? It would have been kinder if she had lost her mind completely, rather than sit here and count the minutes until Antoine Gautier returned. What kind of horrible tortures did he have planned for her? She was already weak from hunger, and she would get weaker. Was he going to leave her here to starve? No, he would want a more complete revenge than that. He would be back.

"Oh, Tristan, why can't you rescue me this time? But I fear I was too clever for you. You are hundreds of miles away, searching for me on the island, if you haven't given up by now."

What was she thinking? She didn't want *him* to rescue her! Bettina looked about the room and felt the tears well in her eyes. Anything would be preferable to what Antoine Gautier planned for her, even life with Tristan. But Tristan wasn't here to help her, and that left only one alternative, a quick death.

With her mind set on her only solution, Bettina got up and

slowly walked to the open window. There was no balcony outside, not even a ledge that might lead to another window.

Below her to the right was a small awning over a back door, but directly below the window was a pile of firewood. The pile was large, with cut branches sticking up in all directions like pointed spears. There was certain death waiting for her in that pile of branches, a quick death.

Bettina lifted her legs out of the window and sat there for a moment, savoring her last minutes of life. She smiled ironically, thinking that she had run away from the handsomest man she had ever met. She had left him for this.

"Oh, Bettina, you have been such a fool," she said aloud with a heartfelt sigh.

She released her hold on the sides of the window and took a deep breath. All she had to do was lean forward and that would be the end. But a part of her still clung to life, even though that life meant prolonged torture, and she climbed back into the room.

You have to jump, Bettina. I can't. You could scream for help. No, that would bring Antoine Gautier, and I would still have to jump. Then jump away from that pile of branches.

She looked out the window again, but the pile was just too large to avoid.

"The awning!"

Bettina threw her bundle of clothes out the window; then she climbed out herself until she hung precariously by her hands from the windowsill. She tried to reach the awning with her foot but struck only air. She saw her mistake now. She should have stooped on the windowsill and jumped toward the awning. But it was too late, for she was too weak to pull herself back up.

One hand slipped, and her body twisted away from the building. She groped frantically with her free arm, and she caught the sill just as her other hand slipped. Her body twisted the other way, giving her a clear view of the awning. It looked impossible to reach from her position, for it was at least six feet below her and two feet away. But she had to reach it. It was her only chance to live.

It was more difficult this time to turn her body back so she

149

could reach the sill, but she finally made it. She knew she had only a few more seconds before both of her hands gave way, but she remained calm. Using her feet to hold herself away from the rough wall of the building, she swung herself back and forth.

She was still reluctant to let go, but consoled herself with the thought that she would have died, anyway. She swung away once more, then back toward her target. She let go. She landed on her knees in the middle of the old canvas awning and quickly grabbed the sides, but her weight toppled the rotted supports and she slammed full force into the closed door, then slid the few feet to the ground.

Bettina gasped for air, then didn't know whether to laugh or cry. She wondered now why she had been so reluctant to attempt escape. Then she glanced up at the window so very high above her and trembled at her own daring. But, thank God, she was free and alive. Now she prayed she could find the Comte de Lambert without running into any more evil men.

Bettina pushed herself up, picked up her bundle, then ran to the end of the alley. She cautiously looked around the side of the building. Antoine Gautier was weaving drunkenly down the street toward her. Bettina ducked her head back and pressed against the building. She held her breath as she waited for Gautier to pass the alley. He staggered past and then tripped and fell only a few feet from her. Bettina thought she would faint while she waited in suspense for him to get up.

He rose slowly to his feet and continued toward the entrance of his building without even glancing in her direction. Bettina gave him a few minutes to enter the old inn, which also gave her heart time to slow its beat. Then she dashed out of the alley and ran down the street in the direction from which Gautier had come. She stopped the first person she came to, a young boy, and asked directions to the Lambert plantation. He told her it was on the outskirts of town, but he informed her proudly that he had seen the *comte* on the docks that very morning.

Bettina continued toward the docks, wishing she were leaving town instead. When she reached the dock, she went up to an old man leaning against an empty crate, whittling on a short stick.

"Excuse me," Bettina ventured. "Do you know where I can find the Comte de Lambert?"

"What do you want with him, boy?"

"It is a matter of importance," Bettina replied. She vowed she would never wear a man's clothing again.

"Over there." He pointed to a large ship. "De Lambert is the one giving orders."

Bettina hurried on, relieved to find the *comte* so quickly. She saw that the ship the man pointed to was not unloading crates as the others were, but human cargo, black men with their hands and feet shackled with irons. When she came closer, a fetid odor assailed her nostrils, almost making her sick.

She saw the man giving orders, a man of medium height, with wavy black hair, but he was standing with his back to her. Bettina called his name. He glanced at her with obvious irritation, and she noticed the golden-brown eyes and strong, handsome face, but then he turned back to what he was doing.

Well, what did she expect, dressed as she was? Everyone mistook her for a boy. She walked slowly up to him.

"Are you Comte Pierre de Lambert?" she asked, forcing him to turn around again.

"Away with you, boy! I have no coins to spare."

"Are you —"

"Away with you, I said!" He cut her off sharply.

"I am Bettina Verlaine!" she shouted back at him, losing her temper.

He laughed at her and turned away again. She yanked the scarf from her head, then pulled her hair out from beneath her shirt and let it tumble down her back.

"Monsieur," she called sweetly. When he turned once again, Bettina threw the scarf in his face and stalked away from him.

"Bettina!" he called, running after her, but she didn't stop. When he caught up with her, he swung her around to face him, amazement on his face. "You must forgive me, Bettina. I thought you were dead. Marivaux returned with my ship and told me what happened. I thought you were a young boy just now, come to taunt me. The whole town knows that I was waiting for you to come, and they know what happened."

Her anger left as fast as it had come, and she smiled warmly at the young man who stood before her.

"I am sorry I threw the scarf at you."

"But I was a cad to bark at you the way I did. We will say no more about it. Come," he said, leading her to a carriage a few feet away. "I will take you home now. We will talk later, and then I have a surprise for you."

"A surprise?"

"Yes, I think you will be most pleased," he replied with a lazy smile. "But tell me one thing now — how did you manage to come here?"

"On a merchant ship."

"But it was not a merchant ship that attacked the *Windsong*."

"No, it was not," Bettina said. "There is much that I have to tell you, but as you said, we can talk later. Right now I need a bath and a change of clothes."

"Of course, *ma chérie*. It will not take long to reach the house."

"Ah, Madame Verlaine. I am glad to see that you are feeling better today," Pierre de Lambert said as Jossel Verlaine walked into his study unannounced. "It was a shock to you not to find your daughter here on your arrival yesterday."

"I am not feeling better, *monsieur*. But I refuse to believe that my daughter is dead. You must search for her!"

"Please sit down, *madame*," Pierre said, motioning to a chair beside his desk. "I have found your daughter — or, rather, she found me. Bettina has been shown to the room next to yours. She is presently bathing."

"But why didn't you tell me this immediately!" Jossel exclaimed and started to rush from the room.

"Madame Verlaine!" Pierre called sharply, halting her before she reached the door. "I must insist that you wait before seeing Bettina."

"But why? Is something the matter with her?"

"No — she seems to be fine. But I have yet to find out what happened to her after she was taken from the *Windsong*. I must

152

ask that you let me speak to her first."

"But I am her mother!"

"And I am her betrothed. There are certain things that I must know before —"

"What are you implying, *monsieur?*" Jossel interrupted him. "It is enough that Bettina is here and alive."

"If Bettina is to become my wife —"

"*If!*" Jossel nearly shouted. "Let me inform you, Comte de Lambert, that I was against this betrothal from the very beginning. I always wanted Bettina to choose her own husband. I still do. Now that André is dead, Bettina does not have to honor the agreement you made with my husband. I came here to tell her this."

"Please, Madame Verlaine, you misunderstood me," Pierre said, flustered.

"I believe I understood you perfectly, *monsieur.* If Bettina is no longer innocent, it is no fault of hers. And if you do not wish to marry her, I will take Bettina and we will leave your house immediately!"

Pierre was annoyed but managed to hide it. He should not have told the woman that her daughter was here, for then he could have sent her away and kept Bettina as his mistress without her mother's knowledge. The whole town knew what had happened to Bettina Verlaine, so he could not possibly marry her now. But he could not let her go, either — she was much too beautiful to lose.

"Madame Verlaine, I am sorry if I have misled you. I have every intention of marrying Bettina. But since I will be her husband, I thought she might like to tell me her story first. After all, she did come to me. Afterward, she can rejoice in seeing you, and forget about her terrible ordeal."

Jossel calmed down and considered what he had said. "Very well, *monsieur.* I will wait in my room."

"You will not go in to see Bettina?"

"I will wait until you have spoken with her. But I wish to be called immediately when you are finished."

"I will inform you myself."

Pierre watched her leave the room and gritted his teeth, an

153

angry scowl on his face. He would like to shoot Captain Marivaux for letting pirates capture Bettina. Even if she was still a virgin, no one would believe it. Now he must stall for time and think of some way to get rid of the mother. He felt sure he could handle Bettina if she were left in his care.

Chapter 23

"Bettina, you are even more beautiful than I remembered," Pierre said when he came into the drawing room and closed the doors.

"You are very kind, *monsieur*," she replied demurely. She felt a bit self-conscious.

"You must call me Pierre, little one, since we —"

"Don't call me that!" Bettina interrupted harshly. "Tristan called me his little one, and I never want to hear it again."

"I am sorry, Bettina."

"Forgive me," Bettina said quickly, feeling like a fool. "I did not mean to snap at you. It is just that the memory of that man is still vivid in my mind."

"Who is this man you speak of?"

"Tristan is *capitaine* of the *Spirited Lady*, the ship that did battle with the *Windsong*."

"He is a pirate, of course?" Pierre asked, his yellow-brown eyes studying Bettina's face.

"He claims to be a privateer under the protection of England."

"Pirate or privateer — it is the same thing more or less. Did he — ah —"

"Rape me? Yes — many times," Bettina said without blushing. "He lied to me and tricked me as well. He told me he was bringing me here for ransom. But instead he took me and my servant to an island he claims as his own. He would have kept me there for months if I had not escaped."

"This island, does it have a name?"

"I don't know. From a ship it looks deserted. There are natives who live inland, and there is a large house away from the shore that the Spaniards built long ago."

155

"And how did you manage to escape this Tristan?" Pierre inquired.

"I left the house while he slept, and was able to hail a passing ship at dawn. But we must go back to rescue my old nurse!"

"Your servant is still on this island?"

"Yes."

"But she is probably dead by now, Bettina."

"She is not! I only left her there because I thought you would rescue her. And I want revenge against Tristan. He must die."

Pierre looked at her with startled eyes. "Bettina, this is absurd. The pirates that plunder these waters are ruthless. They would as soon cut a man's throat as look at him. You do not know what you are asking."

"I am asking for revenge and to have my servant rescued. If you cannot do this for me, I will find someone who will," Bettina said, trying to control her anger.

"Very well," Pierre said, shaking his head. "But I have no ships here at the moment. It will take some time."

"Wasn't that your ship you were unloading today?" Bettina asked.

"No. It belongs to a friend of mine. You will meet him tonight at dinner. I was merely seeing to the cargo of slaves that I purchased, but that does not concern you." He paused, looking at her thoughtfully. "Will you be able to find this island again?"

"I have a map." Bettina handed him the folded piece of cloth that Captain Rawlinsen had given her.

"Well, at least with this you will not have to go along," said Pierre, putting the map in his pocket.

"But I wish to go with you," Bettina said heatedly. "I must see for myself that Tristan dies."

"We shall see. But now, if you will wait here, you may have the surprise I mentioned earlier." He left the room, hoping that her mother could dissuade Bettina. To even think of attacking a pirate stronghold was ridiculous.

"Mama!"

Bettina could not believe her eyes when she saw her mother appear in the doorway. She ran to Jossel and clung to her, fearing

156

that she was just an illusion.

"It is all right now, my love. I am here." Jossel spoke softly, stroking Bettina's hair.

Hearing her mother's tender words, Bettina's composure dissolved and she burst into tears. She felt like a small child asking her mother for love and protection. The tears turned into heart-rending sobs that Bettina couldn't stop if she tried. Her mother was here, and everything would be all right now. Bettina was no longer alone.

It was a long time before the tears dwindled and Bettina's breathing returned to normal. They sat on the sofa, but Jossel still held Bettina wrapped in her arms.

"You do not have to speak of it if it is too painful, Bettina."

"No, I want to tell you, Mama. I must know if I am wrong in the way I feel. I am filled with such hatred that sometimes I think that I have changed into another person."

Bettina told her mother everything that had happened, from the moment when the *Windsong* first sighted the *Spirited Lady*, to her escape from the island and her talk with Pierre. She omitted nothing of her time with Tristan, even admitting that her body had betrayed her many times into enjoying his love-making.

"Maddy could not understand why I hated Tristan so much. And Pierre thinks it is foolish that I want revenge. He is my betrothed — he should also want revenge. But I could tell that Pierre would rather forget about the whole thing." Bettina paused, looking at her mother with pleading eyes. "Am I wrong to hate Tristan so? Is it wicked of me to want to see him dead?"

"This man raped you continually, and you have every right to hate him. But you are alive, Bettina. He could have raped you once and then killed you, but he did not. It is wrong to wish someone dead. With the life he leads, this Tristan will die soon enough. Do not let his death be of your doing. To seek revenge is to destroy yourself."

"But to see him dead is all I have thought about."

"This is not good, my love. You must forget this man. You must put your hatred and your memory of him aside. What has been done cannot be changed. It is a fate that befalls many women, but they survive and so will you," Jossel said, pushing the hair back from Bettina's face. "You are lucky, *ma chérie,* for you can choose what to do with your life. You can marry the *comte* if you wish, or, once dear Maddy is rescued, we can all go back to France."

"But I thought it was all arranged — that I had to marry the Comte de Lambert."

"Not anymore, Bettina. André made that agreement, but — but André is dead."

"Dead!"

"Yes, he died the day we returned from Saint-Malo. It was an unfortunate accident. He fell from his horse and hit his head."

Bettina shivered, remembering her own fall from the white stallion. Although he was not her real father, he was the only one she had ever known, and she felt sorrow.

"I am sorry to give you this news after what you have been through," Jossel said.

"It is all right, Mama. It must have been hard on you, being all alone."

"I must be honest with you, Bettina, I told you before that I never loved André. Living with him all these years has not been pleasant. And any fondness I had for André was destroyed many years ago when he began to pressure me for a son. I was shocked by his death, but I did not mourn him. I felt only a sense of freedom."

"It must have been awful, living all those years with a man you did not love."

"I had you to live for. You gave me happiness," Jossel returned.

"But you are still young, Mama. You can still find love."

"I doubt that, *ma chérie.*" Jossel smiled. "But I am a wealthy widow now, extremely wealthy. I never dreamed that André was so rich. I can afford to give you anything you want now, to make up for all those years you were kept from me. But this means that you do not have to marry the Comte de Lambert if you do not wish to. We can stay here for a while, and if you find that you love him, then you have my blessing. If not, then we will leave."

"I have grown so accustomed to thinking of Pierre de Lam-

158

bert as my future husband, it is hard to think otherwise," Bettina said with a half-smile.

"Well, at least André chose a young man for you. And he is handsome."

"Just being young and handsome does not make him a good man," Bettina said, remembering Tristan's startling good looks. "But as you said, we can stay here for a while. I will need time to know Pierre better."

They continued talking until the Comte de Lambert came in to escort them to dinner. The dining room was rather cramped with a huge polished mahogany table, which was presently set for four. A tall man who appeared to be in his late forties, with curly black hair and dark-gray eyes, was seated at one end of the table. He rose courteously when they entered the room.

"This is my other guest, the owner of the ship we spoke of, Bettina," Pierre said. "He has been staying with me for some time now, awaiting the return of his ship."

The man took Bettina's hand and bowed before her. "Don Miguel de Bastida, *mademoiselle*. It is an honor —"

"Bastida!" Bettina gasped. "You — you are the one Tristan searches for."

The man turned pale. "Do you know this man Tristan?"

"Yes, unfortunately I do. Can you tell me, *monsieur*, just out of curiosity, why does Tristan want to kill you?" Bettina asked.

"I would have asked you the same question, *mademoiselle*. I have been informed by different people for many years now that a young man called Tristan searches for me, yet no one can tell me why. You say he wants to kill me?"

"That is what I gathered from a conversation I overheard. Tristan mentioned that he had been looking for you for twelve years and that he feared you might die before he could find you. He — ah — called you a murderer."

"A murderer!" Don Miguel laughed. "The man must surely have me mistaken for someone else. But I would like to meet this Tristan. Do you know where he is now, *mademoiselle?*"

"I gave the Comte de Lambert a map that shows Tristan's island hideaway."

"Don Miguel, this is hardly an appropriate conversation to

159

have over dinner," the Comte de Lambert said quickly.

"I am sorry, Pierre. You are right, of course. You must forgive me, ladies, for it is not often that I dine with such charming company. I forgot my manners."

"That is quite all right, Monsieur Bastida," Jossel replied, glad that the *comte* had interrupted the conversation, though Bettina did not seem to be upset.

"You are Spanish, Monsieur Bastida. How is it that you speak French so fluently?" Bettina inquired.

"I have been to France many times in my travels. Also I have dealings with many of the French settlements here in the New World. It was necessary to learn your language."

"I must compliment you, *monsieur*. You have learned it well."

The conversation continued with small talk throughout dinner and afterward, when they retired to the drawing room. Don Miguel de Bastida was a charming man, and he seemed quite taken with Jossel. Bettina noticed how different her mother looked from the last time she had seen her in France. Then Jossel had been under the strain of her daughter's leaving home. But now she looked much younger and very beautiful with her silky white-blond hair braided about her head, wearing a green velvet dress that set off her dark-green eyes.

The Comte de Lambert seemed preoccupied every time that Bettina glanced at him. She twice noticed a worried frown on his face, but he hid this quickly with a lazy smile when he saw her watching him. He was a handsome man, though not nearly as handsome as Tristan. Even with the scar Tristan bore on his cheek, he was still — Why did she keep thinking about Tristan?

As it grew late, Bettina tactfully excused herself. She was not really tired, but she wanted to be alone. Pierre insisted on escorting her to her room, and when they reached it, he followed her in and closed the door.

"Is the room satisfactory?" he asked, coming up behind her.

"Yes," Bettina said, glancing around at the luxurious furnishings. "Your house is quite beautiful, from what I have seen of it."

"I had it completely refurnished when I decided to marry you. You can see the rest of it tomorrow. Ah, Bettina, I have waited

160

so long for you to come." He turned her around and crushed her to him, covering her mouth with his hard, demanding lips.

"Please, Pierre, it is late and —"

"Do not send me away, Bettina," he cut her off, still holding her close. "We will be married soon, and — and I want you so."

"Pierre!" Bettina gasped, pushing him away.

His face turned angry, almost cruel. "I cannot stand the thought that he had you first!" Pierre said heatedly. Then his face softened and he continued to plead with her. "Please, Bettina, I will be gentle, I will make you forget this Tristan."

Bettina was shaken by Pierre's behavior, but she was also angry that he would assume she would jump into bed with him before they were married.

"Do you intend to rape me, too?" she asked in a cutting voice.

"Of course not," he replied.

"Then leave my room, Pierre. It is late and I am tired."

"Forgive me, Bettina. You have had an exhausting day, and I was thinking only of myself."

She permitted him to kiss her again, softly this time, then he left the room.

Chapter 24

Try as she might, Bettina couldn't sleep. The disgusting scene with Pierre kept coming back to her, making her more and more angry. Just because she was no longer a virgin did not give him the right to presume she would sleep with him before they were married!

She had heard her mother go to her room a few minutes before. Bettina was so glad that her mother was here. She was not dependent on the Comte de Lambert now, and as her mother said, she didn't have to marry him if she didn't want to.

It was over an hour since Bettina had gone to bed, but she just couldn't seem to fall asleep. It was unusually hot in the room, and she was tempted to remove her shift and sleep naked. Even with the large French windows open, the breeze that she could hear in the trees outside failed to come into the room.

Bettina got up and walked out onto the wide veranda. The entire one-storied house was supported off the ground on short pilings, and the veranda completely surrounded it.

Thick gray clouds covered the entire sky and hid the full moon. Bettina supposed it would rain soon. Perhaps then her room would be cooler.

She walked a little way down the veranda, seeing the lights of the town in the near distance, but she stopped when she heard voices. Turning, she saw that she was standing just outside the drawing room, and had almost walked in front of the open doors. Very little light spilled out on the veranda, for there was only one candle left burning in the spacious room.

"You are indeed a lucky man, Pierre," Don Miguel was saying. "If I were ten years younger, I might try to win Bettina Verlaine away from you. But I am too old now to keep such a beautiful young girl happy. Her mother, on the other hand, would make me a suitable wife. It is amazing how young the widow looks, despite the fact that she has a full-grown daughter. But perhaps even Jossel would find me a bit too old to satisfy her."

"Nonsense, Miguel, you are still as fit as ever," Pierre replied. "Why not stay here a little longer and try to win the lovely widow. You could do worse."

"What? Are you trying to get rid of the mother-in-law before the wedding?" Don Miguel laughed.

"There will be no wedding," Pierre said bitterly.

Bettina gasped, moved closer to the wall, and stood immobile beside the wide-open doors, hearing the conversation as clearly as if she were inside the room.

"You are joking, of course — or are you a fool?"

"If only I were joking," Pierre said in a voice mixed with rage and regret. "You have been in town. You have heard the talk about Bettina. When the *Windsong* crawled into the harbor and her crew spread the tale, Bettina was quickly called the pirate's whore because no attempt had been made to exchange her for ransom. I cannot possibly marry her now."

"You are indeed a fool if you give her up just because of what your neighbors will say about her."

"You do not live here, Miguel," Pierre returned. "This is a small island, and I cannot have continued gossip about my wife. It would cause endless difficulties."

"So you will just let the pearl slip through your fingers? If I were —"

"I intend to keep the pearl," Pierre interrupted. "I just have not figured out how to do it yet."

"You mean you will keep her as your mistress?" Don Miguel asked, surprised.

"Of course. As you said, I would be a fool to give her up."

"But how do you propose to accomplish this? I was under the impression that Bettina Verlaine expects to be your wife. Her mother also expects this."

"Yes, well, the mother must go, leaving Bettina in my care. Then it will not take long to bed Bettina, and afterward I shall explain why it is impossible for us to marry."

"You are a libertine, Pierre," Don Miguel laughed. "To have all the advantages of a beautiful wife, without the entrapment of marriage."

"Well, this is not how I wanted it to be. I wanted Bettina for my wife. I could have made her a queen if only — if only this man Tristan had not forced her to be his whore!"

"It is ironic that this same man has affected both of our lives, and yet neither of us has met him," said Don Miguel.

"Then you truly have no idea why he searches for you?"

"No, I have spent many sleepless nights trying to understand why he looks for me. I have been told he is a young man, with blond coloring, and extremely tall. At first I thought he might be a bastard that I never knew of, but the more I learned of him, the less likely that notion was. I just do not know."

"You said he is young?"

"This does not suit your ego, eh?" Don Miguel chuckled. "But what does his age matter? I doubt Bettina was treated compassionately by him. Pirates are a ruthless lot. I should know; I was one myself in my youth."

"You never mentioned this before!" said Pierre, astonished.

"It was a long time ago, and very few people know of it. I fell in with a bad lot, and we took to raiding for the sport of it. And since raiding was also profitable, I continued my — ah — somewhat enjoyable career for quite a few years. But I have mended my ways now — it is best forgotten."

"Well, your secret is safe with me."

"That does not worry me, but this Tristan does. Until tonight, I always assumed that he merely wanted to find me to settle some debt or the like. But thanks to your Bettina, I now know that I have a dangerous enemy. That map she spoke of, why did she give it to you?"

"Ha — she wants me to go to the island where Tristan took her to rescue her old servant, who is still there, and to kill Tristan." Pierre laughed contemptuously. "She wants revenge for what he did to her."

"She is a spirited girl — I would not have guessed it from our meeting tonight. But why not give me the map, and I will

164

save you the trouble of doing what she asks."

"I burned it."

"You what?" Don Miguel exploded.

"I had no intention of going there — my ships are not armed for battle, my crews are not soldiers. I planned to tell Bettina the map was lost, and that would put an end to it. But why do you wish to go there?"

"I am not a man to sit and wait for my enemies to find me. I must find Tristan first."

"Bettina came here on a merchant ship. The *capitaine* would know where this island is — it was he who gave Bettina the map," Pierre said.

"Is he here? Is his ship anchored in the harbor?" Don Miguel asked hopefully.

"Bettina was merely put ashore. But I will ask her the name of the *capitaine* and his destination in the morning, if you still wish to find this pirate before he finds you. But in my opinion, it is a foolish venture."

"It is not you whom this man wants to kill, so find out what you can. I could live out my life without Tristan's ever finding me, but I cannot take that chance."

Even after the two men had gone to bed, Bettina still stood transfixed outside the drawing room, leaning against the wall. The conversation between the two men kept going through her mind. She felt so cheap and used, and Pierre was despicable! To think that he intended to make her his mistress and was going to lie to her about the map! He planned to get rid of her mother, and then he would force her to submit to his will or no doubt throw her into the streets!

Bettina shivered despite the warmth of the night and quietly tiptoed back to her room. She was angry. Yes, she was definitely angry. She wanted to tell her mother what she had overheard. She wanted to leave this house right away. But it was late, and her mother was probably asleep already. Bettina would have to wait until morning to put an end to Pierre's loathsome plans.

Were all men so ruthless — taking advantage of women because they were weaker? Bettina hated to think of what would have happened to her if she had not chanced to hear Pierre and

165

Don Miguel talking. But she had, and she and her mother could take lodgings in the town tomorrow.

Bettina suddenly remembered Madeleine. She still had to be rescued before they could return to France. But Don Miguel de Bastida was going to go to Tristan's island. Of course! She would send for him and have her mother commission him to rescue Madeleine. He would kill Tristan on his own, so Bettina need not feel guilty about his death. So Tristan would die, Don Miguel de Bastida would be paid for something he would have done anyway, and Madeleine would be rescued. Yes, it would all work out perfectly.

Chapter 25

Sometime in the middle of the night, Bettina slowly drifted out of sleep. She could hear rain on the veranda and assumed the storm had just started. With reluctance, she crawled out of bed and made her way to the French windows, for the air was quite chilly now and she had left the windows open. The room was completely dark, and the rain muffled all sound.

Luckily, there was no furniture between the bed and the windows to trip over, but before Bettina was halfway across the room, someone grabbed hold of her hair and she was pulled back against a sopping-wet body. She parted her lips to scream but was rewarded with a dry rag shoved in her mouth. Her arms were secured and quickly tied behind her back, and before she could spit the gag out of her mouth, another strip of cloth was placed over her mouth and tied behind her head, pulling her hair in the process. She tried to run forward, but she was pushed to the floor and her feet were secured tightly with rope.

Bettina was sick with terror. It must be Antoine Gautier, though she had done her best to forget him and hadn't imagined he would be crazy enough to kidnap her from the *comte*'s plantation.

He had left her lying on the floor for a moment, but now he was back, leaning over her. A few drops of water fell onto her face from his wet hair, but she couldn't make out his features in the darkness.

"Sorry to have to tie you up, little one, but you've been a bad girl and I'm through taking chances with you. It's raining pretty bad out there, so I'm going to roll you up in a blanket. Though why I should be so considerate after what you've done, I don't know."

167

Outrage exploded inside Bettina's head. What was Tristan doing here? He would have to have left the island within a day or two of her escape to appear here now. He should have searched the island for days, weeks — why hadn't he? And why had he come for her — why? He would have brought her to Saint Martin in another month or two anyway.

He rolled her up in a heavy blanket, and after making sure she could breathe, he picked her up and quickly carried her out the French windows. She could hear nothing except the rain as he walked along the veranda and then down some steps. She could feel drops of rain hitting the top of her head, and her feet were getting wet, but when he stopped and set her on her feet, she could no longer feel the rain.

"We will wait here where it's dry until Jules comes. We searched separately for you to save time. We have to get back to the ship before dawn, and I had a hell of a time just trying to find this place."

Bettina cursed whoever had given him the directions to find her. But when she was found gone in the morning, her mother would realize what had happened and would insist that Pierre come after her. Her mother would do whatever was necessary to rescue her daughter.

"Tristan, I found her."

"I don't know whom you have there, Jules, but it's not Bettina. I have her right here."

Tristan had his arms wrapped around her, forcing her to lean back against his chest.

"But I lit a candle as you suggested. This one has long white-blond hair," Jules replied.

"I did the same, and I tell you *this* is Bettina," Tristan returned with growing impatience.

"Did you see her face?"

"No, but —" He paused, and Bettina could feel his arms tighten around her. "Blast this infernal darkness! We'll take them both. There's no more time to dawdle — I want to be out of these waters before the ship is sighted. Whoever the other one is, one more woman on our island won't make any difference." Bettina tried to scream out, but no sound

168

escaped her lips. She knew that Jules had captured her mother, too, but there was nothing she could do about it. Oh, God, now how would she be rescued? Pierre didn't have the map anymore. And Tristan said he was through taking chances with her. What did he mean by that?

Bettina was lifted from the ground, and Tristan threw her over his shoulder. He started walking fast, half-running. Soon, her arms hurt and her feet were cold, and she felt a growing frustration at not being able to move her limbs. Tristan hadn't had to tie her up, she thought resentfully, for his strength had always overpowered hers. He had tied her up like a runaway slave just to humiliate her.

Wet branches and leaves brushed against her bare feet, and the rain still poured down in an angry torrent. Her stomach ached from being bounced on Tristan's shoulder, and by the time he finally stopped, the rain had soaked through the blanket.

Tristan bent her legs and laid her down, and she knew from the rolling motion that she was in a small boat. The boat rocked more when Jules climbed in, and she sensed that her mother was laid down beside her. In a very short time they would be aboard the *Spirited Lady*, and once again she would be completely at Tristan's mercy.

Bettina felt a growing sense of dread and desperation, but she was helpless to do anything about it. Her mother must be terrified. Jossel would have overheard the conversation between Tristan and Jules, just as Bettina had, and she would know where they were being taken — and by whom. But Jossel didn't know that Pierre had destroyed the map. She didn't know that there was no one to rescue them.

Bettina was picked up and hoisted over Tristan's shoulder again. She could tell he was climbing, and after another few minutes, she knew that she was in his cabin. He laid her down on the floor and roughly rolled her out of the blanket.

Bettina glared at Tristan as she lay helplessly on her side. Her eyes were the darkest of greens, and if they could have killed, Tristan would have been dead. He studied her critically and then laughed heartily.

169

"I knew it was you, little one. You have an unmistakable fragrance about you."

Jules carried her mother into the cabin, bound in a blanket also. He stood her up and gently unwrapped her. Bettina's anger soared even higher, remembering how Tristan had purposefully treated her roughly.

"I see you had the right one, Tristan," Jules said with a grin as he started to untie Jossel. "This one looks to be my age. Perhaps she won't mind sharing my cabin."

Bettina tried to protest and struggled to sit up, but she couldn't. Tristan looked at her and grinned mischievously. It was obvious that he didn't intend to untie her quite yet.

Jossel rubbed her arms when they were untied, but otherwise she stood still, even when the gag was removed from her mouth. Bettina could see the fear in her mother's eyes, and she felt sick with misery that she couldn't comfort her.

"Who are you, *madame?*" Tristan asked.

He stood in front of Jossel, his legs astride and his hands on his hips. She was a small woman, and Tristan towered over her like a menacing giant.

"I am Jossel Verlaine, and —"

"Blast it!" Tristan bellowed, making Jossel shrink back from him. "Do you know what you've done, Jules? This woman is the girl's mother!"

"So?"

"I have enough trouble with the vixen. I don't need her mother to contend with!"

"It is your own fault that the wench is difficult to handle," Jules replied. "I told you long ago what to do with her, but you wouldn't listen. You are too soft with women, Tristan. I see no problem in bringing the mother along."

Tristan looked at Jossel's pale color and wide green eyes. His face softened considerably, as did his voice when he spoke to her again.

"I'm sorry if I frightened you, *madame,* but it was a surprise to find you here. Bettina has spoken of you before, and I assumed you lived in France." When Jossel didn't answer, Tristan continued. "I do not intend to harm either you or your daughter.

You may rest easy on that account."

"Then please untie her, *monsieur*," Jossel said timidly, not knowing what to think of this big man.

"Not yet."

"Surely you do not intend to punish her for escaping from you?" Jossel asked.

"So she told you about me, eh?"

"I wager it wasn't a pretty picture she painted," Jules broke in with a humorous chuckle.

"Haven't you something to do, Jules?" Tristan scowled darkly at him.

"Nothing at the moment," Jules replied. He sauntered to the table and sat down.

"Bettina told me everything," Jossel said with a bit more courage.

"Everything?" Tristan asked, an amused expression on his face now.

"Yes."

"Well, I can assure you, Madame Verlaine, that I am not the monstrous pirate she would have you believe."

"Then if you are an honorable man, you will let us go. You will also release Madeleine Daudet."

"*Madame,* I said I was not a monster, I did not say I was an honorable man," Tristan said. "Bettina belongs to me. I warned her against trying to escape, and since she didn't heed my words, I will deal with her as I see fit."

"*Monsieur* —"

"I'm not finished," Tristan cut her off. "I will not tolerate any interference from you. If you wish to remain with your daughter, I suggest you heed my words. What I do with Bettina is my affair. Have I made myself clear?"

"Quite clear," Jossel whispered.

"Good. You may sleep in Jules's cabin. He will vacate it for you, I'm sure, since he wouldn't want his wife hearing of any dalliance."

"I suppose I must," Jules replied grudgingly.

Tristan walked to the door with them, and then whispered to Jossel out of Bettina's hearing, "I won't harm her, *madame,* so don't fear for her."

Jossel was utterly astonished by Tristan's gentle words, but she smiled at him hopefully before Jules pulled her along to his cabin.

Bettina watched Tristan as he closed the door, leaned back against it, and grinned. His hair was sopping wet, and his clothes were plastered to his body, displaying the bulging muscles on his arms and chest. He was still clean-shaven, but she could hardly see the scar anymore, for his face was completely bronzed by the sun.

"Your mother is a striking woman; quite beautiful, in fact. It is easy to see that you are her daughter," Tristan said. He pushed himself away from the door and sauntered to the washstand by the bed.

He removed his shirt and tossed it on top of the two wet blankets piled on the floor. He then took a towel from the washstand and began to rub his hair briskly. Damn it, when would he untie her?

"Ah, Bettina, what am I going to do with you?" He stood before her now, rubbing the towel across his chest. "I will admit I was furious when I discovered you'd left the house. You're lucky I didn't find you that morning, or I probably would have given you a sound beating, as Jules thinks you need. But I've had time to calm down."

As Tristan walked to the table and poured a tankard of rum, Bettina began to fear that he was going to leave her trussed up on the floor. He had told her mother that he would deal with her as he saw fit. What was he going to do?

He looked at her, his powder-blue eyes alight.

"What punishment would fit your crime, Bettina? I told you I would keep you prisoner if you tried to escape me, and that I will do. But you not only tried to escape, you succeeded — for a little while. Your one mistake was in letting the horses out of the corral, for one of those beasts came running across the backyard and woke me. And when I started out after you, the white stallion came charging out of the forest as if the Devil were after him. Were you bruised by the fall? I doubt you were, for your luck held that morning. I reached the shore just as you boarded that blasted ship. I would have been here the day before,

172

but I encountered a storm that took me off course."

So that was how he'd found her so soon. She should have closed the corral; she should have known the horses wouldn't wander far.

"So what punishment shall it be, little one?" He crossed to her again and crouched down beside her, lifting her chin with his finger. "I could still beat you. Jules seems to think that would do the trick."

She jerked her head away. But then she felt his hand on her breast, and it was like fire, even through the material of her shift.

"Why did you run away from me? Because of this?" he asked in a deep, teasing voice.

He moved his hand lower. She tried to move away from him, but she was already pressed against the built-in bed and could move no farther. She was afraid now. How would he punish her?

Untie me, she wanted to scream at him. And then her eyes widened in terror when he drew his knife. She tried to scream, but little sound escaped through the gag. He smiled at her, though his eyes showed no warmth.

"Relax and accept your fate, Bettina, for I've decided on a fitting punishment for you."

She stared in horror as Tristan drew the knife up the front of her shift. He cut the material at her shoulders and tore the ruined cloth away from her. He stood up, tossed the shift and the knife aside, and stared down at her nakedness. His eyes examined every inch of her body, and she could feel the heat rise to her face.

He moved to a chair, sat down facing her, and continued to look at her silently. She could read no emotion on his face, not even lust. She wanted to die — no, she didn't. She wished *he* were dead! If only she could scream her hate at him. She would tear his eyes out when he untied her.

She closed her eyes, for she couldn't bear to watch him staring at her unclad body. But after a few minutes, Tristan crossed to her with the silence of a cat. He picked her up and laid her gently on the bed, then sat down on the edge beside her. She looked at him, and his eyes were soft again. He was no longer angry, but she knew what he was determined to do.

173

"For once I can do as I like, without having to hold you down or listen to your insults," he murmured. He began to stroke her tender flesh, using both hands to caress her, scorching her skin with his touch. "This is what you ran away from, Bettina. This is what you fight to deny yourself."

Stop it! Stop it, damn you, she screamed inside her head, but Tristan buried his face in her neck. He used his lips now, and his tongue, and he left a trail of fire as his mouth descended to her breasts. Her desire swelled and surfaced, overpowering her resistance.

"What you are feeling now is not disgust, little flower. It is pleasure, pure and simple — you know it, and I know it. You curse me, but you want me. Your passion conquers your hate, and your body cries out for the fulfillment that only I can give you."

Tristan stood up and removed his breeches and boots. Then he turned her over gently and untied her feet, running his hand up her leg and over her buttocks when he finished. Bettina tried to get up, but he pressed his knee in the middle of her back, forcing her to be still. He untied her hands and then quickly retied them above her head.

He turned her over, then eased between her legs before she could kick out, but she was beyond reason or resistance. He removed the cloth from her mouth, and they kissed hungrily. She didn't care. She didn't care about anything except the fire that Tristan had started and must end. Why had he bound her arms? She wanted to hold him, to cling to him, to feel his muscles rippling, to run her hands through his wet hair. But all she could do was sense the whole of him with her body, and it was maddening yet ardently exciting. Nothing else mattered at this moment — nothing.

Chapter 26

They had sailed beyond the storm, and the morning sun shone through the open cabin window. Bettina lay on the bed, with nothing covering her except a film of perspiration slowly drying in the salty breeze. Her body still tingled with the aftereffects of Tristan's lovemaking.

How could Tristan make her want him so passionately, she wondered, when she hated him so? The humiliation she had felt earlier was nothing to the ecstatic pleasure that followed. Was she so wanton that a man's touch could make her tremble, that a kiss could make her give him everything?

But Pierre didn't affect her with his kiss. Only Tristan stirred the fires within her.

What was the matter with her? It wasn't her fault, but Tristan's. He was a devil, and he had the power to work magic with his fingers. After all, she would never go to him and ask him to make love to her. It was only after he touched her and continued to touch her that she desired him. He *must* be a devil. How else could he have the strength of ten men, such an incredibly handsome face, and such a magnificent body?

She glanced at Tristan now, as he stood before the open window looking out to sea. He appeared worried. Good. She hoped he had a million troubles, and she hoped she was his main vexation.

Bettina started to get up, but remembered that Tristan hadn't untied her yet. She frowned. She had assumed that the humiliation he put her through was to be the punishment he spoke of, but . . .

"Tristan, untie me," she demanded.

He looked at her with a raised eyebrow and a half-grin, and

175

she blushed at her own nakedness. His eyes sparkled, and his hair fell in waves on his temples. It was the color of molten gold with the sun shining on it.

"Did you say something, little one?"

Oh! She knew damn well he'd heard her. Well, she would play his game and humble herself, but only long enough to gain freedom.

"Will you please untie me? My — arms hurt," she said.

"Prisoners are usually kept in rusty irons," he remarked. "You should consider yourself lucky that you're tied with rope."

She couldn't tell if he was teasing her, but he made no move to come forward and do as she'd asked. She gritted her teeth. She wanted to curse him, but she had to get free first.

"Please, Tristan." With an effort, she managed to sit up, but she still couldn't lower her arms. "You cannot mean to leave me like this."

"Why not? At least with your hands bound, I need not worry that you will attack me when my back is turned."

"My arms hurt! Do you intend to torture me just because I escaped you? Damn you! I told you I would leave you if you raped me again — so I did! I would have stayed on your island if you had let me be."

"I'm sure you would have. I'm sure you would be quite content if I never touched you again, as I did a little while ago," he taunted her. "But you are just too tempting to leave alone, Bettina. If I want to kiss you, I will. If I want to make love to you, I will do this also. You forget what I told your mother earlier — you belong to me."

"I want to see my mother," Bettina said.

"What, like that?" he laughed.

Bettina blushed again, but she tried to control her anger. "Will you untie me or not?"

"I suppose so. But only on a few conditions."

"Well?"

"You will stop fighting me, and —"

"Always the bargaining and the conditions. Aren't you man enough to handle me, Tristan?" she teased, sensing a perfect chance to get back at him. "Pierre was."

"So it is Pierre now, eh?" he asked coldly. "Are you on such intimate terms after two days' acquaintance?"

"More than intimate," Bettina replied, averting her eyes from his.

"What is that supposed to mean?" he demanded. He crossed to her and lifted her face up to his. "Answer me!"

"Untie me first."

"You will answer me first, blast you!" Tristan raged.

"Will I?" Bettina asked, her voice coated with honey. She was surprised and delighted that mentioning Pierre could make Tristan so angry. "I can be very stubborn, Tristan. Would you like to see how stubborn I can be?"

He turned away, slamming his fist into his hand and mumbling curses under his breath. Was Tristan jealous of Pierre? she wondered. How would he react if she lied and said she had made love with Pierre? Perhaps he would no longer want her if he thought another man had bedded her.

He turned back toward her, and without a word he roughly untied her hands. He stood back while she rubbed her arms and her wrists, and then she slowly pulled the cover from the bed and wrapped it around her body.

When she didn't speak, Tristan lost his patience. He tilted her face to his and noticed the clear, dark blue of her eyes.

"You have been released; now answer my question." He made an effort to speak calmly.

"What question?" she asked innocently.

"If you wish to play games, Bettina, you won't like mine. Now answer me!"

"What is it you wish to know, Tristan?"

"You said you were more than intimate with de Lambert. What did you mean by that?"

"I thought what I said was perfectly clear."

"I will have a straight answer!" Tristan raged. "Did he rape you?"

Bettina laughed. "You amaze me, Tristan. How could you possibly think that Pierre would have to rape me? He is my betrothed. I told you before that I would succumb to him willingly."

"That was *after* you were married! Do you expect me to be-

177

lieve that you went eagerly to the man's bed on the first day you met him?"

"I do not care what you believe," she replied. She had gone too far to back down now.

"Did you *let* him make love to you?"

"Yes!" Bettina shouted.

Tristan's face went livid with rage, and his fists clenched at his sides. He stalked from the room, slamming the door behind him, and Bettina gave a sigh of relief. But Tristan came back a minute later.

"You lie!" he shouted. "You wouldn't have made love with him. Not with your mother in the same house!"

"It — it happened before I knew my mother was there — before she knew that I'd arrived. Pierre came into my room. He said that he had waited so long, and that he loved me," Bettina said, trying to make her lie sound plausible. "We were to be married soon. I saw no reason to wait. After all, I was not a virgin — thanks to you. And I found that I could not deny my future husband anything."

"You still lie! You wouldn't fall into the arms of a stranger, even if he was your betrothed!" Tristan stormed, pacing the room in his fury.

Bettina was afraid. She had never seen Tristan so angry before. She decided to admit the truth, but to leave some doubt in his mind.

"It would soothe your ego to believe I am lying. Very well, I made up the whole thing, simply to make you angry. I lied. Are you happy now?"

He stopped pacing the floor and turned to her, but his face was darker than ever.

"What is the matter, Tristan?" she asked, raising an eyebrow. "You would not believe me before; you insisted I was lying. Well, I admit it. Don't you believe me now?"

"Why should I believe anything you say?"

"Why, indeed?" she asked, and decided to attack. "Come now, Tristan. You had no reason to fly into a rage in the first place — unless, of course, you love me. Do you love me, Tristan? Is that why you came after me?"

178

"I — blast you! I told you before there is no room in my life for a woman, or for love."

"Then take me back to Saint Martin."

"No — not until I'm finished with you," he said coldly.

"I escaped you twice, Tristan. I will do so again!"

"You were a fool to try it this last time. You could have been picked up by slave runners, pirates, or any number of cut-throats."

She hadn't even thought of that. "Well, I was not. It was a merchant ship I sighted, and the *capitaine* was good enough to take me to Saint Martin — without reward. There are still a few decent men in this world."

"Perhaps there are, but you won't be given a chance to escape again. I warned you I would keep you prisoner if I had to."

"I want to see my mother," Bettina said, changing the subject quickly.

"No."

"But she will be worried about me. I want to comfort her."

"I said no. Now, do you want something to eat?"

"What I want is a needle and thread. If you —"

"Again the answer is no," he interrupted her.

"But why not?"

"Because without clothes, you won't be tempted to leave my cabin."

"No?"

"I think not," he replied with a half-grin, and then he left the room.

Bettina quickly went to his chest, but when she opened it, her face flushed angrily. It was empty. There was nothing in the cabin for her to wear!

Chapter 27

Bettina marched fretfully back and forth across the cabin, with only a blanket covering her. It was late in the afternoon, and the ship had been anchored in the small cove for over an hour now. Bettina's patience had left her and had been replaced by a seething anger. What was Tristan waiting for?

The last two weeks had been miserable for Bettina. She had been forced to stay in the cabin with absolutely nothing to do. She wasn't allowed to see her mother at all, and Tristan brought all her meals. He was the only person she had seen in two weeks.

The cabin door opened, and Bettina turned abruptly to see Tristan saunter into the room. She glared at him murderously, her eyes large, flashing emeralds.

"When will you take me ashore?" she demanded shrilly.

"Now, if you like," he returned calmly. "You can put these on, since you were once so fond of wearing them."

She grabbed the clothes that Tristan held out to her, then turned away and donned the large breeches and V-necked shirt, using a piece of rope he was generous enough to include for a belt.

"I have no shoes," she reminded him in a saucy voice.

"That's too bad, little one. I wasn't about to grope around in the dark that night looking for your shoes. I guess I'll just have to carry you when we get to shore."

"That will not be necessary!" she snapped. "Where is my mother?"

"She is already on the island. Come."

After twenty irritatingly slow minutes, Tristan pulled the small boat ashore and, with the help of the two men who were with them, carried it up the beach and put it with the other boat.

He must have taken only a handful of men with him to come after her, for there was no one left on the *Spirited Lady*. She also saw that Captain O'Casey's ship was no longer in the cove.

Tristan took her hand and dragged her along after him. When they reached the forest, he picked her up and carried her despite her protests until they came to the lawns in the front of the house. Then he set her down.

Jossel and Madeleine waited by the front door for her, but when Bettina tried to run ahead, Tristan jerked her back beside him, his grip on her hand like steel. He kept hold of her, and when they reached the front door of the house, he took her on inside, not letting her stop to talk to her mother and servant for even a moment.

"Let go of me!" she shouted, trying to pull away from him.

But Tristan ignored her demand and continued to the stairs, pulling her roughly behind him. When he came to his room, he thrust Bettina inside and then closed the door, leaving her alone. She heard the key turn in the lock, and she tried to open the door, but it wouldn't budge. She could hear him walking away. She pounded on the door furiously, then listened again, but Tristan was gone.

Damn him! He was going to stick to his word and keep her locked up. She couldn't stand much more of this confinement, seeing only Tristan, with his damnable smile and his lustful demands.

She paced the floor. An hour passed, and then another. She wanted out! She froze when she heard the key turn in the door; then it opened, and Tristan came in with a tray of food in one hand. He locked the door again and set the tray down on the small table beside the bed.

"How long do you intend to keep me locked in this room?" she asked, trying desperately to sound calm.

"Until you give me your word that you won't escape again," he answered in a curiously patient voice.

"Damn you, Tristan!" Bettina cried. She stamped her foot in fury. "I cannot stand this anymore!"

"Then give me your word."

"You go to hell!"

"Such a temper," he laughed. "Your servant told me once that you were a gentle and loving girl. Is it only me that brings out your fiery temper?"

"Until I met you, I never had cause for rage," she said contemptuously.

"No? I hear you have lived most of your life in a rage." He smiled when she looked at him in surprise. "Yes, your servant told me about you and your father. Am I just a replacement for him, Bettina? Have you lived with anger so long that you must have someone to direct it toward?"

"Enough Tristan!" she wailed in a torn voice. "My father is dead!"

A look of concern appeared on Tristan's face. "I — I'm sorry, Bettina."

"I don't want your sympathy!" she snapped angrily.

Tristan sighed heavily. "You really should try to curb your hotheadedness, Bettina. I won't put up with it much longer."

"No? What will you do? Tie me up and gag me again? Or beat me this time? You enjoy making me suffer, don't you?"

"No, I only want to give you pleasure," he replied softly. "You bring the suffering on yourself."

Bettina pulled one of the velvet chairs over to the window facing the mountain and sat there watching the changing colors of the sky. The sun had set below the mountain a long time ago, but its dark mass was silhouetted against the pinks, purples, and reds of the sky behind it.

A slight breeze blew in through the open window, and Bettina pulled the blanket closer about her shoulders. A little while ago, Tristan had brought in her evening meal, but she ignored him until he left to go back downstairs to drink with Jules.

A week had gone by since they'd returned to the island, and she was still locked in this room with absolutely nothing to do. Tristan had taken away the clothes he let her wear to come ashore, and he had removed both her clothes and his from the room.

He kept the door locked even at night. He kept the key beneath the bedpost on his side of the bed while he slept. He had invited her to remove it when she saw him put it there, saying she could have her freedom if she could lift the bed, with him in it. But she couldn't — he knew she couldn't.

After the first day, Bettina wouldn't talk to Tristan. She hadn't spoken to him at all for six days. She wouldn't even fight him when he made love to her, which surprised him quite a bit. When he took her, she avoided responding to him until the last minutes; then her body took control. Afterwards, she turned cold again.

But these last few days, Bettina had begun to look forward to Tristan's visits. She was starved for company and questioned him about what was going on as soon as he came into the room. But he told her little and would say nothing at all about her mother.

But tonight, tonight she had decided to take a stand.

He would be back soon, so she didn't have very much time. She got up and pulled the chair over to the door. She then moved the heavy Spanish chest and set this up against the door, leaning the chair against it. The other chair followed, and the small bed-side table. She only wished she had the strength to move the bed.

She sat on the bed and waited. It wasn't long before she heard the key turn in the lock. She flew off the bed and braced herself against her sturdy barricade. Tristan tried to open the door once and then again, but it remained shut.

"Bettina, open this door — now!"

"Like hell I will!"

He shoved on the door again, and this time it started to open. Bettina strained against it, feeling her feet slipping on the rug. But then she heard Tristan walk away, then return with help.

"How many times must I say it, Tristan? The vixen needs to be put in her place," Jules said gruffly.

"Tristan, I — I am not dressed!" Bettina yelled in dismay. She grabbed the blanket, wrapped it around her, and tucked it above her breasts, just in case they succeeded in opening the door.

"I suggest you get under the covers, Bettina — and hide," Tristan yelled back. Jules burst out laughing.

She didn't hide, but braced her weight against the barricade again when the two men started leaning against the door. This time her feet actually slid across the rug and she almost fell on her face as the door opened.

Tristan stepped inside and closed the door, and Bettina could still hear Jules laughing as he went back to his room. She backed away from Tristan and watched while he silently moved the furniture back.

"Well, why don't you speak?" Bettina added. "Go ahead. Show me how angry you are."

"I'm not angry. It was a good try, Bettina. At least your spunk has returned. I was beginning to think you had grown docile."

"Tristan, I must get out of this room. I cannot stand it anymore!"

"You know what it takes."

"Very well! I promise not to escape again if you will tell me when you will let me go."

"You are in no position to make bargains, little one," he replied, sitting down in the chair he had just returned to its place.

"But why won't you tell me when you will return me to Saint Martin?"

"Are you so anxious to see your Pierre again?" he asked coldly.

"No. You — you can take me to any island, as long as I can gain passage there. It need not be Saint Martin," she said, trying to pacify him.

"But then you will go to Saint Martin. What is the difference?"

"You told me there is no room in your life for women. You cannot continue to keep me here if you spoke the truth."

"I'm not going to keep you forever, Bettina. I just haven't decided how long it will be."

"I do not ask for a specific date, Tristan, just an amount of time. One month, two, three?"

"Let us say one year, perhaps less."

"One year!" she exploded. "No — that is too long! Surely you do not intend to stay away from the sea that long?"

"No, probably not. I could leave you here alone from time to time, but only if I have your word that you won't escape."

Bettina turned her back on him and gritted her teeth. A year was such a long time! How could she endure a year with him? But he said he would leave from time to time. Perhaps he would be gone for most of the year. And since she had discovered what kind of a man Pierre was, she wouldn't be going back to him. She wasn't really in a hurry to go anywhere. But she had to get out of this room.

"Will you allow the time I have already spent with you as part of the year?"

"If you insist."

"Very well, Tristan," she said dejectedly.

"Your word."

"I give you my word I will not escape you, on the condition you will let me go in one year — or less."

He laughed triumphantly. "Come here, Bettina."

"To be submissive was not part of the bargain, Tristan," she replied tartly.

Chapter 28

Bettina awoke to a beautiful morning, with the sun streaming in through the window and birds singing on the roof. She was impatient to be up and about. She quickly shoved Tristan out of bed, telling him to go and get her clothes. He pulled his breeches on grudgingly and did as she asked. When he returned with her clothes, he climbed back into bed without a word and went to sleep again.

Bettina had forgotten that her shift was torn, but she wasn't about to waste time sewing it now — she wanted to see her mother. Both of her dresses were of soft material, so it wouldn't matter if she wore her shift or not.

She chose the lilac cotton dress and donned it quickly. She left the room, not even bothering with her hair, allowing it to hang loose and flow down her back. Her bare feet felt the chill of the cold floor as she hurried down the corridor and descended the stairs.

She saw Madeleine sitting at the long dining table with her mother, talking away in her cheerful manner. Madeleine stared at Bettina in surprise when she saw her, but Jossel immediately rose to her feet and met Bettina before she reached the table.

"Oh, my love, are you all right?" Jossel asked as she embraced Bettina. "He said he would not harm you, but he would not allow me to see you."

"I am fine — now," Bettina replied and led her mother back to the table.

"Does — does Tristan know that you have left his room? He would be —"

"He knows, Mama," Bettina interrupted. "I struck a bargain with Tristan last night. I gave my word that I would stay here

186

for one year. Counting the time I have already spent with him, it will actually be less than eleven months."

"You agreed to this?"

"I had no choice. He set the amount of time, and I had to give my word that I would not escape in order to leave that room. I could not stand being locked up any longer."

"It was a foolish thing you did, escaping again," Madeleine scolded. "Tristan was like a madman when he told me you'd hailed a ship and were gone. I was worried sick over you."

"I'm sorry, Maddy. But I was coming back for you. I wouldn't have left if I didn't think you would be rescued."

"Oh, I was all right, pet," Madeleine returned. "In fact, I have grown to like it here. I no longer have kitchen duties, but I still supervise those two young girls who serve here whenever Tristan is home."

"Who are those girls?" Bettina asked curiously.

"Aleia and Kaino," Madeleine answered. "Their older sister, Maloma, is married to Jules."

"Married? Yes, I did hear Tristan say Jules had a wife here."

"A wife and three children by her. Cute little tykes, they are — all girls."

"And does Tristan have a wife and children here, too?" Bettina asked sarcastically.

Madeleine and Jossel exchanged curious glances, and Madeleine said, "Tristan has never taken seriously any of the village women. He visits the whores there occasionally, but that is all. Many of his crew have married village girls, though, and they have built their own huts on previous visits here. The rest of the crew stays in the village."

"Is there a priest, then, who performed these marriages?" Bettina ventured. "I would like to go to confession."

"No, the couples went to the village chief for his blessing, that is all. But I think I have convinced Jules to bring a priest here to give these marriages God's blessing."

"Why do you concern yourself, Maddy?" Bettina asked.

"Tristan's men married these native girls honorably; they do not intend to desert them. I only feel they should be married properly."

187

"It is Jules you are thinking of. Honestly, Maddy, you are impossible. Must you mother everyone? Jules does not deserve your concern."

"I have come to know him also, Bettina," Jossel said. "I find it hard to believe he is the same man who nearly whipped you to death."

"He is the same man, and he would still like to see me whipped. If I harmed Tristan, Jules would be the first to bare my back."

"She is right, Jossel," Madeleine said reluctantly. "You were not there the day she nearly killed the *capitaine*. Jules, he can be like a wild demon, but only where Tristan is concerned. He protects the *capitaine* as a mother protects her child."

Jossel frowned and looked at Bettina sadly. "I fear I have not protected you as I should have, *ma chérie*."

"Oh, no, Mama, you must not blame yourself. There is nothing you can do for me without endangering your own life. I will manage — it will only be for one year."

"You sound as if you have given up, Bettina. It will not be a year. The Comte de Lambert has the map you gave him. He will rescue us," Jossel said.

Bettina sighed and told her mother of the conversation she had overheard between Pierre and Don Miguel. "So it will be a year unless Tristan decides to let me go sooner," Bettina finished.

"Does Tristan know that you no longer intend to marry the *comte?*" Jossel asked softly.

"No, and you must both promise not to tell him or anyone about it," Bettina replied, and waited for her mother and Madeleine to nod in agreement.

"But if he knew, perhaps he would marry you," Jossel returned.

"Mama, my feelings for Tristan have not changed since I last spoke to you about him. I still hate him, and I would never, never marry him. And he has also said he will not marry me. He will not change his mind."

"But a year is a long time, Bettina. If you should bear Tristan a child, then he would surely —"

"No! Do not even think it!" Bettina cried. "It will not happen!"

"Calm yourself, my love. Of course it will not happen. I did

188

not mean to upset you," Jossel said quickly, wishing she were as sure as Bettina was.

"I'm sorry I shouted, Mama. I have been doing that a lot lately," Bettina said with a faint smile.

"And with good reason, I imagine."

"Very good reason," Bettina laughed softly.

"If only Ryan had come back, our lives could have been so different," Jossel said wistfully.

"Ryan? Who is this Ryan?" Madeleine asked.

Jossel's face turned slightly pink. "Bring Bettina some of that hot bread Aleia baked, please, Maddy, and some milk."

"You never told Maddy about Ryan?" Bettina asked after the old woman had left.

"No, but I think she suspected there was someone in my life all those years ago. She knew how happy I was for a while. But it would serve no purpose to tell her now."

"I suppose you are right. But I have not asked how you have fared, Mama. Have any of the men — ah — bothered you?"

"Heavens, no," Jossel laughed. "What would these men want with an old woman like me?"

"Mama, this is no matter to take lightly. You are not an old woman, which you know very well, and you are beautiful," Bettina scolded.

"Do not worry about me, Bettina. Your *capitaine* has taken very good care of me."

"He has!" Bettina exclaimed. "But he would tell me nothing, not even if you had a roof to sleep under."

"He does not strike me as such a bad man, though he forces you to sleep with him, and on this I have been reminded not to interfere. But he has given me his protection. I heard him give the order that I was to be left alone and respected."

"Honorable actions do not fit his mold," Bettina said sarcastically.

"Tristan has been more than generous to me," Jossel replied. "He gave me the room next to Madeleine's. And he has supplied me with plenty of material for dresses, and it is such expensive cloth. He also found me a pair of shoes when he saw that mine were left behind."

189

"Tristan did all of this for you without being asked?"

"Yes. I did not expect to be treated so kindly. But I think Tristan did it because of you, because I am your mother."

"More likely so he would not have to deal with my wrath," Bettina returned bitterly.

"No, Bettina. I think he really cares for you. He did not like keeping you locked up."

"That is absurd. He enjoys making me suffer!" Bettina snapped, her eyes turning green at the mention of her three-weeks' confinement.

"Many times he started up the stairs with determination, then stopped in indecision, as if he were fighting with himself. He would go a few more steps, then turn around abruptly and storm out of the house. He did not know I saw him, but I believe that he started up the stairs to release you."

"You are interpreting his actions the way you want to believe," Bettina replied. "You would like to believe Tristan is an honorable man and that he cares for me. Well, he is not honorable, and he does not care for me. He wants me only to satisfy his lust, no more."

"Does Tristan speak French?" Jossel asked, suddenly changing the subject.

"No. He is an English seadog who speaks only his native tongue," Bettina replied contemptuously.

"You did not tell me he was such a handsome man."

"What does it matter how handsome he is, when his soul is black with sin?"

"You do not find him even a little bit irresistible?" Jossel ventured.

"Certainly not! Tristan may be a devil, but his powers will not soften my heart."

"I only want you to be happy, Bettina."

"I will be happy when I leave this island, not until then," Bettina answered.

"You sound like an angel when you speak your language, little one," Tristan said softly.

Bettina started and turned her head to see Tristan standing behind her. "Must you walk so quietly?" she demanded. "How long have you been standing there?"

"For a few minutes. I didn't want to interrupt your conversation with your mother. I'm sure you have much to tell her," Tristan said. He sat down in the chair next to her.

Bettina turned back to her mother with wide, angry eyes. "Why did you not tell me he was there?"

"He motioned for me to say nothing. That is why I asked if he spoke French. I did not know if you would want him to learn how you feel about him. But his face did not change when you spoke of him — he did not understand."

"He knows how I feel, Mama — he knows I hate him."

"You've had enough time to discuss your complaints with your mother," Tristan said sourly. "You will speak English now."

"I was merely telling my mother how much I hate you," Bettina replied in a saucy voice.

"How much you *think* you hate me."

"What are you implying? Do you think I do not know my own mind?" Bettina asked heatedly.

"I think you deceive yourself. Is it hatred you feel when you cling to me in bed?" he asked with a taunting smile.

"You will not speak of that in front of my mother!" Bettina gasped.

"Why not? Would you have her believe that you hate me all of the time?"

"You are a devil, Tristan!" Bettina stormed. "I am not responsible for the magic you work in bed, but it does not affect what I feel in my heart. If I did not hate you, would I have asked Pierre to kill you? And I hate you even more since you have brought me back!"

Bettina stood up and walked to the front door, but Tristan ran after her and stopped her. They stood by the open door in a shaft of warm sunlight, well out of Jossel's hearing.

"Where do you think you're going?" he asked, a dark scowl on his face.

"Away from you!" she snapped and turned to walk out the door, but he held her arm and jerked her back against him.

"Shall I prove to your mother the truth of my words — that

191

you will yield to my embrace?" he asked, his voice cold and unrelenting.

Bettina couldn't stop the tears that welled up in her eyes. "Stop it — please. You have already humiliated me in front of her. Must you continue to do so?"

"Stop your blasted crying! You deserve this for your outburst. Where is your damnable temper now?"

Bettina continued crying while she pushed against him. She felt like a fool.

"Let go of me." She tried to sound demanding, but failed pathetically. "I told my mother everything. I told her what happens to me when you rape me — how my body betrays me. You do not have to prove it to her."

"No, but perhaps I should prove it to you," he replied huskily.

Bettina angrily decided to prove something to him. She glanced at the table and saw that her mother had tactfully left the room. She wrapped her arms around Tristan's neck, pulled his lips down to hers, and kissed him passionately. She put all the feeling she could muster into the kiss, caressing him with her hands, molding her body to his. Her own senses soared, but when she felt his desire begin to rise, she pushed herself away from him.

She wanted to laugh at his startled expression, but she gritted her teeth and remembered why she had kissed him. "Now you know, Tristan, what I could give you if I didn't hate you. You may exact passion from my body when you rape me, but there is still a part of me that is not affected by your touch. This part of me you will never reach, because it is only mine to give. You will never have my love."

Bettina turned and ran up the stairs to her room, ignoring the food Madeleine had left on the table for her.

Chapter 29

Bettina had tossed and turned fretfully most of the night, causing Tristan considerable annoyance. Now she was still tired, but she knew it must be noon or later and she had to get up — she couldn't put it off any longer.

She mechanically donned a new pink shift and a rose-colored dress. A month and three weeks had gone by since Tristan had brought her back to the island. She should have had her monthly time the week after Tristan had released her from his room, but she hadn't. However, she wouldn't believe the obvious. She refused to even think about it. But now she was a week late again, and she could no longer deny the truth. She was two months' pregnant.

What was she going to do? How could she bear to raise the child of a man she despised? Would she hate the child, too? No, she couldn't hate her own baby, she was sure of that. But Tristan probably had bastards scattered all over the Caribbean. Her child would make no difference to him.

Bettina started to comb the tangles from her hair, but then she stopped and threw the comb down on the floor. She ran out of the room and halfway down the stairs.

Tristan was at the table, bending over some papers. As Bettina stared at him, the rage surfaced and exploded inside her head. She clasped her hands to try to stop their trembling; then she ran down the rest of the stairs and came up behind Tristan. He straightened and turned, hearing her approach, and when he did, Bettina swung her closed fist full force across his cheek.

"What the hell was that for?" Tristan growled, rubbing his face.

"Damn you, Tristan!" Bettina screamed. "I am pregnant!"

193

"Sweet Jesus, is that any reason to attack me?" he grumbled. "I don't mind a slap from a woman if she thinks it is deserved, but you always have to use your blasted fists!"

"I should have waited until I could find a dagger so I could lay open your black heart!"

"I don't know what you're so mad about." He grinned. "You should have known it would happen sooner or later. Besides, if it is only one month, how can you be sure?"

"Because it is over two months — two!" she yelled. She ran back up the stairs before he could say more.

Tristan heard the door to his room slam, and he chuckled. But then his face darkened like a storm cloud when he realized that a little over two months ago, Bettina had been in Saint Martin.

He ran up the stairs and burst into his room, crashing the door against the wall. Bettina shrank back when she saw the violence on Tristan's face. He grabbed her cruelly by the shoulders and shook her.

"Whose child is it?" he raged.

"What?"

"Blast you, woman! Whose child do you carry?"

She stared at him with an incredulous look on her face. "Have you gone mad? The child is —"

Bettina stopped short. She remembered the doubt she had planted in his mind, and started to laugh.

He shook her again, violently, until she stopped laughing. "Answer me!"

"The child is yours — of course," she replied in a mocking voice. "Who else could be the father?"

"You know damn well who!"

"Come now, Tristan. I told you I lied about Pierre. Didn't you believe me?" she teased.

"I will have your word that the child is mine!"

"No, you will not! I will not give you that satisfaction," Bettina replied, becoming angry again. "It does not matter if the child is yours or not. Once I leave here, you will never see it again. And if it upsets you so much that I am pregnant, let me leave now!"

"You were so upset that you came downstairs and attacked *me*."

"You have ruined my life! I could have been married to Pierre by now if it were not for you. You force me to stay here against my will and give birth to a bastard. I have reason to be upset, but you do not!"

"I have a right to know whose child you carry!"

"What right do you have? You are not my husband; you are not my lover. You are merely the man who rapes me. What right do you have?"

Tristan pulled her to him and kissed her savagely, hurting her in his embrace; then he shoved her away from him angrily. "Blast you, Bettina! You are a witch!"

"Then let me go. Please, Tristan. My shape will grow soon, and you will have to go elsewhere to satisfy your lust, anyway. Release me now," Bettina pleaded.

"No. But I must leave. You have bewitched me and kept me from my purpose."

"And what purpose is that? Delivering your stolen gold to England?" she asked sarcastically, moving away from him.

"The gold has already been disposed of."

"So you go to steal more gold. You are a pirate, Tristan, though you hide behind the English for protection."

"And you see things only the way you wish to see them. But this voyage is not for profit — it is for personal reasons."

"But you spoke of a purpose. What purpose?"

"It is nothing you need to know about," Tristan said, and turned to leave the room.

"Do you go to find Don Miguel?" Bettina asked.

Tristan swung around and looked at Bettina suspiciously. "How do you —"

"If you will remember, I was there when you spoke of Don Miguel to *Capitaine* O'Casey," Bettina interrupted him. "Don Miguel does —"

"Stop saying his name with such familiarity!" Tristan said brusquely, his clear blue eyes suddenly alight with a fire that came from his very soul. "He is Bastida — the murderer!"

"Why do you search for him?" Bettina ventured.

"Because of something that happened a long time ago. It is no concern of yours."

"But even Don Miguel doesn't know why you look for him. He has never met you."

"What in hell are you talking about? What makes you think he doesn't know?"

"I had dinner with him at Pierre's house. He said —"

"Bastida was there?" Tristan asked incredulously.

"Yes."

"Mother of God! He was so close — so very close. Blast it, Bettina! You see what you've done to me?"

"I have done nothing to you!" she cried indignantly.

"If I had not been so intent on finding you, I would have asked the townspeople of Saint Martin the same questions I ask in every port. I would have found Bastida at last!" Tristan said vehemently. "Is he still there?"

"You blame me because you did not find Don Miguel, when it was not my fault. I will not answer your questions about him."

Tristan crossed to her in two quick strides and grabbed her arm tightly. "You will answer me on this, Bettina, or by God, I will beat it out of you!"

She turned pale, for there was no doubt in her mind that he meant what he said.

"I — I don't think he will still be there. He was waiting for the return of his ship, and it arrived the day after I did. I gathered he would be there only a few more days."

"Do you know where he was going or where he lives?"

"No."

"What about his ship? Do you know the name?"

"No. I only know it brought a cargo of slaves that Pierre purchased."

"So far, you have told me nothing useful. I gather you spoke to him of me. What did he have to say?" Tristan asked in a calmer voice.

"He said only that he has heard that you search for him, but he doesn't know why. He thinks you must have him mistaken for someone else because he has never met you," Bettina replied. Don Miguel might find Tristan first and end her misery. She would not warn Tristan that Bastida was now searching for him.

"So Bastida thinks he doesn't know me," Tristan reflected, letting go of Bettina's arm. "Well, he knows me; he just doesn't remember. But before I kill him, I will make sure he knows why I'm sending him to hell."

"Why do you want to kill him? What has he ever done to you?"

"I told you it is no concern of yours."

"Have you considered that he might kill you instead? He may be much older than you, but he is still a powerful man. You could be the one to die."

"That would certainly make you happy, wouldn't it?" Tristan asked coldly.

"Yes, it would! You have caused me nothing but misery. You know I hate you, and now I know you hate me, too. You would have beat me, though I am with child, just to obtain information about Don Miguel!"

"I wouldn't beat you, Bettina," Tristan said with a heavy sigh. "I will never raise a hand against you — you should know that by now. It was a hollow threat, and I was angry enough to make you believe it. But I had to know what you could tell me. I must find Bastida. I have sworn to kill him, and I will never rest until I do." He turned and walked out of the room.

Bettina was left in confusion. She still didn't understand why Tristan wanted to find and kill Don Miguel de Bastida.

Chapter 30

The tavern was small, and the many tables crowded closely together about the room were empty this late at night. The best food in town could be had here, but the brothel upstairs received more clientele. Tristan was seated at one of the tables with an amused expression on his face, watching sailors and merchants climbing up and down the stairs at the back of the room.

"Tristan, it is madness to linger here," Jules said, casting furtive glances about the room. "I'm beginning to think you've lost your judgment. We can eat on the ship. Let us go."

"Relax, Jules. There is no danger here," Tristan said, leaning back in his chair.

"No danger! That man de Lambert probably has a reward out for your head. After what Bettina told him about you, he would know it was you who took her again. Are you tired of living?"

"You're beginning to sound like an old woman. No one knows us here."

"I didn't want to come to Saint Martin to begin with, but you were so sure you would learn something of Bastida here. Well, all you have learned is that he left in a hurry. No one knows anything else."

"The Comte de Lambert would know. He would know in what direction Bastida sailed, perhaps even his destination."

"Mother of God! You *have* lost your sanity. You can't mean to go to his plantation and ask him!"

"Why not? If he can tell me where Bastida is now, it is worth the risk."

"Then I will go with you," Jules returned.

"No," Tristan said adamantly.

"You are a young fool. It's not because of Bastida that you

want to see de Lambert. It is because that blond vixen intends to marry him. Admit it."

"Perhaps you're right."

"Did it occur to you that he may not want her when she returns to him with your child?"

"How did you know of the child?" Tristan asked angrily, coming forward in his chair.

"I couldn't help but hear Bettina when she gave you the news. I didn't mention it before because you've been in such a foul mood since we left the island."

"Well, Bettina may be pregnant, but I have doubts that the child is mine. She may bring de Lambert his own child when she returns to him!" Tristan said bitterly.

"But that is impossible," Jules laughed. "She was here only two days."

"That does not make it impossible!" Tristan bit off, tiny blue flames in his eyes.

"You sound jealous. Don't tell me you've fallen in love with the wench."

"You know I have never fallen for a woman. There is only one thing in my heart — and that is hatred. But to see Bettina grow big with a child that might be de Lambert's — the doubt is like a dagger twisting in my stomach."

"Then give her up."

"That's the trouble. I'm not tired of her yet. She —"

Tristan stopped short and looked toward the door with amazement. Jules turned his head and saw a man dressed regally in gray silk. His cloak and scabbard were black velvet, and his bearing spoke of nobility. The man crossed the room and approached the plump woman behind the bar who made the arrangements for the girls upstairs.

When the madam saw the gentleman, her face lit up with a welcoming smile. "Comte de Lambert, you are back so soon."

"I would like to see Colette again," he said.

"So my new girl, she has lit a fire in you, eh? Poor Jeanie, she will be disappointed that you have found a new favorite."

Jules was afraid to look at Tristan, but when he turned, he saw that outwardly Tristan appeared calm, but his knuckles gleamed white. Tristan rose slowly, like a hungry lion stalking unsuspecting prey.

"For the love of God, Tristan," Jules whispered angrily. "He will know you."

"Just stay where you are and stop looking as if you were facing the gallows," Tristan said coldly. He turned and approached de Lambert. "*Monsieur,* might I have a word with you?"

Pierre de Lambert stopped at the foot of the stairs with one hand on the rail, annoyed at the delay. But when he saw the huge stranger walking toward him, all thoughts of Colette and pleasure vanished. The man was unusually tall, with golden hair curling slightly at the nape of his neck. He was dressed like a common sailor, in tight breeches and a white, open-necked shirt with billowing sleeves caught at his wrists. He wore a black baldric over one shoulder to support a wicked-looking sword, and his hand rested lightly on the hilt.

Pierre felt a slight tingling of recognition, but he knew that if he had ever seen this man before, he would have remembered. He eyed him warily and waited for the man to speak.

"I overheard the madam address you as the Comte de Lambert. If you are indeed the *comte,* you might be able to help me," Tristan said amiably. His eyes were like blue ice, and his smile fixed.

"How can I help you, *monsieur?*"

"I am looking for a friend of mine," Tristan said. "I have been told he was a guest of yours recently."

"Whom do you speak of?" Pierre asked. "I have many guests at my plantation."

"Don Miguel de Bastida He —"

"What is your name, *monsieur?*" Pierre interrupted, edging his hand slowly to his sword.

"Forgive me. My name is Matisse. Perhaps Don Miguel spoke of me. He saved my life a few years ago in battle."

"Don Miguel spoke of no battles while he stayed with me, nor did he mention your name."

"Well, I suppose he is not one to boast of his marksmanship," Tristan laughed, feeling sick. He would have preferred to draw his sword, but he couldn't kill the man just because Bettina might

200

be carrying his child. "Can you tell me where I could find Don Miguel? It is important to me."

"Why?" Pierre asked skeptically, though he was sure this Matisse couldn't be who he had thought he was. No, the pirate who had stolen Bettina wouldn't dare to approach him.

"As I said, Don Miguel saved my life. I would like to repay him — perhaps be his personal guard so that I might save his life one day."

"Well, I am sorry, but I cannot help you. Don Miguel left rather abruptly over three months ago, and I was too upset over a personal matter to be concerned with his destination."

"Then you have no idea where he could be?"

"I imagine Don Miguel is still somewhere in the Caribbean. He had some old business that he wanted to take care of before he returned to Spain."

"Did he say what kind of business?" Tristan asked hopefully. "It might lead me to him."

"I doubt that, Monsieur Matisse. Don Miguel's business will not keep him long in any port," Pierre said. "Now I must bid you good night — I have someone waiting for me."

"Of course," Tristan said, and turned to walk back to his table. The smile on his lips vanished as quickly as a snuffed candle, but the fire still burned in his eyes.

"I am surprised you didn't come right out and ask him if he had bedded Bettina. You wanted to, didn't you?" Jules asked heatedly when Tristan sat down.

"Yes, but I couldn't expect the truth from him on that subject. So you heard my little performance?"

"I couldn't help but hear! You were a fool to speak to the *comte*. I saw his face when you told him you were looking for Don Miguel. For a moment he guessed who you really are. I'm surprised he believed that tale you spun about Bastida."

"Well, he did," Tristan replied dryly. "I told you there was nothing to worry about."

"Yes, but you took the risk for nothing. We still don't know where Bastida is. We could search these waters forever and not find him."

"I suppose you want to give up?"

"Well, it wouldn't hurt to return to the island for a short visit," Jules said.

"We've only been gone a month and only put into four ports thus far. If you miss your wife that much, you should have stayed with the women as I asked you."

"I'm not worried about their safety. Joco and the men we left behind will protect them. But I am not the only one who is thinking of home. The rest of the crew is, too — and you also, my friend. You didn't come to Saint Martin just to learn of Bastida. You came to see what Bettina's betrothed is like. Are you disappointed that the *comte* is not old and pockmarked?"

"Why should that bother me?" Tristan asked calmly. Then he suddenly exploded, "What the hell is he doing in a blasted whorehouse? If I were him, I would be out searching every island from here to the Colonies. But where does he do his searching? In a whore's bed! I'll wager he doesn't have one ship out looking for Bettina."

"Is that what you want him to do? Do you want him to find her?"

"No."

"Well, then?"

"I just don't understand why he isn't trying," Tristan said more quietly.

"You don't know that he isn't, but let's not wait around to ask him when he comes down. The food is cold, anyway. I'm for returning to the ship — now."

Tristan laughed. "What's happened to you, old friend? Taking small risks never bothered you before."

"Yes, but I have only just come to know my new daughter. And Maloma is pregnant again. With only girls so far, I would like to see a son before I die."

Tristan frowned as they left the tavern, reminded of the tormented and sleepless nights he had spent this last month, thinking of Bettina and the baby growing within her.

Chapter 31

The house was pleasantly cool throughout the morning, and only the persistent beating of the afternoon sun warmed the thick white stone walls. Bettina walked slowly down the stairs one afternoon, a month and a half after Tristan left, wearing a comfortable, sleeveless dress of yellow cotton and carrying a large towel over one arm.

In France, Bettina had worn only the most fashionable clothes, though she detested doing so. She thought clothes should be becoming but also comfortable to wear, but André had never allowed her to dress in such simple garments. But on this tropical island, Bettina gave up the two petticoats and the extra bodice and skirt that were always revealed under the outer dress. She simply connected the skirt and bodice of her dresses, instead of leaving them slashed in front. One shift sufficed for modesty, and she could do without the large lace collars and the slashed and puffed sleeves.

She had even decided in the beginning not to bunch up her skirts for the extra width it added to her hips. Let Tristan stare at her slim hips long enough, and they might turn to a more rounded shape. That had been her hope, but Tristan didn't seem to mind that she wasn't well rounded.

Bettina surveyed the large dining hall with a smile. The brightly colored tapestry that Joco had produced from the cellar now hung over the fireplace, and she had made white curtains for the few windows. The windows were too small and too high to allow much light into the room, and she decided that they needed enlarging, but she would have to wait and discuss that with Tristan. Five thickly stuffed chairs in light colors had been added about the room, and Joco was presently out back building a sofa.

203

Luckily, Tristan had never disposed of the booty from the last captured Spanish ship, and Joco had been able to find furniture and materials to improve every room in the house.

The booty was kept in the cellar, and none of the women were allowed to go down, but had to summon one of the men if they needed something. Bettina only noticed after Tristan left that the room was kept locked at all times. Joco assured her that nothing mysterious was in the cellar; just captured goods, odds and ends, and a supply of food. But Bettina thought it strange that Tristan had been able to produce a pair of shoes for her that just happened to be her size, and a pair for her mother.

Bettina had spent the morning in her room with Maloma. They had become friends, and since Maloma was also pregnant, they had much in common. They were making little quilts for the infants, but although Bettina enjoyed the entire morning spent sewing and idly chatting, she still couldn't keep Tristan completely from her thoughts.

A month ago, Maloma began to swell with the child she carried. She would give birth only two weeks before Bettina, but Bettina's figure remained as slim as ever.

Bettina didn't doubt that she was pregnant, but she had hoped she would lose her trim shape quickly. She wanted to be enormously big before Tristan returned to the island, so that he would have to look elsewhere to satisfy his lust.

Tristan had left angrily, taking only half the men with him. He hadn't even told Bettina goodbye, but had left the same day they argued so fiercely. But she didn't miss him, she told herself continually. She didn't know when he would return, but she hoped it wouldn't be for a long, long time — in fact, never.

Bettina went by the kitchen area and lingered there a moment, smelling the aroma of fresh bread baking. Then she left through the back door and stepped her way around the lumber in the yard. She stopped by a stocky young man with curly blond hair who was hammering away at the frame of the new sofa. She smiled approvingly at Joco when he looked up at her.

"You have a talent for carpentry, Joco," Bettina said, surveying his work. "Has this ever been your trade?"

"I'm ship's carpenter, *mam'selle*. I like to work with wood."

"How long have you been with *Capitaine* Tristan?"

"Ever since he bought the *Spirited Lady*. Never saw no reason to want to sail on any other ship. The cap'n treats his crew squarely. But now that I've got a wife and two children, I've been thinkin' of givin' up the sea."

"So you intend to settle down?" Bettina asked. So there were honorable men among Tristan's crew, she thought.

"I'll be givin' up the sea, all right, now that my two sons are old enough to need a father. I was gonna ask Cap'n Tristan if I could settle here. I've got a little hut on the north shore that I can improve, and this island is just right for raisin' a family."

"I suppose it is," Bettina said, glancing about at all the tropical beauty surrounding her. "Well, good day, Joco."

Bettina left him and walked across the back lawn to the forest. She was going to a secret place she had found one day when she went exploring by herself. She went there often, for in that secluded area, Bettina could make believe that this island was her home, that the past months were only a dream, and that she had never met a man called Tristan. But no matter how hard she tried to concentrate on pleasant things, Tristan always found his way into her thoughts.

It was spring, and the island was twice as beautiful as when Bettina had first come. The sky was clear, leaving the blazing sun no place to hide, and the towering mountain stood alone, without the swirling mist that usually clung to it.

Bettina saw Thomas Wesley weeding a bed of flaming poinsettias that he had planted around the tree he called shower of gold. The tree had bloomed recently in a burst of bright yellow buds and petals. Bettina had wondered at the immaculate lawns and flower beds, but she met Thomas Wesley after Tristan gave her the freedom of the island, and she learned that he was responsible for the beautiful gardens.

Bettina waved to Thomas before she entered the forest and started down the path. For most of his life, Thomas Wesley had been head gardener on some great estate in England, but he had always wanted to be a sailor and visit other lands. He had come to the New World on a merchant vessel, but then he had met Tristan and signed on the *Spirited Lady*. When they found this island with its lush jungle five years before, he had just had to stay. Tristan had agreed, and in five years, Thomas had turned the grounds surrounding the house into gardens worthy of a palace. He was happy here — you could see it in his face — and Bettina enjoyed talking to him.

Soon Bettina left the path and had to work her way around vine-covered trees and heavy undergrowth. It wasn't as difficult as the first time, for her visits were creating an obvious trail.

She continued toward the mountain and the center of the island. The mountain had been her destination the day she had first decided to explore. She had planned to climb the foothills until she could stand in the midst of the swirling gray clouds. She wanted to lose herself in that primitive splendor, wanted a single sunray to break through the clouds and touch her as it had the heart of the mountain her first day on the island. But she never fulfilled that desire, for she had found another island wonder that day.

Bettina passed palm trees of all heights and varieties, standing side by side with tall pines, their scent filling the air. Coconuts lay on the ground, and magnificent flowers were everywhere — blue, lilac, yellow, and pink.

Soon Bettina could hear the trickling of running water — a stream running down from the mountain. A few steps more and she finally reached her little paradise — a hidden pool formed by the stream. There were new hibiscus blooms on the opposite bank, large flowers the size of her outstretched hand. They were brilliant reds and yellows, and a lone white one that she knew she would be tempted to pick before she returned to the house.

Bettina walked into the blazing sunlight that half-covered the grassy left bank of the stream. She dropped the towel that she had brought, and began to undress. To her left, silvery carpeted steps seemed to climb up to the mountain itself, and a miniature waterfall fell down them to fill a shallow, rounded pool with crystal-clear water. The pool was surrounded by tall trees, thick ferns, and flowers, and heavy branches fell over the stream on both ends, nearly touching the water. Bettina was hidden as if in a small room.

As she stepped into the cool water, Bettina wondered fleetingly if she would be able to keep her paradise a secret from Tristan when he returned. Then she chided herself. Why couldn't she stop thinking about that man, even for a little while?

Chapter 32

"Are you here with me, Tristan, or is your mind back on the island again?" Jules asked.

"Did you say something?" Tristan looked up, his blue eyes dreamy. Then they darkened with disgust as he glanced about the crowded, smoke-filled room. The stink of unwashed bodies assailed his nostrils. "Tortuga is the Devil's own breeding ground," he said distastefully. "Why the hell couldn't Bastida be here with the rest of the cutthroats and murderers?"

"You used to like to come here and raise a little hell yourself, as I remember," Jules reminded him. "At least here you know what you're up against."

"Got your courage back, eh?"

"I prefer this hellhole any day, to walking into the hands of your enemies."

"I'm sorry I put you through that scare back on Saint Martin," Tristan said soberly.

"You would have swung for it, not me. Three ports since Saint Martin, and we still haven't learned anything about Bastida's whereabouts. When will you give up the search, Tristan?"

"When I find him," Tristan replied, finishing off his second tankard of rum.

"You know, the men spoke to me before we entered the harbor. They're anxious to return home."

"Why? Haven't I given them leave in every port? They've had plenty of women."

"They want to return home with a priest."

"A what?" Tristan asked disbelievingly.

Jules laughed. "It seems quite a few of our shipmates want to have a proper wedding."

"Bunch of fools! The old chief's blessing was good enough before. I suppose you are in accord with this?"

"As a matter of fact, yes. Madeleine has been after me for some time now," Jules answered, humor in his voice. "She swears I'm living in sin with Maloma."

"So this is her idea — I should have known. Where are you going to find a priest, anyway? And if you do find one, why would he want to come with us?" Tristan asked.

"Who is to say he wouldn't? Once he hears how many men and women are presently living in sin on our island, the good fellow might even elect to stay."

"Well, if you and the men are lucky enough to find a willing priest, I won't deny your wishes. But I still think it is ridiculous."

Jules looked thoughtful for a moment. "Will you be paying a visit to the widow while we're here?"

"I hadn't considered it," Tristan answered. The lovely widow Hagen hadn't even entered his mind, though she lived only a few blocks from this very tavern, and he always visited her when he came to Tortuga.

"What excuse have you for not finding a congenial bedmate for a night or two?" Jules asked with an innocent expression.

"Do I need an excuse?" Tristan raised a brow.

"It's not like you to pass up bedding a wench."

"I have had other things on my mind. Must I remind you that this is not a voyage for profit or pleasure?" Tristan asked irritably.

"No, but without the widow's help, you wouldn't have bought a ship to search for Bastida. And she has probably been informed that the *Spirited Lady* is in the harbor. She will be disappointed if you don't visit her."

"If you are trying to make me feel guilty, old friend, it won't work. I've paid my debt to the widow."

"You were grateful enough when she sold you the *Spirited Lady* for such a paltry sum."

"That was six years ago, and you forget that Margaret Haven is a very wealthy woman," said Tristan. "Her husband left her half a dozen ships when he died. She was more than willing to let the *Spirited Lady* go for the small sum I had."

"It was *you* she wanted."

"You flatter me, Jules. The lady has had countless lovers since I first met her. She just likes men. Besides, the widow would demand too much time. We won't be here that long."

"You could make the time," Jules replied lightly.

"I could, but I don't intend to."

"What is the matter with you, Tristan?" Jules said. "You know the widow knows every ship that comes into the harbor. She also knows you search for Bastida. One visit to her would be worth hours of combing the docks for information."

"Why are you so intent on my seeing the widow?" Tristan asked in exasperation.

"We have been searching for Bastida for over two months, and yet it is Bettina Verlaine who occupies your thoughts. I had hoped the widow could make you forget her for a while," Jules answered.

Jules was right. Bettina and her child had plagued Tristan day and night these past months. He doubted the widow could make him forget about Bettina, but she might tell him something of Bastida.

Tristan sighed heavily. "Very well. I will meet you back on the ship in a few hours."

"Take your time, my friend. There is no hurry," Jules replied jovially.

Tristan smiled and shook his head. He left the smoke-filled tavern and stepped into the blinding sunlight; then he sighed again. He had no real desire to see the widow, though he had always been anxious to visit her before. She was a beautiful woman, only three years older than he, and passionate beyond belief.

Tristan passed a small jeweler's shop and decided to go in. A pearl necklace might pacify the widow's temper when he informed her that he wouldn't be staying the night with her. But then — Blast it, why shouldn't he stay the night with her? One day wasted wouldn't matter, and it would be nice to make love to a woman who didn't constantly scream her hatred, who opened her arms and her legs gladly.

Tristan started to leave the jeweler's, for there was no need to purchase a gift for Margaret now, but then a pair of earrings caught his eye. They were sapphires, tiny gems mounted in rings of silver, and suspended in the center of the rings were large dark-blue sapphires that reminded Tristan of Bettina's eyes when she was happy. He would like to see her eyes that color all the time, and in his mind he could picture the sapphires dangling from Bettina's ears, contrasting beautifully with her silky flaxen hair, and matching her dark-blue eyes.

He purchased the earrings, and also a long strand of pearls — just in case.

Margaret Hagen saw Tristan come up the stone walkway leading to her three-story house. Before he had a chance to knock on the door, it opened, and he was met by a pair of angry dark-violet eyes. But the anger disappeared quickly, and Margaret threw her arms around Tristan's neck and kissed him intensely, molding her soft body against his.

"Ah, Tristan, I've missed you so," she whispered against his ear. Then she pulled him into her house and quickly shut the door. "I was so angry when you didn't come this morning," she scolded. "But now that you're here, I can't stay mad at you."

She took his hand and started to lead him upstairs, but he pulled her into the parlor instead. "You haven't changed, Margaret," he laughed softly.

"But *you* have — in more ways than one. You used to carry me up those stairs to my bed before I could even greet you. Have you been with another woman this morning? Is that what kept you?" she asked heatedly.

"No, I stopped to purchase a gift for you," he said lightly, and produced the pearls from the pocket of his longcoat.

She beamed with delight, and she turned and lifted her black shoulder-length hair so he could fasten the pearls around her neck. She faced him again and smiled as she fingered the pearls lovingly.

"I know these didn't take you all morning to purchase, but I won't reproach you anymore." She took his hand and led him to a black-and-gold sofa. "Now tell me, why did you shave off your beautiful beard? Not that I mind, but you look so much younger without it."

211

"It was something I had to do. But since then I've gotten used to being without it."

"Why would you have to shave? That is ridiculous," she replied.

"It's a long story, Margaret, and I'm afraid I don't have the time to relate it," Tristan said. "I will be sailing in a few hours."

"But why?"

"You know that I can never rest until I find Bastida. And although preying on Spanish gold is very profitable, it keeps me too long at sea. If I am to find that murderer, I have to devote all my time to hunting him down, and that's what I've decided to do."

"Why don't you give it up, Tristan? You will probably never find Bastida."

"Our paths will cross one day, of that I am sure," Tristan said, his voice full of bitter hatred.

"Then I might as well tell you. Bastida was here about two months ago."

"Blast it!" Tristan exploded, slamming his hand down on his thigh. "Why didn't I come here first? That's twice now I could have found him, only my mind has been elsewhere!"

"I doubt you would have found him here, Tristan. He was here only a few hours. It seems he is also searching for someone or something."

"What can you tell me?"

"Not very much, I'm afraid. Bastida was asking about a merchant ship, and he stayed only until he was satisfied it wasn't in the harbor."

"Why a merchant ship?"

"I have no idea. But if he is searching each island as you are, with only a day's stop on each one, then the odds are greatly against your finding him until one of you happens on the same place," Margaret replied.

"Perhaps you are right."

"Then you will stay here for a while?" she asked hopefully, running her hand over his chest.

"No," he answered, and stood up quickly. "I must be leaving."

"There is another woman, isn't there?" she asked, making an effort to smile.

Tristan decided to tell her the truth. "Yes, I suppose you could say that."

"Is she pretty? Of course she would be," Margaret said. "When you said your mind has been elsewhere, you were referring to this woman. You must love her very much."

"I don't love her, but I want her. She has obsessed my mind," he replied irritably.

"And how does she feel about you?"

Tristan laughed shortly. "She detests my very soul, and yet I can't blame her. Perhaps it is because she hates me that I still want her. She is a challenge."

"I find it hard to believe that any woman could hate you, Tristan." She stood up and kissed him lightly on the cheek. "But if you're sure you don't love her, I can wait until you get her out of your blood."

"Well, don't give up your countless lovers while you're waiting," he teased.

"You know I could never do that," she laughed. "Unless, of course, you were willing to marry me. I could give up any man if I had you, Tristan. You would surely be worth the loss."

Tristan left the widow's house in a carefree mood. He had intended to stay the night with Margaret, but somehow he just couldn't. The old desire for her was gone. He didn't know what was the matter with him, but he didn't want to worry about it at present.

There was no point in continuing to search for Bastida now. He would wait awhile until Bastida found whoever it was *he* was searching for and returned to Spain. But for now — now Tristan would go home.

Chapter 33

After a long two and a half months of absence, Tristan could hardly contain his excitement when his island was sighted. He had been a fool to leave Bettina just when he had learned she was carrying his child. He had missed her so. She would be four and a half months' pregnant now, but he prayed she wouldn't be too big to make love to.

Tristan paced nervously across the foredeck until his ship sailed into the small cove and the anchor was dropped. Then in a loud, booming voice, he informed the crew that they could take their leave immediately. He would order the men who had stayed on the island to come and secure the ship. If the men on board were as anxious to see their women as he was to see Bettina, he might have had a mutiny if he had delayed them on the ship.

Father Hadrian stood by idly, watching the men hastily lowering the small boats. He wondered if he should speak to the captain about keeping these men from their so-called wives until after the marriage ceremonies. But seeing the happy anticipation on the faces of the crew, he doubted they would listen to reason.

No, he would just have to close his eyes and pray that the ceremonies took place quickly. Besides, Captain Tristan would offer no help. The priest had been told about the Frenchwoman the captain was keeping on the island, and the young man had made it quite clear to Father Hadrian that he would tolerate no moralizing about his way of life. He thought it absurd that some of his men wanted to marry when they didn't have to, and he had no intention of marrying his lady.

In less than twenty minutes, the boats were ashore, and after another ten minutes of half-walking, half-running, Tristan stood just inside the doorway of his house, completely amazed at the changes.

"It looks as if the women kept busy while we were gone," Jules said when he came up beside Tristan. "I must say it is a definite improvement. They've turned this old fortress into a home. And look, they've even hung curtains!"

Tristan glanced at the white curtains and smiled. At least Bettina hadn't made a wedding dress with the material, as she had wanted.

Tristan laughed as his crew made a terrible racket running past the house on the way to their homes. The shouting and laughter brought Maloma to the top of the stairs, and Tristan stared openmouthed when he saw how big she had grown. They had never stayed home long enough before to see the women grow with child, and he prayed again that Bettina wasn't that big yet. But he wondered why she didn't appear.

"I will see you later, Tristan — much later," Jules said over his shoulder as he started for the stairs.

Tristan smiled as he watched Jules join his wife. Davey volunteered to take Father Hadrian to the village, where he had asked to stay, and Tristan was relieved that the good father would not be sleeping in the room next to his.

Tristan started to walk toward the stairs, then began to run.

"*Capitaine,* she is not in your room."

Tristan halted abruptly and swung around to see Jossel standing in the doorway to the kitchen. He walked to her, scowling, imagining the worst of possibilities.

"Where is she?" he demanded brusquely.

"There is no reason for you to be upset. Bettina went for a walk — as she does every afternoon," Jossel said calmly.

"Where?"

"I have no idea in which direction she goes. She always walks alone."

"It's good to see you back, Cap'n," Joco Martel said when he came from the back of the house. "Was your voyage successful?"

"No, but I left you in charge here, Joco, and I'll have your

215

hide if you can't tell me where Bettina is right now!" Tristan bellowed.

"She's in the forest, Cap'n," Joco replied weakly. "She always goes the same way, leavin' the path where it turns toward the village."

"Straight or to the right?"

"Straight."

"And now tell me why in blazes you've let her go into the forest alone?"

"You trusted 'er before you left, Cap'n, and she 'ad a fit when I tol' 'er she should 'ave someone with 'er. She insisted on goin' alone, and I didn't really see no 'arm in it," Joco answered nervously.

"Blast it! That woman has no right to insist upon anything. I gave you instructions when I left. You were to carry out *my* orders, not hers!" Tristan stormed.

"My daughter is no longer a child, *Capitaine*. She can take care of herself. And she has always cherished her privacy. In France, she always took walks through the countryside alone," Jossel said.

"This is not France, *madame!* There are wild pigs living at the foot of the mountain. If Bettina walked too far, she could be attacked and killed!"

"Killed!" Jossel turned pale.

"She was never gone long enough to reach the mountain, or I would 'ave gone after 'er," Joco said quickly.

"How long has she been gone?"

"Only an hour," Joco replied.

Tristan said no more, but left the house by the back door. Running, it took him only a few minutes to reach the bend in the path. As he left the path and followed the trail of trampled grass that led toward the mountain, he wondered if Bettina had found the same shallow pool that he used to come to. If that was where she went on her walks, he could understand her wish for privacy.

When Tristan saw that the trail indeed led to the stream, he slowed his pace and decided to surprise Bettina. But when he came to the trees bordering the stream, he was the one who was surprised. Bettina was lying on the soft grass beside the pool, completely at ease, and completely naked.

The blood rushed through his veins as Tristan's eyes covered her entirely. Her whole body was a golden tan. She lay on her back with the sun caressing her, one leg raised, her hands clasped behind her head, and her damp hair spread on the grass above her. Tristan stared for long moments at her slightly protruding belly and the plaguing doubts surfaced again. A child slept there, but whose child? But Tristan pushed the thoughts of the child from his mind, for the throbbing in his loins was the only thing that mattered now.

"Tristan!" Bettina gasped when she opened her eyes to find him standing above her.

She stared at him for what seemed like an eternity, unable to say anything. She felt desire rise in her, almost like an ache. He stood, legs astride, with his hands on his hips. The sun lit the edges of his hair to liquid gold, and she wanted to run her hands through it, to touch his bronzed cheeks, to taste his lips on hers.

Bettina watched with anticipation as Tristan removed his shirt, then his knee-length boots and breeches. But when he was naked, and she saw the look of triumph on his face as he bent down to her, she finally broke out of her trance. She quickly rolled out of his reach and grabbed her dress to hide her nakedness, then scrambled to her feet, holding the dress in front of her.

Tristan laughed heartily. "It took you long enough to remember that you hate me. But then, you don't really hate me, do you, Bettina? Why don't you give in to what you were feeling a moment ago?"

Oh, God, why had she stared at him so long? He must have seen the desire in her eyes.

"I don't know what you are talking about!" she retorted. Her cheeks were bright pink, but she was in control now.

"Yes, you do, little one," he said huskily and started to approach her.

"Tristan, stop!" she screamed, backing away from him. "Come no closer to me!"

"I'm going to make love to you, Bettina, and you know it.

217

You want it. So why don't you give up this pretense?" he asked softly.

"You are mad!" she cried fearfully. "If I wanted you to touch me, would I ask you to stay away? I still hate you, Tristan — have no doubts about that."

"You're lying, Bettina, especially to yourself," Tristan said quietly. He leaped forward and grabbed her about the waist.

"Tristan, please!" she begged as he pulled her to the shade and lowered her to the ground. "If you make me fight you, it will harm the baby!"

He mounted her despite her pleading, and held her arms stretched out at her sides as he leaned over her. "You're not going to fight me, little one. I have thought of this moment every day I was away from you, and you know there is nothing that will stop me from having you now." He released her arms and leaned on his elbows, careful not to press his full weight on her. He held her face with his hands and kissed her softly, then smiled lazily at her. "You will have to give up your resistance for a while, for the baby's sake. The child will give you an excuse not to fight me, so relax and enjoy it while you can."

"But I do not want an excuse! Why don't *you* take the excuse and find another to force yourself upon?" Bettina asked heatedly.

"It's you I want — and it's you I'll have. You don't want to fight me, Bettina. It's only your pride that makes you continue to do so."

"That is not so!" she cried indignantly.

"Why must you be so stubborn?" he asked in exasperation. "You have a reason now to give up — without losing your pride. For God's sake, I won't taunt you for it!"

"No!"

Tristan kissed her passionately then, stopping her mouth. He entered her, burying himself deep inside her. He felt her nails begin to dig into his back, and he tensed, waiting for pain. But then she ran her fingers through his hair and caressed his back. The fires that were always between them grew, and as the pleasure exploded inside Tristan, she kissed him intensely, sending him to heights that he could reach only with this woman.

When Tristan rolled to her side and lay on the grass beside

her, Bettina sat up and clasped her knees, her hair covering her body like a white silk cape. She stared moodily at the little waterfall.

"I've missed you, Bettina," Tristan said softly from behind her. He moved her hair aside and caressed her back. "I've thought about you constantly — every day, and especially at night, when I would lay in my cabin remembering how we shared it."

"I am sure when you went ashore you found suitable companions to relieve your misery," she replied sarcastically.

"You sound jealous, little one," Tristan laughed.

"That is absurd!" she bit off angrily, turning toward him. "I have told you time and again to find another."

"That's easy enough to say, even when you don't mean it. Consider your true feelings, Bettina. You've missed me, too, haven't you?"

"Of course not. How could I miss you when I prayed that you would never return. And why did you return so soon? Did you find Don Miguel?"

"No, I've decided to wait some time before I continue the search."

"How much time?" she asked.

"These last months that I've been away from you have seemed like an eternity. I've decided to stay here until the year you promised me comes to an end."

"But — but you cannot!" she cried. "When I gave you my word that I would stay here for a year, it was only because you said you wouldn't be here the whole time."

"And I haven't been. You already had two and a half months alone, and that is enough."

"Then I suppose I must be thankful that I am with child, because it will free me from your advances when my time grows near. Then you will *have* to find another," she replied tartly, standing up to dress.

Tristan frowned at her words as he reached for his own garments. What if the child were born with black hair? Worse, what if the child were graced with Bettina's white-blond hair and dark eyes? Then he would never know the truth.

"You look troubled, *Capitaine,*" Bettina teased him as she

bent to pick a bouquet of violet flowers. "Are you finding it difficult to decide who will replace me?"

He stared at her for a long moment, his eyes falling to her waist. Now that she was dressed, her shape looked the same as when he left her.

"I saw Maloma at the house," Tristan remarked, ignoring her question. "She has grown quite large already, and yet you have changed very little. Are you sure that it's four and a half months that you've carried the child?"

Bettina laughed gaily, her eyes sparkling blue. "You would like to believe that, wouldn't you? Then you would have no doubt that the child is yours. Well, I am sorry to disappoint you, Tristan, but my calculations are correct. Now, if you do not mind, I am going to return to the house."

He grabbed her arms as she started to pass him, making her drop the flowers she held. "But you say the child is mine?" he demanded.

"I have told you it is."

"You said you lied about de Lambert, but in truth you could be lying now."

"Believe what you like, Tristan. I told you before that it doesn't matter."

"But it does matter!" His voice rose to a high pitch, and his hands tightened on her arms. "For the love of God, Bettina! I can't stand this doubt anymore. Swear to me that the child is mine!"

There was pain mixed with rage in his eyes, and Bettina felt a strong desire to see the relief on his face that only she could give. But then she remembered why she had planted the doubt in his mind to begin with. She had hoped to make him suffer, and he was suffering. She would not remove the doubt and give him peace of mind. This was a satisfactory revenge for all the misery he had caused her.

"Every time I gave you my word, Tristan, it was because you left me no choice to do otherwise. But I have a choice now, and I choose not to give you my word on this. I told you the child is yours — that is enough."

"Damn you, woman!" he stormed, his eyes turning to icy

crystals. "If you won't swear to it, it is because you can't do so! The child must be de Lambert's!"

"Believe what you like," Bettina whispered. Her heart beat so loudly she felt sure he would hear it.

Tristan lifted his hand to strike her, but then he shoved her away from him.

"Get back to the house!" he commanded in a cold, threatening voice, and then turned his back on her.

Bettina walked past him without a word, and hurried along the trail. After a little way, she looked back to see if he followed, but the trail was empty behind her. She smiled triumphantly to herself. She had weathered the worst of the storm, and the rest would be quite enjoyable. He would be angry and frustrated, perhaps so much that he wouldn't want to share a room with her — she hoped. She could feel her freedom drawing nearer.

Joco Martel was waiting anxiously just outside the back door. "Did you see the cap'n? Is — is 'e still angry 'cause I let you go into the forest alone?" he asked quickly.

"Why should he be angry over that?"

" 'E feared you might go too close to the mountain, 'cause there's wild pigs up there," Joco replied.

"Da captin so upset, he make others same," Maloma laughed. "You mama been walking floor with worry since he go find you."

"This is ridiculous. I was perfectly all right — until Tristan found me," Bettina said irritably.

Maloma laughed again. "You better tell you mama dis. She in big hall with Maddy and my Jules."

"I will. And don't worry, Joco. I doubt the *capitaine* will speak to you about this. When he returns, he probably *will* be angry, but for something else entirely."

When Bettina entered the dining hall, she saw that her mother was indeed pacing the floor in front of the fireplace. Madeleine was on the new sofa with Jules, berating him for letting Tristan go after Bettina in such an angry mood.

"Bettina!" Jossel cried when she saw her. "Thank God, you are all right. If I had known there are wild animals on this island, I would never have let you go out alone."

"I have never gone near the mountain, mama, so there was

no need to fear. I always went to a little pool I found in one of the streams, but I will go there no longer." Not after what just happened there, she added to herself regretfully. It used to be a beautiful spot where she could find peace and forget about Tristan.

"Where is Tristan?" Jules asked casually.

"He stayed behind — to calm down, I hope."

"So you had a fight about the child, eh?" Jules ventured, a knowing gleam in his brown eyes.

"How did — What makes you think that?" Bettina asked.

"I knew it would happen, though I thought he'd wait until after he —"

"Jules!" Madeleine cried. "You will not speak so!"

Jules stared at Madeleine and Bettina and Jossel tried hard to suppress their laughter. Jules was not accustomed to taking orders from a woman, even one who reminded him of his mother.

"I — ah — think I will go up to my room and rest for a while," Jossel said quickly. "I will join you later for dinner," she added, and left.

Bettina smiled. "Now that Mama has gone upstairs, you may continue what you were going to say, *monsieur.* And you keep quiet, Maddy."

"It — it escapes me now," Jules said uncomfortably, and stood up. "And I have things to do, so —"

"Come now," Bettina interrupted him. "Let us finish our conversation. You were going to say you thought Tristan would wait until he had bedded me."

"Bettina!" Madeleine exclaimed.

"Oh, hush, Maddy. I know such things are not talked about, but we are not exactly in a drawing room in France." Bettina turned back to Jules. "You were right, *monsieur,* but how did you know we would argue?"

"Tristan has been tormented these last months. The young fool fears he may not be the father of the babe, and this greatly troubles him. I suspected he would have it out with you when he returned." Jules paused and looked rather embarrassed. "He — ah — he *is* the father, isn't he?"

Bettina laughed softly. "Of course he is. I told him so, but

222

I am afraid he chose not to believe me."

Just then, they heard Tristan's angry voice, and a moment later he threw the door open, slamming it back against the wall, the loud crash echoing in the hall. He stopped and scowled when he saw them by the fireplace; then he walked to the table and sat down heavily in a chair with his back to them.

Bettina decided not to antagonize him any further with her presence, and she quietly mounted the stairs, hoping he wouldn't notice her depart. A frightened Madeleine followed behind Bettina. Jules, however, sank into a chair beside his friend.

"Bettina tells me that you don't believe the child is yours," Jules ventured.

Bettina heard Jules, and she stopped at the top of the stairs to listen, hidden by the wall of the corridor. When Madeleine reached the corridor, she was surprised to find Bettina standing there, but when her young ward motioned her to silence, she, too, stayed to listen to the conversation in the hall.

"I know the child isn't mine!" Tristan growled, his face a mask of bitter frustration.

"You're being unreasonable, Tristan."

"The hell I am! That woman lies to suit her purpose, as I do. But when she gives her word, I know it's true, and she won't give it on this matter."

"You have insulted her by even asking for her word!" Jules exclaimed.

"Ha! I will do more to that woman than insult her! I wanted to beat the truth out of her today, and I've still a mind to do so."

"I can't let you do that, Tristan," Jules said calmly.

"You can't?" Tristan fell back in his chair, astonished. "Since when do you defend that vixen? You have told me time and again that she needs a beating."

"When she deserved it, yes, but she doesn't deserve a beating now. And even if she did, I would have to stop you because of her condition. You could harm the child — *your* child — and I can't let you do that."

"I tell you it's not mine! I know Bettina is lying, only I don't know why. When the child is born, you will see the truth of my words. And perhaps then I will discover Bettina's game."

"Perhaps then you will see what a blasted fool you have been!" Jules said harshly.

Later, when Bettina came down for dinner, she passed Jules on the stairs. She stopped the big man and kissed him lightly on the cheek to thank him for defending her. Jules blushed considerably, the bright red showing through his bronzed tan, and Bettina continued down the stairs, leaving him shaking his head in bewilderment.

Tristan sat darkly by himself at the head of the table. He had not seen her kiss Jules, and he glowered at her as she sat down beside him in her usual place. He said nothing as she quickly filled her plate. She had half-expected him to fight with her again, and so she was relieved by his silence.

Tristan didn't touch his food, but drank an enormous amount of rum, though, surprisingly, he seemed to stay quite sober. After the others joined them, the meal progressed in unnerving silence, and Bettina ate hastily so she could retreat back to her room.

After several useless hours spent trying to fall asleep, Bettina heard footsteps in the corridor just outside her door. She had been sure that Tristan wouldn't want to share his bed with her that night, but as the minutes passed, she began to feel uneasy, wondering why he was still standing outside the door.

Then the door burst open forcefully, crashing against the wall, and Bettina sat up quickly. When she saw Tristan's expression, she knew that he had slammed the door on purpose, to make sure she was awake. He closed the door quietly and stared at her coldly for some moments before slowly approaching the bed. He leaned against the bedpost and continued to stare at her.

Angry and embarrassed, she started to speak, but he halted her with his own deep voice.

"You will remove your shift now, Bettina. Despite everything that has been said and done today, I'm going to make love to you." He spoke calmly, but his eyes were a hard, icy blue.

Bettina couldn't believe what she heard. He was filled with

224

rage, and yet he still wanted her. Or did he just want to punish her?

She started to protest, but he stopped her before she could say a word, his voice menacing.

"That was not a request, Bettina, but an order. Remove your shift!"

Bettina shivered, though the room was quite warm. Tristan had told Jules that he wanted to beat the truth out of her, and she realized with sickening dread that neither Jules nor anyone else could protect her now.

Bettina slipped out of her shirt, then pulled the covers up to hide her nakedness. She could stand anything, but she had to think of her baby and protect it from harm if she could.

Though she had done what he demanded, there was no triumph on his face. His expression remained cold, even when he yanked the covers away from her and began to remove his own clothing with deliberate slowness.

"I want you to understand that I will no longer tolerate your feigned resistance, Bettina," he said harshly. "I have treated you with care because you are so lovely and I didn't want to mar your beauty. I have been too lenient with you, and that has been my mistake."

He lay down on the bed and pulled her to him, daring her to resist him. His voice was a deadly whisper as he continued. "You are my possession. I should have lashed your back the first time you showed your hellish temper. I should have chained you to my bed so you could not escape me. But most of all, I should never have laid eyes on you. Then I wouldn't have this pain that eats at me. And God help me, even though I know you carry de Lambert's bastard, I can't stop wanting you."

His lips came down on hers, hurting her with savage pressure. She knew that Tristan was torn. He hated her, hated her for many reasons, but inevitably, his need for her won out over the hatred. And after a few moments, Bettina was also lost in his desire.

Chapter 34

Summer came, bringing with it a glorious new burst of color. Beautiful flowers that Bettina had never seen before bloomed everywhere. She was introduced to delicious new fruits and couldn't eat enough. Her favorite was the large red-yellow mango, twice the size of her fist, and Thomas Wesley made a special trip from the village, where he lived, to bring her two of these tantalizing fruits each day.

The days were hot, but made comfortable by the constant trade winds, and the nights were pleasantly cool, making the island a paradise in which to live. But the paradise was shattered by turmoil within the house. Tristan's black mood had only worsened in the month since he had returned to the island. Bettina avoided him as much as possible, for whenever he saw her growing shape, his anger flared anew.

Bettina had never returned to her little pool in the forest. She imagined it would be even more beautiful with new summer flowers everywhere, but she told herself stubbornly that Tristan had ruined her enjoyment of the secret place. Instead, she went often with her mother and sometimes Maloma down to the small cove where the ship lay at anchor. There she took off her shoes, raised her skirt, and walked along the beach in the cool, wet sand, letting the small waves lap at her legs.

Bettina found contentment walking with her mother. They talked of pleasant things or just walked silently, each lost in her own thoughts. When Madeleine joined them, they talked of France and the friends left behind, but mostly they spoke of the big celebration, held three weeks before, to honor the nine couples united in marriage by the priest.

The party had been a grand one, and was not spoiled in the

least by Tristan's sour mood. Despite his opposition to the marriages, he allowed the dining hall to be used for the occasion. There was music and dancing. A feast was served that took all day to prepare and was entirely consumed as the night wore on. Most of the Indian villagers came, bringing with them a huge roasted pig, and they danced, too — wild, beautiful dances of their own culture.

Bettina found it easy to lose herself in the happiness of the young native girls who were now married in the church. But Jossel was depressed every time marriage was mentioned. Bettina knew her mother wanted her to find such happiness also. But Bettina didn't see how that would be possible until she had left the island.

One morning, Bettina stayed alone in her room to put the last trims on a baby's pink dress that she had started a few days before. She was surprised when Tristan walked in through the open door, for he very seldom came to his room in the morning. He crossed to the bed where she was working, and saw the little dress.

"So you hope for a daughter," he said sardonically, leaning against the bedpost. "I can see how this would amuse you if the child were mine, but what excuse have you to wish a daughter on your beloved *comte?* Every man wants a son, and I'm sure that whorechaser is no different."

Bettina ignored him, for she knew he wanted a fight. When he failed to gain a response from her, Tristan moved to the chair by the window and began to polish his sword. They ignored one another, though they were totally aware of each other's presence. After a while, it became a contest to see who would speak first or leave the room in irritation. But then an angry, flushed Jossel came into the room, and she drew both Bettina's and Tristan's attention.

"Honestly!" Jossel exclaimed in French. "What is the matter with him?" She nodded at Tristan.

"Why not ask him?" Bettina said quietly.

"He would not tell me, but *you* can. I have tried not to interfere, but your quarrel has gone on too long."

227

"Mama, can't this wait until we are alone?"

"No. He does not understand our language, and I wish to speak of this now. I was just told that he made the servant girl, Kaino, run from the house in tears this morning. She brought him his food, and it was not hot enough to suit him! She refuses to return. She is scared out of her wits that he will find fault with her again!"

"He only voices threats, Mama. He will not see them through," Bettina replied.

"The servants do not know this. With his blustering and raving, they fear to go near him."

"I will talk to the girls. I will explain that he is only finding a release for his anger, that he will not do them harm," Bettina replied.

"But Madeleine tells me that you could put an end to Tristan's evil mood."

"Do not say his name, Mama! He will know we are talking about him," Bettina gasped.

She looked at Tristan, but he was preoccupied with cleaning his sword and seemed to be paying no attention to them. She frowned slightly, wondering why Tristan had let her converse so long in French, when he had always stopped her before. But then, as if he had somehow seen into her mind, he stood up scowling, and stalked from the room, mumbling angrily about women and their blasted secrets.

Jossel was too upset to notice Tristan's abrupt departure. "Can you put an end to the way Tristan has been acting?" she asked her daughter.

"I probably can," Bettina whispered.

"Then for God's sake, why do you hesitate?"

"You do not understand, Mama."

"Then explain it to me!" Jossel said in exasperation. "Why has Tristan been such a monster since he returned a month ago?"

Bettina sighed and stared at the door Tristan had left open.

"Tristan thinks the baby I carry is Pierre's."

"Madeleine said this was the problem, but I could not believe her," Jossel said heatedly. "The notion is ridiculous. You were at Pierre's house for less than a full day. Tristan must be mad to think you would be intimate with Pierre before you were married!"

"I gave him reason to think I was."

"But why?"

"I was furious when he stole me back. And then he humiliated me more than I could stand, to punish me for running away from him. I had to get even with him. So I lied to him and said I slept willingly with Pierre.

"Tristan became so enraged that he scared me, so I admitted I had lied. Only — only I did so in a way that left doubt in his mind. He forgot about it until I told him I was pregnant. Then he demanded to know whose child I carried. I told him truthfully that the child was his, only again I left doubt. When he asked me to swear that the child was his, I refused, and he assumed Pierre was the father."

"But why have you done this, Bettina? Why don't you tell him the truth?"

"I *have* told him the truth," Bettina replied.

"Then why have you purposely planted this doubt in his mind?" Jossel asked.

"You talked me out of seeking his death, so I chose a different revenge. And this revenge was sweet to begin with, only —"

"Only you are sorry now?" Jossel interrupted.

"Yes."

"Then tell Tristan what you have done."

Bettina avoided her mother's gaze. She stared sadly at the little dress in her hands. "It is too late to make matters right. I have thought about it often. Even if I told him everything, he would not believe me. He would think I was lying just to pacify him. He would always doubt me even if I gave him my word."

"You don't hate Tristan anymore, do you?" Jossel asked softly.

"Oh, Mama, I just don't know. The desire I have for him confuses me. Sometimes I want him as much as he wants me. And yet at other times I still hate him. He is so arrogant, so infuriating, and I can never forget what he has done to me."

"He took you against your will, but now you admit you want him also."

"But that is not the point!"

229

"No? Then take my advice, my love, and consider what is the point. The year he asked for soon comes to an end." With that, Jossel walked out of the room, leaving Bettina staring blankly at the floor.

Chapter 35

Bettina spent the rest of the morning and most of the afternoon debating with herself. She even forgot to go downstairs for lunch. But she finally decided that she had nothing to lose by confessing everything to Tristan, and much to gain. She missed his lazy smile and the buoyant laugh that lit up his eyes. She missed his winsome charm, and especially his tenderness.

She wanted the old Tristan back. Now, she felt happy that she was going to bear his child, and, strangely enough, she wanted him to share her happiness. She didn't know why it was suddenly so important to her to have Tristan the way he used to be. But with a firm feeling that she could make him believe her, Bettina left the room she shared with Tristan to find him and make things right between them.

She ran down the stairs, and, seeing no one in the hall, she looked out the back door.

Tristan heard Bettina come down the stairs from where he lay on the sofa by the fireplace. He sat up and saw her walk toward the back door. He started to follow her, but was halted by a commotion in the front yard.

Bettina also heard the noise from the front of the house, but before she could go to investigate, she saw a rowdy bunch of men running across the backyard toward the village. She frowned, for the men were strangers. Then she heard a low-pitched female voice in the big hall.

"Tristan, you handsome seadog, I hardly recognized you! So you finally shaved your beard. I like it — I always knew I would."

"It's been a long time, Gabby," Tristan said affectionately.

Bettina turned, confused, and saw a woman with unruly bright copper curls falling halfway down her back. She was

231

dressed like a man, but her breeches were cut well above her knees, shamefully displaying long, shapely legs. She even sported a sword hanging from a leather baldric, and a long, coiled whip hung from her other hip. She stood proudly in the middle of the room, facing Tristan.

"Sweet Jesus! I can't believe what you've done to this old house. If I didn't know better, I'd think it had felt a woman's touch," the red-headed woman said. "You bastard! You haven't brought that widow here, have you? Damn you, if she's finally talked you into marrying her, I'll —"

"That's enough, Gabby." Tristan cut her off, seeing Bettina standing in the back doorway. "Margaret isn't here, nor has she ever been."

"Good. That's her loss and my gain," Gabby laughed. "I've been looking forward to spending some time alone with you here. I'm going to shut us up in that cozy bedroom of yours for days, and to hell with my crew!"

"You haven't changed," Tristan laughed. "You're as immoral as ever."

"You wouldn't have it any other way, would you, love? Now give me a proper greeting before I begin to think you've spent yourself on those village whores."

A knot twisted in Bettina's stomach, and she knew it wasn't her child kicking. The copper-haired woman threw her arms around Tristan's neck and pulled his lips down to hers. She kissed him passionately, and — damn his black heart — he was enjoying it, returning her kiss wholeheartedly.

When someone touched her arm, Bettina gasped and turned to see a rough-looking man with a shining bald head. He wore no shoes, and only a narrow vest partially covered his bare chest. Bettina instantly recognized the expression in his dark eyes.

"I knew I'd have a long wait in the village, so I come here for a bite o' food, an' look what I find instead." He spoke more to himself than to Bettina as his eyes covered her body. "Are there more like you around, or will I have to be sharin' you wit' me shipmates?"

Bettina wondered if Tristan would bother to rescue her this

time, or would he be too busy in the other room? She decided to try reason.

"*Monsieur,* I am pregnant! Surely you can see this?"

He drew her to him, a lecherous smile on his lips. "What I see is that you're a damn sight better than what I'd find in the village. It's been too long since I've had me a white woman."

"Leave me alone, *monsieur,* or I will scream!" Bettina said quickly, her voice rising to a high pitch.

"Now, you wouldn't want to go an' do that, or you might disturb me cap'n. She's all for watchin' a bit o' sport, but I'm thinkin' she's havin' her own by now."

Bettina shook off the man's hand and started backing away, but as the man slowly pursued her, Tristan happened to see him. The man lunged for Bettina and grabbed one arm to jerk her to him again. She cried out in a shrill voice, but Tristan was already there. He pulled the man away from Bettina, then stepped in front of her, blocking her view with his towering frame.

The red-headed woman had followed Tristan, her face a mask of fury. But before she could say anything, Tristan's huge fist had connected with the man's face, sending him sprawling to the floor and breaking his nose with the single blow. As the man brought his hand to his nose, blood poured through his fingers and down onto his bare chest. His eyes were filled with terror as he stared at Tristan.

"Damn you, Tristan!" the woman Gabby stormed. "You had no call to lay my man low! Have you gone —"

She stopped short when Bettina stepped from behind Tristan. The big room was filled with an ominous silence as the two women stared at each other for the first time, Bettina's turbulent green eyes meeting the steel-gray eyes of the other woman.

"Who is she?" Gabby demanded.

Tristan smiled and said, "The lady's name is Bettina."

Gabby became furious. "Blast it! I don't give a damn what her name is! What is she doing here? And if my man wanted to have her, why did you stop him?"

Tristan's eyes narrowed. "This could have been avoided, Gabby, if you had given me a chance to speak earlier. But now

233

I'll tell your man instead." He turned to the man, and his eyes were like glistening ice. "Since your face wears the proof of my words, the message will carry more weight coming from you. Bettina is not the only white woman on the island. There are two others — her mother and her old servant — and none of them is to be touched. But this one especially is in my care," he said, motioning to Bettina. "I will kill anyone who comes near her! Carry my warning to all your shipmates, and you damn well better make sure they heed what you say!"

The man scrambled to his feet and out the back door as quickly as he could.

"What do you mean she is in your care?" Gabby exploded, her body stiff with rage.

Bettina spoke before Tristan could answer, a half-smile on her soft lips. "Tristan was being kind in his choice of words, *mademoiselle*. He should have said I am his property."

"He married you?" Gabby asked in astonishment.

"No."

"So you are a slave, then!" Gabby laughed heartily. "I should have known."

"A slave with few duties, *mademoiselle*," Bettina smiled. "In fact, I serve Tristan only in bed."

Bettina walked out of the room without looking back to see Tristan's amused expression. She had gained very little by what she told that woman, except that Gabby was now furious at Tristan. But how long would that last? How long before Tristan was kissing her again?

Gabby was beautiful, and she had a stunning shape. Now that Bettina had lost her own slim figure, would Tristan turn to Gabby to satisfy his needs? Bettina had told him too many times to find another. Would he take her advice now? Would he tell her to leave his room so he could share it with that copper-haired woman? And why did this thought hurt like a knife piercing her heart?

Bettina turned left at the top of the stairs instead of going to her own room. She stopped for a moment to stare absently out the window at the little jungle of greenery on the flat surface of the roof. Summer flowers bloomed there now, different shapes

234

and sizes on a canvas of green.

She wondered why Thomas had failed to bring her fruit today, or, for that matter, why the house had been so empty when she had gone downstairs earlier? At least one of the two native servant girls could usually be found cooking, and members of Tristan's crew usually relaxed at the big dining table. Where was everyone?

A fear surfaced in Bettina that her mother might not be in the house, either. She hurried the few steps to Jossel's room and opened the door quickly, but she was relieved to find her mother looking out the window.

"At least *you* are here," Bettina sighed.

Jossel turned from the window, a worried frown on her forehead. "I saw some men running toward the village."

"Yes, I saw them, too. It seems we have visitors," Bettina said dryly as she moved to the chair beside her mother. "But where is everyone? When I went downstairs a while ago, I found the house empty."

"That was Tristan's doing," Jossel replied a bit irritably. "When I came down from your room this morning, after we talked, he asked me and everyone else to leave the house."

"Why would he do that?"

"He said he wanted to be alone, but he was acting very strangely. He did not order us to leave, but asked us politely. I could not decide what caused the change in him," Jossel said. "But anyway, the servants went to the village with Maloma to visit their parents, and Jules took Madeleine to show her the house he is building. I did not feel like going out, so I came to my room instead. When I saw those men, I was afraid to go downstairs, for fear I would provoke Tristan's anger."

"You probably would have, for you would have disturbed him in an embrace," Bettina replied.

"Then you told him the truth? Everything will be all right now?"

"No, Mama. It was not me he was embracing, but the female *capitaine* of those men you saw."

"A *woman* commands those rough-looking seamen?" Jossel asked, her green eyes widening.

"Yes, and she is very beautiful. I heard her talking to Tristan.

He has known her a long time, it seems, and they were lovers before. She came here just to be with him," Bettina said sadly.

"Even if what you say is true, you forget that it is you Tristan wants," Jossel reminded her.

"Not anymore. I saw him kissing her, Mama. He was enjoying it. And look at me. Do you think he would choose this round body of mine to sleep next to him, when he can have her slender one instead?"

"Are you just going to give up? You admitted you want him. So fight for him!"

"I have nothing to fight with."

"You carry his child! Tell him the truth."

"I was going to, but it is too late now that *she* is here. He will be sure to think I am lying — he will think I am jealous of her."

"Are you?" Jossel ventured softly. "Are you jealous of this woman?"

"Perhaps. I hated it when I saw him kiss her. I felt sick inside. But it is only because I have had Tristan to myself for so long."

"Is that the only reason?"

"Oh, stop it, Mama. I do not love him, if that is what you are trying to make me admit. There are many kinds of jealousy — not just that of love."

"What do you intend to do?"

"I know Tristan is going to tell me to leave his room tonight so he can share it with her. I would like to stay here with you, Mama."

"Of course you can stay with me. You need not have asked," Jossel replied. "But I think you are wrong."

"No, I'm not wrong, Mama. You have not seen this woman yet. Tristan could not resist her even if he wanted to. I will come here right after dinner. I will not give him a chance to ask me to leave his room."

Bettina was dejected, but she hadn't wholly resigned herself to giving up Tristan. She kept hearing her mother's words: You want him, so fight for him. But she had so little to fight with. All she could do was take special care with her hair and dress, and this she did in the time left to her before the evening meal.

236

She chose a dress of white-and-gold brocade that she had recently completed. It was a special dress she had made for the wedding celebration, but she had been unable to finish it in time, and so had not worn it yet. The square neck of the dress was extremely low and revealed her swelling breasts. The sleeves were long and full, gathered at the wrists, and the long slash was held by four gold bows, the openings revealing her bare arms. To accommodate her growing shape, Bettina had made the dress without a waist, gathering the material just below her breasts with gold ribbons.

Madeleine returned and helped Bettina with her hair, all the while giving her outspoken opinion of the woman sea captain. Maddy, like Jossel, thought Bettina had nothing to worry about, but Bettina couldn't forget the fact that Gabby was at that moment downstairs with Tristan.

With her hair braided and wrapped about her head with interlaced gold ribbons forming a net of gold and white, Bettina was ready to face what lay ahead. She was pleased to see that when she stood erect, her large shape was hidden by the many folds of the waistless dress.

When Madeleine opened the bedroom door, they heard boisterous laughter coming from below. Bettina distinctly recognized Tristan's booming laugh, and felt a pain shoot through her heart. She sent Madeleine ahead of her, for she needed a few more minutes to collect her poise and clear her mind of worry. With this done, she left her room quickly, before she lost courage again.

When Bettina descended the stairs, she was surprised to find the long table filled with members of Gabby's crew. Those who faced her stared in wonder, causing the men on the opposite side of the table to turn also, for Bettina was like a shining light coming out of the darkness. Tristan couldn't take his eyes from her, either, but Bettina met his gaze only for a moment; then she looked at Gabby. The woman had taken Jules's customary seat next to Tristan, and she was leaning exceedingly close to him.

Gabby had not changed or bathed, probably refusing to leave Tristan even for a minute. But it was unnecessary, for the woman demanded attention with her beauty, and she was quite angry at the moment because all attention was directed at Bettina.

The big room was unnervingly silent as so many eyes followed Bettina to her seat directly opposite Gabby. Bettina could see the fire in Gabby's gray eyes as the two women continued to appraise each other. Tristan sat back and observed both women. One corner of his mouth lifted in an amused grin.

"You failed to introduce me to your friend, Tristan," Bettina said quietly, breaking the silence.

Tristan looked into Bettina's startling green eyes and cleared his throat a bit nervously.

But Gabby said coldly, "I am Gabrielle Drayton, captain of the *Red Dragon*. Tristan told me how he *acquired* you, Bettina. But he would not tell me your full name — which is?"

"I told you earlier that I have reason for withholding that information, Gabby," Tristan said coldly. "At my request, you will let the matter be."

Bettina looked at Tristan quizzically; she remembered that he had also refrained from telling Captain O'Casey her full name when he had introduced them. The name Verlaine was nothing to be ashamed of, but then Bettina looked at her mother and smiled, for in truth, she had no right to the name. And since she was illegitimate, she had no right to the name Ryan, either.

Gabby stiffened when she saw Bettina smile at an older woman, obviously her mother. So the wench was proud to hear Tristan come to her aid. She was assured of his protection, but Gabby would see how long this would last.

"I was not aware that slaves are dressed so regally these days, or that they are now allowed to eat at the same table as their betters," Gabby remarked. "Have class distinctions changed, Tristan, or is it just Bettina who is so honored?"

Jules choked, and Jossel rose angrily to her feet to protest, but Bettina answered quickly, a sweet smile on her lips.

"Tristan is a kind master. He —"

"Do you always answer for Tristan?" Gabby interrupted, her voice full of venom.

"That's enough!" Tristan growled, the muscles in his cheeks twitching dangerously. "I told you clearly what the situation was, Gabby, so stop this pretense and let her be!"

"You told me many interesting things, including the fact that the child she carries is not yours." Gabby laughed shortly. "Who is the father, then? One of your men? Perhaps your good friend Jules here? Did he get to her first, Tristan?"

"You go too far, woman!" Jules bellowed, slamming his huge fist down on the table. "I have never touched the lady — nor has any other man. Only that misguided jackass sitting at the head of the table has had that pleasure!" Tristan smiled at this, though no one noticed, for Jules held their attention as he continued angrily, "And you are mistaken in thinking Bettina a slave, for she is not. She is here only because she gave her word to stay. She will be leaving at the end of the year."

"Really?" Gabby's laughter filled the room as she turned to Bettina. "Don't you like it here?"

Gabby's laughter was like a drum beating inside Bettina's head. She glanced at Tristan and saw that he was staring down at his tankard, an amused expression on his face. She could feel tears welling in her eyes, and she rose quickly before they spilled forth. But as she ran up the stairs, Gabby's laughing seemed to grow louder. The tears streamed down Bettina's cheeks as she went to her room to collect her clothes, then ran to her mother's room.

"I brought you something to eat, Bettina, since you did not touch your food tonight," Jossel said when she entered the room. "You should not have let that woman upset you. She did it on purpose, you know."

Bettina was curled up in the chair by the window, wearing only a pale yellow shift. "Is Tristan still with her?" she asked calmly as she took the plate of food from her mother.

"Yes, but they are not alone. He started to follow you, only that — that bitch taunted him into staying. Oh! She infuriated me so, I could have torn her eyes out!"

Bettina smiled with an effort. "Those should have been my words, Mama, only I do not feel like saying them. You saw the way Tristan has been since she came. She has made him forget his anger. His black mood is gone because of her."

"So you are giving up again? Have you considered that Tristan is only trying to make you jealous?"

"How could he be? He did not know I was watching when he kissed her. Now, let us not discuss it anymore. It is late, and I am exhausted."

"It is no wonder with all you have been through this day. But you must eat. You must —"

"I know, Mama," Bettina interrupted with a smile. "I must think of the child."

Chapter 36

The wings of time seemed to be clipped, for a week dragged by with nerve-racking slowness. Bettina spent this week in tortured misery, though she tried hard not to show it. But the nights took their toll on her, and she could do nothing to hide her reddened eyes, caused by lack of sleep and spent tears.

She lay awake each night, long after her mother had drifted to sleep beside her, hoping and praying that Tristan would come for her, that he would drag her back to his room. She foolishly imagined Tristan asking her forgiveness, telling her that she was the only one he wanted, that Gabby meant nothing to him. But her imaginings couldn't last long, for reality would slip back to her mind and the tears would spill silently down her cheeks again. After sleeping in her mother's room for seven nights, Bettina knew Tristan wouldn't come. But God, why did it hurt so terribly?

No one except her mother knew where she was spending her nights now, for no one saw her come and go from Jossel's room. The others assumed nothing had changed, but Tristan and Gabby knew better, Bettina reminded herself.

She supposed that Tristan had been relieved to find her gone that first night because he hadn't had to tell her personally that he had another to take her place. He hadn't even bothered to look for her that night, or any night since, and this was what hurt the most — that he could just completely forget about her.

The days were bad enough, seeing Tristan and Gabby talking and laughing together. But Bettina could hardly bear the nights, for she knew that Gabby was lying in Tristan's arms, that she was sharing his room and making him happy.

Tristan was in the best of moods each day, always smiling.

241

Madeleine and Maloma couldn't understand why Bettina was so forlorn, or why Jossel looked at Tristan with such hostility, which he found amusing. And when Madeleine asked Bettina what was bothering her, she only made excuses.

In the late afternoon of the eighth day following Gabrielle's arrival, Jossel found Bettina by the corral, staring moodily at the beautiful white stallion. It was very seldom that Jossel Verlaine lost her temper, for she was a quiet woman by nature, but Tristan had just ordered her to take a message to Bettina. Jossel had told him what she thought of him, only to have him scoff at her anger. She was still upset, but as she came up behind Bettina, drawing her daughter's attention, she successfully controlled her anger.

"Tristan insists you join the rest of us for the evening meal," Jossel said, gritting her teeth so she wouldn't say more.

"Why, so he can ignore me as he has done this last week? I cannot stand to see that woman's obvious pleasure in gaining Tristan's complete attention."

"I am only giving you his message," Jossel replied. Then she added thoughtfully, "He was annoyed last night when you did not come down to eat, and personally I would like to see him upset again."

"You do wonders for my morale, Mama," Bettina smiled. "If I happen to have a headache tonight, will you be able to bring me up something to eat?"

"You can be sure of it," Jossel laughed.

"Is Tristan in the hall?" Bettina asked, serious again.

"Yes."

"Is she —"

"He was alone when he spoke to me," said Jossel.

"Well, I have something to ask him. If he does not agree, I will be having a lot of headaches in the future," Bettina said, her voice edged with humor.

"What are you going to ask him?"

"Let me speak to him first, Mama, then I will tell you," Bettina replied. She set off across the lawn, leaving her mother to wonder what she was up to.

When Bettina entered the darkness of the hall, she was discouraged to see that Tristan was no longer alone. He was standing with his back to the fireplace, facing Gabby, who was relaxed on the sofa. Aleia was lighting the candles in the chandelier.

Bettina met Tristan's gaze, and his lazy smile made her determined to speak to him now, but when she reached the sofa, she stiffened at the sound of Gabby's voice.

"Well, if it isn't the little mother-to-be."

Ordinarily, Bettina would laugh at such a remark, for she was taller than Gabby, but at the moment, she didn't find it amusing in the least.

"I trust you are feeling better today?" Gabby continued, referring to Bettina's absence of the night before.

Gabby was attired in a lovely black lace dress, with a gray underdress of silk that matched her eyes. She looked beautiful, she knew it, and she was pleased to see that Bettina noticed it.

"May I speak to you — alone?" Bettina asked Tristan calmly, ignoring Gabby.

"You really must teach this girl some manners, Tristan," Gabby remarked indignantly.

"I agree," Tristan replied, grinning. "But not now."

He took Bettina's hand and escorted her outside into the front yard, leaving Gabby fuming on the sofa. After they'd walked some distance from the house, Bettina stopped and faced him.

"Tristan, I want you to release me from my promise. I want to leave the island now."

"Haven't you always wanted to leave?" he asked with a mocking smile, his blue eyes alight with laughter.

"Yes, but —"

"Why should my answer be any different from the last time you asked to go?"

"You know why!" she stormed, and her eyes instantly turned a turbulent green. "You have no reason to keep me here any longer!"

"Now, why do you say that, little one?" he teased her.

"Will you let me leave here now?"

"No," he replied.

"Very well, Tristan," she returned coldly. "You are stubborn, but then you always have been."

"I'm glad to see you give up so easily," Tristan chuckled. "Now, come. It is almost time for the evening meal."

He took her arm to escort her back to the house, but she pulled away from him.

"I will not be dining with you this night," she said haughtily.

"No?" He raised an eyebrow.

"I am afraid I am going to have a terrible headache in a few minutes. In fact, I expect to have many headaches and other ailments in the coming days."

"You will not start this game again, Bettina!" he said sternly.

"You go to hell!" she blurted. She turned and hurried back to the house.

"Bettina, what did you say to Tristan earlier?" Jossel asked excitedly when she came into her room, carrying Bettina's meal. "He was acting oddly at dinner."

"I asked him if I could leave the island, but he refused. So I told him of the ailments I expect to have in the coming days," Bettina replied quietly.

"Then that is probably what had him troubled tonight. You should have seen him, *ma chérie*. He just sat there without touching his food or saying a word. Even that woman could not draw him out. She became angry after a while and went upstairs. Tristan watched her go, then sighed and followed her. I came up right after them."

"So he is with her now?"

"I imagine so," Jossel replied reluctantly. "But I still say he is trying to make you jealous."

"It has gone beyond that, Mama. Tristan has made her his woman, and I have to accept it. I don't want to speak of them any longer."

Bettina put the tray of food on her lap and began to pick at it absently, but Tristan was still troubling her thoughts. She just couldn't understand why he still wanted to keep her. Unless — unless he was punishing her for the last months of anguish she had caused him! But in order for him to think that his taking Gabby would hurt Bettina, he would have to think that Bettina cared for him. And Tristan would be a fool to believe that Bettina cared for him just because she lost herself to him in passion. No — there must be some other reason why he wanted to keep her.

Madeleine burst into Jossel's room just then, but stopped short when she saw Bettina. "What are you doing here, pet?" she asked, then continued, "She is gone!"

"Who is gone?" Jossel asked patiently.

"That woman — Gabrielle. She has left!"

"How do you know this?" Jossel questioned, glancing at Bettina's startled face.

"She came down the stairs, changed to her sailing clothes, and her face was red with anger. I was still at the table with Jules and Maloma, and Gabrielle looked at me with murder in her eyes. Then she turned to one of her men and yelled at him to get her chest, and she sent another to find the rest of her crew and meet her at the cove. Then she stormed out the front door!"

"Are you sure she is leaving the island?" Jossel ventured.

"Yes. Jules said that she had never stayed this long before. He expected her to leave days ago."

"Mama, you must help me!" Bettina said urgently, coming to her feet. "Now that Gabby is gone, I will not go back to his room. I refuse —"

"Go back?" Madeleine interrupted. "You mean you stayed with your mama this whole week? Why did —" Madeleine broke off when the door opened again and Tristan walked slowly into the room.

"No!" Bettina cried as Tristan came directly to her and grabbed her hand.

He didn't say a word as he pulled her gently yet firmly behind him down the corridor to his room. Only after he closed the door and leaned back against it did he release her hand. She backed away from him.

"We are even now, Bettina. Though a single week hardly equals the months of torment you caused me, I have decided to be merciful," Tristan said in a low-pitched voice.

"What are you talking about, Tristan?" Bettina demanded.

"Don't you know, little one?"

"If I knew, would I ask you?" she stormed, green eyes flashing wildly. "You are talking in riddles!"

"I was referring to this week, Bettina. And how Gabby came at just the right time, giving me a solution to my problem."

"Of course *I* was that problem," Bettina said coldly. "Gabby's coming was most convenient for you, I am sure. Why did she leave so suddenly?"

"Because I told her to go."

"Do you really expect me to believe that?"

"Believe what you like," said Tristan, smiling.

Bettina stared at him. A frown creased her brow. Tristan had used the same phrase she had used so many times. What game was he playing now?

"Am I confusing you, Bettina? I thought you would realize the truth by now. I sent Gabby away because she had served her purpose — too well. There was no point in continuing the game if you wouldn't come down and observe it."

"Are you trying to say that all the attention you gave Gabby was only to make me jealous?"

"Of course."

"And I suppose when you made love to her, that was also to make me jealous?" Bettina stormed. "You will not get me back with these lies!"

"I don't have to get you back, Bettina — I never lost you. Come with me," Tristan said softly. He opened the door and walked to the room at the other end of the corridor.

Bettina followed him, only out of curiosity, but she was surprised at what she found. The room was in complete disarray. The tub was full of dirty water, with puddles around it. Crumpled towels were on the floor, along with the beautiful bedspread. The sheets were all mussed, and Bettina saw copper hairs on the pillows.

"Why is this room such a mess?" Bettina asked.

"This is where she stayed on previous visits, and she always left the room in this fashion. She won't let anyone pick up after her, and she won't do it herself. She would only let Kaino in to bring her water for the tub — you can ask the girl yourself."

Bettina glanced about at the thick dust and noticed that the

246

table by the bed had a message written in the dust — fifteen little words that filled Bettina's heart with joy:

you wanted her when you could've had me i'll never forgive you for that tristan

"You have not been in this room since she left?" Bettina asked quietly as she drew her hand across the message, wiping it clean.

"No."

"And I suppose you will tell me now that you slept elsewhere this whole week, that you did not share this bed with that woman?"

"I swear it is the truth. I give you my word!"

"I find that hard to believe, Tristan. She is a beautiful woman. She offered herself to you. How could you refuse her?"

"She intrigued me once, but that was a long time ago," he said. "It's only you I want now."

"How can you say that when I have lost my shape, and — and she is so slim?"

"Ah, Bettina," Tristan sighed. "What does it take to make you believe me? I have given you my word — what more do you want?"

"I want to know why you did this, why you let me believe she was sharing your room."

"To make you jealous — I told you that!"

"Then —"

"If you are going to ask me questions all night, let us go back to my room where we can be comfortable."

She let him pull her back along the corridor, and into his room. She was angry with him, but she was also so elated she thought she would burst. She felt like laughing, only she couldn't let Tristan see her joy.

"If you will relax and be quiet for a few minutes, I think I can answer the few questions that you have yet to ask," Tristan said as he sat down on the bed to pull off his boots and remove his shirt. "Right before Gabby came, I was lying on the sofa in the hall, trying to decide what to do about you. I heard you come downstairs, and when you went into the kitchen, I started to follow you. But then Gabby walked in. I knew that you could hear everything she was saying. And when she kissed me, I pro-longed it only because I knew you were watching. That was as close as I came to her the whole time she was here."

"Then why did she act so smug and satisfied every time she saw me?" Bettina asked. She stood looking out the window.

"She knew what you thought, just as I did. She was too proud to let you think otherwise. She knew you had moved out of my room, and she thought she could win me over. That was the only reason she stayed as long as she did. If you hadn't run to your mother's room the night Gabby arrived, I would have had to sleep on the sofa downstairs in order to make you believe what I wanted you to believe. As it is, you fell right into my plans."

"Why have you bothered to explain this to me?"

"Because I want you back in my bed as if nothing happened," Tristan replied tenderly.

"Do I have a choice?"

"No," he said, smiling.

Bettina was pleased with his answer, and she turned to look out at the moonlit yard so he wouldn't see her joy. But there was still something that puzzled her.

"Tristan, tell me one more thing," Bettina said. "When Gabby came, your disposition changed completely, and you were happy. Now, perhaps she was not the cause. Perhaps it was because you found pleasure in thinking I was miserable—which I wasn't, mind you. But now that this farce is over, why have you not returned to being the tyrant you were before Gabby came?"

"I was happy before she came, Bettina. That is why I sent everyone out of the house that day — because I didn't want them to know it. Gabby's coming gave me an excuse to show it openly."

Bettina swung round to face him, her green eyes enormously wide and filled with seething anger. He had spoken in French! He spoke fluent French!

"It is as well we get this all over with now," Tristan said in English once again. "But before you assail me with loathsome names, consider everything I know, Bettina — everything you told your mother a week ago. I left the room that morning, but I did not go downstairs immediately. I waited outside the door

248

and heard everything. Can we not call ourselves even?"

Bettina gritted her teeth and turned away from him. She recalled every time she had spoken French in front of Tristan, and felt furious at his deception. No wonder he had interrupted her the time she had asked Captain O'Casey to help her escape! And he had heard her whole confession to her mother.

"Well, say something, little one."

"I hate you!"

"No, you don't. You want me," Tristan whispered.

"Not anymore!" she cried. "You have deceived me for the last time!"

"Blast it, Bettina! You should be glad I deceived you this time!" He crossed to her and grabbed her shoulders, forcing her to look at him. Then he continued in a softer tone, "You wanted me to know the truth about the child, the truth about what you had done, but you were afraid I wouldn't believe you. Well, you were right. I wouldn't have believed you if you had told me yourself. But after hearing you tell your mother, when you thought I had left and you were alone, this convinced me the child is mine. I should have been furious with you, but instead I was overjoyed that you would bear my child."

Bettina did not pull away from Tristan when his arms wrapped around her. And when he kissed her, a sweet, gentle kiss, she welcomed it, savored it. She was tired of arguing with him. And he was right, as always. She was glad he knew the truth.

"Is all forgiven?" Tristan asked, holding her head against his chest.

"Yes," she whispered, and looked up into his smiling blue eyes. "But how did you learn to speak French so well? Is it taught in your English schools?"

Tristan laughed deeply. "The only schooling I've ever had was from a crusty old English sea captain. I signed on his ship as cabin boy when I was fourteen. And out of necessity, he taught me to read and write, and to speak English."

"But you *are* English!" Bettina said in surprise.

"No, little one, I'm French. I was born of French parents in a little fishing village on the coast of France," Tristan said.

"Then why do you sail for England?"

"I have no ties with France, and England has been good to me. France is my country, Jules's also, but we haven't gone back to her since we left twelve years ago. We've sailed with the English and lived in the Caribbean since then. This is my home now."

"So Jules is also French?"

"Yes. When Casey pronounced Jules's name properly, I thought for sure you would realize it. That is why I couldn't tell you my surname is Matisse. It would not be wise for my crew to know they sail under a French captain. You will keep this to yourself?"

"If you wish," Bettina laughed. She looked at him curiously. "But why have you kept my surname a secret? You would not tell Gabby or Casey my full name; yet they know I am French."

"I only wanted to keep your name itself a secret. There is no doubt a reward out for information about your whereabouts. Though I trust Casey, I don't trust his crew, and I certainly don't trust Gabby. If they don't know who you are, they can't sell any information about you. And I want it kept secret that you are on this island."

Bettina smiled. This was the most Tristan had ever told her, and she felt warmed by his new trust in her. But where did Don Miguel de Bastida fit into Tristan's life? Would he ever tell her about that part of his past?

"Now answer one question for me."

"What is it?" Bettina asked.

"When you and your mother talked that day in this room, she said something that didn't make any sense — that you were at de Lambert's house for less than a full day."

"There was a storm, if you will remember. You were caught in it yourself," Bettina said quickly.

"Yes, I was caught in it. It came from the west and continued east, which took me off course. But your ship was far enough ahead of me to escape the storm. You would have been on Saint Martin two days before I came."

"I — I had trouble finding the *comte,* that was all." She had forgotten about that horrible first day on Saint Martin, and she hated being reminded of it.

"What happened?"

"Nothing," she answered, biting her lip.

"What happened, Bettina?" he asked again. He knew she was hiding something from him.

"Very well, Tristan," she sighed and sat on the edge of the bed. She told him everything that had happened to her before she finally found Pierre, even that she had actually wished he would rescue her.

"And after all that, I bind you up and rape you again," Tristan said dejectedly. "No wonder you wanted to get even with me. I should be horsewhipped!"

"You didn't know what I had been through, Tristan. You were only trying to teach me a lesson, which I learned well enough."

"Did de Lambert take care of this Antoine Gautier?" Tristan asked.

"I didn't tell him what happened, nor my mother. It was over, and I wanted to forget about it. You are the only one I have told. But I doubt Pierre would have done anything. You were right about him, Tristan. He is a self-centered man, just as André Verlaine was."

"Well, it seems every time you run away from me, you end up in danger," Tristan said with a half-grin. "I will have to remedy that by never letting you out of my sight again."

He came to her then, with desire in the depths of his blue eyes. And as he pushed her gently on the bed, she forgot about everything else.

Chapter 37

Tristan helped Bettina from her chair at the table and walked with her to the sofa in front of the fireplace. The fire had been lit along with the huge chandelier above the table, and other candles on the walls also, for though it was only the middle of the afternoon, the hall was dark and chilly with an approaching storm.

Tristan stirred up the fire, then came and stood in front of Bettina, looking down at her large belly where her hands rested.

"Is he stirring again?" Tristan asked bashfully. The child was such a complete part of Bettina that he felt he couldn't share the experience with her — not yet, anyway.

"Yes," she laughed. "It seems as if he is turning somersaults."

She reached out, took Tristan's hand, and placed it on her large middle. She smiled while she watched the pleasure on Tristan's face as he felt his child move within her.

"Do you still wish for a daughter?" he ventured, taking her hand in his.

"A daughter would be nice, but as you said, every man wants a son."

His eyes gleamed at her reply, and he bent to kiss her tenderly. "I will be back shortly, Bettina. There's no supply of wood for the fire, and I'll have to gather some before the storm begins."

When Tristan left, Madeleine joined Bettina by the fire, and they talked about the double wedding that was planned for the following week. Maloma's two sisters would be the brides, and Madeleine couldn't be more excited if she were their mother herself. She loved weddings.

It was the middle of July, and Bettina had to wait until the middle of September before her child would be born. After seven long months of carrying her baby, she wished the rest of the time would go by quickly. But the past month, despite the discomfort caused by her large shape, had been filled with happiness.

She touched her sapphire earrings, which she wore every day, and remembered that Tristan had said he hoped they would always match her eyes. Her eyes had remained blue since the night Gabby left, and she saw no reason for them to change in the near future. She let each day take its course and didn't try to analyze her feelings for Tristan or think about what would happen come December when her year with him would come to an end.

Tristan treated her with the gentlest care and saw to all her needs personally. He acted like a husband in every way, and Bettina was content. They never spoke of marriage or love, but their happiness was obvious for all to see.

"We have visitors," Jules called out as he came in the front door.

Bettina sighed heavily, remembering the last visitors they had had. But she was relieved when she turned and saw Captain O'Casey standing in the doorway, looking back at the threatening sky.

"I wonder if me men will make it to the village before this storm breaks," Casey remarked to Jules with a chuckle. Then he turned and showed obvious surprise when he saw Bettina and Madeleine by the fire.

Bettina stood up to greet Casey, and she laughed when his eyes widened even further at her swollen shape. Then he smiled warmly and started to approach her.

Glass crashed on the floor, and Bettina turned to see her mother standing motionless with a broken vase of flowers lying at her feet. Jossel's face had turned as white as her hair, and she stared with wide eyes at Captain O'Casey. Casey was also stunned, unable to move.

"Jossel?" Casey whispered in a torn voice. "Dear God, can it be?"

Bettina was filled with confusion as she watched her mother run to Casey and throw her arms around him. He held her to him as if he were afraid to let her go, and Bettina knew then who he was, even before her mother spoke his name.

"Ryan — my Ryan! I thought I would never see you again!" Jossel cried, tears of joy running down her cheeks. "Why did it have to be so long?"

"It was fourteen years before I was free to return to you, but after so many years had passed, I was sure you wouldn't have waited. Even though I still loved you, I thought it best not to disrupt your life."

"I told you I would wait forever."

"Fourteen years seemed like forever. And you were so young when we parted — only sixteen. A young heart changes," Casey said, holding her face between his hands.

"I gave up hope that you would come back, but I never stopped loving you, Ryan."

They kissed, oblivious to all who were watching. Bettina couldn't take her eyes from her father. Why hadn't she sensed the truth when she first met him? He was still as her mother had described him — an Irishman with flaming red hair and laughing green eyes.

Bettina glanced at Madeleine and was surprised to find her smiling.

"I knew your mama never loved André Verlaine, and I suspected many years ago that she had found another man to love," Madeleine whispered to Bettina. "I am glad they have found each other again."

"It seems they don't even know we're here," Jules laughed when he came up beside Bettina.

"Can you blame them?" Bettina asked. "They have not seen each other for twenty years."

Bettina leaned back on the arm of the sofa and watched her parents with loving eyes. She wondered how Casey would react on learning he had a full-grown daughter, and one who would soon make him a grandfather.

Jossel and Casey looked tenderly at each other, lost to everyone but themselves. They had so much to say, so much to make up for, that they didn't know where to begin.

"How did you come to be here, of all places?" Casey finally asked. "Is your husband here also?"

254

"André died last year."

"So we can be married immediately?" Casey said hopefully, taking her hands in his.

"Yes, my love. And as for my being here, I came to the Caribbean for our daughter's wedding, but it never took place. Tristan brought me here when he kidnapped Bettina from Saint Martin."

"Bettina," Casey whispered. "When I first saw her, she reminded me of you, but I never dreamed she was my daughter."

"You have met her?"

"When Tristan first brought her here," Casey answered. "The lass asked me to help her escape. By the saints, I've been a fool!" He looked at Bettina now, and his eyes narrowed at her protruding belly. "Did the lad marry her?"

"No, but —" Jossel was cut off when Tristan came through the kitchen door.

"Casey! It's good to see you again," Tristan said.

"You won't be thinkin' that for long, me friend," Casey growled. His fist slammed into Tristan's jaw.

Tristan stumbled backward from the force of the blow and fell up against the wall. He shook his head and rubbed his jaw. Then he looked at Casey in confusion.

"Blast it, man! Why in hell did you do that?"

"There'll be more where that came from, lad," Casey said without humor, as he stood waiting for Tristan to come at him.

Despite her clumsiness, Bettina ran across the room quickly and stood in front of Tristan, facing her father with pleading eyes.

"I don't want him harmed," Bettina said in a low voice.

"You can't mean to defend the lad after what he's done to you!" Casey shouted.

"I tried to tell you, Ryan, that they are happy," Jossel said quietly.

"Will someone tell me what is going on?" Tristan asked, losing his patience.

Casey ignored Tristan and looked to Jossel. "Did you tell her about me?" he asked, frowning.

Jossel smiled knowingly. "I told her last year, when she left home to be married."

"You two know each other?" Tristan asked in surprise.

Casey sighed as he looked at Tristan. "I don't know what to do about you, lad. I'd like to tear you limb from limb, but me daughter doesn't want you harmed."

"Your daughter!" Tristan looked from Casey's stern expression to the smiling Bettina. Then he stiffened and said, "I don't believe it!"

"It's true enough," Casey returned. "It's me daughter you've been sleepin' with all these months, and had I known before, she'd not be in the condition she's in now."

"Is this true, *madame?*" Tristan asked Jossel.

"Yes," she answered proudly.

"Mother of God! Both parents under my roof!" Tristan exploded. "Why you, Casey? Sweet Jesus! Of all the men in this world, why do *you* have to be her father?"

"That's a fool question, lad," Casey answered. "Bettina's mother is the woman I love, and have loved for twenty years."

"Very well. You're her father, but that changes nothing," said Tristan.

"It changes one thing, Tristan. You're goin' to marry me daughter."

"I will not!" Tristan bellowed.

"Then Bettina will be sailin' with me as soon as the storm is over."

"Like hell she will! She has given her word she will stay with me for one year. Would you have her break her word?"

"Is this so, Bettina?" Casey asked.

"Yes."

Casey sighed heavily. "If you won't be marryin' her, lad, then you won't be sleepin' with her, either. And I'll be stayin' here to make sure you don't."

"No one tells me what I will or won't do, Casey, especially in my own house!"

"Then you leave me no choice but to take Bettina away."

Tristan could see that Casey meant what he said. What could he do? He wasn't prepared to give up Bettina yet.

256

"Why don't you ask her what *she* has to say about this?" Tristan returned.

"It doesn't matter what she has to say," Casey replied. "She's me daughter, and I'll not see her sleepin' with a man she's not married to."

"Blast it, Casey! I can't do anything to her, anyway, with the way she is now. What difference does it make if she shares my room or not?"

"A good point," Casey said, smiling. "Since you must leave her alone, why are you bein' so obstinate, lad?"

"I still want her beside me when I sleep," he said stubbornly.

"I'm sorry, Tristan, but I can't allow it."

Tristan saw that he had lost, and he could think of nothing to do about it.

"Then you had better see Father Hadrian before the storm breaks. I insist you marry *your* lady also, *if* you plan to share a room with her," Tristan said sarcastically, and walked away.

Casey saw Bettina's saddened expression, and said, "I am your father, lass, though Jossel's husband raised you. I was wrong to leave you and your mother behind, and I've regretted it for more than half me life. But I was a poor man and I couldn't see takin' your mother away from the luxury she was accustomed to. I've thought of you so often, though in me mind you were a son. But I'm glad now that you're what you are. I've never been able to be a father to you, Bettina — until now. Don't hate me for doin' right by you where Tristan is concerned."

"I could never hate you, Casey," Bettina replied, touched.

She came into his arms and hugged him closely, feeling as if she had known him all her life. But then she looked at Tristan again, and her eyes filled with tears. She left the hall quickly without another word and went to her room. In privacy, the silent tears turned into heartfelt sobs.

"Was I wrong, Jossel?" Casey asked after watching Bettina run up the stairs.

"I cannot say," Jossel replied. "Bettina has been very happy recently."

"When I was here before, Bettina hated Tristan. He was

257

keepin' her here against her will. Has that changed? Does she love him now?"

"Yes, but she has yet to admit it to herself," Jossel answered. "Perhaps this is the best way. If Tristan is separated from her long enough, he might relent and marry her. But I think you will have a hard time keeping them apart in the meantime."

"I will worry about that," Casey smiled. "But Tristan mentioned a priest. Is there one on the island now?"

"Yes. He brought one here because some of his men wished to marry properly."

"Then why are we still standin' here, I'd like to know?" Casey asked with a chuckle.

Jossel laughed merrily, unable to contain the happiness that was bursting inside her. After so many wasted years, the man she loved with all her heart would finally be hers. If her daughter could only find this same joy, she would be the happiest woman alive.

Chapter 38

Jossel and Ryan O'Casey's wedding day was blessed with the worst storm of the season, and unfortunately they were caught in it on their way back from the village. They were soaked to the skin by the time they reached the house, but they were so absorbed with each other that they didn't seem to notice.

Casey was in the best of moods, for Jossel was his wife and nothing on this earth would ever part them again. When they entered the hall, not even Tristan's resentful attitude could dampen his mood.

"I see you wasted no time in doing the honorable thing," Tristan remarked after Jossel had gone upstairs to change her wet clothes.

"It's what I wanted to do, lad," Casey replied. He peeled off his wet shirt and went to stand by the fire.

"What would you have done if Father Hadrian had not been on the island to give you his blessing, Casey?" said Tristan. "After twenty years of separation from the lady, could you have restrained yourself until you had found a priest?"

"It's hard to say. But I'm thankful that I won't be put to the test. Now, bein' we're nearly the same size, lad, how about lendin' me some dry clothes — I left me things on the ship."

"I should let you catch your death of cold."

"Now is that any way to treat your child's grandfather?" Casey chuckled.

"Sweet Jesus! I don't need to be reminded that my child will have *you* for a grandfather," Tristan grumbled. "And don't think you'll have any say where the child is concerned."

"You forget, Tristan, that Bettina will be leavin' here at the end of the year, and the child goes with her."

"Blast you, Casey! Must you stab me at every turn?" Tristan raged and turned on his heel, leaving Casey with a contented smile on his lips.

Bettina could not remember when she had seen her mother so happy. They were all still seated at the table, though they had finished the meal sometime before. But Casey, as he held Jossel's hand in both of his, was relating what had happened these last twenty years to keep him away from France.

He had already told of the first five years that it took him to amass a small fortune. Even Tristan listened attentively, for he had never heard Casey speak of his past. Tristan was reminded that he spent almost the same amount of time to save enough gold to purchase the *Spirited Lady*. Only their goals were completely opposite. Whereas Casey had amassed his fortune for the sake of love, Tristan had scrimped and saved with hatred goading him on, for only with his own ship could he search for Bastida at will.

"And so after five years I was on me way back to France," Casey continued. "But after seven weeks at sea, we encountered the worst storm that I've ever seen. For two nights and a day the small vessel was battered and tossed about, sustainin' heavy damage. After the storm was over, it was discovered that six men had been swept overboard, and the ship would be crawlin' the rest of the way home.

"Then, two days later, it was our misfortune to be sighted by a private vessel. Turks they were, and a merciless lot. Seein' how crippled we were, they wasted no time in attackin' us, and in less than an hour we were boarded. They were disappointed with our small cargo, and quickly decided to sell all those who were left alive, in order to make their venture worthwhile.

"The next nine years were a bit of hell, and it was only my will to return to France that kept me alive in the beginnin'. But bein' shackled to the oars of an Egyptian barge for what seemed like an eternity slowly eroded my will to live. But finally the opportunity came to escape, and I took it, along with the rest of the poor souls who could barely be called men. We had chosen the right time, for that hellship was carryin' a fortune in gold and jewels that day. When it was divided among those of us who were left, I found that I was richer than I was when the Turks attacked us.

"It took me a year to gain back me strength, but in my heart, I felt it was too late to return to France. I purchased a ship, and for three years I waged my own personal war on any Turkish vessel or slave ship I could find. But then I lost my taste for revenge. So these last two years I've hired my ship out to carry cargo up to the Colonies, and done battle with a few plate ships that saw fit to attack me first, but I've continued to chase down any slave ship I come across and free the poor devils within."

"If only you had not been so proud when we were young, Ryan, we could have been together all these years," Jossel said wistfully, thinking of all that Casey had suffered, and all the time she had spent in a loveless marriage.

"What's done is done," Casey replied, bringing her hand to his lips. "We're together now, so let us forget the past." He looked at Tristan and smiled amiably. "If it were not for you, lad, I wouldn't have found Jossel again. You have my deepest thanks for bringin' her here."

"You're a blasted hypocrite, Casey," Tristan replied, though not harshly. "Your lady is here only because I brought her daughter here. Will you thank me for bringing Bettina here also?"

"Can you not forget your resentment, Tristan, and see that I am only doin' what's right for Bettina?"

"What I see is that you had no qualms about making love to a married woman, getting her with child, and then leaving her," Tristan said bitterly. "Where were your high principles then?"

"I loved Jossel, and her marriage was not a happy one. If I'd had the means, I'd have taken her with me then, but I didn't. I always wanted to marry her, so my intentions were honorable even then. Can you say the same?" Casey said calmly.

"Why are you so obsessed with marriage?" Tristan asked in exasperation. "I've taken care of Bettina and seen to all her needs. We were both content with the way things were — until you came here."

"Answer me this, Tristan. If you had a daughter — and you might have one soon — would you let some young scoundrel make her his whore?"

"Bettina is not a whore!" Tristan exploded, his face livid. "Nor is she married."

"Married! I am sick to death of that blasted word!" Tristan stormed, his eyes a dangerous white-blue. "Does marriage guarantee that a man and woman will remain faithful to each other? No! Is it a testimony of undying love? Not in most cases. It keeps a child from being labeled a bastard, but there are too many bastards in this world for that to matter."

"It is easy for you to scoff at marriage, Tristan, for it is only the woman who is condemned for livin' unlawfully with a man," Casey reminded him.

"Who here condemns Bettina?" Tristan asked angrily. "She lives among friends!"

"Friends would be the first to pity her," Casey answered.

"Enough of this, please!" Bettina cried, unable to listen to any more. She rose from the table and went to stand before the fire, gazing down at the dancing yellow flames.

"Bettina is right, Ryan," Jossel scolded in a whisper. "If you and Tristan insist on discussing her so frankly, with no thought to her feelings, then do it when she cannot hear you."

"Your advice is unnecessary, *madame,* for there will be no more discussions on this subject," Tristan said coldly.

He left the table and slowly approached Bettina by the fire. When he stood behind her and rested his hands on her shoulders, he could feel her stiffen at his touch.

"Are you all right, little one?" Tristan asked in a gentle voice.

"Yes."

Her answer was but a whisper and left doubt in his mind. He turned her around to face him and saw that her green eyes were filled with shining tears, making his heart ache. He wiped her tears away, then held her face in his hands.

"I'm sorry, Bettina. I don't want you to think that because I don't want to marry you I don't want you anymore. I want you more than I've ever wanted anything. But marriage scares me to death! I have lived my life independently, with no responsibilities — needing no one."

"You do not have to explain yourself to me," Bettina said with a smile, her eyes deep pools of blue. "I have grown quite fond of you, Tristan. In fact, I — I think I am in love with you. But I do not want you to marry me unless you want it with all your heart. It is enough that you want me."

He kissed her tenderly for a long moment, feeling as his greatest wish had just been granted, but also feeling uncertain. He knew he wanted Bettina, but he didn't know if he loved her or not. Since he had never been in love with a woman before, he wasn't sure if it was love or just desire that he felt for her. But he felt very happy that she loved him.

"Bettina, when your year is up, would you stay here with me — live with me as you have been?" Tristan ventured.

"If it were only up to me, I would stay. But I don't think Casey will let me," Bettina replied.

"Casey again! Your blasted father is going to push me too far yet!" Tristan said harshly as he released her.

"I cannot apologize for him, Tristan. He is my father and he only wants what is best for me."

"What *he* considers is best!"

"Maybe so, but it is his right," Bettina returned, lowering her eyelids to hide the pain that suddenly filled her.

She started to walk past him, but he took her hand to stop her. "Where are you going?"

"Everyone else has already gone up to bed. I was going to do the same."

He saw that the hall was indeed empty; then he looked back at Bettina, his eyes softly pleading with her. "If we can't go up together, then stay with me a little longer."

Her hurt at Tristan's outburst disappeared with his tender words. She let him lead her to the sofa, where he pulled her back against him, his arms wrapped around her. As he held her gently, they could hear the rumbling of thunder outside, drowning out the soft crackling of the fire.

"If I come to you in the middle of the night, will you not cry out?" Tristan asked.

"It would be difficult, for Mama has moved her things into the room next to yours, and Casey took your chest to Mama's old room. He wants us as far apart as possible."

"I'm not even master of my own house anymore!" Tristan

said in exasperation. "Is there nothing you can do, Bettina?"

"I will talk to Mama tomorrow and ask her to speak to Casey. Perhaps she can get him to relent."

"I suppose I must be content with that for tonight. But Casey damn well better give in."

Chapter 39

Bettina awoke with a start, calling Tristan's name with torment in her voice. She looked at the empty place in the bed beside her, the nightmare that had awakened her lingering vividly in her mind. She had dreamed that after years of devoting herself to Tristan, giving him all her love, he had suddenly cast her out without a second thought because another woman had caught his eye. What Tristan had said in her dream kept reverberating in Bettina's mind: "You must remember that we were never married. It had to end someday."

She looked about the room, gloomy with the storm raging outside, and suddenly felt depressed and on the verge of tears. Tristan wanted her, of that she was sure, but why couldn't he love her also? She had finally admitted to herself, and to Tristan, that she loved him, and she was slowly realizing just how intense that love was. She had given him a chance to declare how he felt about her, but he had only asked her to stay with him.

He spoke of no greater emotion than desire. Could she be content with that? Could she bear to give him all her love and not be loved in return? But on the other hand, could she bear to leave him and never see him again?

Bettina pulled back the covers to get up, and shivered in the chilly breeze that swept in through the open window. This would have been a perfect morning to linger in bed, enjoying Tristan's warmth. She hoped he missed her as much as she missed having him beside her at night. She also hoped she could talk Casey into putting an end to their separation.

Bettina slowly donned a light-blue dress with full, long sleeves to keep her warm on this stormy day. The sky was covered with heavy gray clouds, and she couldn't judge what time of morning it was, but she hoped she would find her mother alone in her room.

After taking the few steps to the room next to hers, she was disappointed to find it empty. But as she started to go downstairs, her mother appeared at the turn in the corridor.

"It is so late, I began to worry about you," Jossel said.

"I must have overslept," Bettina said. "I didn't fall asleep until very late last night." Bettina bit her lip, wondering if her mother would help her talk to Casey. "Mama, can we talk in my room?"

"Yes, of course."

They entered the room, and Bettina motioned for her mother to sit down, while she herself moved to the little wooden cradle that Tristan had made only the week before. She touched it gently, setting it in motion; then she turned to face her mother.

"Mama, you must know that I am very glad you and Casey have found each other, that you are finally married to the man you have always loved."

"You do not sound as glad as you say you are, *ma chérie,*" Jossel replied with a slight smile.

"I *am* glad for you, Mama, but I guess I am feeling sorry for myself. You found your happiness when Casey came here, but I lost mine."

"I know you are upset. I was as surprised as you when Ryan forbade you and Tristan to share this room. But this separation could be the best thing for you, Bettina. Ryan is certain that if Tristan is kept from you long enough, he will come around to doing what is right. We talked about it for a long time last night."

"Tristan and I also talked, Mama. He will not marry me, for he fears such a total commitment. But he has asked me to stay here with him. It would be the same as if we were married, only without the actual vows."

"But he could leave you at any time!"

"He could do that even if we were married."

"A man feels a different responsibility to his wife," Jossel replied.

"I know. But Tristan is against marriage, and he will not be pushed into it. But I love him, Mama, and I want to stay here with him."

"So you have finally admitted it to yourself. I knew you loved him, even when you still professed your hatred so strongly," Jossel said with a knowing nod of her head.

"Perhaps I did love him then, but I am sure of it now. Will you talk to Casey?" Bettina asked hopefully, "I do not want this separation, Mama. It has only been one night, and already I miss Tristan terribly. I want him beside me at night. I need the reassurance that even though I am big with child, he still wants to be with me."

"I will speak to your father as soon as we are alone," Jossel said. She stood up, took Bettina in her arms, and hugged her. "But if Ryan does not relent, do not give up hope, Bettina. I think you underestimate the power you have over Tristan."

Bettina came down to dinner that night with a heavy heart. Her mother had talked to Casey in the afternoon, and had just given Bettina his answer. Casey was confident that given enough time to think about it, Tristan would see that marriage was the only way. Bettina only wished that she shared some of Casey's confidence. But now she had to tell Tristan that her mother had failed to change Casey's mind.

Though Bettina deliberately ate slowly, the time seemed to fly by, and, very soon, the moment she had dreaded was at hand. Jossel took Casey up to their room and motioned for Madeleine to go upstairs also, for she knew Bettina and Tristan needed privacy.

Tristan had been cordial throughout the day, and Bettina knew that he expected her to tell him that Casey had relented. Would he become furious again?

Bettina left the table without waiting for him, and moved to the sofa. Besides the prospect of arguing with Tristan, she was also extremely uncomfortable tonight, and her back hurt.

The torrent of rain had continued all day and was still hammering away at the house. Flashes of lightning could be seen from the high windows, and occasional cracks of thunder broke the silence in the large hall.

Bettina stared at the fire, concentrating hard on the flickering flames. Tristan sat down sideways on the sofa so he could face her, and took her hand in his.

"Did your mother talk to Casey?" Tristan asked quietly.

"Yes."

"And?"

Bettina took a deep breath. "He has not changed his mind, Tristan. For some reason, he is confident that you will change yours."

"Then you will defy him," Tristan said calmly. Bettina knew it was a command. Then he added, "You are a grown woman, Bettina. You are old enough to do as you please."

"If it were my stepfather who had forbidden us to live together, I would do as you ask, for André was an uncaring man. But Casey is my real father and he cares for me. He is not doing this to spite you, Tristan, for he is your friend, regardless of what you may think now. He feels he is doing the right thing for me, and I will not go against his wishes."

"Is this the way you want it?" Tristan asked, hurt.

"I hate sleeping in your bed alone, Tristan. I want you there with me. When I told you yesterday that I think I am in love with you, I should have been more explicit. I love you with all my heart, Tristan. You are the very breath of my life." Bettina paused. "Give my father time, Tristan. When he sees that you will not give in, perhaps he will."

Tristan did not answer, but surprised her by leaning back on the sofa and pulling her into his arms. Without talking, he held her for a long time, until they heard the storm end in the late hours of the night.

Chapter 40

It was well into the month of August, the time of year when frequent hurricanes stormed throughout the Caribbean. Maloma would give birth to her child near the end of the month.

The last month, though not a happy one, had been tranquil. Tristan hadn't argued with Casey again, and generally seemed cheerful. Surprisingly, he'd even joined the celebration of Aleia and Kaino's double wedding.

Tristan kept busy during the days, for he had decided to clear a large area of the forest on the leeward side of the island in order to plant sugarcane. Since most of his men wanted to settle down and raise families, they were eager to help Tristan clear the area and plant the crop for a share in the profits. A small refinery would also have to be built, but this could be done after the crop was planted.

The last four weeks had been very slow ones for Bettina. The burden of carrying her child was weighing down on her, and she envied Maloma, who didn't have as long to wait. She also missed Tristan.

She could not spend her nights with him, and Tristan was exhausted in the evenings after working all day. He often drifted off to sleep with her in his arms. She would wake him then, and walk with him to the top of the stairs, but there, with only a tender kiss, they would part and go to their separate rooms.

In the middle of the night, Madeleine woke Bettina to tell her Maloma's time had come earlier than expected. Jules had finished his house, which was only a half-mile from the big stone fortress, and he and Maloma had moved into it over a month before.

Jules had come for Madeleine, for he had so much respect for the old woman that he wanted her to be the midwife instead of one of the village women. He had also roused Tristan from sleep, and Madeleine, Bettina, and he left quickly for Jules's house.

Madeleine checked on Maloma's condition, then came out of the bedroom to inform them it would be many hours yet before the actual birth. Madeleine told Tristan to start kettles of water boiling, and Jules, since he was in no condition to help in the preparations, was to go to the village to fetch Maloma's mother.

The sky was turning light blue then Jules returned to the house. Tristan, seeing Jules's dazed state, thrust a tankard of rum in his hand. This was the first time Jules had been present at the birth of one of his children, and he didn't know what to do.

As the morning progressed, Maloma's mother offered to fix a meal, but nobody felt much like eating. So she took the other three children out into the yard so they wouldn't be underfoot. When the first screams came from the bedroom, Tristan watched Jules turn pale, and then paler still with each scream that followed. He felt sick himself, never realizing until now how much a woman suffered to give birth to a child. Would Bettina have to endure the same pain?

When the final tormented scream came, Jules cried out to God to spare Maloma's life, thinking she would surely die from such anguish. Even Tristan turned white, and he stood motionless during the silence that followed, until the distinct cry of a child drifted out to them. He then relaxed and clapped his friend on the back, but Jules ran into the bedroom, deaf to the congratulations that were called after him.

A few minutes later, Madeleine came out of the bedroom chuckling to herself.

"Is Maloma all right?" Tristan asked impatiently.

"She is fine," Madeleine answered, trying to suppress her mirth. "And so is her son. It was a difficult delivery."

"Then may I ask what is so damned amusing?"

"It is your friend Jules." Madeleine laughed again. "He is

270

in there swearing he will never touch his wife again. He would not listen when I told him it would probably never be so hard on her again."

Tristan started to chuckle, now that it was over, and then he, too, burst out laughing.

For the next few days, to the amusement of all, Jules wouldn't set foot from his house, for he refused to leave Maloma's side. And Tristan made a decision that he convinced himself was the only thing left to do. He couldn't go on wearing himself out each day in order to find peace in exhausted sleep at night.

"I guess I've been acting like a blasted fool, haven't I?" Jules said when he finally came to visit Tristan.

"To say the least," Tristan laughed. "I've even heard that you've sworn never to touch your lady again."

Jules laughed sheepishly. "Well, I've changed my mind about that. Maloma is coming along fine. She's even been up and about this morning."

"And your son?"

"He seems tiny and frail, but they assure me that's the way he's supposed to be. He's so small, I'm afraid to touch him."

"You'll get over that, I'm sure," Tristan replied with a smile. "Have you named him yet?"

"Yes. Guy — Guy Bandelaire."

"A fine French name," Tristan remarked; then he looked at Jules thoughtfully. "I have decided it is time I left for Spain. Bastida has had eight months to take care of his business in the Caribbean, and I feel certain I will find him there this time. I will also bring back the machinery needed for the sugar refinery."

"Very well. When do we leave?"

"I want you to stay here, Jules," Tristan replied firmly.

"It is too dangerous for you to go alone! Even though we are not at war now, you will still be on Bastida's home ground. He will have the advantage!"

"For once, Jules, do as I ask! I need you to stay here more than I need you with me. I may not return until after the new year begins, and you are the only one I can trust. Bettina wants to stay, but if Casey tries to take her away with him, you must prevent it. I will not take unnecessary risks if I can be sure Bettina will be waiting here for me."

"I don't like it, Tristan," Jules grumbled. "You have never looked for Bastida without me."

"Will you do as I ask?"

"I suppose so," Jules said reluctantly.

"Good. Casey need only know that I've gone after the machinery, for he would probably object if he knew otherwise. I will take those of my men who are willing to go, and also some of Casey's crew. I'll tell Bettina the truth, so she won't worry as the months pass. And if Casey becomes anxious and starts insisting that I'm dead and not coming back, you can tell him why I have been delayed."

"Casey isn't going to like the risk you are going to take, when in his opinion you should have settled down and married his daughter."

"The old bear is convinced I will come around eventually."

"And will you come around?" Jules ventured, his brown eyes studying his friend's face.

"I doubt it," Tristan replied quickly, and then, with a half-grin, added, "You know how I feel about marriage. You've been with me long enough to know me well."

"Yes, I know your views about marriage, but I also remember what you said when you first found Bettina, that you only wanted to keep her for a little while. You changed your mind about that soon enough."

"I didn't want to keep her long because I knew she would take my mind from Bastida. She has succeeded in doing just that, but this voyage will wipe Bastida from my mind forever."

"When do you plan to sail?"

"Tomorrow morning."

"Have you told Bettina?" Jules asked.

"No, I haven't seen her alone yet, but —"

"Then you might as well get it over with now," Jules interrupted him, seeing Bettina coming down the stairs. "I'll leave you alone."

Tristan turned and saw Bettina. The thought of leaving her suddenly seemed absurd, but he had made his decision and he

272

would see it through.

When she joined him, her face alight with the pleasure of seeing him, he took her hand and brought it to his lips. Then he led her to their favorite spot before the fireplace. He decided it would be best to come straight to the point, and to do it quickly, before he changed his mind.

"I am sailing for Spain in the morning, Bettina. And before you object, know that this is something I have to do. I have to see Bastida dead before I will ever be content to settle down."

"Then you will not be here for the birth of your child?"

Tristan was surprised that she was taking his news so calmly. "No, but this is one reason why I am going now. I don't think I could bear to go through what Jules did."

She smiled faintly. "I will miss you, Tristan, but no more than I have missed you this last month. Perhaps it will be easier this way. Will you be gone long?"

"Yes, but you will have the child to occupy your time — the months will pass swiftly. When I return, you will be slim again, and if I have to kidnap you from my own house in order to make love to you, then I will do so."

She laughed now. "I will look forward to your kidnapping me this time."

"So will I, little one. In fact, the thought of it will sustain me in the coming months."

Chapter 41

Bettina carefully controlled her emotions when she said good-bye to Tristan, just as she had the day before, when he'd told her that he was leaving. But as soon as his ship sailed around the forested point that hid the little cove, she burst into tears.

She felt in her heart that it would be a very long time before Tristan returned, for he would not find Don Miguel de Bastida. Tristan would end this trip eventually and come home, but he would leave again and again to search for a man he would never find. But she didn't want him to be successful. She would rather suffer through his long absences than have him find Don Miguel and possibly die.

For two days, Bettina worried about Don Miguel and the mystery surrounding him. She questioned Jules about him, but since Tristan hadn't told her anything, neither would Jules. The only thing she could think of was that Don Miguel might be responsible for the scar on Tristan's face. But how could Tristan hate the man so passionately because of a scar that didn't even mar his handsomeness?

It was as if by thinking about Don Miguel de Bastida so much, Bettina had willed him to the island, for on the afternoon of the second day, he sailed boldly into the little cove. No one knew that he had come until he burst through the front door of Tristan's house with a dozen armed men behind him.

Bettina was on her way downstairs, and when she saw Don Miguel, she was forced to sit down as a wave of dizziness swept over her. Casey was at the table with Jossel, and he rose quickly to his feet, ready to do battle even though he was unarmed. Jossel stared with wide green eyes when she recognized Don Miguel, for she remembered the conversation he had had with Bettina about

Tristan, and she could well guess his reason for being here.

Don Miguel took off his hat and bowed to Jossel quite formally. "It is a pleasure to see you again, *madame,*" he said in French.

"Who are you, *monsieur?*" Casey asked angrily in the same language, before Jossel could say a word.

"Don Miguel de Bastida," he said with a humorless smile.

"Bastida! So you are the one Tristan searches for."

"Yes, and I have come here to end his search," Don Miguel replied. He sheathed his sword and said, "Now, where is this young man who wants to see me dead?"

"You have come too late, for Tristan sailed two days ago. He will not be back for at least a month," Casey replied. He stepped around the table to face the man.

"Come now, *monsieur,*" Don Miguel said impatiently. "Must I search this island for him? His ship is anchored in the cove. He must be here."

"That ship is mine!" Casey returned heatedly. "I have no reason to lie to you, Bastida. I couldn't care less if you have it out with Tristan!"

Bettina slowly descended the rest of the stairs and caught Don Miguel's attention.

"Ah, Mademoiselle Verlaine. I see you have been unable to escape from this Tristan again."

"I have no wish to escape any longer, *monsieur,*" Bettina replied, trying to remain calm.

"Pierre will be disappointed," Don Miguel said. He stared at Bettina's large belly and asked, "Is Tristan the father of your child?"

"That is no concern of yours!" Casey stormed.

Don Miguel laughed shortly. "Yes, Pierre will surely be disappointed. But enough of this! I have no intention of waiting here for Tristan to return." He looked at Bettina and smiled, though there was no warmth in his dark-gray eyes. "*You,* mademoiselle, will collect your things quickly. You are coming with me."

Jossel gasped, and Casey turned quite livid with rage.

"You are not taking my daughter anywhere!"

"*Your* daughter? I was under the impression that her father was dead."

"Her stepfather is, but I am her real father!"

"This is most amusing, but it does not matter," Don Miguel said. He motioned to his men to seize Casey. "She will come with me, and I'm sure that Tristan will follow. I have a small residence in Santo Domingo, and I will wait for Tristan there. Do not worry, for no harm will come to the girl if all goes well. After I take care of Tristan, I will deliver your daughter to Saint Martin."

"But she cannot travel in her condition!" Jossel finally spoke as Casey struggled to throw off the men who were holding him.

"It will not take long to reach Santo Domingo. She will be all right."

Don Miguel turned to one of his men and told him to watch Bettina as she packed her things. There was nothing she could do but go with him. Unfortunately, Jules and the rest of the men were miles from the house, still clearing the new fields, and they wouldn't be back for hours yet.

When Bettina was escorted back downstairs, Don Migel turned to Casey with a parting warning.

"Do not try to rescue the girl yourself, *monsieur.* If anyone comes but Tristan, I will kill her. And he must come alone, do you understand?"

Don Miguel de Bastida wasted no time in leaving the island. On his ship, Bettina was shown to a small cabin that was scantily furnished with a hammock, a little table, and one chair.

When the door closed and she was alone, she sat down in a daze. How could this be happening? She should have said something. She should have told Don Miguel that Tristan wouldn't return for five or six months, but then Don Miguel would only have come back again when Tristan was home, and they would have faced each other then. And Bettina wanted to prevent that.

Don Miguel expected Tristan to come to Santo Domingo to rescue her in two months or less. But Bettina knew that Tristan had gone to Spain and wouldn't be back for many months. A plan grew in her mind, and she decided on a story to tell Don

Miguel. Though it would not be the truth, she must make him believe her.

When the sun disappeared, Bettina was invited to Don Miguel's cabin to dine with him. She went willingly, for she was anxious to set her plan in motion. She had resigned herself to the possibility of never seeing Tristan again, but she would do her best to save his life.

When Bettina entered Don Miguel's cabin, she saw that her own room was a small closet compared to his. The room was luxuriously furnished, but held none of the instruments and charts that usually cluttered a captain's cabin. Don Miguel obviously did not command his own ship, but employed someone else to do so.

They did not speak until after Don Miguel's personal servant had left the room. Then Bettina's curiosity prompted her to open the conversation.

"From the sea, that island looks uninhabited. How did you know it was where Tristan lives?" Bettina asked, trying not to sound too interested.

"I had a map," Don Miguel answered as he studied her face. "Though until I found that hidden cove, I was beginning to think I had been misled."

"But Pierre burned the map I gave him! Where did —"

"So you knew about that," Don Miguel interrupted her with a laugh. "Well, the map I have was drawn by a female's hand."

"That is impossible!"

"On the contrary, it is quite possible. I had searched everywhere for the ship that rescued you from that island, but I had no luck. Then last month I met a remarkable woman — a Gabrielle Drayton. She was more than happy to help me locate Tristan."

Bettina tried hard to hide her anger and loathing. Color sprang to her cheeks, and she wanted to curse Gabby aloud for betraying Tristan. Instead, she opened a new line of questioning.

"Why do you want to find Tristan?"

Don Miguel looked surprised. "You know the answer to that as well as I, Mademoiselle Verlaine. You yourself told me that Tristan wants me dead. Knowing this, I could not wait for him to find me and take me unawares."

"If that is your reason, then I am afraid you have gone to a lot of trouble for nothing, Monsieur Bastida. Tristan has given up searching for you," Bettina said.

Don Miguel laughed. "You must think me a fool. The man has spent most of his life hunting me down. It is inconceivable that he would give up the search."

"I assure you he has," Bettina returned. "Tristan considered it a waste of time to continue searching for a man who would soon die, anyway."

"Die? I have many years left. What nonsense is this?" Don Miguel asked, flustered.

"It is my doing, *monsieur*. When Tristan kidnapped me from Saint Martin, I was furious. The one thing he wanted most in the world was to kill you. I knew this, so I told him he would never have the chance. I told him I had met you and that you had aged beyond your years, that you were in fact dying of an incurable disease. I purposely destroyed his hopes in order to strike back at him."

"You lied to him!"

"Yes, but Tristan believed me. I had my mama also swear it was true. He was furious that he had been cheated out of your death, but he soon forgot about it — and you. He decided there could be no pleasure in killing a dying man."

"Well, he will be surprised to find me well and strong when he comes for you," Don Miguel returned with humor in his voice.

"He will not come for me. In fact, he will probably thank you for taking me off his hands," Bettina said quite easily. She took a sip of the dark-red wine that had been offered to her.

"Now I know you lie!" Don Miguel replied angrily. "You carry his child!"

"I carry his bastard, which he couldn't care less about. As soon as I conceived, Tristan cast me aside for another. He had grown tired of me, anyway. And since I no longer had to suffer his attentions, I saw no reason to escape again — the island was a pleasant place to live."

"If all this is true, why did your father not take you away?" Don Miguel asked.

"He was going to as soon as I gave birth."

"For some reason, I do not believe you, Mademoiselle Verlaine," he said.

"When Tristan does not come, you will see the truth of my words. And when you grow tired of waiting, *monsieur,* what do you intend to do with me?"

"Either way, I will give you to Pierre as a present."

"I see," Bettina whispered, her eyes downcast.

Casey wouldn't come after her for fear of endangering her life, and Tristan wouldn't be back until the new year. She would be living on Saint Martin by then, with Pierre, and Tristan wouldn't want her back, she thought miserably.

Chapter 42

Bettina was a prisoner in Don Miguel's small house. It stood on the outskirts of Santo Domingo, with the nearest neighbor a mile away, and was surrounded by high walls in the Spanish fashion. The single door in the front wall opened into a large entryway that served as a drawing room. On the right of this were two bedrooms, with a small den between them. The kitchen and dining room were on the opposite side of the house.

The outside doors and the heavy wooden shutters over the windows were kept locked at all times. Bettina knew there was a walled patio outside her bedroom, but not once had she been allowed to walk in it, or feel the soft breeze against her face. She had the freedom of the house during the day, but she preferred to stay in her room. And at night, the door to her room was locked.

Bettina's room was small, but nicely furnished. The bed was large, four-postered, and quite comfortable. A handcarved chiffonier stood behind the door, and a beautifully carved chair with a velvet seat and back was in the corner by the bed. There were several tables, and against the remaining wall, opposite the shuttered window, was a huge bookshelf that held a few books and many polished statues of marble, jade, and ivory. The little sculptures ranged from a few inches to a foot in height, and depicted different animals.

There were only two servants in the house, a cook and a maid, but Don Miguel had given them strict orders not to converse with Bettina. Even if they had attempted to do so, it would have been useless, because the two women spoke only Spanish. Bettina saw the cook only once, but the maid brought her meals and water for her baths. Bettina tried many times to speak to the maid, to communicate with her hands, but the older woman completely ignored her.

Bettina grew more depressed as the days went by. She saw Don Miguel only in the evenings, when they dined together. He spent each day on the docks, carefully observing every ship that came into the harbor. Each evening, Bettina repeated that Tristan wouldn't come; then she would say no more. Though she was starved for conversation, she couldn't bring herself to talk civilly with this man. She knew that he was setting a trap for Tristan, but Don Miguel would tell her nothing about it. And she could think of no way to warn Tristan, if by chance he should come.

Bettina had been at Don Miguel's house for three weeks. The end of September was nearing, and she still worried about Tristan. At least she had no time to worry about the fact that her child was a week overdue.

Many times she thought her time was at hand, for she would experience cramps and pressure in her womb. But then the cramps would disappear and she would be filled with disappointment, for she wanted the birth over. These small discomforts were so frequent that soon she didn't even notice them anymore. She had awakened this morning with the pressure in her womb much stronger, but she put it down to yet another false alarm.

When the maid unlocked the door and came into the room with Bettina's breakfast, Bettina noticed that the little woman seemed unusually cheerful. The room was dark because of the locked shutters, but the usually sullen woman was humming a merry tune as she lit the candles. Bettina supposed the maid was anticipating the fiesta she and the cook would be going to that day. Don Miguel had told Bettina last evening that he was giving the servants the day off so they could enjoy themselves in town.

She remembered thinking at the time that he had purposely told her about the fiesta to make her feel more depressed, for he said that it was too bad she would have to stay in the house by herself. But the silent, cold treatment she received from the maid made her feel as if she were by herself each day, anyway.

Today would be no different from any other day, she told

herself as she ate a few bites of food, then pushed the tray aside and got up to dress. But as soon as she stood up, she clutched her middle, afraid to move. The cramps she had felt while lying in bed now seemed twice as strong.

As soon as she was able to move, Bettina left her room, praying silently to herself that she would find the servants still in the house. She went directly to the kitchen, hoping to find the cook there, but it was empty. Bettina refused to become alarmed, but searched quickly through the rest of the house. But with each room she went in and out of, she was finding it more and more difficult to remain calm. And when she opened the door to the last room, Don Miguel's bedroom, she felt a panic within her such as she had never experienced before.

Bettina knew without a doubt that her time had come as the pressure came again, and the water burst from her, running down her legs to form a puddle at her feet. Bettina lifted her shift with trembling hands, but it was already soaked. The panic she felt was not the fear of giving birth, but the fact that she would have to do it alone. Why today of all days did she have to be completely alone in this house?

She moved to the nearest chair in the entryway and sat down in a daze. All she could think about was Maloma screaming in agony as she gave birth to her son. But then another contraction brought her back to her own situation, and, as soon as it passed, she got up in a panic and began to check all the windows and the outside doors to see if any had carelessly been left unlocked. She wanted to get out of this house; she wanted help! But rationality soon returned, and she realized she was wasting precious time.

The time went quickly because she didn't know how much of it she would have. In the hours that passed, Bettina managed to boil water that she would need and carry this to her room. Between the steadily increasing contractions, she found clean sheets and changed those on her bed, and also brought clean linen to wrap her baby in. She found and cleaned the knife that she would need to sever the cord from the baby's navel. Then, still able to move about, she changed her shift and wiped up the water that had poured from her earlier.

All of her efforts were slow ones because she had to stop and wait for each contraction to pass. But it was late in the afternoon now, and the spasms of pain had grown so frequent and so unbearable that she could no longer contain her agony, and her screams echoed through the empty house.

When Bettina heard the front door open and then slam shut, relief flooded over her. Now she would not have to give birth alone. No matter how distant the servants had been toward her, they were women themselves, and they couldn't refuse to help her. But she realized that the fiesta in town would not be over yet, and one of the women had probably just come for something she had forgotten. Bettina would have to summon the woman before she left again. She struggled to get off the bed where she had been lying, but as soon as she stood up, another contraction gripped her. She started to scream.

Suddenly, the door to her room burst open and Don Miguel stormed into the room, his face a mask of anger. He strode up to her, and before she could speak, he slapped her viciously across the face. She fell back on the bed, and the sudden movement caused her even worse agony, but her pride refused to let her cry out.

"You lying bitch!" Don Miguel yelled, his fists clenched at his sides. "He is here — Tristan is here!"

"That — that cannot be!" she stammered. "He is —"

"Enough of your lies!" He turned on his heel and left the room, but Bettina could hear him storming in the other room. "To think I had begun to believe your lies, to believe he would never come! I grew lax in my vigilance, and now it is too late for the trap I had planned!" He came back into the room holding a thin rope in one hand, and looked wildly about the room as if searching for something.

"But how can you be sure it is Tristan?" Bettina asked frantically. "You — you must be mistaken!"

Don Miguel looked at her with a mixture of fear and rage in his eyes. "I saw him myself as he moved among the crowds in the streets! He fit the description I had of him, and when I moved closer, the big man he was with called him by name. They are asking the peasants where I live. And he is a clever one, that

283

Tristan. He did not sail into the harbor as I expected, but has hidden his ship up the coast so he could sneak into the town unobserved. I had no time to summon my men — I must face Tristan alone now!"

Bettina stared blankly at Don Miguel. Tristan was actually on the island. How could it be? He should be on the other side of the world. And dear God, why did he have to come now? Why not yesterday, or tomorrow, anytime but now, when she was about to give birth and could not help him in any way?

"You do not have to face him," Bettina said quickly. "You could flee before he comes."

"I will end it once and for all. I have the advantage of being an excellent swordsman. I have never been beaten, and I will not be beaten today."

He grabbed her wrist, yanked her off the bed, and pulled her over to the large, heavy bookshelf. She stared at him stupidly as he began to tie the thin rope about her left wrist.

"What are you doing?" she asked.

"I am making sure you will not stab me in the back while I am taking care of Tristan."

She had momentarily forgotten about her baby, but now she could feel the beginning of another contraction. The terror showed plainly in her eyes as Don Miguel secured one wrist and wrapped the rope around a shelf well above Bettina's head, then began to tie her other wrist.

"You cannot do this!" Bettina screamed. "I am in labor — I have been since morning. My baby —"

She could say no more as her body strained in agony, and she cried out in a shrill voice. She tried desperately to pull her hands down to hold her middle, but Don Miguel had secured them tightly above her head. The bookshelf tilted forward dangerously.

"This is excellent — more than I had hoped for." Don Miguel laughed malevolently. "Your screams will distract Tristan and make him careless."

When the pain subsided, Bettina looked up with tear-filled eyes, deep pools of shimmering green. "For the love of God, let me lie on the bed!"

"This was the only rope I could find, and it is too short to tie you to the bedposts."

"I can do you no harm in my condition. My baby is about to come!" Bettina cried.

"You obviously love this Tristan, or you would not have lied as you did to prevent our meeting," Don Miguel said impatiently. "And women can do miraculous things for the sake of love. I cannot take the chance."

"Then lock me in this room if you do not trust me, but please — I must lie down!" Bettina pleaded.

"Unfortunately, the key is not where it is usually kept, and I do not have time to search for it. And alas, my dear, I am not chivalrous enough to put your comfort above my own life. Besides, with the door open, your screams will sound much louder and will help to bring Tristan to a quicker death."

"But — but my baby will die this way! I must have my hands free! I swear to God I will do you no harm, only please, please, release me!" Bettina begged him, the tears streaming down her cheeks.

"No! It is just as well the baby will die. I do not want another Tristan hunting me down in my old age," Don Miguel replied harshly. He walked out of the room, leaving Bettina staring after him with wide, horror-filled eyes.

Bettina could only pray now that Tristan would come quickly, that he would overcome Don Miguel and come to her aid before her baby fell to his death. But she knew she was praying for the impossible. Her pains were so unbearable now that she knew she must be nearing the end.

Bettina tried twisting her wrists in an effort to free her hands, but there was no slackening in the rope. She considered toppling the heavy bookshelf over, but when she looked up, she saw that there were three shelves towering above her head. The bookshelf would fall on her, and though she didn't fear for her own life, her baby could be killed.

The agony gripped her again, and screams were forced from her. When Tristan came, if he came in time, she knew she must somehow stifle her screams. She had to endure — she had to! She couldn't let him know that she was about to give birth, for he must be alert and think only of Don Miguel and the battle at hand. Dear God, give Tristan skill, give him strength, let him be the victor!

When Bettina relaxed, she could feel the perspiration trickling down her temples, down her sides, and between her breasts. She twisted her head to wipe her brow on her upraised arm, then glanced miserably at the bowls of water on the table by the bed. She had prepared everything that she remembered Madeleine had ordered for Maloma, but her efforts had all been for nothing. She looked at the knife she would have used to cut the umbilical cord and give her baby life apart from her. Her baby would have had a better chance to live, she thought, if she had plunged that knife into Don Miguel's heart.

Chapter 43

After questioning countless Spanish-speaking Santo Domingans, Tristan finally came across an old man who had been to France in his youth and knew a little of the language. The old man gave him directions to Bastida's house, and after wasting time arguing with Jules, who wanted to come along, Tristan left alone for the outskirts of town.

The hired horse was as slow as a blasted mule, and just as ornery, and this only added to Tristan's frustrations. He realized that he would probably be walking into a trap, but he dared not endanger Bettina's life, or the life of his child, who would surely be born by now. Jules had passed Bastida's warning on to him, and he was left with no choice but to go alone.

It was nearing dusk when Tristan reached Bastida's house. He approached the front door slowly, but he began to think the old man had given him false directions when he noticed the shuttered windows. The house looked deserted from the outside, but when he tried the door, it opened easily into a well-lit entryway. He glanced about quickly for signs of ambush, but the room was empty and eerily silent.

Leaving the door open behind him, Tristan walked a few paces into the room, his footsteps like those of a cat on the polished floor.

"Bastida, show yourself!" Tristan called out angrily. A moment later, he came face-to-face with the man who had haunted his dreams for so many years.

It had been almost fifteen years since Tristan had set eyes on this man, but he had changed little since then. He was thinner, perhaps, and his features were more blunt and lined with age, but he was otherwise the same.

"So we meet at last, Tristan," Don Miguel said in a light tone as he came into the room, his sword on one hip, a dagger on the other.

"You recognize me?" Tristan asked, his hand going immediately to the hilt of his sword. But Bastida disappointed him with his answer.

"No, but I saw you earlier in town and heard you called by name. Perhaps if I knew your full name, I might —"

"You never knew my name, Bastida!" Tristan said sharply. "It did not matter to you then, so it is of no consequence now." He glanced quickly at the doors that led off the entryway; then he looked back to Bastida, his eyes like ice. "Where is Bettina?"

"In there," Don Miguel answered, pointing to an open door.

"And my child?"

Bastida laughed fiendishly. "She is giving birth to the bastard now."

Tristan paled and started for Bettina's room, but Don Miguel stepped in front of him. Tristan drew his sword and stood back, and Bastida did likewise, a malicious smile playing on his lips.

"Bettina! Bettina, are you all right?" Tristan called out.

"Yes, yes. Don't worry about me."

Relief flooded his features when he recognized her voice. He had heard no screams, so he assumed she was in the early stages of labor and there was no hurry to help her.

Don Miguel smiled appreciatively. "That girl has more stamina than I gave her credit for," he said with a shake of his head. "It is too bad that you will not live to see her again."

"We shall see who will live to see the end of this day," Tristan replied. He was poised in the traditional fencer's stance, prepared to thrust forward.

But Don Miguel smiled. He stood relaxed, his arms crossed over his chest and the rapier in his hand pointing to the ceiling as it rested on his shoulder.

"Surely before we begin, you will refresh my memory. I may not even be the man you have searched for all these years. Someone else may have used my name and —"

"That is possible," Tristan cut him off, lowering his sword to the floor. "But it is not the case. Though I learned your name

288

that accursed night you came into my life, it was your face that was burned into my mind. You have changed little, Bastida. *You* are the one I have sought."

"But I have no memory of you," Don Miguel said calmly.

Tristan took a step closer and touched his cheek. "You do not remember this scar you inflicted on a boy of twelve?"

Don Miguel shook his head slowly as he eyed the thin line on Tristan's cheek. "I have left my mark on many."

"Then perhaps you will remember the words you spoke at the time, after you laid my cheek open with the point of your sword. 'This will teach you never to raise arms against a mightier opponent. Your father was a fisherman as you will also be, and a fisherman is not a worthy match for a *don*.' I never forgot those words, Bastida, and as you can see, you predicted my future falsely. I am an equal match for you."

"I said such things often in my youth," Don Miguel replied. "Surely you have not hunted me all these years because of that scar?"

"You still have no memory of me?" Tristan asked. His rage began to surface.

"No. Your name and face have no meaning to me, nor what you have told me this far."

"Then I will tell you what took place that night, for it is still in my mind as if it happened only yesterday. It was a night in summer, some fifteen years ago, when you and your noble friends came to my village on the coast of France. Most of the village men were out in the fishing boats. In ten minutes you had killed every single man who had tried to protect his home. Then you had your sport with the women.

"My father had stayed at home that night, and he was one of the last who died by your blade, Bastida. I watched you kill him from the window of my parent's house.

"My mother forced me to hide under my bed as you came toward our house, Bastida. I watched you and your noble friends throw her on the ground and rape her, many times.

"You killed my mother and spit on her lifeless body. I crawled from my hiding place and ran after you. I attacked you with my bare fists, and you opened my cheek with the point of your sword and kicked me to the ground, only a few feet from where my father lay, telling me I was no match for you.

"Now you know why I have sworn to kill you, Bastida! When you murdered both my parents, it was a mistake to leave me alive," Tristan said, the fires of the past lighting his eyes. "Now my parents will be avenged!"

"Or you will join them," Don Miguel replied easily.

"Do you remember me now?"

"What you described happened in many raids. I have no memory of you, but I vaguely recall having to kill a fair-haired woman who came at me with a knife. I confess I have led a sinful life, but am I any different from you?" Don Miguel asked, his mouth turning up at one corner. "Did *you* not rape Bettina Verlaine?"

"I may have raped her, but I did not kill her husband in order to have her, nor did I share her with my crew or kill her afterward. I kept her, and she will bear my child and become my wife."

"Most commendable," Don Miguel laughed derisively. "But if you insist on matching skills with me, she will never be your wife. I may have led a ruthless life, but I do not plan to see it ended today."

Bastida came forward now, his sword arm extended, and their blades clashed together. Bastida had not boasted falsely of his ability, and with quick thrusts and movements he immediately put Tristan on the defensive. But Tristan was not without skill himself, and he successfully parried Bastida's flickering blade until the older man, with a cunning twist of his wrist, drew first blood.

Bastida retreated a step, a taunting smile on his lips at seeing the blood trickling down Tristan's chest. The two men circled each other warily; then the clashing of swords resounded in the air again. Tristan took the offensive, forcing Bastida across the room with a furious attack. Bastida tired quickly, and Tristan's blade reached his target again and again.

Tristan was like a wild bull charging the matador's cape, which was Bastida's shirt, dyed crimson from his own blood. Tristan had the strength of youth and the quickness of a darting cobra, and with a sudden upward thrust, Bastida's sword was ripped from his hand.

The point of Tristan's blade rested against the older man's chest, and for a moment there was a madness in his eyes that turned Don Miguel's blood cold. But before he could lean forward to put an end to the man who had haunted him, Tristan was distracted by an anguished low moaning coming from the next room.

The color drained from Tristan's face, and his hands began to tremble. Forgetting all about Bastida, who stood wide-eyed before him, Tristan turned and ran for the room where Bettina was. Behind him, seeing his chance for victory, Bastida drew his dagger and raised his arm to hurl it at Tristan's broad back.

A sudden blast of gunfire exploded in the room. Tristan swung around to see Bastida falling slowly to the floor, the dagger still in his hand. Then his eyes turned to the front door he had left open, and he saw the massive frame of Jules Bandelaire standing there, his great pistol smoking.

Tristan smiled weakly. "I suppose I must be thankful for once that you're a stubborn Frenchman who refuses to obey orders."

"And rightly you should be," Jules grunted as he sauntered into the room. "You had him at your mercy, and instead of running him through as the bastard deserved, you gave him your back for a splendid target. By rights, it should have been you lying in a pool of blood. You're so damned smitten with that girl that you run to her at the slightest cry. The wench will be the death of you yet."

"Tristan!"

Bettina's scream was like a knife through Tristan's heart, and he completely forgot about Jules as he ran into the room. The bed was empty, and he glanced frantically about the room.

"Mother of God!"

He ran to her, his face as pale as hers. In one swift motion he cut the rope with his sword; then he dropped it and lifted her in his arms. She screamed from the sudden movement, sending a cold chill down his spine, but in two quick strides he brought her to the bed and laid her down gently. She opened her eyes and they were calm, filled with relief, as she stared up at him.

"My God, Bettina, why didn't you tell me? Why did you let me delay so long with Bastida?" he asked. He wiped the blood from her chin, blood from the cuts on her lips where she had bitten them to keep from screaming.

"He wanted you to hear my cries, thinking they would upset you and make you careless. I couldn't let that happen. I am sorry I cried out when I did, but I —"

"You should have cried out sooner, blast it! I have to get you help," he said sternly, apprehension showing on his face.

"It is too late for that, Tristan. You will have to —"

Tristan was struck with horror as her screams filled the room again. Jules came to the door, but seeing Tristan by the bed, with Bettina fiercely clutching his hand, he quietly closed the door and left them alone. A few minutes later, Tristan brought his daughter into the world.

Bettina stared in wonder at the tiny infant Tristan placed in her arms. She proudly noted the golden wisps of hair and the light blue she could see through half-closed eyelids. Then she looked up at Tristan and frowned.

"I — I am sorry I could not give you the son you wanted," she said in a hoarse whisper.

Tristan sat on the edge of the bed and bent to kiss her brow, then smiled with a shake of his head.

"What does it matter that our first child is a girl? There will be others, many others, and I will love them all. But this one, this tiny red-faced girl, will hold a special place in my heart."

She could see in his eyes that he was not disappointed, and her heart filled with joy. With a sigh of relief mixed with contentment, Bettina slept.

It was morning when Bettina awoke. The shutters in her room had finally been opened wide and the sun was spilling into the room. The feeling of peace and happiness that she had felt before exhaustion claimed her came back to her now as she felt her daughter stir on the bed beside her.

In the next half hour, she experienced the pleasure every mother must feel at being able to nourish her child from swollen breasts. As she held her baby in her arms, the child appeared

292

to be asleep, except for the continuous sucking motion of her little mouth.

Tristan came into the room a while later, and sat down on the edge of the bed, taking Bettina's hand in his. His eyes were soft and tender as they gazed down at her and at his sleeping daughter.

"How do you feel?" he asked.

"Happy."

"That's not what I meant, and you know it," he said in a voice that was supposed to sound stern, but didn't.

"I am fine, really," she said with a warm smile, and saw the tension leave his face. But then she touched his cheek tenderly. "Tristan, what you told Bastida, did all that really happen?"

"Yes," he answered, and no hate flashed into his eyes as it used to whenever Bastida's name was mentioned.

"It must have been awful living with that memory all these years, and you were so young when it happened. How did you manage after that — or — or would you rather not talk about it?"

"I don't mind talking of it anymore, but I think you should rest right now," he replied.

"I don't want to rest!"

He shook his head at her stubbornness, but the corners of his lips turned up in a smile. This was a part of Bettina that would always be there, like her maddening temper. But these were traits that made her what she was — the woman he loved.

"Very well, little one. I had known Jules ever since I could remember, for he lived alone in the house next to mine, his parents having died years earlier. Fortunately, he was up the coast that night, and when he returned, he became my guardian. He helped me to bury my grief, but he could do nothing about the hate I harbored. Two years later, he and I left the village and traveled north until we came to a large coastal town with a harbor full of ships from friendly countries. Jules wanted to go to sea, and the only thing I wanted was to find Bastida. So we signed on with the first ship leaving, which was an English vessel."

"And now your search is finally over."

"Yes, but it was over before I came here. I never went to Spain.

293

After only a week and a half at sea, I realized that I could forget the past, forget about Bastida, all because of you. I turned the ship around and sailed for home. I knew then that you were the only one who mattered to me. I love you, Bettina, so much that it hurts. I should have realized it the first time I left you, when I had desire for no other woman but you. You have become a part of me, and I can't live without you."

"Oh, Tristan, I have prayed to hear you say this!" Bettina cried, tears of joy coming to her eyes. "When I was brought here, I thought I might never see you again. And now you are here, telling me you love me as I love you."

"You will never be rid of me, little one. I was a fool to leave you to go in search of Bastida; only I realized it too late. Jules came after me in your father's ship and found me on my way home. When he told me what had happened, we came straight here. For two days I could think of nothing but killing Bastida. But then my thoughts were replaced with fear that he might harm you, or that you might not be here. Even then, knowing that I was on my way to finally face Bastida, it was only you I could think of. But it is all over now. The past is dead. We will never be parted again, my little French flower, and we will be married as soon as we reach home."

Chapter 44

They didn't reach home until the end of October, for Tristan delayed their departure from Santo Domingo until Bettina had regained her strength. They made one stop, however, to purchase what was needed for the sugar crop, because Tristan didn't plan on leaving the island again for a very long time.

But now they sailed into a little cove, with Casey's ship trailing close behind. Bettina stood on the deck of the *Spirited Lady*, with Tristan's arm wrapped around her waist, and baby Angélique asleep in her arms. She was staring at the horned mountain in the distance, for it was as it had been the first time she saw it, shrouded in thick gray clouds, but with one shaft of the sun's rays lighting its heart. She felt as if the mountain were welcoming her home, telling her that she would find only happiness here on this little island. She smiled and leaned closer to Tristan.

Casey and Jossel greeted them before they even reached the house. Jossel was crying tears of relief, and Casey slapped Tristan on the back, telling him he had been confident that his daughter would be saved, which was an outright lie, for he had been worried sick.

Angélique was awakened by all the noise, and she started to whimper, bringing herself to everyone's attention. Jossel took her granddaughter from Bettina's arms and exclaimed over her beauty. And she was a beautiful baby, with tiny little golden curls falling over her forehead, and wide blue eyes, the same color as the sky in the morning.

"Seems she's taken after her father," Casey remarked, peering over Jossel's shoulder at Angélique as Jossel led them into the hall. He turned around to Tristan, who followed behind with

Bettina. "I heard you were convinced for a while that the babe wasn't yours." Casey laughed, a twinkle in his light-green eyes. "Would you still be in doubt?"

"The babe is mine, as is her mother," Tristan replied firmly.

Jossel smiled. She could see how proud Tristan was that Angélique had his coloring. She didn't have the heart to tell him that Bettina's hair had been this same yellow-gold before it turned white-blond a few months after her birth. But at least the eyes were unmistakably Tristan's.

Madeleine came running from the kitchen and burst into tears when she saw Bettina and her baby. Maloma joined them with her baby snuggled in the crook of her arm, and Jules, after greeting her, went down to the cellar to bring up flagons of rum to celebrate the homecoming. Bettina hated to leave the cheerful group, but Angélique was beginning to fuss for a feeding. She took her from Jossel, who was disappointed to give her up so soon; then Bettina started for the stairs after telling Tristan she wouldn't be long.

Tristan watched her go, his eyes glowing with love. But then Casey thrust a tankard of rum into his hand with a hearty laugh.

"I warned you that you might be havin' a daughter, that I did," Casey said. "Perhaps you can understand now why I kept you from Bettina, but then maybe it's too soon for you to be feelin' what a father feels for his daughter. And then again, maybe you won't be around to see that little one grow." Casey grinned. "Will you be there to chase the lads away from Angélique, or will that be left for me to do in my old age?"

"I'll be there, you sly old fox," Tristan replied, grinning. "And I'll be even worse than you when it comes to protecting my daughter's honor. And you can stop worrying about your own daughter, Casey, because I am marrying her today."

"I knew you'd come around, lad, that I did," Casey said with a chuckle. Then he turned to his wife. "Did you hear that, Jossel? They'll be wed today!"

"But Bettina has no wedding gown!" Jossel said. "I want my daughter to have a proper wedding that she will always remember."

"I'll take care of the gown," Tristan said.

"Good, it's settled, then," Casey said.

"But there is so much to do!" Jossel protested, considering that things were going along much too quickly. "The wedding must wait — at least a few days — to give me time —"

"No!" Tristan said adamantly, causing Casey to laugh boisterously.

"I give up," Jossel sighed, throwing her arms up in the air. "There is nothing left for me to do but see to the preparations for a feast."

And then Jossel smiled, for even though this day was not as she had always dreamed it would be, it was nevertheless what her daughter wanted. Bettina would marry the man of her choice, and she was happy. And this, of course, was all that mattered.

"It is all settled," Tristan said when he came into his room, finding Bettina playing with Angélique on the bed. "Casey has gone to bring Father Hadrian." He joined her on the bed lying on his side with Angélique between them, but when he looked at Bettina, he was surprised by her saddened expression. "Are you having doubts about marrying me, little one?"

"Of course not! You know how much I love you."

"Then why aren't you as happy as I am?"

"I am," she said faintly. "It is just that I wish I had a white gown to wear."

"You will have," Tristan replied, lifting her chin up with a finger. "Jules will bring it up shortly."

As he said it, Jules came through the open door carrying a large trunk that he set down at the foot of the bed. Bettina recognized the trunk immediately, and she turned to Tristan, who was glowering at Jules.

"I asked you to wait until I had a chance to tell her, blast it!" Tristan said angrily.

"Well, her mother insisted I bring it up from the cellar right away. She said the gown needed to be laid out to ease the wrinkles," Jules replied. "If you'll look at Bettina, you'll see you've worried for nothing."

Tristan turned to Bettina and could see the happiness on

her face. She leaned over and kissed him tenderly.

"So you lied to me about leaving all my trousseau behind," she scolded, but a smile played gaily on her lips.

"It was only for your sake that I did so," he replied quickly. "You needed something to keep you occupied while on my ship, and making a new wardrobe was the perfect solution."

"But why didn't you let me have my trunks after you brought me here?"

"How would you have reacted at that time if I had?"

She laughed, knowing full well she would have been furious. "So that is why the cellar door was always locked — so I would not find out that my trunks were there."

"Are you angry?"

"No, beloved. I wanted a gown, but I did not want to delay our wedding day to make one. You have settled the problem. Is this why you refused to give me the white satin when I asked for it?"

"No, I just couldn't stand the thought of supplying you with material for a gown you would wear to wed another man. I guess I loved you even then."

"But I made this gown for the same purpose. It doesn't bother you now?"

"You made that gown to marry a man you had never met. I am that man."

Bettina slipped away from the celebration to give Angélique her last feeding for the night. She went to Jossel's room, for at her mother's insistance Angélique had been moved into her grandparents' room for the night. She was wide awake when Bettina came into the room, gurgling playfully in her little cradle. After being awake most of the evening, there was a good chance that she would sleep soundly until morning, and Bettina anticipated spending an undisturbed night with her husband.

She fed Angélique silently, lost in happy thoughts of the day. She was remembering how beautiful the wedding had been, the words that had bound her to Tristan, the expression on his face, the love she saw in his eyes. It was a day she would remember forever, and the best was yet to come.

With Angélique nourished and fast asleep, Bettina laid her back in the cradle and quietly closed the door. Tristan met her at the bottom of the stairs, and without giving Bettina a chance to bid everyone a pleasant night, he grabbed her hand and pulled her playfully back upstairs to their room. He picked her up before he opened the door to carry her inside, then kicked it shut behind him. When they were alone, his movement slowed as if he wanted to savor each second with her.

The soft patter of rain could be heard outside the windows, and a cool, fragrant breeze stirred the curtains, bending them in a rounded arc like the canvas on a ship. Tristan set her down gently in the middle of the room, barely able to see her in the darkness. His fingers fumbled with the bindings on her wedding dress, and finally she had to push his hands away to do it herself, for Tristan was like a nervous young lad about to encounter his first taste of love.

Without speaking, for words were unnecessary, Tristan moved to light a single candle; then he turned back in time to watch Bettina step out of her satin gown and remove the rest of her garments. He could hardly believe that she was his and that at last he would have her again. This last month, he had refrained from taking her, giving her a chance to recover completely from childbirth. He had looked forward to this moment as if it were the first time he would have Bettina, and he smiled now, thinking how foolish he had been to fear marriage. For having Bettina as his wife, knowing that she was bound to him forever, filled Tristan with an inexplicable contentment. He loved her beyond reason, and knowing that she loved him, too, gave him a constant feeling of euphoria — he'd never dreamed he could be this happy.

Seeing the candlelight shimmering on Bettina's ivory skin as she stood with her back to him letting down her hair, Tristan undressed quickly, throwing his clothes aside in his haste. When she turned around, they stood transfixed for a long moment, looking into each other's eyes.

"I love you so much, Tristan," Bettina murmured. A dreamy smile was on her lips as she clasped her hands behind his neck.

"Has my spirited lady been tamed, little one?" he asked teasingly.

"Very much so," she replied, her eyes like shining sapphires in the candlelight. "Will you miss her?"

Tristan's eyes gleamed with love when he answered. "Turbulent waters are an adventure to ride, but I prefer to sail calm seas. The vixen is gone, and in her place is my wife."

Tristan's lips found hers then, and he kissed her fervently. And with his mouth still burning against hers, he picked her up and carried her to his bed. There, in a burst of passion that consumed them both, their bodies mingled and their love soared to ecstatic heights.